WHEN
STARS
BURN
OUT

WHEN
STARS
BURN
OUT

ANNA VERA

WHEN STARS BURN OUT

Copyright © 2015 by Anna Vera

For information regarding permission, contact:
AnnaVeraBooks@gmail.com

ISBN-10: 0692564691
ISBN-13: 978-0-692-56469-1

Cover and Internal design by Najla Qamber Designs
Edited by The Polished Pen / Max Dobson
Proofread by Crenel Publishing

Subscribe to Anna Vera's newsletter for updates and exclusive content:
www.AnnaVeraBooks.com/subscribe

Find her on Instagram or Twitter @AnnaVeraBooks

To the underdogs

THIRTY YEARS
EARLIER

A DARK SKY OPENS to a flush of neon-green light. The light falls, slow and sweeping. It stains the rooftops and empty midnight roads of a small city sleeping soundly at the darkest shade of night.

The podcraft arrives silently. Though the light should act as a beacon, the craft goes about its business invisibly, descending to land in a soft-spoken neighborhood in Snowflake, Arizona. The craft exhales a string of four people dressed in cloaks of solid black, their faces similarly uneasy.

The neon-green light is fast to disappear as the craft returns to the sky. Darkness falls, a black net cradling Earth in arms of depthless shadow, leaving behind the four people—who clearly do not belong—at the center of a vacant street.

Leading the group is a young man: lengthy, with almond eyes as pitch-black as the night sky, and lips perpetually taut. He stands at the base of a street lamp casting out a dim, orange haze alongside the others, all women.

"We're breaking protocol being here, Pavo." The woman speaking holds up a chin, her dark eyes a perfect mirror to the man's she is addressing—her brother. "A single report of us being here could ruin everything."

"Nobody will see us." Pavo glares at another woman, one with a cascade of magenta-colored hair, standing rather severely at his sister's side. "*Will* they, Io?"

Io's fingertip reaches her temple; all at once, her expression sharpens with supreme focus. When she looks up again, it's with a blare of confidence.

"Nobody for a five mile radius," she confirms gleefully.

"See, Onyx?" Pavo frowns at his sister. "Satisfied?"

Onyx doesn't reply, watching as Pavo goes off the road and approaches a small house. A light glows behind a set of pale, lacy curtains—artificial and flickering. Television.

Somebody is awake.

Pavo strolls up the sidewalk, leading the rest of the group to a front porch decorated with houseplants sporting mismatched pots and a single warped wooden chair.

Checking with Io, he asks, "Do you have him restrained?"

Io nods, fingertip still pressed to her temple.

Without another word, he walks inside. The three women, only a few years younger than their leader, Pavo—who's no older than thirty—enter the house, operating with robotic circumspect.

Pavo walks into a dimly lit living room, the television at its center a sparkling smear of static. Before it is a man, so stationary he could be mistaken for dead, sitting upon a sofa straining under the bulk of his weight. Though he appears to be asleep, the man's eyes are wide open, gaping as extensively as his mouth.

Paralysis.

Though the man's aware of what's going on—of the strange interlopers dressed in black cloaks, with peculiarly dark eyes, and a host of mysterious abilities—he isn't able to move a muscle.

Pavo snaps his fingers at Io. "Wake him."

Io's eyes skirt to Pavo's sister. Onyx gives her a quiet nod of approval. She walks closer, eyes locked on the man sitting squat in his drooping couch.

"How awake would you prefer?" Io inquires.

"Don't give him complete control—that would defeat the purpose of this experiment." A brief glance at the group's fourth member, and he adds, "Get closer, Peridot. You've got to witness everything first-hand or not at all."

Peridot steps away from Onyx's side, treading gingerly to the man on the couch. With her there, Pavo instructs Io to lift a little of her power, partially relinquishing her grip on the man's ability to move—so he's still controlled, but coherent.

Immediately the man wilts, limbs heavy. A deathly huff of breath drags itself through his lips. The group tightens rank at the man's periphery, and the closer they come to him, the more ferociously the man begins to sweat; a band glitters across his forehead, perched upon his upper lip, dripping from his temples.

He glares at his uninvited visitors, unable to speak—or to *scream*, rather—as he'd like. The network of capillaries webbed over his face burst. His eyes flare wide with the signature panic of prey facing predator, and the corners of his sclera become colored by a hideous puce-hued bloodshot.

He wheezes, a question loud in his eyes: *Who are you?*

They know far better than to answer.

1

THE OFFICE'S VENTILATION SYSTEM whirs, pumping recycled air through an agonizingly small air duct overhead.

I swat my hand, fanning myself. The cramped office smells like a sticky exhaled breath: hot and wet and disgusting. I try to keep my mind on Marathon's cool, fresh air.

Relax. You'll be there soon enough, Eos.

My mentor sits across from me, a desk dividing us. She scribbles letters in a language I don't understand over a smooth slip of white paper. Her fingers—nimble, thin, and bony as the rest of her—grip her red-inked pen a little too vigorously.

We've spent forty-five minutes like this.

A hot drip of sweat rolls down my spine, settling at the base of my back. I fidget in my seat.

"Is there a . . . problem?" I finally ask.

Onyx's black eyes click up to mine—devoid and unreadable as outer space. Then they return to the slip of paper covered in a swath of red loops and swirls, hieroglyph-like symbols.

Mentor's Language.

I stretch, cracking my knuckles. "Does *everybody* get a slip?"

"No," Onyx clarifies promptly. I'm shocked by her tone—it's

as unyieldingly sharp as a rose's thorned bite, and though she's prone to this breed of severity, today it feels . . . *different*.

"Why am I—"

"Shut up, let me write, and I'll tell you."

"Yes, ma'am," I say, falling silent. I thrum my fingertips over the desk's smooth surface, failing to stop fidgeting in a way that speaks to my nerves.

Today is my final evaluation. If I pass, that means I'm ready to deploy to Earth as a soldier and fight the Muted—the vicious, bloodthirsty monsters infected by the plague. I've spent years of my life dreaming of the nights I'll spend staring down the scope of a rifle, waiting for a Mute to come strolling into view . . .

If only Onyx would hurry up with the paperwork.

I chew a nail. "You nearly done?"

"You don't want me to be done, Eos Europa."

"And why wouldn't I?"

Onyx slams her pen down with a snap against the plastic surface of the desk. "What do you think this slip says, Eos?"

She pushes the paper forward. There's no way in hell I can decipher it. All I know is it sports a series of letters impossible to identify for those illiterate in the language, scrawled in red ink.

"No. I don't." Though I continue to stare at it. "Is this part of the test or something? Finding a way to—"

"I can't pass you."

"You . . ." I trail off, her words sinking deeper. "What?"

"I'm afraid you've failed your Final Exam."

"Which means . . . that I can't deploy," I add stupidly, feeling like I've been lanced through the chest with a blunt spear.

It's not possible. Nobody fails.

Nobody.

Onyx has the decency to look guilty, at least.

"Why?" I gasp.

"You know why, Eos."

"It's not the skillset thing, is it?" I fan my palms out over the desk's surface. The *skillset thing*—or not having an ability of the supernatural variety, thanks to my defective genetic coding—has been the bane of my existence for as long as I can remember.

"I get my genetics aren't ideal," I say, "but I can still fight and shoot and wield a knife. I can still kill the Muted effectively, and is that not my Purpose?"

Onyx casts me a truly pitying stare. "The Project authorized a single missed point on the exam, that is correct. They realize specimens, despite their design, aren't all perfect."

"How many points did I miss, then?"

Onyx opens a drawer, extracting a manila folder, and puts it gingerly on the desk. After she flips it open, I see it holds my test results, charted in a series of sporadically placed dots.

I notice a few dots are way off. *Outliers.*

Onyx taps the outliers. "You failed your Psych Eval."

Impossible.

"I'm afraid you do not fulfill the requirements necessary to be deployed as a—"

All of a sudden, I'm laughing. Maniacally.

This is absurd.

"So you're saying I'm not psychologically sound?"

"Not enough to be an adequate soldier." Onyx refers to the chart beneath her index finger, providing a brusque explanation for each outlier. "You have an overinflated self-esteem," she says, fingertip sliding to the next. "You're overconfident in your own abilities. You possess delusions of grandeur. You're bold to the point of being brash . . ."

I yank the paper away from her, wrinkling it. For a tedious beat of silence, we stare each other down: her black eyes pinned to my muddy green ones.

"Are you calling me a diagnosed narcissist?" I challenge.

"This is your termination order," she replies, apparently not intending to dignify my question with a response. "You're not to become a soldier, but instead work as a groundskeeper—"

"Groundskeeper!?" I whisper, nostrils flared.

"If not that, you may work as a technician, keeping the cogs of our spaceship oiled." Onyx stares unblinkingly. "Or, you may work in the kitchen preparing food."

The reality of my future wafts over me like stale air, and all I can do is stare with my jaw agape, feeling the color slowly drain from my face.

"No," is all I manage in the end. "*No.*"

"You've missed two points; I cannot pass you."

"You are second-in-command," I argue desperately. "Pull a few strings or something!"

Onyx heaves a sigh, apparently bored. "There's nothing else that I can do for you, Eos."

She begins packing the file, and in a jolt of panic I reach to take it away, to stop her—to stop *this*. Because as soon as it's over, so are my chances at a life worth living. At a life fulfilling my one true Purpose.

But as my hand springs forward, so does hers, catching my wrist inside her bony fingers. Instantly—as soon as we're making skin-to-skin contact—the buzz of her skillset ability thrums from her grip in a wash of heat accompanied by a distinctive sound . . .

A high-pitched, vibratory peal.

Onyx releases my hand. The sound dies, replaced by words as cold and barren as a winter night. "To qualify for fighting as a soldier, you must not only have a solid *psychological* standing, but also a solid *physical* standing."

A stamp appears; she presses it down on my file: *Unfit.*

"You have neither," she finishes, stuffing my manila folder file back in the drawer.

"You can't do this," I decry. "You can't fail me!"

"I believe that I just have," she replies, eyes dull as she nods at the slip resting at the center of the desk. There's a blank space left at the bottom, waiting to be filled with my preferred career.

Preferred career.

What an absolute joke.

The legs of my chair skid loudly over the linoleum flooring as I shoot to a standing position, barely succeeding to keep my lips dammed—holding back a slew of words I'd love to say, but know would later regret.

"Thank you," I croak angrily. "For nothing."

Onyx stands with just as much vigor as I have—the legs of her chair, too, skidding loudly.

"You're aware, I hope, of what awaits soldiers?"

"Glory?" I answer, knowing full well she's expecting a totally different response. "Honor? A legacy?"

"Death," she corrects coolly.

"Death," I say, treading to the office's door, "awaits us all."

My mentor replies by way of strutting forward to meet me at the office's exit, her lips taut as a clasp as she forces the slip into my hand and says, "Someday you'll thank me for this."

Thank you for what, exactly?

WHEN STARS BURN OUT

She straightens herself, readjusting her jacket as though in the effort of remaining dignified. "You will inform your league of your new Purpose. Tell only Cybele, Helios, and Merope. I'll be the one to alert Apollo."

Onyx nudges me out of her office door with a swift jab to the side and adds, before I can outrun the cruel words she sends chasing after me, "They will deploy to Earth without you."

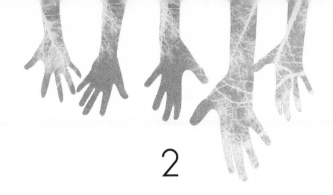

2

WHEN I'M BACK IN my pod, I lean miserably against the sill of the room's circular window, begging myself not to blackout.

Kitchen aid. Groundskeeper.

This can't be happening.

I can't help but curse myself for a fool. Has anybody besides me failed their Psych Eval before? Am I really so insufferable as to endanger others?

My fist collides with the window.

I lift my eyes, peering through the pane of glass, which looks out on an outdoor arena: a large, city-sized greenhouse covered by a dome of thick glass. Everybody calls it *Marathon.*

My first thought is of the arena's fresh air.

My second is of its always-at-your-disposal supply of guns.

Ah, yes. Let's shoot off some steam.

Before I go, I give one final look to Earth—a smear of color in the distance, a blend of churning, textured clouds. It hangs in the black sky like a glittering ornament.

Up close, though? It's hideous.

A place of rot and decay, where the living are less alive than those already dead. A place that is expiring. A big, bleeding black mark striking a line through *what could've been.*

I've dreamed of defending Earth's remains, defending the history going up in smoke. With a blood-slick knife in my palm and a halo of Mute corpses fanned out at my feet. With dawn rising up against a dying night. Hope restored and faith renewed and a life worth living—not just for me, but for everybody.

Being a part of that, it's all I've ever wanted.

That honor. That *glory.*

I cringe against a swelling chaos in my ears, a deafening rip in my reality, as my memories rise and bob like an untethered buoy to the surface of my thoughts.

Everything I've worked for is *gone.*

Everything I've tried to become isn't *who I am.*

Everything is full of holes, stabbed porous by a red-inked pen gliding over the smooth surface of a slip of paper.

Punching through my pod's doorway, I slip back out into the halls of the Ora. Before I know it, I've weaved through the twisted innards of this bulky, metal spaceship and am standing before a pair of steel doors marking the entry to the arena.

And I've yet to be spotted by anybody I know.

Thank god.

I press a hand to the door's fingerprint identification pad and two steel, slab-like doors shoot open. A gust of fresh air. A hiss as they close at my back, as I enter a room sized similarly to that of a large walk-in closet—brushed steel, exhibiting racks and racks of all sorts of guns, ammunition, weapons . . .

My instinct is to bypass all the shiny, new guns in favor of an old revolver called a Smith & Wesson. It was recovered years ago by a post-deploy specimen who brought it back by accident. While we were training—to time manual reloading—I'd picked it up and felt an instant connection.

It fit my palms perfectly, and it had . . . *character.*

We don't use bullets, obviously. We use pellets, which still hurt like hell, but at least they aren't dangerous. I load a few into my gun and head to the actual arena, taking in the acres and acres of gorgeous vegetation: harvested a generation ago, managed by controlled climates and excellent—

Groundskeepers.

I shake the title out of my mind just as I hear the hissing of opening doors at my back—and a beat later, a voice.

"How did it go?"

Merope Poplar, a member of my league.

And also my best friend.

She's standing in a dirt-smudged uniform, her porcelain cheeks smeared in charcoal face paint. I notice the corner of her lip is cracked, bleeding.

"Where's Lios?" I inquire casually, focusing on loading and reloading my gun unnecessarily. "He'll fix up your lip. You three been sparring today?"

I'm eighteen years old. Merope's nineteen. We're the closest in age in our league, with everybody else being years older. Not only is she my best friend—a sister, really—but she's also gifted with the skillset ability of Empathy.

Meaning I can't hide anything from her. Ever.

Well, nobody can, but I *especially* can't.

"I asked you about your Final Exam," she reiterates with narrowed violet eyes. "You were in Onyx's office for nearly two hours. What was taking so long?"

Merope swipes sweat off her face and smears the charcoal face paint everywhere. She looks vaguely like a raccoon. A pretty, violet-eyed raccoon, whose glare is fraying my periphery with all its burning intensity.

To hell with it. Spit it out, Eos.

My tone is distinctly sardonic as I say, "Well, according to our mentor, I'm not physically or psychologically fit to fight as a soldier alongside you on the front line."

"Physically . . . or psychologically?" Merope probes. I keep my lips tight, eyes averted. "You . . . No, there's no way," she adds with a lighthearted scoff, as though I'm joking.

"I failed," I confirm.

"What do you mean, you failed?"

"I think that statement is self-explanatory."

"Eos," she gasps, breathless. "Tell me this isn't . . . You're supposed to deploy with . . ." Her little fingers claw nervously at her braided hair, releasing it in tufts of frizz. "I need you by my side when we deploy!"

"Merope," I say in warning. "You're making this worse."

"What's your new Purpose, then?" she asks, still messing with her hair—so black, it's almost blue. "How will you be serving our Purpose?"

"I get to be a groundskeeper or kitchen aid."

"We've got to talk to Onyx."

"She has made it very clear that there's nothing anybody can do to change this," I argue hotly. *This is all bad enough without making some kind of a scene.*

Merope sighs deeply. I take her hand in my own, lacing our fingers together. We exit the weapons room, spilling out into the muddy lawn of Marathon—into air that's thin as a wisp, a balm to my fiery mood.

Rays of sunlight fall in beams from a dark sky, filtered by the glass, which is UV protectant—like Earth's atmosphere, but a little stronger, probably.

Farther off, specimens practice sparring in a quagmire.

The irrigation system must've just turned off. The lawn is muddier than it normally is, so much so there's a deep puddle of water resting just beside the sparring specimens. Two are against each other, while the rest linger in a ring around them, watching through critical lenses.

Jupiter, the Tertiary Counselor, gives a shouted commentary evaluating the fighters' techniques.

"No skillsets!" he bellows as Ares, a specimen whose skillset ability is manifesting fire, shoots sparks from his fingertips. "This is hand-to-hand combat *only*."

Ares's opponent is a member of our league: Apollo, who's got black hair and eyes, with fair skin. His muscles ripple under his skin-tight shirt. Nearby, a few girls openly swoon.

I scoff as Apollo throws a punch at Ares, hitting his mark perfectly—right in the jaw.

Merope shakes her head slowly. "He's good looking, I'll give him that," she offers.

"Not you too?" I say, rolling my eyes. Merope's cheeks take on a pink blush. "He's nothing but a smug bastard."

As though to emphasize my point, Apollo dips and dodges a left hook strike with ease. His combat skills are executed with an alacrity Ares simply isn't used to facing—given his skillset, he hasn't ever *needed* to be good at sparring.

With that, Apollo tackles Ares, and after a few moments of hastened wrestling, he's got him in a choke hold. Ares's dark face swells, bloating. He taps.

"Apollo wins," Jupiter declares, apparently bored.

"Any other takers?" Apollo asks. He winks at a girl standing nearby, igniting a chorus of excited tittering.

The smuggest of all bastards.

Before I know it, I've shot up a hand. "I'll take you."

"No skillset—"

"That *won't* be an issue," I say, interrupting Jupiter before he gets too carried away with himself.

No skillset, no problem.

This is my kind of fighting.

I peel off my jacket and leave it heaped, alongside my gun, at Merope's feet. She whispers, "Kick his ass."

"No problem," I mutter as I approach Apollo. He looks as he always does: beautiful, but vaguely confused.

Apollo glances at Jupiter. "But she's a girl."

I scoff. "You don't miss much, do you?"

Jupiter waves a thin-fingered hand in the air, indicating we should bump fists—a gesture of good sportsmanship.

Apollo's fist bumps mine. "Don't hold back."

"Oh, I will," I say, steadying my pace, matching the rhythm of my footwork to his. "Or else I'll kill you. You don't want that."

"Kill me?" he echoes with a laugh—and throws a punch at my face, full-throttle. I dodge it by an inch. The ring of people around us gasps, then cheers.

My small victory seems to aggravate Apollo. He dives a fist at my face again. I drop, rolling. Mud splatters under my weight as I fall, leaving my bare arms sleeved in brown-gray.

Apollo leaps, aiming to tackle.

I roll again.

The mud is frigid and slick. I feel it seep through my clothes like icy fingers. Apollo misses but doesn't fall. I take a handful of water and splash it in his face, leaving a spattering of mud flecked over the bridge of his nose like freckles.

He hastily wipes the mud off his face. *Furious.*

Seething, he says, "Fighting like a gir—"

"Fighting to *win*," I interject, capitalizing on his distraction by throwing a fist into his stomach. A moment of silence follows, filled only by his wheezing.

Bent forward on his hands and knees, he gasps, trying to catch his breath. *Life doesn't spare a kick when you're down. I won't spare you either, Apollo.*

I pummel three additional jabs, bloodying his nose, leaving his thin, pale lips split. He yells, lunging for me. A second later, we're rolling together, splashing in the mud, just as he and Ares had moments ago.

The crowd around us is a stew of color as I roll and tumble, and roll again. Their voices are dulled by the loud rhythm of my breath as I keep it steady, controlled.

I'm caked in mud. It drips from my hair, leaves a gritty residue in my mouth, drying patchily on my cheeks. I catch a glance at Apollo, and he's just as dirty—his face alive, lit up like fire in all his poorly concealed rage.

I roll onto my back and lift my legs, striking a heel into his thigh as hard as I can. He falls in the wrong direction, tipping forward, *landing on me.*

"Get off," I growl, shoving at him wildly. He regains control of himself, sitting perched on top of me the way Lios always does before tickling me to tears.

He lies down, parallel to me, while wrapping his legs around me like he'd rather die than let go. Then, fast as that, he's got an arm around my neck.

Wrapped there, cinching tighter.

Just as he'd done to Ares.

Rolling backward, he drags me along. His hold on my neck tightens, but I refuse to tap out. Even Jupiter says, "Eos, it's best to recognize your limitations—"

I throw a jab into Apollo's ribs.

He cringes, tightening his grip. I feel my periphery quiver and fade, darkening. I'm shocked to also detect the distinctive sensation of a skillset ability when it's active: a strange *buzzing*.

I try to say, *No skillsets!* but the words are blocked.

Unlike the feel of Onyx's skillset—a high-pitched ringing, a vibratory peal—Apollo's feels like a song. It rolls out of his flesh with a rhythm, a steady beat akin to the thud of a heart.

Weird. Very, very weird.

I've never felt a skillset like this before.

Apollo shifts nervously, his skillset's feeling increasing like a whisper might to a yell, then to a scream.

Again, his grip tightens, and I'm sure I'm going to blackout this time—but just then, I recall we're fighting beside a pit of mud and stagnant water . . .

I've lost enough today. I won't be losing this too.

Despite being league members, we're basically strangers to one another. This is the most I've interacted with Apollo for at least two years—the last interaction being obligatory, and under the hawk-like supervision of Onyx. But during that obligatory lesson, Apollo showed me one thing about himself:

He doesn't like water.

I throw every ounce of my strength into rolling us over to the side, to the left. Before Apollo realizes what I'm doing, we're already slipping down the muddy slope, rolling over one another as we tumble.

When we stop—by sheer *luck*—I've ended up on top of him.

I lunge, pushing his head backward so it's fully immersed in the foot-deep muddy water. Apollo bucks and thrashes under my hips, completely panicking over being submerged.

"Eos wins," Jupiter drawls lazily from beyond, and I lift my grip on Apollo's face immediately. He thrusts himself out of the water, gasping. His face is a patchy kind of red and his black eyes stare daggers at mine.

"What?" I snap, climbing out of the water.

Apollo snorts. "You cheated."

"How?"

"You know I'm phobic of water," he snarls, grabbing me by the wrist—hard. A quick *yank,* and he's dragged me within reach of his right fist, which punches unsuspectingly into my jaw.

My head is whiplashed, lip split instantly.

Everything is silent.

I run my tongue over my lower lip, tasting blood. My eyes don't yield from Apollo. I wouldn't be surprised if he put a knife in my back later, once it was turned.

"Coward," I reel, stopped by Jupiter, who has thrust his arm between the pair of us. "You pathetic coward."

"Cheater," Apollo parries back.

"*You* used your skillset," I decry, but Apollo isn't listening to anything I'm saying. The patchy pink to his cheeks has faded to a dull, sickly pale—and a moment later, I see why.

Pavo is approaching us.

And beside him, a very angry Onyx.

Her voice is like a cracked whip. "Apollo!" His posture straightens at once. "You've knowingly defied my orders!"

"I . . . I was just . . ."

"You're coming with me."

"I'm sorry," Apollo says in earnest, chancing a quick glance back at me as he follows—an odd, unreadable kind of expression masking his pale face.

But I don't have time to scrutinize it any further because less than ten seconds later, Pavo's beside me. "Good work."

"Thank you, sir."

"Apollo's reign has ended," he jokes. "He's been undefeated until today—until *you*."

"I wasn't aware of that, sir."

"Don't lie," Pavo commands with a stale breath. "You knew, yet you challenged him regardless. You're the kind of specimen who will serve well as a soldier."

After all the excitement of defeating Apollo, the reality of today floods back in, cold as ice.

I gulp. "I . . . There's . . ." I look up, seeing Merope stand off to the side of us, my jacket draped over her arm. Sticking out of the pocket is my termination order.

"What is it, Eos?" Pavo asks.

"Might I meet you in your office in a minute?"

"Of course." Pavo's lips yield to a rare, congratulatory smile before he treads off toward the arena's exit. I'm left squeezing the mud-water out of my hair, feeling a little woozy.

A beat later and Merope's at my side, looking sheepishly at my split-lip before pointing to her own. "We match."

"That we do," I say irritably.

"At least I got mine from a fair fight—not a suckerpunch."

"How did he become such a dick?" I hiss as Apollo exits the arena at last. "We were all raised by Onyx together, yet none of the rest of us suckerpunch people in the face."

The shuffling of footsteps heralds an approach.

Merope and I both look up to see who it is and are relieved to see it's Cyb and Lios—the last members to our league, both as spattered in sludge as Merope and I are.

"We heard about the spar," Cyb says, her pale brows arched in an atypical testimony of her approval. "Passed Apollo on our way back in the arena. Had his tail between his legs, didn't he?"

She looks up at Lios: a tall, godlike specimen. He's always been the best looking of us all with his bronzed skin, red-brown hair and bright sapphire eyes.

Lios laughs, draping an arm over her shoulders. Though I've always seen Lios as a brother, Cyb hasn't—they've been linked romantically for years.

I'll never forget following Lios into Marathon one day in the hopes of him practicing sparring with me—only to discover him practicing something else entirely.

I'd found him pinning Cyb against a rock wall, her pale legs wrapped around his bare, bronzed hips. I was younger. Not really aware of sex—well, *aware* of it, but not aware of it in relation to myself. Until that moment, I didn't really think much about it.

Being eighteen and still a virgin, though, I'll admit I think about it a lot more now.

I snap back to reality a moment too late. Lios is eyeing me strangely, with concern.

"You're being quiet," he says. "What's wrong?"

"Nothing." I spit the lie instantaneously. Merope gives me an encouraging stare that says, *Come on, Eos, just get it over with.*

I sigh, shaking my head. "Actually, no."

We're alone in the arena now, with sparring lessons being

over for the day. It's just us, the chilly air, and the slurp of mud sucking enthusiastically at our shoe soles.

Lios drops his arm from Cyb's shoulders, passing his hand through my hair instead. "What's up, kiddo?"

I stare miserably back at my league, wondering . . .

Wondering how I'll tell them the truth without looking like the total, utter failure that I really am . . .

"I didn't pass my exam."

"No." Lios's sapphire eyes are edged. "How?"

"Failed my Psych Eval," I say, scowling at Cyb to gauge her pending reaction. "Apparently my ego's too big . . ."

"We'll talk to Onyx," Lios declares suddenly.

"*No*," I nearly yell in reply. Everybody stares. "No, there's nothing we can do. I already told Merope—we aren't going to try talking to Onyx."

"And why wouldn't we?" Cyb asks.

"Because I don't—" I pause, swallowing. "I don't know that after all this, after everything . . . I think it's best if I stay, if I work where I can't accidentally endanger anybody."

Could it be? Has Onyx actually gotten to me? Her speech about my being a danger, a liability. And after sparring today, the way Apollo looked at me. "*Cheater*," he'd said . . .

All because I thought not to tap out but to employ his worst fears against him. *To fight dirty. To go there.*

Would I have, if I weren't so bullheaded—so confident in my ability to beat him, to win?

"Endanger?" Cyb barks, raking her buttery hair aside, fixing her silver-gray eyes on mine. The southern hemisphere of her skull is shaved nearly to her scalp, a swath of brunette under the peroxide blond. "Is that the horseshit Onyx has been feeding you all morning?"

"We're worse off without you, if anything," Lios adds.

"Can I just—" I stop, dabbing a finger to my split lip and brushing a hand down my mud-coated arms. I look desperately at my league. "Can I just forget about this for a while?"

For a second, everybody is quiet. Then Lios steps closer, his thumb brushing my bottom lip, Healing it immediately. I give him a weak smile. Merope thrusts my revolver forward in a way that says, *Yes, of course.*

"Let's go shooting," she suggests.

"Shooting." Cyb snorts, smiling slyly. "That *has* always been your favorite form of catharsis."

I try to smile, accepting my revolver. "Not today."

"Not today?" Merope echoes, looking disappointed to have failed at cheering me up. "Are you sure?"

I pull out my termination order—now wrinkly, splattered with mud—and say, "I've got to turn this in."

"Now?" Merope asks.

"I told him I'd be there in a minute." I gesture to the arena's exit in reference to Pavo. "But I'll . . . I'll see you afterward?"

My league exchanges glances.

Lios decides he'll be spokesperson. "You want to go alone?"

"We'll go with you," Merope says.

"No, it's fine." I don't know why, but I feel a crack snake its way through my steeled stoicism. I walk away before they can see it breaking me apart and say, as loud and strong and as brave as I can make myself sound, "It'll be boring. I'll do this alone."

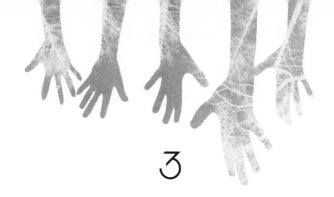

3

DAVO'S OFFICE IS THE largest in our branch of the Ora.

As the Lead, he carries all the authority, including assigning and managing branch-related jobs. He probably thinks I'm here to discuss deploying with my league in a month's time.

How wrong he is.

I look at the blank space at the bottom of the slip, which remains distinctly *unfilled*.

When I arrive, I push the door open. "Sir?"

But nobody is there. The whole office is empty, except for its furniture and a few scattered papers, one of which sits on top of all the others, typed and written in English.

I freeze up in the way everybody does when presented with a morally repugnant—but *tempting*—opportunity. I glue my eyes to the adjacent blank wall. *Don't look. There is no need to look. It is not your business, Eos,* I tell myself in a chant.

But if it were so private, why leave it out in the open?

I chew my lower a lip, fighting an internal war.

Oh, damn it to hell.

I'm skimming through it, at least.

Attention: ORA BRANCH 50

Mentors and Specimens of Branch 50 have been gifted the honor of executing mission PIO Morse. The success of this mission determines the fate of the Project itself, and is to be executed with absolute precision.

Four leagues from Branch 12 were selected to execute the task of capturing the PIO Morse target and failed in less than thirty seconds after landing on Earth. All leagues are suspected to have died, yet without physical proof, no conclusions can be drawn.

The first league deployed from Branch 50 will be that of the leading officer's. Should this league fail, as the last four have, the league charged by the counsel's second-in-command shall deploy as a replacement. If both leagues fail, PIO Morse will be passed on to another Branch.

Unauthorized movements of any kind will result in the prompt execution of the perpetrator at hand (without trial) and all involved. PIO Morse is not to be discussed with any persons outside of the mission unless approved by—

What the hell is—

"Eos Europa?"

"Yes, sir?" I snap to attention as Pavo walks in, his eyes as blaringly off-putting as his sister's. "My apologies. I thought you were inside, so I let myself—"

"No matter." Pavo refuses to sit. His eyes, depthless and oddly suffocating, ransack mine. I try twisting my expression into something akin to *disengaged,* but don't fully succeed.

He snatches up the letter and without hesitating—without a single, suspicious glance at me—shreds it into fine, wispy pieces, swiping them off his desk and into a nearby trash can.

Finally he says, "To what do I owe this visit?"

Trying to keep my hand from trembling as I do so, I dig a fist into my pocket and extract my termination order. The slip is wrinkled, ink bleeding out like red cobwebs. I thrust it forward so he can take it, begging my impassiveness not to fissure.

Pavo accepts it and reads fast. "I'd thought . . ." He stops and glances vacantly at the wall opposite him, clutching the slip tight in his thin fingers. "I'd thought for certain you'd deploy."

"Likewise, sir."

"Onyx has failed you. Under what grounds?"

"I think it's written on the slip, sir."

"Right—of course." Pavo pauses to read it. Then, after a few moments of silence, he huffs a sigh. "Your Psych Eval. Tragic."

"Yes, sir."

"The slip isn't finished," he says at last, indicating the blank space at the bottom—a jeering insult; salt sprinkled over an open, aching wound.

I swallow dryly. "Oops."

Pavo extracts another red-inked pen, leaning forward so he can write on his desk, and to my absolute astonishment I see a spider crawl sheepishly out of his pocket.

"Sir," I practically shout as it clings to his untucked shirt.

"What shall I write in this space, Eos?" he asks, unaware.

"I'd prefer groundskeeper, I guess." I gulp in an inadequate effort at swallowing, my sole focus off my own turmoil and on the mystery that is that spider.

Spiders do not exist on the Ora. They exist on Earth.

Which means . . . Pavo has recently visited . . .

"Hm." Pavo poorly feigns intrigue. "Why is that?"

"I enjoy being outdoors," I say, and it isn't a lie. Pavo writes the request in, filling up that gaping blank space, and folds the slip into a crisp, white envelope.

His eyes meet mine. They're distant, as though suddenly he's forgotten why we're standing here. And practically on cue, I see the spider scamper over the surface of his desk.

There's only one explanation for this . . .

I don't know what possesses me. I walk past him, eyeing the arachnid sharply. Pavo pauses, watching—his face twisted with disconcertion—as I hover my fingertip ominously over the spider's long-legged body.

And press down on it. *Hard.*

Why would Pavo go to Earth? For what reason?

And how did he manage without the CORE's permission?

Pavo clears his throat, apparently disinterested in defending himself in an argument that's indefensible. Spiders don't live very long lives, and that alone indicates he's visited Earth recently.

"Does the lead officer need the CORE's permission to take a podcraft to Earth, Pavo?" I inquire mock-innocently, wiping the guts of the spider off on my pants. "Or does a man such as yourself have superiority over those basic limitations?"

Pavo wets his lips. "Superiority, of course."

"You've gone to Earth recently." Not a question.

"Why don't you," he goes on sternly, with an entirely colder disposition, "focus on what's pertinent to you: *groundskeeping*."

I stare daggers. Calling him out wasn't supposed to set him

against me, but to gauge if he's ally-potential. If he's got access to a podcraft without the CORE's permission, and if he wanted me to deploy so badly . . .

No, Eos. Don't go there. That's crazy.

I croak out a halfhearted "thank you" and head for the exit of his office. I've nearly left when I hear him add, "You'll begin your new duties tomorrow, Eos. At dawn."

"Marathon?" I ask.

"Indeed, that's where you'll start off." Behind me, I hear the shuffling of paperwork. "You're dismissed, Europa. I bid you an enjoyable future in your chosen occupation."

Chosen, I think with an indignant sniff. *More like sentencing.*

I LEAVE PAVO'S OFFICE feeling like I've been un-capped and spilled all over the floor.

I'd promised to meet Merope afterward. A huge part of me wants to tell her everything—the way Pavo glared distantly at the blank wall after hearing I wouldn't deploy, and how weirdly bothered he'd seemed by that fact.

And that spider!

When, and *why*, would Pavo have recently visited Earth?

Despite wanting to tell Merope about all this, I figure it's best kept to myself. For now, at least. She'll be deploying in a month with the rest of my league; they've got bigger things to bother themselves with.

So this afternoon I skip past her pod. Mine is located farther down the hallway, almost at the very end, and thankfully I make it there entirely unnoticed.

My pod's doors hiss in my wake. I go ahead and dial a code

into the keypad that keeps it locked to all but the authorities, my desperation for privacy at an all-time high.

The room is small and dark, lit up in a wash of blue-green light cast off Earth, filtering in through my window. Alone for the first time since failing, I feel the deeper sides of myself shift and strain, threatening a collapse.

I keep it quelled.

So you failed. What does it matter? Prove yourself to be the best groundskeeper the Ora has ever had. You may never see one of the Muted face-to-face, let alone kill one, but the upside is that you'll—

I hiss through gritted teeth. *There is no upside.*

Suddenly I'm all too aware of the linoleum floor, the sheets of metal quilting the walls. How easy it would be for me to rip them up, leaving this pod in smithereens.

Compose yourself, Eos.

And so I do.

Taking the swirling chaos inside, I roll it into a condensed ball of marbled emotions, and tamp it mercilessly into the deep, dark recesses of myself—like a secret drawer, where I'll keep it all hidden away forever.

Though, that drawer *does* shudder slightly when I turn and see what's lying on my bed. A folded uniform. Gray. A jumpsuit with a large pocket over its breast sporting an embroidered name that I wish so badly wasn't mine.

Branch 50: Eos Europa

Groundskeeper

I exhale sharply, willing myself to refrain from picking it up and throwing it haphazardly across the room. Instead, I find the wherewithal to carry the uniform to my desk and leave it there, folded neatly for tomorrow morning—set to begin at the ungodly hour of 4:00 AM.

I sit on my bed—its old, coiled mattress springing as wildly as a trampoline beneath me—and glare at my uniform.

I drop my gaze to my upturned palms, begging for a skillset ability to suddenly emerge. My hands lie open, facing the ceiling like sunflower heads following the trajectory of the sun, and give in to a private beg. *Do something. Please. Anything.*

Nothing happens.

Do something, damn you!

I'd never assumed I'd be powerful. I'd only assumed that at the very least, I'd be competent.

That's what my genetic coding was for, after all.

But I'm a glitch. A bug.

A lemon.

THE NEXT MORNING IS so cold I can't stop shivering.

The atmosphere feels thin. My gray uniform doesn't do much to stop the chill. *Why* meeting at 4:00 AM on the weekend is necessary is beyond me—yet here I stand, shaking in the damp and miserable cold of Marathon.

I rake a hand through my silver hair—an unusual side-effect of my modified genetics—with waves as frizzy as a dandelion's spores, and take in the Master Groundskeeper, a man who has proclaimed himself *"Huckleberry."*

An earthly, native-born name if I've ever heard one.

"You're going to work like a slave," he says without a hint of good humor. "Get used to being dirty. Get used to mud crusted under your fingernails, and rocks in your boots, and days passing without a spoken word to anybody but the trees."

I cringe. "Sounds delightful."

He plows on. "The solitude is something you're just going to have to adapt to—hours, days, years of regular isolation. This is a solitary job, and it can sometimes get lonely."

Huckleberry's eyes lift, adopting a shade of sympathy, but also joy, like the look people take on when they're knee-deep in commiseration. "That's why I recommend reading."

"You do a lot of reading?"

Oh, of course he does.

Huckleberry.

"I do." The Master Groundskeeper gives me a sly wink as he pulls out a lofty, sun-bleached volume titled *A Collection of Shakespeare's Works.*

After an abrupt toss, he says, "This is a favorite of mine."

"You're giving it to me?"

"I'm letting you borrow it—for now," he clarifies.

"Well, thanks." I run a fingertip over the gilded, embossed letters of the tome and smile weakly.

We turn a corner shortly afterward, finding ourselves in a large plot of tilled soil. Heaps of plants—still entrenched in their temporary, plastic crates—wait to be repotted, their leaves green but slightly wilted.

So we'll be planting today . . .

I sniff, my nose running against the cold. Overhead, a large fluorescent light fixture casts rays of a deathly white glow over all the arena, leaving it colorless.

And to know, I think bitterly, *that my league is sound asleep in their pods right now, dreaming blissfully of their pending deployment. Meanwhile, I'm here.*

Here and looking distinctly like a prisoner who's fulfilling a long sentence of community service orders, with a book serving as her sole replacement for daily human contact. Because that's a real thing that's really happening.

This will be my life.

This will be my life *until I die.*

Huckleberry says, "I'm going to teach you the best ways to raise crops on a spaceship of this size and caliber. Though it's still cold outside, now is the best time for planting." He glances at me appraisingly. "You'll learn why."

I reply via deadpan stare, thinking, *Oh, I'm sure I will.*

The Ora's every branch is assigned a time zone, ours being all territories from Arizona to Montana. It's mid-winter there right now, and though I know I'll learn why later, I can't imagine how raising crops *now* is advantageous.

Huckleberry grunts, dropping to his knees before a crate of large-leafed plants. I watch as he digs his bare hands into a heap of mud and begins forming little holes.

After a stilted pause, he glowers up at me.

I sigh. "Are you going to make me—"

"Yes, I am," he grumbles.

"Right. Okay then," I concede, setting my things neatly out of harm's way then kneeling beside him. A blooming chill seeps through to my kneecaps, indicating the soil's wetness.

I chew a lip and say, "Now what?"

"Here." Huckleberry thrusts a plant into my hands before I'm able to adequately argue about it. He doesn't speak again, letting me learn through observing his techniques and copying them as he goes.

Eventually we fall into a rhythm of planting.

We start talking a little too.

I notice a plant with a cluster of dead roots and snip them away without Huckleberry's guidance, and his face lights up in a way that a parent's might after their kid's first steps.

"There ya go," he says brightly, his face a map of webbed and broken capillaries; eyes wreathed in wrinkles after a lifetime of working in the sun.

And perhaps, ages ago, smiling occasionally.

"See? Not that bad," he says.

"Well it's not rocket science," I say modestly.

"It's harder than it looks, but you're doing quite well. I think you've got yourself a green thumb."

"We'll talk again tomorrow, if they're still ali—" The words die on my tongue. Across the way is my league, all four of them standing in the fast-paced wake of Onyx.

As usual, Merope's the first to notice, her skillset granting her a heads-up. The others follow her gaze shortly after and see me here, *digging bare-handed in the mud.*

I feel my face burn.

I thought they'd be sleeping. *Stupid.* They're scheduled to deploy in a month! Of course they're going to spend as much time as possible training and preparing.

Preparing for PIO Morse, probably. What I'd *give* to be a part of such an important Purpose.

To top it all off, I think I've just insulted Huckleberry.

"It's a hard job," he mumbles, his voice thick with gravel as he follows my line of vision, "but somebody has to do it. Right?"

I yank another flower out of its pot. "Right."

An unmet gaze gnaws at my periphery. I tell myself it's okay to look up—just once more, and that's it.

Onyx is looking right at me, face as blank as an unpainted

canvass, lips taut. I don't look away, waiting for her to be the one to break eye contact—and when she does, I'm grateful for it.

Our temporary exchange was like that of two strangers.

Then she leaves, taking my league with her.

Aside from that, I didn't receive a single signal to indicate anybody had even noticed—*or remembered, or cared*—about me. Even Merope kept her eyes averted, and she's supposed to be my best friend. Are they really so ashamed of me they'd be willing to forget about my existence altogether?

I feel like I've been slapped.

Maybe I really am a nonentity now. Maybe Huckleberry is right and it's time I got used to being lonely and ignored. That's what happens to people like me, right? To the people who do the behind-the-scenes work?

I pick up a watering can. "Let's plant these," I mutter.

He stops me, placing a weathered, dry hand on my forearm in a lumbering and heartfelt gesture. "It's not that bad."

"What's not that bad?"

Huckleberry's eyes find mine again. "Being me."

My chest constricts.

God, I'm such a self-righteous, self-absorbed, self-everything ass!

"I'm sorry," I say, resting a hand on his. He heaves a sigh, lifting his pale-blue eyes skyward, toward Earth and the moon and the stars.

"I failed my exam twenty-seven years ago," he divulges. I keep my hand on his. I do the math and realize that'd make him around forty-seven—which doesn't make sense. *Every* specimen knows the Project began breeding specimens like us no earlier than thirty years ago . . .

I let it pass, noticing Huckleberry's grave demeanor.

"It was all I ever wanted," he goes on. "To fight as a soldier placed on the front line—just like you."

"How do you know I want that so badly?" I whisper.

"Those." Huckleberry's eyes point to my arms, spotted with cuts and bruises leftover from sparring. "I work the arena more than anybody else; I'd see you out here every day, trying to get people to practice with you."

For some incredible reason, I feel my throat tighten.

"Those specimens you just saw . . . They your league?"

"Yes," I say.

Huckleberry fixes me with a sad stare. "They will all die," he says chillingly, speaking with such utter certainty I'm left gaping and speechless. "They will die, and we will always be left behind, wondering if we could've helped them."

Then he drops his gaze to a tuft of thistles, and with bare hands, he begins ripping them up from the roots. And while he takes his anger out on the weeds, I take it out on my palms—my nails digging deep, hands forming fists.

And for the first time ever, it occurs to me that my league could actually disappear like all the others—"in less than thirty seconds"—and how would I handle that?

Have they already been debriefed on PIO Morse?

Likely, a quiet part of me says. *And if you go blabbing to them about it, you'll only look like a jealous fool . . . and a snoop, who's read a document so top secret, admitting to knowing about it could forfeit her own life . . .*

No, I won't tell them I know about it.

I'll keep it to myself like everything else.

I HAVEN'T SPOKEN TO anybody in my league for three days.

Merope stopped by last night—an act of desperation that led her to wasting nearly thirty minutes rapping her knuckles loudly against my pod's doors, despite the late hour. I'd sat up ramrod straight in bed, heart pounding.

Let her in, I'd begged myself. But I didn't.

Eventually she stopped knocking and resorted to pleading and bargaining, and I almost caved in then, but only didn't for fear of looking like a total imbecile.

Later, I told myself, *I'll tell her I wasn't even in my pod. That I would've answered had I been.*

When she stopped pleading and faded into total silence on the other side of my doors, I went still. I hadn't realized how it'd feel to hear her *give up.* In a fit of masochism, I'd leapt up and darted to the doors, pressing an ear against them to listen to each and every one of her footsteps as they walked away, widening the gap between us.

And I could've stopped her. I could've opened those doors with a press of a finger and invited her in, and we could've talked all this petty bullshit over.

But honestly, if I'd done that, what would I have said?

That I've been avoiding everybody intentionally?

How *pathetic.*

We've been all but birthed from the same womb, and yet this is what's standing between us. *My shame. My pride. My bitter and unyielding jealousy.*

I've built up a wall without realizing it. Instead of spending my final days with my league, I've been wasting away under the scalding afternoon sun with Huckleberry.

My time outdoors has gleaned a bronze to my pale cheeks and a few streaks of white highlights in my silver hair. I've grown used to dirt under my nails, the feeling of the hot afternoon sun seeping through the silky weight of my hair and rolling down my scalp like hot wax.

And despite looking like I've accepted this as my future, I haven't yet. It's still dreamlike. Maybe I'm still in denial. I can't shake off the pang of loss; the memory of a gun weighing down my palms, the cold bite of its steel. Like a phantom limb, I feel like it's there, but it isn't. And won't ever be again.

But my body still aches for it.

I've reached my final day of training. Just as I'm getting my potting tools put away, Huckleberry approaches me, nodding at the book at my side.

"Who's your favorite character?" he asks.

I dust off my hands, cracking open the book to where my bookmark is placed: *Much Ado About Nothing*. "I like Beatrice."

"She's a strong female character—unlike her sister, Hero."

"Hero is strong in her own ways."

"Perhaps," Huckleberry argues, wiping sweat off his forehead in the dying sunlight. Never before did I foresee myself in a gray groundskeeper uniform discussing *Shakespeare's Works* with some old guy without any friends, but here we are.

He looks at me softly. "Congratulations. Starting tomorrow, you'll begin working the grounds independently."

"Independently?" I chirp.

Huckleberry looks over his beefy shoulder. "You're going to be responsible for the Plantation. It's a great starting job, caring for all the plants, the crops. You'll do well."

"But I . . . I'll be working alone, then?" Huckleberry gives me a solemn nod as he starts walking away. I shout, sounding more desperate than I'd like, "What about returning your book?"

"Keep it," he says. And he doesn't turn to look back.

4

I FINISH WAITING FOR the irrigation system to run its full course, offering the supervision required of me between the dusty pages of *Shakespeare's Works*.

When the lawn is so wet it's soggy, I crank off the irrigation system, place my book aside, and raise a hand to shade my eyes from the beams of buttery sunlight.

I can see Earth, a looming ball of indigo patches and jagged continents, topped in a swirl of clouds.

I'll never get there.

I'll live and die, and never get there.

Shaking off a grimace, I finish my work—rolling up ropes of green hoses, storing equipment—and return to the new locker that I've been assigned in one of the lower levels of the spaceship, where other *unqualified-to-fight* specimens go. We're all corralled together in a locker-by-locker neighborhood of despair.

My closest neighbor is a girl who's always covered in an oil-slick layer of black grease. She's a technician, keeping the cogs and joints of the ship lubricated, working alongside an assembly of approximately twenty others.

We don't normally bump into each other, but today I leave the arena a little later than usual. Her hair is black and coiled in a tight mini-bun, kept well out of her bubbly, round face.

She was in Pavo's league before getting disqualified for what they called an "irrelevant skillset"—anything that can't actively help others, or kill the Muted—and for being mentally *unsound.*

Naturally, we get along well.

I snag her eyes as I approach my locker, dragging off a pair of dirty gloves. "Nova."

"Eos," she says by way of greeting while slamming the door of her locker with a little too much enthusiasm. I see she's crying.

I stare, eyes pinched. "Bad day?"

Nova regards me miserably. "My league received their official deployment date." I raise my brows. "Twenty-four hours from now and they're going to be on Earth."

"Lucky bastards," I growl, returning my eyes to my locker.

"But it's not just that . . . There's another thing." She leans on my locker, speaking as I dig through it. "But you have to swear you won't breathe a word of it."

"You must be desperate, to be confiding in me." I give her a long stare before indulging her. "Okay. Go for it."

"Something really bad is happening."

"How bad?"

"The last four leagues deployed have disappeared as soon as they stepped foot on Earth's soil."

I wet my lips, suddenly fully alert. "Disappeared?"

PIO Morse.

Four leagues disappearing, presumed dead.

But how does Nova know this?

"Their microchips suggest they died."

I try to disguise my panic. "*Suggest* they died?"

"The cause isn't clear." Nova scrapes a nail against grime on my locker absently. "Their organs failed simultaneously . . ."

"What could cause that?"

"Nobody knows," Nova says, eyes gravitating to mine like two dull moons. "But I don't think it's the Muted."

I raise my eyebrows in a *yeah-I-don't-think-so* kind of way.

"The Muted are vicious killers, but not even *they* are capable of killing *that* quickly—the way a dose of poison, or decapitation, or a bomb going off might."

"Right," I agree grimly. "Who told you all this?"

"My brother."

"Oh." Just then, I remember—her brother is Ares, the boy who sparred Apollo before and lost. "He's the specimen whose skillset is manifesting fire?"

Nova gives a slow, disdainful nod.

Nova and Ares are two of the only biological siblings birthed here on the Ora, all because of Ares's skillset. With an ability as rare as his, they tried blending the same genetics twice to produce a sibling with an equally special power.

But when Nova was born with eyes capable of seeing colors outside the known spectrum—an ability entirely irrelevant to the act of killing the Muted—it was a huge letdown.

So now she's a technician, and her brother is going to be one of the biggest contributors to our Purpose in recorded history.

"I'm afraid for Ares," she says, chewing a nail. "What if he and his league disappear like all the others?"

"Pavo has it under control. Those other four leagues were from other branches." I arch a brow. "Everybody knows we're the best branch in all of the Ora. Whatever it is that happened to the others, won't happen to us."

But despite how convincingly I say so, fear runs an icy finger down my spine. What could possibly lurk at Earth's surface, so ferocious and menacing as to be capable of killing more than one trained specimen simultaneously?

It couldn't be native-borns. *We're allies.*

So what could it be?

I store my work things in my locker, closing it. "Let's meet tomorrow, shall we?" I offer casually. "I'm going to go ask a few questions; I won't say much, and I'll only speak to those I trust."

"You're going to talk to your ex-league, you mean?"

I grit my teeth at *ex-league,* then nod. "They leave in just three weeks," I add softly. Voicing it aloud makes me feel unwell.

"Tomorrow," she agrees. I pat her on the shoulder by way of saying goodbye, but she stops me, gripping my sleeve with a startling wildness that stops me cold.

"What is it?" I say.

"Have you ever *wondered . . .*" She stops, pursing her lips as though they were speaking without permission, and stares at the fire alarm in the corner. With a shake of her head, she adds, "I'll see you tomorrow."

"Okay." I nod slowly, plagued by the strangest sense of utter foreboding as I leave.

I stroll absently through the Ora's dark hallways, lights sputtering and dying overhead as I pass. *What's killing them? What's waiting for us?*

Specimens churn in surges as they pulse through the arteries of the spaceship's innards, flowing down hallways and spewing into others, like blood through veins.

I find myself in front of my pod all too soon.

It occurs to me that I won't be sleeping here another week from now. I'm being relocated to a lower-level pod, closer to the lockers pertinent to my ranking.

Soldiers are reveled, located on the main-level, while the rest of us lurk in the shadows, tucked away in the spaceship's bowls, ignored and unappreciated.

I've been avoiding this place, but I will miss it.

I press a fingertip against the glass pad and the doors open with a swift sigh of air, abandoning the shadow-cloaked throat of the hallway in favor of my room. Not a second later, I'm startled by a shift in my periphery.

I freeze.

Merope gets off my bed, where she was sitting. The springs wine and jiggle, still compressed by Lios, who remains seated at the foot of the mattress.

Cyb is leaning against the window, looking out.

I back up a few steps.

Merope's hands are in her pockets. "Don't get mad."

They're dressed in deployment uniforms: black fabric that feels foamy to the touch, tucked under native-born attire so they blend in upon arrival. They have guns holstered, ammunition in bags, an excited edge to their demeanors—the way all specimens do when they're readying to deploy.

I am paralyzed by jealousy.

"Why would I be mad?"

"You've been avoiding us." Cyb's grey eyes look colorless in the dim lighting. "Don't you want to say goodbye?"

"Goodbye? Why so soon?"

"We could be deploying as early as tomorrow."

"What?" A spate of fear takes flight in my chest and cracks like erupting fireworks. "I thought you were deploying three weeks from now?"

Yet again, I think of PIO Morse. Their Purpose is special and extraordinary—they won't be following typical deployment protocol or procedures.

I chew a lip, realizing if they deploy tomorrow, it would be in anticipation of Pavo's league disappearing like the four other leagues before it.

Merope walks closer, violet eyes edged, regarding me with open scrutiny. "What do you know, Eos?"

She knows I know.

Is there anything I can hide from her skillset?

Lios and Cyb swivel their heads sideways, beholding me with such sterility, an outsider would assume the four of us were a group of strangers—not best friends, not *family.*

When I don't reply, Merope grips my wrist in hers, her hold as strong as a vice. Though she's able to detect us Empathetically from a distance, her skillset ability amplifies with physical touch.

Every skillset feels different. Apollo's, so far, has felt the most unusual. While Onyx's feels like a smear of white noise, his was a pounding heartbeat.

Merope's feels like dipping your toes into hot water, having a wave of it roll up your legs and seep into your body.

I try pulling my wrist away. "Don't read me!"

"Why not?"

"All you have to do is ask and I'll answer."

"*Answer,* then!" she snaps in a very *un-Merope-ish* way.

I grab a fistful of my gray uniform, twisting it nervously in my hands, drowning in the impatient quiet.

Admitting what I know is also admitting I didn't tell them.

I've been so obsessed with myself—*my path, my career*—and being unjustly angry at my league for getting what I've always wanted . . .

I can't believe I justified keeping PIO Morse to myself.

"I know about PIO Morse," I say at last.

"What!?" Lios exclaims reflexively. But when I try to repeat what I've just said, I realize I can't. It's as though my jaws have been glued shut by an invisible force.

Because they *have* been glued shut by an invisible force.

Cyb's skillset.

She glares at me so intensely, I feel like I've got a thousand accusatory fingers pointing at me from all directions.

"You do not," she whispers gravely, "need to repeat that."

Lios's jaw tightens. "Eos, I don't know how you found out about our mission, but you cannot—*cannot*—let anybody else know you're in on this. Do you understand?"

Cyb's skillset releases; I rub my stiff jaw.

Merope asks, "How did you find out?"

"When I went to turn in my termination order, Pavo's office was empty, so I let myself inside—"

"You went inside?" Cyb echoes, appalled.

"Just to lay the slip on his desk. But that's when I saw he had a letter open, and it wasn't in Mentor's Language." I lift my shoulders apologetically. "Couldn't help myself."

"You read it," Lios says, shocked and impressed. Cyb lets out a long-winded hiss of breath. "I can't believe Pavo would be so careless as to leave it out."

"Well?" Merope interjects, absently rubbing a thumb over her inner wrist—scarred lightly by a microchip implant, a true mark of a soldier. "What did the letter say?"

"The basics," I say cryptically.

"Which are?"

"Pavo's group is deploying first. It said PIO Morse's success was vital to the Project—and if it isn't achieved by our branch, it'll be passed on to another."

When nobody replies, I realize this is old news.

"And," I add breathily, "if Pavo's league fails, you're the ones who're going to replace his league on Earth. Immediately."

A deathly stillness ensues.

Cyb cocks her head, lips a rictus of hopelessness. "It's kind of strange, isn't it, that there is even a need for a backup league in the first place?"

This is when I realize they don't know everything.

I've got to tell them.

"PIO Morse isn't an easy Purpose to fulfill," I confess, a raw edge to my voice, looking at Merope—every part of her coiled and ready to spring.

"You think there's actually a *chance* Pavo's league will fail?"

"There's a very, very real chance," I tell her.

"How is that?"

"The last four leagues, all from Branch 12, have failed to complete this mission. They are believed to have died almost immediately after landing on Earth."

Lios rakes a nail over his stubbled chin. "From what?"

I echo Nova's earlier response. "Nobody knows, but it killed them in a way a Mute isn't capable of doing. We're left without a single clue as to what it is—"

"Except," Merope interjects suddenly, "that whatever it is, it doesn't want our Purpose fulfilled."

Cyb addresses Lios. "What could it be?"

He doesn't answer. None of us do. If the Muted aren't to blame, it's impossible to say what is—unless it's the native-borns trying to kill us, but why would they? They don't know all the details of the Project. They only know that specimens exist and are meant to help protect them.

We're supposed to have as little interaction with them as possible for this reason, but what if somebody, specimens from another ship, slipped up? What if they told the native-borns we are living safely in space while everybody else dies?

Even though we're trying to save the world, would that even matter to them? Would they be so furious with the Project for keeping some people alive, and leaving the rest, that they'd go so far as to kill specimens?

If we die, you die—that kind of thing?

I clear my throat. "Have you been briefed on the details?"

Merope spits an angry sigh. "We're not to be briefed until thirty minutes prior to when we're set to deploy. They don't want to risk anybody else finding out what we're doing."

"At least now we know why Onyx is treating it like a damn suicide mission," Cyb adds gravely.

Lios turns to me. "What else do you know?"

"Nothing." *For now,* I add mentally. *For now, until I've had a chance to squeeze Nova for every drop of information she's worth.*

I think of her last words to me. *Have you ever wondered . . .*

She *knows* something.

When I look up, Lios is staring at me. It's like he can see straight through my skin, the way only family can. He looks as though he's standing on some kind of emotional precipice he's been pushed to the edge of, and is at risk of falling.

Then he says, "I wish you were coming with us."

I could cry.

I've been feeling so derailed, so lost.

I'm feeling just like Huckleberry said I would, like I've been left behind to wonder, forever, if I could've helped them if only somehow I'd been there.

Looking Lios dead in the eye, I say, "I *will* see you again."

Merope laces her fingers through mine, squeezing my hand tightly in hers. "Meet us tomorrow in the assembly area?"

I lean sideways, into her. "What time?"

"Evening."

"The assembly room it is, then. For dinner," I say.

Suddenly Lios is pulling me into a hug. Merope leans in and a second later, Cyb's off the bed, joining the rest of us. We stay that way for a while.

And then they leave.

Lios swipes a handful of fingers playfully through my hair before pulling me into another hug. He whispers in my ear, "See ya tomorrow, kid."

I press my face into his chest. "See ya."

Cyb pinches my cheek. That's all she offers me—and for her, that's actually a lot. She trails behind Lios, linking hands, going to the same pod, the same bed.

"Their last night together," Merope mutters. "In private."

"I wonder what they plan on doing?"

"I've got a few ideas."

"I know," I say, walking her to the door. I point an index finger jokingly to my dimple. "I was being sarcastic."

"Oh, of course you were." Merope's eyes drift not to the exit of my pod, where I'm waiting for her to leave. Through my pod's window, a star falls, dragging along a glittering trail.

The moon looms beside our ship. It's swollen, entirely black except for a fingernail-clipping of white. We can see every dip, every pit and pulverized crater. And even farther beyond, we can see Earth hanging in the distance—lying low, lying in wait.

"Lios has always loved Cyb, huh?" Merope whispers, eyes peering distantly. "Cyb's always loved him back. What kind of magic happens to procure that kind of mutual satisfaction?"

"You can't be talking about *love at first sight*."

"Maybe I am." Merope turns, eyes lifted. Her face is pale as the moon itself, hair like spilled ink. "If it exists, they definitely have it together, don't they?"

"I guess." I shrug. "Do you think you'll ever . . . ?"

"Nah." Merope's answer surprises me. "You're the closest thing I've got to a soul mate."

We pause, and I can practically feel our final moments drift and fly and fall away—and when I try to grab for more, there's nothing but air.

"I don't know what I'll do without you, E."

"You'll be okay, M."

"What if I die?" Merope's question catches me completely off guard, and I realize her violet eyes are shining. "What if I die and I'm never able to say goodbye?"

"You know I hate goodbyes," I say casually, but an image, sharp and refined as glass, takes hold of me like the unshakeable grip of a nightmare: *Merope attacked and lying alone on the side of a road. A sky of blinking stars. A bed of rocks and pine needles, softened only by the bloom of her own syrupy blood rolling out from under her.*

And absolutely nobody there to rock her in their arms and tell her the only lie we, as people, want to be told:

Shh . . . It'll be okay.

5

THE NEXT MORNING IN the arena, I'm assigned the task of hole digging. *Seriously.* I dig holes all day and, afterward, another poor fool is bequeathed the job of watering down the soil, taking three-seed bunches and planting them in the holes I've dug.

This is now my life.

So after a particularly excruciating day, I decide I'll indulge in a shower before meeting my league in the assembly area later this evening. But first: *Nova.*

I wait for her at the lockers, watching the clock tick by, fast and unrelenting. I fold a fresh uniform and unfold it again, trying to kill time and find a reason to stick around.

Where is she?

Eventually the other technicians come in, rising from the black bowels of the spaceship. Two—Libra and Gemini—stop by my locker, flanking my sides like an ambush.

"Can I *help* you?" I ask indelicately.

"What've you done to Nova?" It's Libra speaking, a girl who's one of Jupiter's post-deploy specimens. She was once a front line soldier for his league, but after losing her left eye, she was rendered "unfit" for going back to battle. Now she has a leather patch there, framed by spirals of strawberry-blond hair.

I glance askance at her cohort. Gemini was also mentored, at one point years ago, by Jupiter. Why, exactly, he's been deemed unqualified to fight, I'm not sure.

And don't particularly care.

I clear my throat. "What have *I* done with her, you ask?"

They both stare daggers. The other technicians detect the twang of tension in the air, finding reasons to change quickly and leave the locker room altogether.

"*I* haven't done *anything* with her."

"You two talk a lot," Gemini states accusatorily.

"Yes, sometimes. Today we were hoping to meet for dinner to vent about the tedium of our futures," I lie. "She was supposed to meet me. Where is she?"

Libra shoots Gemini a fast glance. They make some kind of a strange, silent exchange. Then Libra says, "She's gone missing."

This does, admittedly, chill my blood a little.

"Missing?" I echo.

"Hasn't been seen since last night."

"And why," I investigate, feeling suddenly nervous, "did you jump to the conclusion of my involvement?"

If anybody overheard us . . .

If anybody has any reason to believe that I'm involved, that I know too much . . .

When neither Libra nor Gemini reply, I slam my locker door hard enough to startle them. Libra blinks slowly, squeezing her eye shut in exasperation, before saying, "*Rumors.*"

"What kind of rumors?"

"Her brother Ares said she'd spoken with you."

"Yes, in passing."

"So . . . you don't know where she is?" Gemini asks, his brows as thick as caterpillars.

"No, I don't. And if I did, I would've said so already."

They eye me suspiciously.

"My shift is over," I proceed brusquely, shouldering my way through them, clearing my path. "If Nova isn't coming, then I'll get on with my day."

"You *really* don't care?" Gemini bemoans in my wake.

"I don't have to." I turn, brandishing the pair with a glare so steely, they both flinch. "We're on a ship. In space. It is literally impossible for her to be anywhere else except *here.*"

Again, I turn my back on them. "My recommendation is you stop interrogating me and start looking for her. What do you think about that?"

I turn the corner, leaving them gaping in my wake.

I TRAIPSE UP THE spiraling staircase and am spat out in front of the assembly area: a large, domed room reminiscent of the inside of a hollowed egg.

Inside, a throng of specimens churns like an undercurrent.

I walk in, heading to the bathrooms, my mind still poised on the cusp of the unanswered question: *What now?*

What. Do I do. Now?

The bathrooms are empty—a small mercy.

I strip the lanyard I have dangling at my neck—with keys to all the places I work—and my clothes off, and find my favorite stall at the far end of the room. I twist on the hot water, which sputters initially before settling into a steady stream, leaving my skin a sensitive, sunburned pink.

After a few minutes of intense ruminating, it becomes clear that I've got one option: *I've got to find Nova, even if it makes me look suspicious, and even if it affiliates me with her further.*

Caution be damned. What I need are answers, and if she's the only one who can give them to me, then I've got no choice but to take a few personal risks. If I can't fight side by side with my league, the least I can do is fight here to figure this out.

I turn off the water just as voices erupt in echoes leaping off the tiled all-white bathroom walls. I freeze, listening to the rattle of lockers opening and closing, of voices becoming clearer.

"We should've deployed an hour ago!"

Again, I freeze. *Pavo's group hasn't deployed yet?*

I glimpse through the gap in my shower curtain to identify the owner of the voice: *Calypso Mar, one of Pavo's specimens.*

Calypso's pale, lightly freckled body strolls into view. She's stark naked. My eyes leap back inside my stall where I proceed to stand silently, dripping cold and wet.

Another voice replies, "Well, I'm glad of it."

"Castor, stop. You're being terrible."

"Because I delight in spending extra time with you?"

"No, of course not," Calypso adds, a smile warping the tone of her words. "I just—I feel bad, I guess. Ares's sister is missing."

"Nova, right?"

"Yeah . . . Ares won't deploy until she's found."

"So that's why Pavo dismissed everybody for an hour?"

"Basically."

"How many minutes," Castor asks, speaking in a coquettish, purr of a voice, "of that hour do we have left?"

"Forty-five," Calypso replies just as flirtatiously.

Oh god. What if they do something stupid and have sex in the showers, and all the while I'm forced to bear witness?

No. That's it.

I'm going to reveal my cover and leave.

Just as I rake aside the curtains, I hear "... but you've heard the rumors ..."

Luckily their voices carry just loudly enough to drown out the sound of my ruffling shower-curtains. I duck back in. Fast.

Rumors, Calypso, did you say?

Please. Go on.

This I'm willing to listen to.

In my haste, I miss the muttered reply from Castor, only catching the tail end. "... my skillset's capable of answering all these questions, you know."

After pausing for thought, comprehension dawns.

Castor's skillset is the ability to foretell the future in a series of glimpses—by degrees, and with variables, but still. It's helpful and advantageous, and not to mention hailed by the mentors.

I lean a fraction out of the shower, watching. Castor extends a hand to Calypso. With a single moment of physical touch, she will be able to foresee Calypso's future.

Calypso hesitates. "We said we'd never do this."

"Everything is different now, Cal," Castor cajoles. "What if there's a bomb? I could foresee it. We could save everybody. We could change *everything*."

"I don't know if I want to see what's coming."

"Please, Cal. Let me help you."

"What if what you see is unstoppable?"

"We will figure it out," Castor assures, trailing a fingertip from Calypso's temple to her freckled chin. She speaks so sadly, so *affectionately*, I almost look away.

I hear Calypso sigh in resignation and hold out a shaking hand for her girlfriend to take.

Castor accepts it delicately, engaging her skillset. "We'll just take a quick peek," she says casually.

There's an extended pause. I stand dripping wet and trying not to shiver. I dip my head through the gap, eyes locked on the pair as they stand rigidly, side by side.

Castor drops her girlfriend's hand, her face stiff as stone.

"What?" Calypso demands.

"The missing leagues," she says robotically. "You find them."

"We find their bodies, you mean?"

"No. You find *them*." Castor looks like she's just had the life sucked out of her—face as pallid as death, fingers quivering. She is even blinking back tears.

Calypso keeps her head slightly bowed, peering up through her pale, pinched eyebrows. "Their microchips indicated they all died of total system—"

"I know."

"That means they are dead, Castor."

"That means only that their microchips *say* they are dead."

"What?" Calypso breathes, panic-stricken, before pitching forward to take her girlfriend's hands in her own. "Tell me what you saw, Cas. Tell me everything."

Castor pulls away from Calypso's touch, flinching. A beat of silence follows, utterly tragic—even for me. "I saw your future."

"And?"

"I can't protect you."

"Why not?" Calypso asks, verging on tears.

"I could stop a bomb. I could stop a Mute's attack. I could even change the situation's circumstances." Castor looks up at her girlfriend with misery. "But I cannot save you from yourself."

Calypso's lip trembles. "Save me from . . ." She shakes her head slowly, loosing the pool of tears perched on her eyelids. "I have no idea what you're talking about!"

"You deploy tonight," Castor says, slogging on pants and a graying shirt. "Your league will disappear, like all the ones that deployed before you, but you won't die or be held hostage, or—"

"Why in the hell do we stay, then?" Calypso cries.

"You will stay willingly."

"Willingly?" Total silence. I choke back a gasp, my thoughts swirling wild as a cyclone. "But . . . but we'd be traitors."

Castor's eyes meet her girlfriend's dazedly, as though she's just awoken from a painful nightmare.

"Yes," Castor whispers. "Yes, you would be."

I PRACTICALLY SPRINT DOWN the hallway, hair dripping wet.

What the hell have I just accidentally learned?

If Castor's right, specimens aren't being killed upon landing on Earth's surface—they are choosing to stay, *willingly,* on their own accord. But why?

What could possibly be so tempting?

Specimens aren't born so much as bred, specifically to grow up and fulfill their Purpose. To betray it is unfathomable. *I can't think of a single reason I'd betray it, myself.*

I pick up my pace, shouldering my way through a heard of specimens migrating from the assembly area into the hallway, my thoughts buzzing and flickering like a half-screwed in light bulb, when a jolt of recollection strikes. *Microchip removal.*

That is the answer.

Castor specified that the other leagues weren't dead as much as they were made to *appear* dead.

By the abrupt removal of their microchips.

Without a pulse to monitor, of course the chips will relay total system failure to CORE's radar systems!

I feel my muscles tighten, joints locking up.

It's not a matter of *what* awaits specimens on Earth, it's a matter of *who*. And because microchip removal is practically an art form, taught only to specialists, whoever is awaiting leagues on Earth is definitely a full-fledged, security-breaching *traitor*.

A traitor persuading others to become traitors.

But with what argument?

And why?

I wiggle my way into the assembly area. It's nearly dinner, so naturally the place is packed with specimens of all servitudes and ranks, intermingling with one another. The moist odor of overcooked vegetables and chewy, unthawed meat is as rife in the air as the twang of spreading gossip.

"Move!" I grunt in exasperation to Juno, a nearby specimen with hair shaved down to her scalp. She eyes me aggressively as I pass by, unfazed.

I've got to get to my league. Now.

A beat later, and they're in sight, sitting together at a table lodged in a cubby-like corner. It's where we always sit.

Merope has already caught my eye, forewarned by her ability to sense me Empathetically. The others follow her gaze, faces splitting into smiles, which fade abruptly at Merope's calling.

"Something is wrong," she says, inaudibly, but I'm able to read her lips and am preparing to reply when the loud, shrill wail of an alarm rips through all conversation.

The whole assembly room stops, pivoting in unison to see where the commotion is issuing from. The entryway is a clot of frantic specimens, all raising their feet up as though trying not to step in something.

Water.

The area has been flooded.

A few moments later, accompanying the fire alarm, a series of sprinklers go off—probably activated by a trigger pulled from a lower level in the ship.

The alarm sounds shrilly, an agonizing, repetitive scream.

Somebody shouts, "Fire! There's a fire!"

But there isn't a trace of smoke in the air. And given how well-protected the Ora is in regards to preventing fires, the idea of one starting is difficult to believe.

I hear Jupiter, the third mentor and Tertiary Counselor of our branch, step up and attempt to take control of the situation.

"Specimens!" he shouts. "Return to your pods. The ship isn't on fire. There is nothing to worry about. An alarm near the arena has been triggered by accident."

Near the arena?

Meaning the place where my work locker is located?

"The false alarm is under investigation." Jupiter's words fade as I turn fast on my heel, ignoring Merope's shouts at my back, and run toward the watery chaos.

I feel like I've just been jabbed in the throat.

The lockers.

The alarm was pulled . . . by my locker!

"Eos Europa!" Jupiter booms as I pass, his long-fingered hand snatching ahold of my elbow. "Where is it you're going?"

"The triggered alarm . . . was it in the locker room beside the arena's entryway?" I ask quickly.

"Yes, actually. The CORE notified us that it was."

I hold up the lanyard around my neck. My work keys, giving me access to Marathon, dangle suggestively before Jupiter's dark and ominous eyes.

"Sir," I begin, not knowing at all where I'm going with this, but going for it nonetheless. "I—I just realized I've left the doors to the arena open. I planted crops this morning, and they are at risk of drowning if the area isn't closed off from the showers."

Jupiter looks furious. "What?"

"I'm sorry," I beg. "Let me take care of it. I'll be quick."

Jupiter studies me for a stretched second, his gaze as hot as coals pressed against flesh.

"Be quick," he barks eventually, and I launch myself into the dark hallway, icy water swallowing my ankles. The chaos from the assembly area fades, dying at my back as I trudge through the water pooling higher and higher, deeper with every level.

Jupiter doesn't know. Doesn't know the alarm wasn't falsely triggered, but *intentionally* triggered. He doesn't know that just a day ago, a girl stared longingly at it for reasons I didn't think twice about initially, but now understand.

It was a back-up plan, the alarm. A last resort.

Nova.

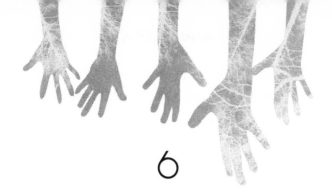

6

THE WATER SEEPS INTO my shoes, leaving them soggy and squelching and startlingly cold. I ignore the feel of them, sprinting down the spiraling hallway that descends to the lower levels of the spaceship.

Minutes later, I turn the corner and catch a glimpse of a redheaded figure jogging through the water, which now stands at nearly mid-shin. She swears viciously, her voice raw.

Calypso.

As though sensing my presence, she turns, darting a furtive glance over her shoulder. Our eyes meet—hers red and puffy from crying just moments ago. She must be going to the loading dock to deploy, stationed at the Ora's lowest level.

"The alarm has been turned off," she tells me.

I refrain from the urge to say, *No shit, I have ears,* given the loud pealing of it stopped like a heart nearly fifteen minutes ago.

Instead, I ask something pertinent to me.

"Shut off by whom?"

"Pavo," she says. *Oh, is that so?*

"I'm going to close off Marathon. Has Pavo gone back to the loading dock, or is he still patrolling the area?" Calypso eyes me warily, so I add, "Maybe he's already shut the doors for me."

Lie, lie. Lie some more.

"He's at the loading dock. We're deploying now," she says in a hasty, feverish tone. "I'm late."

"Right. Good luck," I reply, but her back's already turned on me as she stomps through still-standing water to the lowest level offered on the Ora: the loading dock.

Okay. What now, Eos?

To the lockers.

I trudge onward, reflecting on how badly it would all end for us if the ship were actually on fire. Acknowledging the potential disaster a fire could cause, the ship has been equipped with top-of-the-line security and precautionary measures; the alarms and sprinklers in every room are just one of many radical safeguards in place to ensure a multi-billion dollar project doesn't literally go up in flames.

It doesn't help that the Ora is like the Titanic in that there aren't nearly as many podcraft necessary to take us all back to Earth if shit did hit the fan. They're too expensive, podcraft, and can only carry seven people at a time—tops.

Finally I reach the lockers, realizing abruptly that they're all wide open, left ajar.

I stand still, taking it all in. The chain of lights overhead sputter and buzz. Water rolls back and forth, receding like a tide over the gray linoleum flooring as our branch of the Ora tilts, readying to launch the podcraft with Pavo's league.

My locker is open. A few others are too. The clock at the opposite wall has stopped ticking. There is a stillness to the area that suggests a kind of dormant unrest. It raises the hair on my arms, tickles the nape of my neck like a cold, stale breath.

I step in, breathing silently. Water drips, rolling off the lip of the locker cabinet and slipping in beads down white walls. For a few steady seconds, that's all I hear. *Drip, drip, drip.*

Then, *BANG.*

I flinch, startled.

The sound is from someplace around the corner, and after the echo of the original sound fades, there's another.

SPLASH.

I lurch forward, peering into the lower level bathrooms.

Debris falls from the ceiling in chunks; a solid square sheet of aluminum crashes into the water, leaving behind a black gap in the ceiling like a missing tooth.

I inch closer, compelled by instinct.

Why has only one sheet of the grid-like ceiling fallen?

Air whistles out of the air duct overhead, but that isn't the only thing I hear. A voice. A whisper.

"Up here!"

My eyes dart up, flitting immediately to the black hole in the ceiling. I see a face peering back at me, looking down from the small, square-shaped gap in the vent.

"Nova," I say breathily. "What the hell are you doing?"

"Get up here before they find you," she urges, eyes nodding to the shower stall beneath her. If I climb it, it will hoist me just high enough to climb into the ceiling's hole.

I stare, abhorred. *She really is crazy.*

"Hurry!" she orders, the timbre of her voice suggesting a genuine, underlying panic.

The shower stall walls are slick with water, and I slip a few times in my effort to climb it. Finally, I grab ahold of the shower curtains, managing to scale up the wall's side before ripping them off their rod altogether.

Nova holds out a hand. "Here," she says.

I take her clammy palm and she heaves, dragging me up just far enough for me to use my own strength and elevate myself the rest of the way.

The sheets of aluminum are a false, dropped ceiling. Higher up overhead is the real ceiling—so high it's seemingly endless, as dark as the roof of a mouth.

We scoot away from the edge, keeping ourselves hidden.

I fix Nova with a critical glare. "Do you care to explain why you decided to disappear?"

She gulps, refusing to reply for a few tedious seconds as she picks at a scab on her ankle. "I've been hiding from Pavo."

Hiding from Pavo?

She's lost it.

I humor her. "Why are you hiding from Pavo?"

Nova runs a tongue over her lip. "He's trying to kill me."

I'm suddenly wildly aware of how truly suspicious we look together, hiding in the ceiling.

"Turns out my skillset isn't as irrelevant as they thought."

"What?" I badger, mouth dry.

"My skillset ability enables me to see colors that don't exist for other people, to see a broader scale. Harmless as it seems, it's given me the ability to see things invisible to others."

"What kinds of things?"

"Things like energy—solar, electrical." Nova pauses for a few seconds, as though trying to decide if I'm worthy of being told any of this. Then she adds, "Souls."

"Souls," I echo, trying not to sound as skeptical as I feel.

"Souls emit energy. It's called an aura." Nova scoots a little closer to me, eyes lit up like matches. She traces a finger along the contour of my body. "And I can see them. They glow, like a rainbow sometimes, but other times they're a solid color."

"What do the colors mean?"

"The colors are indicative of mood—and one's future." I can't stop glancing through the ceiling's hole. If I've got the bad luck of Jupiter remembering I'm down here, he will be looking for me soon.

Or if my luck is even worse, Pavo will stop by.

"He's trying to kill me," Nova reiterates.

"Yeah, you've mentioned that—*why*, though?"

"Everyone has an aura," she says so quietly I almost can't hear her over the groan of the ship and the subsequent splash of rolling water. "Everybody *except* the mentors."

Nova tries grasping my hand, but I recoil away from her as fast as a cobra's strike in reverse. "You're not well, Nova."

"Nobody can know the mentors don't have souls like us, that they are different in ways we can't—"

A noise disrupts her. Splashing. The undertones of a voice barely muttered. Every second it draws itself closer to us, and I can't decide if I'm going to leap out of the gap in the ceiling and run for my life, or hold perfectly still and silent, and hide.

But before I can do either, Nova hastily whispers, "I needed to tell somebody. Eos, your group deploys next. You've got to warn them that things are not as they seem—"

"Shut up!" I hiss as the footsteps approach. She doesn't.

". . . and now it's up to you," she cries, eyes so dark and full of tears, they look like pools of wet tar. Her skin is as dark as the shadows shrouding her, leaving me to focus mainly on the stark whites of her eyes. "Tell your league that when they get to Earth, they must abandon their Purpose and run."

This gets my full attention.

"What?" I gasp. "What did you just say?"

"When they get to Earth, they must betray the Project."

"But that would make them traitors," I say, regurgitating the exact sentiments expressed by Calypso just hours ago.

Nova shuffles backward in a way that causes a disturbing amount of noise.

"Stop moving," I hiss, not realizing what she's doing until she's already doing it—lifting the lip of another sheet of metal at her right side.

"Who's the real traitor?" she whispers, crying as her nails rip the sheet of metal out of place, sending it crashing into the shallow water below us. Two gaps in the ceiling now: the one leading to me and the one that's a diversion. "Is it the liar, or the person being lied to?"

I reach for her but am too late. She falls through the ceiling and back into the water just as I hear Pavo enter the bathrooms in a tirade of frantic splashing.

The angle I'm sitting at positions me just perfectly. Through the gap at my side, I can see a mirror.

And in the mirror, I can see Nova.

Pavo slows his approach. I can practically hear his lips lift into a sinister smile. "Done playing hide-and-seek?"

"Where's my brother?" Nova asks.

"Deployed. Halfway to Earth by now."

"Are you going to tell him the truth?" Nova's voice is solid as steel and impressively strong. "Are you going to tell anybody what is really going on here? What the Ora really—"

In a flash, Pavo is gripping Nova's throat in his fist. I can see her feet swing, barely grazing the water below, as he lifts her up high and fixes her with a startling black gaze.

The pair shift out of view. A second later, I hear a heavy thud against the water and am glad I didn't fully see it—because somehow, *somehow*, I know it was Nova's body that just fell.

I hear Pavo's footsteps splash off. When I can, I dip my gaze through the gap in the ceiling, my hair falling in a silver halo around my face.

"Nova?" I whisper. The blood rushes to my face as I dangle upside down out of the hole. "Nova—are you okay?"

Then I see her.

Nova's body lies motionlessly in the water, her eyes devoid and empty, and suddenly I find myself swallowing back an acidic influx of hot bile, failing to stay composed.

I choke back a visceral scream.

Pavo killed Nova, just as she'd said he would.

I STUMBLE, FINGERTIPS TRAILING over a railing running alongside the curved wall of the hallway.

Everything is opaque, stained in gray shadow. I barely have the coherency needed to properly navigate myself through the ship's twisted low-level innards.

I feel like I'm wandering, looking at what's ahead of me but not really seeing.

My mind's eye is locked on Nova's limp and lifeless body.

I stop walking.

I don't even know where I'm going.

The hallway is so absurdly dark. The frigid water from the fire alarm sprinklers hasn't even reached this deep, soaked up and swallowed by drains on its way down the spiraling hallway that circles the ship's core.

Where is Onyx?

I haven't spoken with her since the day she spent forty-five minutes writing up my termination order, but in the face of a friend's death, it's Onyx who I feel compelled to go to.

I will tell her everything.

Everything her brother has done. Everything I've—

A voice. "Eos?"

I turn dazedly and see my league standing before me, all four of them dressed in similar, panicked expressions.

Everybody except Apollo looks terrified.

I realize Onyx isn't with them.

For some reason I address Apollo with my question instead of anybody else. "Where is Onyx?"

Apollo's brows pinch with intrigue. "Are you . . . okay?"

"Tell me where I can find Onyx."

Apollo glances back at our—*his*—league, as though asking for permission to speak freely.

I stare daggers. "Where is she, Apollo?"

"She's meeting us right now, at the loading dock."

"The loading dock?" I breathe, looking at Merope.

She looks like she's near tears, not because she's deploying tonight and she's afraid of leaving—but because Pavo's league deployed just moments ago, and is already gone.

Disappeared. Just like the others.

I shove Apollo aside in order to get to her. "Pavo's league?"

Merope looks so haunted, she's almost unrecognizable: eyes cut wide, lips pale. She looks like a ghost.

"Thirty-four seconds after landing on Earth, they all began falling off radar. Just like the rumors," she says distantly.

I cast a glance at Cyb and Lios, each looking grave.

Suddenly, I feel furious.

"They have to call off your deployment," I spit. "Unless they have a new game plan, they can't expect for subsequent leagues to succeed when the others—"

"Oh, we'll succeed," Apollo says slyly.

I'm about to ask how that is, when a voice echoes through the hallway. My head snaps behind us, finding the source. Even from a distance, I know it's Onyx.

I sprint off and am turning the corner, just close enough to finally announce myself, when I'm arrested mid-step by the sight before me: Onyx's eerie pitch-black eyes find mine, resting uneasily as her brother stands beside her, tight-lipped and angry.

"I tried taking precautions," he raves on, speaking in a loud whisper-shout, not noticing me at all. "But when Mind Scanning didn't work on her, I realized—"

Onyx raises a hand, halting his tangent.

Pavo follows her line of vision, finding me at last. "What are you doing here, Europa?"

"That hardly matters, Brother. I'm sending her back."

"But, Onyx—" I start.

"You're no longer a league member," she crows. "You need to leave this place immediately."

Onyx grips my upper arm and begins escorting me away when I'm held back by something, by another set of equally thin fingers and the buzzing feel of white noise.

Pavo has ahold of my other arm.

There is a very awkward beat of silence during which I'm the rope in a tug-of-war. The tension in the air is so dense it's palpable, leaving everybody on edge.

Onyx glares at him. "Release her," she snarls.

When Pavo speaks, it's through a growl. "The Ora has lost the last five leagues to deploy—including my own, which was by far the strongest from our branch."

Onyx snorts. "That is debatable."

"My league was capable of manifesting fire, controlling the weather, and brainwashing. What skillsets, Sister, do your specimens have to offer?"

I glance back at my league, disgusted by the fact that I've got to agree with Pavo. How could my league possibly be any better off than his?

"Make your point, Brother," Onyx replies dryly.

"I've seen this girl fight in hand-to-hand combat against a male specimen twice her size, and win," Pavo says passionately, his nostrils flared. "And why did she succeed? Because she had familiarized herself with her enemy. She was clever, resourceful, and had identified his weaknesses."

"She failed her exam!" Onyx brays. "It's illegal to send her."

"I don't give a damn if she's failed her exam, or if she's skillset-less, or if she's a *drooling invalid*. She's deploying with your league because she is smart and *she can fight*."

Pavo gives my arm a violent tug and Onyx loses her grip.

Onyx looks like he's just slapped her. "You're mad."

"Sending Eos is an advantage we cannot—*and absolutely will not*—pass up, Sister. This glory is ours to be had, and I won't allow a few petty rules to get in our way."

Pavo's face contorts, forming a grimace that speaks to just how agonizing it would be for him to see another branch granted this precious opportunity.

And then, he's thrusting me toward my league.

"She's deploying," he says. "That's the end of it."

"Brother—"

"Get her microchipped, briefed, and armed with both weapons and provisions. I'll see you all at the loading dock in no more than thirty minutes—they will deploy in an hour."

Pavo walks away without a backward glance at his sister.

Meanwhile, I'm left feeling shaken.

I came here to rat Pavo out for killing Nova, and now I'm about to be microchipped, briefed, and deployed alongside my league the way I've always hoped?

But there's one critical difference: my blind loyalty has been chafed and eroded away, ruined by a few hastily spoken words from a girl I didn't realize was a friend.

I will make sure Nova didn't die in vain.

7

ONYX TAKES A CUP and places it against my lips.

"Drink," she orders. I do as I'm told—even though, for all I know at this point, it could be poison.

Cyb, Lios, and Merope gather around, their faces glistening behind a film of sweat. It's absurdly hot in the laboratory, one of the many reasons the lower levels of the Ora aren't suited for long-term living.

In the corner, Apollo fans himself, apparently bored.

Lios swipes his sweaty hair. "Onyx," he begins, speaking in quiet circumspect. "Shouldn't we start briefing Eos?"

Onyx grunts, robotically taking the cup out of my hand and putting a chilly finger under my jaw. My nostrils fill with the pungent odor of rubber. She positions my arm so my wrist faces the ceiling, resting perpendicular to my side.

Almost immediately, I feel the drugs take. My tongue feels swollen, and the lights are suddenly too bright.

"Tell me about our Purpose," I say before I lose coherency.

"There's . . . a traitor," Merope begins, twisting her fingers in a fit of anxiety. "Her name is Mabel Faye, who was previously in servitude to the Project."

"For how long?"

"Almost a whole lifetime. She's of the First Generation."

Rumors are that the technology for modifying genetics to include supernatural abilities preceded the plague by nearly two decades, at least. By the time the plague, the A-42, struck—the most powerful of the world's governments having already joined together, wisely pooling funds and resources to create what's now known as the *United Government*—these advances in biological understanding had been mastered.

All thanks to the specimens that came before, which were created experimentally. They are known as the First Generation, who helped aid the Project before all others.

"And what did she do?" I ask with a swollen tongue.

"What Onyx is doing for you now," Cyb chimes in, her pale brow arched. "Microchips."

I knew it. "So that's it, then: Mabel Faye is waiting for specimens to deploy to Earth, and once they land, she's taking out everybody's microchips?"

"We *think* so, yes," Merope replies. "She's got backup, likely another traitor. It would be impossible to extract the chips from four specimens so quickly, in under forty seconds."

"Why do so at all?" I ask, dazed and trying to ignore the fact that Onyx is now swan-diving a scalpel between the flesh and sinew of my inner wrist.

I feel the dull pressure of her grip; the tug and strain of the blade as it dips deeper. But I don't feel pain.

Merope strokes my hair. "We don't know why. That's our primary Purpose, though: gathering intel on what she's doing and why she's doing it."

"And," Lios adds, "Mabel Faye is supposedly leaking loads of top secret material on the Project to native-borns." He chews a lip nervously. "We've got to find out how many people know about the Project, and smother it."

"Pavo says she'll tell us a series of lies—brainwash us, claim she has no affiliation with the Project . . ." Merope trails off, her fingers still stroking my hair. "We can't listen to her."

"Whatever she's saying, it's convincing," I say curtly, thinking of how in the hell five leagues were capable of being fooled into betraying their Purpose.

"She's the founder of a quarantine," Cyb says, going on with the debriefing. "A large one with excellent security and lots of resources—easily the best quarantine in Colorado." She stops for a second, hesitating. "If Mabel doesn't come directly to us, the way we suspect she has with the others, the only way to get to her is through the quarantine."

"Meaning gain membership," Lios clarifies. "Find a way to earn her trust—and the trust of fellow members—and sniff out the funny business."

"Why wouldn't Mabel come directly to us?" I ask as, to my far right side, Onyx drops the microchips into my wrist: a small octagonal, pewter-colored chip, which is meant to track my every move, my coordinates. Another to track my pulse, vitals, and my general health. And one final chip, a cherry red orb . . .

Which she leaves out.

Lios says, "We are the first league to deploy almost instantly after a previous league that has disappeared. We're hoping she'll still be too busy dealing with Pavo's league to prepare herself for our unannounced arrival."

"There's no way she knows we're coming," Cyb adds.

"And if," Merope goes on, "Mabel doesn't come directly to us right after we land—*when* we see her later on—she must not know that we're specimens."

I swallow dryly. "We're to pretend we're native-borns?"

"Natives looking to join the quarantine," Lios affirms.

"Easy enough," I grunt.

Onyx stops what's she's doing and suddenly says, "Go to the loading dock." We all exchange glances. "The four of you are dismissed," she reiterates coldly. "I'll finish prepping Eos and we will be there in ten."

After a few additional wordless glances, the four of them file out of the laboratory together, leaving Onyx and I alone while she seals my incision with a Q-Tip dipped in liquid stitches, healing the cut instantly. It leaves a faint scar, a pale silver line as thin as thread, wrapped alongside my inner wrist.

The microchips are inside, set close to my ulnar artery as to monitor my vitals, as well as make it impossible to remove on my own without risking my life.

I've always wanted a microchip scar. It's the ultimate mark of a soldier. Yet today, after what Pavo did to Nova—right before my eyes—I find myself resenting it.

"There's something I've got to tell you," I confess.

"What?" Onyx asks dully.

"I saw your brother kill a specimen this afternoon."

The room, aside from a droning whir of air and the subtle groan of the ship moving, is totally silent.

Onyx's nostrils flare. "Nova," she says decidedly.

"You knew?"

"Her termination was authorized days ago."

"Authorized? On what grounds?"

"That is none of your concern," Onyx says, rolling back her chair and stripping off her rubber gloves. "Though I am sorry you had to see it."

"He strangled her!" I snarl. "You're telling me that's how all ordered terminations are regularly performed? Through the act of strangulation?"

Onyx licks her thin lips. "He strangled her?"

"Yes."

"You're sure? You saw it?"

"Yes," I echo, despite knowing I didn't actually see his fists around her throat; it was all through a mirror, and I'd only been able to see her legs dangling in the air.

But how else would he have killed her?

Onyx studies me, glaring through her depthless eyes, and all of a sudden it's as though I'm jettisoned back in time, thinking of the days we would laugh and play together—when I was young and naïve enough to call her *Mom*.

"Why don't you tell me what's really going on," I suggest.

"What is that supposed to mean?"

"There is more to this," I whisper wildly. "There is more happening here, and you're not telling the truth—but now, right *now*, you can."

I reach for her hand, but she pulls away.

Unfazed, I say, "Tell me. Please."

But suddenly an alarm sounds—a slow, dreary wail. It isn't at all like the fire alarm. More of a call to arms, the kind of blare that might announce a tornado's approach.

Onyx tells me it's time to go, ushering me off the tissue-paper covered table and toward a doorway—but before we step out into the hall, she stops me.

"Find Mabel," she whispers. "Find her."

I look at her, startled by the severity of her eyes.

"I will," I vow.

"No," Onyx snaps, gripping my elbow hard. "Promise me you will stop at nothing until you do."

The alarm continues to blare, a countdown. The podcraft at the loading dock is ready to launch.

"I will find Mabel Faye," I declare again. "I promise you."

Onyx gives me a flighty nod and easy as that, we're walking down the hallway together, descending ever deeper into the dark bowels of the Ora.

When we arrive at the loading dock, I see the others.

They're gathered around a table of weapons. Backpacks and water bottles and granola bars are piled in heaps, and it appears to be something of a free-for-all.

I lift a backpack—it's already full, pre-packed with camping supplies of all kinds, most likely.

Nobody stops to pay me attention. I'm glad of it and leap into the chaos, grabbing supplies, loading guns, and examining a series of knives and other weapons.

Then, a voice. "I *hate* these damned alarms!"

I glance up and realize it's Apollo speaking. He's leaning up against the wall casually, as though deploying in a few minutes is not the most terrifying thing he's ever encountered. The rest of us sport pale, sweaty faces and shaking hands.

"Apollo, now isn't the time," Onyx barks, guiding us to the exit across the room.

I grab a pistol and a few magazines, stopping to consider the spread of knives more carefully.

"You'll pick that one," Apollo says, eyeing a slender stiletto knife at the end of the table. "It's feminine. It's so . . . *you*."

I glare at him, grabbing a vicious skinning knife with a spate of serrated, toothy edges and a hooked end, and raise it up to his bare, ghostly-pale throat.

"Ah." He laughs. "Wasn't expecting that."

I press the blade a little harder. The serrated edges cling to this delicate flesh, pulling enough to aggravate his skin, leaving a track of light pink behind.

Then I lower it. Onyx is right. *Now isn't the time.*

We change into cold-weather clothes: sweaters, jackets, and fur-trimmed boots. There's a pile of hats—haphazard in style, but all goofy—which we pick from. I take a knitted ear-flap hat and when Lios takes one, he selects the ugliest hat available. And on purpose, I'd guess. The hat is as round as a bowl, and brown, like a misshapen mushroom or chocolate truffle.

He puts it on proudly, giving me a sideways wink.

"Let's go!" Onyx shouts. "We're out of time!"

My nerves officially start kicking in, and all too soon we're following Onyx through a large set of steel doors, entering into a cavernous room. The ceiling is so high it can't be seen, a pocket of indecipherable shadow.

Stationed at the room's center is a podcraft: a smaller craft meant for temporary trips to Earth. It is auto-piloted, driven like a drone, and operated by somebody working in the CORE.

The podcraft issues a sweeping neon-green light—lighting up brighter, only to fade gradually, like the slow sweep of breath while you sleep.

But as the time grows nearer to takeoff, the neon-green light picks up speed, eventually transitioning from a breath, to a thudding pulse, to a blink . . .

Then it launches, with or without you.

And just now it flips from a breath to a pulse.

Everybody stiffens, including Pavo, Onyx, and Jupiter.

"Specimens," Onyx commands. "Line up!"

My league and I stand at attention, lined up in front of the three mentors of our branch. My mouth goes dry at the thought of previous leagues—Pavo's, specifically—having done just what we are now, hours ago, but now *they're gone.*

In front of us, Pavo begins pacing. "Your league is our last chance at success. The last chance we have at bringing not only glory to Branch 50, but freedom."

Merope and I exchange a quick glance. *Freedom?*

Pavo grins. "Executing PIO Morse is of such importance, our spaceship, the Ora, has been contacted by its sister-craft, Sors and Fortuna."

We almost never mention the sister-craft, seeing as they are, until we fulfill our Purpose, irrelevant to all specimens. There are three deployable leagues per branch; after they have all deployed, a trial is held to determine which league performed their Purpose the best. Then, the league that's chosen, the cream of the crop, is admitted to the Elite rankings—sent to live in total harmony for the rest of their lives on Fortuna.

It's the future every specimen dreams of. Due to the wide array of genetic differentiations we have, we're unfit to live alongside the natives on Earth. So we're born, we fight, and if we fight well, we live out the rest of our lives in peace.

But two of three leagues won't be picked for the Elite, and they are forced to redeploy—to continue to fight on forevermore, until they are eventually killed. Where they would go should we defeat the plague destroying Earth, I don't know. Most of us try not to think about it.

The other sister-craft, Sors, isn't hospitable. It's a quarter of the size of the Ora—built for a small crew of only a few hundred people, at the most—to monitor Earthly activities. These crew members control the CORE, and are shipped to Earth regularly to keep in touch with what's going on governmentally.

Pavo rubs his palms together. "You're aware of how difficult it is to be admitted to the Elite rankings? Well, in the case of PIO Morse, a very rare exception to the rules has been made."

The podcraft leaps from a pulse to a blink, and though we know it's almost time to take off, we're hanging on Pavo's final words like they're a lifeline. He strolls up and down, eyeing each of us individually, his lips stiff and posture rigid.

"This mission—your Purpose—is so important that they are willing to accept the league which accomplishes it immediately, without trial." Everybody stands a little straighter. "Should you complete this mission flawlessly, the five of you won't even return to the Ora. You will go straight to Fortuna."

I realize I'm struggling to breathe. The possibility of us all going to Fortuna . . . a utopic spaceship without pollution or crime or danger, rife with opportunity . . .

None of us have to die. We could all go there, live together.

Jaw slightly agape, I turn to look at my league. Cyb's silver-gray eyes are spilling with tears. Lios is looking down, pinching the bridge of his nose, swearing silently. Merope and Apollo look as though they could positively *sing.*

And yet there's something holding me back—a certain echo whispering sourly in the back of mind, reminding me of a vow that I've made to somebody.

Nova.

But do I even believe her? How could I possibly buy into the claim that her skillset ability enabled her to see souls? That our three mentors don't have them?

Merope clears her throat. "What about mentors?"

Pavo looks elated that she cared to ask. "Mentors will also be accepted to the Elite rankings—as will your lead and the other authorities in your branch."

So, we'll all benefit from this.

Including Pavo.

The light of the podcraft accelerates from a blink to a rapid and startling flicker, casting us all in a disorienting strobe of neon-green light.

My heart picks up, matching the strobe's pace.

Pavo waves a hand in conclusion. "Find the target, but don't kill her—bring her to me so that I may have the pleasure of doing so myself." His dark eyes take on an evil sheen. "She will pay for defaming the reputation of the Project, for lying to ignorant native-borns. She won't get away with this!"

He gestures to the podcraft, urging us to board. I heave my backpack over my shoulder, readjust my hat over my hair, and try to remain calm.

"Don't forget to cover your tracks," Pavo purrs as we line up to board the podcraft. "One wrong move and your invitation to the Elite rankings will be instantly forfeit."

Cyb boards, followed by Apollo and Lios, and as I scoot closer to my turn, I realize I won't get a chance to say goodbye to one of my newest friends: *Huckleberry.*

Will I ever see him again?

It's my turn. I ascend the small steps leading to the mouth of the podcraft, handing my backpack over to Lios, who tries to situate it beside his, buckling it safely away. Much to my chagrin, my hands shake when I grip the podcraft's hood and begin wiggling my way aboard.

"Tighten this!" Lios shouts over the incredible whir of the podcraft's booming engine. I can barely hear him, but he nods to a seatbelt and fastens it for me, cinching it tight.

Suddenly, Onyx is at my side—a looming, tall shadow.

I glance up at her curiously. "Onyx?"

The podcraft expels a hiss of air, preparing for takeoff, but she makes no move to leave. Her hand finds my hair, and in the most strange, disconcerting way, she strokes it out of my face.

Eyes holding mine, she says, "I tried."

"What?" I shout, though I've successfully read her lips.

"I hope . . ." Onyx pauses, taking a swift step backward and instantly setting herself out of the podcraft. "I hope this isn't goodbye for us, Eos."

Her eyes flash to the seat in front of me, at Apollo.

Then, before I can reply, she grabs the wing-like door of the podcraft and slams it shut. My league and I are plunged in a muted kind of quiet, the engine roaring loudly outside, but softened behind the armor of steel enveloping us.

We begin to move.

Cyb yelps as we lurch forward. Lios, sitting beside me, gives my hand a squeeze. I look to the front seat and see my best friend sitting bravely, her eyes fixed on a small rectangular window at the front of the podcraft.

Through it we see where we're going: a large set of steel doors that open horizontally, like jaws. The podcraft lifts up its rear, tilting us forward, as it perches for takeoff. The jaw-doors grind open, emitting us to a departure chamber.

The podcraft floats inward. The feeling of flying, even just a few feet in the air, is like a finger tickling my stomach. I hear the jaw-doors grind closed behind us, and suddenly there's a cloud of white gas exploding in plumes all around us; it fades, and before us stands another set of doors.

But we don't hear them grind open. We see it happening, but hear absolutely nothing, because the doors are opening up to outer space—an endless sweep of total obscurity, freckled with flaming, brilliant white stars.

And for the first time ever in my life, I truly realize—with a gasping, suffocated feeling of awe—how small, how totally and completely insignificant we all are in the scheme of the universe.

Space is anything but empty.

The podcraft glides out of the open doors, subjecting us to the chilling sensation of being surrounded by absolutely *nothing* and *everything* all at once. I feel the push of the engine as it flares back to life, inaudible in the suction of soundless space propelling us forward as fast as a rocket.

So fast I barely have time to register it, we're skimming the planet's atmosphere. Sparks fly, exploding at the tipped nose of our podcraft. We trip into the unyielding force of gravity and are suddenly plummeting wildly to Earth.

In unison, we're thrown back in our seats. My chest feels as though it is the foundation for a castle built out of bricks—heavy and pressed breathless. I chance a look sideways at Lios and see he's glistening with beads of sweat. His face is pale; he's blinking and wheezing as though he's on the verge of blacking out.

I take his hand in mine. "Almost there," I say, but my voice is swallowed up in the racket of our podcraft shedding an outer-layer of itself, which has suddenly caught fire.

Breathe, breathe, breathe . . .

We bank left and squish into each other, absorbing the force of the turn, and our podcraft steadies. We've made it through the chaos of the atmosphere. I could *cry*.

The planet ripens before our eyes, abstract blotches of color becoming identifiable: dark oceans and pockets of valleys, forests of deep green, and snow-tipped periwinkle mountains. It's all stitched together in a lovely, quilted landscape—and for totally different reasons than before, I've lost my breath.

We dive, plunging into a white cloud. Everything changes.

The sky is dark—so dark, it must be dusk.

The world outside is blocked by heavy clouds, pumped full of ready-to-fall snow, and I realize we're almost there.

We're so close.

After eighteen years, I'm almost there.

Our podcraft steadies itself in a graceful glide. We're still moving quickly, but it doesn't feel like it. For a few seconds, we are entranced blissfully in the views of Earth's surface rolling out like a rug beneath us.

I swallow, chewing a lip. It won't be long until we spot one of the Muted: their shadowed, sinewy bodies, lurking and clawing and shrieking loudly. The new apex predator.

Cyb sighs with relief as the podcraft beeps in a steady, inviting way. We're free to ready ourselves for the swift disembarking that is minutes away.

Everybody begins digging wordlessly through their supply bags and weaponry. I sheath a knife in my boot and keep a pistol tucked in a holster strapped to my leg, a loaded magazine waiting in my left pocket.

Lios, surprisingly, stuffs a granola bar in his face, as though he hasn't eaten in days. I sip from a water bottle, but that's about as much as I can do. Eating *now* feels impossible.

When the sound of ruffled backpacks—zippers being zipped and unzipped—and supplies fades, there's only one sound left to fill the podcraft: the sound of rapid breathing, panicked and as uneven as a nightmare's spur.

The podcraft dips lower, descending into a cluster of trees, their branches drooping under the weight of thick slabs of freshly fallen snow. We hover midair, then descend vertically through a copse of wilted trees, and land.

Nobody speaks.

Up front, I see Merope click something on her dainty left wrist that lights up: *a stopwatch.*

The podcraft's door whooshes open, and a gust of snow-flecked winter wind floods in. It's quiet, the world's noises stifled by a curtain of snowfall, but the noise inside roars as loudly as a storm gathering along a nearby horizon.

My heart is cannon fire.

This is Earth.

8

THE FOREST AROUND US is boundless.

It sprawls in all directions, the horizon composed of black treetops as jagged as teeth, silhouetted against the bright silver sky arched overhead. Snowflakes fall in an onslaught of slow, sleepy spirals, clinging to my eyelashes.

Everything is half stooped under the weight of snowfall, so burdened as to wilt. I inch farther into the clearing our podcraft has landed itself in, positioned at the center of it.

The others spill out of the podcraft, silent as ghosts, and fan out in my wake. I hear the racking of slides and the subtle whine of stretched leather boots, but that's it. The world is silenced by the influx of snowfall, falling as heavy and thick as a set of velvet drapes, dulling the sharp edges of sound.

My focus settles on the dark recesses of the woods—on the gaps between trees, the shadows under low-hanging branches, and the uncannily finger-like, skeletal limbs of foliage sleeping its way through winter.

We're alone.

Everything is totally, utterly calm.

I give a sharp exhale, casting a glance over my shoulder at my league positioned behind me. Apollo's at one end, Lios at the other, the pair separated by Merope and Cyb.

Merope's eyes snag mine. I ask her, "Are we clear?"

She gives a soundless nod in reply.

With her skillset being what it is, she's capable of tapping into the emotional frequencies of any living thing, be it a squirrel or a human being or a Mute.

Or a handful of specimens that went rogue.

Cyb tags Merope with an accusatory glare. "Are you sure?"

"I'm positive," she retorts curtly, though I notice she returns her eyes to the woods, as though she's struggling just as much to trust herself as everybody else is.

Her stopwatch beeps wildly, and she clicks it off.

Lios's asks, "How long?"

"That was the one minute marker," she says, her eyes like coal in the dusky darkness. "Looks like we've surpassed all the other leagues, already."

"She's still dealing with the last league." Apollo walks up, his glossy pistol raised, ready. Snow speckles the mop of black hair on his head.

Cyb eyes him wearily. "I can't see a single sign of them."

I step farther into the silent clearing. "Cyb's right. It looks like every sign of them is gone."

"Snowed over?"

"Obviously, but if they struggled," I add distantly, passing a hand over the bark of a tree, "there would be other signs. Broken twigs, chipped bark . . . dropped belongings."

"Blood." Cyb's face is gaunt.

"Blood," I agree grimly. "It's as though they filed out of the podcraft and walked, in an orderly fashion—" I stop, feeling all of a sudden like I've been doused in ice water.

Merope's lips go white. "What's wrong?"

We are so stupid.

We are so utterly, utterly stupid.

"Her . . . Her skillset," I groan. "We never asked . . ."

"We—" Cyb looks frantically back and forth between the rest of us, her gun dropped to her side. "Did *anybody* ask?"

"No, you're joking!" Apollo sniggers, his lips elevated in a broad, wolfish smirk. "You're telling me everybody here forgot to ask about Mabel's skillset except for me?"

I sigh in relief. "You asked?"

Apollo's face shifts, then stiffens. "Mabel's skillset is the ability to transfer information. So, for example, if she witnesses something first hand, she can transfer that memory—"

"We know," Cyb snaps. "Onyx has the same skillset."

"Well, she can't *control* anybody, then," I say, mulling over the possibilities. "But it looks like she's gathered an arsenal of at least five other leagues—and who knows what skillsets they have to offer, which she may be exploiting."

Just then, a chilling echo drifts over the landscape. Not the echo of wolves howling or the whistle of wind, but the distinctive high-pitched, ragged shrieking of the Muted.

I swallow hard, readjusting my grip on my gun.

"Let's get going," I say.

We begin walking away from the clearing and sink deeper in the folds of the woods. Cyb decides it's the perfect time to give us all an abrasive, unnecessary reminder. "If anybody sees a traitor, they are to be shot on sight."

Apollo snorts, whirling so he's walking backwards, facing us all with those dark eyes. "Who says we have to kill anybody?"

"The Project," Cyb offers rigidly.

"The Project isn't supervising us. It's too busy living in total harmony on Fortuna while the rest of us fight." At Apollo's bold treason, our postures stiffen. "I get they are traitors, but they are still specimens like us."

Lios pins Apollo with a lethal glare. "Enough."

"All I'm saying," Apollo goes on, holding his palms up in a gesture of surrender, "is if we saw a traitor and decided to turn a blind eye, the Project wouldn't ever know otherwi—"

Lios lunges for Apollo.

"What you're suggesting could get us terminated," he relays darkly, grabbing Apollo's collar. "Say another word that may put us all in unnecessary danger, and I'll kill you now and blame it on a damned Mute."

Lios drops Apollo, who is still smiling. "Fair enough."

But Apollo has already made his point—because none of us really want to kill a fellow specimen. What if we stumbled upon any of Pavo's specimens: Ares or Calypso?

Could I kill them?

I grit my teeth, unable to shake the feeling that Apollo has planted a seed inside me—inside all of us. But why?

What are his real intentions?

I HAVE ALWAYS THOUGHT that days on Earth would fade slowly, drizzling from a gray-blue dawn to a buttery day, to a golden dusk and a starry, black night.

I'm not sure if that's ever the case, but I *know* it's not today.

Darkness falls so fast, it's as though the sun has been snuffed out completely. Less than forty-five minutes ago, the forest was lit up in gray, ignited by whatever light filtered through the thick clouds overhead. But now it's dark. *Really dark.*

We haven't encountered a single Mute—thankfully, though also anti-climactically. I long ago holstered my gun and haven't seen reason to take it back out since.

For hours, we traipse through shin-deep snow, our breath expelled in vaporous fumes. The midnight cold is so intense, it feels almost like being wet—as though you're walking in sodden clothes, a kind of frigidity that digs so deep it hits marrow.

Eventually, Lios cracks. "Enough is enough," he says as he drops his backpack and begins digging through it with clumsy, numb fingers.

"Ah." He sighs, extracting a torch. "Thank god."

"Why not use a flashlight?" Cyb asks haughtily as she drops to his side, kneeling. "Are you against modern technology, Lios?"

Lios sniffs indignantly, taking out a flashlight and holding it up alongside the torch as he asks, "Which of these gives off both light and heat?"

Cyb's eyes flash. "You don't have to get sassy."

"I'm not getting sassy."

"You kind of are."

"Is *this,*" he asks, taking her fingers in his and holding them to the newly-ignited torch, "getting sassy?"

Cyb grins, relishing the small amount of heat released by the torch's fire. We follow her lead. It's not a lot, but it's enough.

Apollo finds the wherewithal to retract his hands, pulling out a glistening brass compass.

"We're five miles off," he says, a huff of his breath clouding the compass's glass. We've been heading due north all this time in the effort of tracking down the quarantine. "We're going in the right direction, but with all this snow, we aren't going to get there for a while."

Cyb groans noisily. "Five miles still?"

"If only we'd deployed during the summer—we could run that distance in an hour, tops," Merope, the fastest runner of our whole league, laments.

I give her a narrowed, sidelong glance. "No running."

"Let's just keep up the pace," Apollo concludes, his black eyes desolate in the torch's dim, flickering light. "Eos," he adds, noticing me looking. "Help me, will you?"

"Help you with what?"

"Navigating." Apollo throws the compass, and I catch it just before it hits the snowy ground. "Merope and Cyb, keep your eyes open for the Muted. Lios, why don't you lead the way?"

Cyb snorts, as though to say, *Who made you boss?* But what he's suggesting makes sense: divide tasks, keep constant vigilance, and work together. That's the purpose of a league, isn't it?

So we don't argue.

Lios trudges forward, leading the way. Cyb stations herself at the end of the line, looking behind us. Merope wanders back and forth between the pair, keeping communication consistent, while Apollo and I remain squished in the middle.

He nods at the compass. "We're heading north." Pointing a finger at the compass's large N marker, he adds, "Make sure the arrow stays here—"

"Do you take me for a fool?" I snap, glaring. My fist drops to my side, taking the compass with it. "I'm well aware of how a compass works, Apollo, and given its simplicity, I really struggle to understand why you'd consider it a two-person job?"

"Maybe I just wanted to talk to you."

I elevate my chin. "Start talking, then."

His gaze burns at my periphery—only now do I realize how much taller he is. Aged twenty-three, he's a man. Aged eighteen, and barely so, I'm just a girl.

"What's your favorite color?"

"You're joking," I scoff.

"I bet Lios doesn't know Cyb's favorite color," he remarks coolly, keeping his voice low. "My favorite is red—if you're at all interested in knowing."

I am not. Not really. I heave the strap of my backpack over my shoulder again, the bulk of it crippling. "Why are you really talking to me, Apollo?"

He analyzes me for a few tedious seconds, his gaze like a slow, steady burn. I wet my lips nervously, crumbling under his scrutiny—the strange effect it has, like a paralyzing superpower.

And then I realize: "I don't know your skillset."

"Did you think Onyx kept me hidden away from all of you just for fun or something?" He reaches down, cupping my hand in his, and lifts it up, looking at it like a palm reader. "My skillset is kind of . . . a secret."

"Well, I kind of like secrets," I say, playing along. We stop walking suddenly. He tugs my glove off, finger by finger, until he's holding my bare hand in his, my palm collecting snowflakes.

Black eyes on mine, he says, "But can you keep a secret?"

"Of course."

"Is that a promise?"

"Sure," I say. I smile despite myself. He takes off one of his own gloves after that and runs a fingertip down the center of my palm in a straight line.

Instantly, I gasp: a sharp, intense intake of breath that's not prompted by pain, but rather out of pleasure.

There's a flash.

My mind's eye runs wild and I'm somewhere else: not in the forest with Apollo's hands holding mine, but in a place where there are trees and sloping hills, and rows of rundown, patched rooftops sprouting brick chimneys.

I catch a glimpse of a sign:

ROSEMARY MEDICAL CENTER

Another flash, and I'm looking through Apollo's eyes.

He's sitting in a medical chair. Arm outstretched as a cold, damp cotton swab is dabbed at the crook of his elbow. His jaw tightens hard at the needle's insertion. He doesn't like giving blood samples, but he's done it before. He's done it many times before, even as a child . . .

With every image, my heart races faster.

More, it begs.

They are looking for something. Apollo is different and they are trying to find out why. *Blood tests. Medical exams.* These experiences take up the majority of his childhood.

He hates the doctors. *Hates.*

I feel the hatred like it's my own—teeth gritted, fury like a tongue of fire licking my core—and all of a sudden I feel myself gather air into my lungs, ready to scream.

But Apollo pulls his fingertip away from my palm and it all fades away instantly.

That one simple touch. That one insignificant gesture.

That second-long flesh-to-flesh contact—and I've dipped into his memories, I've seen *who he is.*

My cheeks glow, red and flushed. I feel like every beat of my heart pounds against the surface of my skin, my blood trying to break loose, to spill . . .

I look at Apollo in a way that must be desperate: mouth dropped open and lips trembling; eyes wide, my pupils dilated and swollen, perched above flushed cheeks.

"Do that again," I beg.

Apollo gives me a nervous laugh. "I can't."

I can hardly believe how ridiculous I sound when I open my mouth to a stream of pleading. "What was that? Please, do it just once more. *Come on.*"

Apollo puts a fingertip to my lips, silencing me. "I know it doesn't seem like it, but my skillset is actually dangerous. Linger a little longer, and strange things happen."

"What kind of things?"

"I can't tell you."

"Why not?" I seethe, speaking in a whisper.

"Because you're a stranger to me," he grunts, pulling on his glove as he walks off. "I don't even know your favorite color."

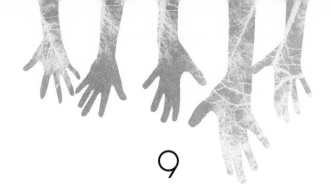

9

WE WALK IN SILENCE.

My thoughts churn wildly, roiling like a stormy sky.

Who is Apollo, anyway? I glance sideways, to a few steps in front of me, where he's trudging through the snow. The urge is still there—alive, ever present.

Touch him, it cajoles. *Touch him again.*

But I've already considered it and it's impossible, given his gloved hands and lack of bare skin. Also, I'd rather not look like a pervert or something. *Stop this. He's toying with you.*

At the head of the line, Lios stops abruptly.

"What's going on?" Apollo asks and is vehemently shushed by both Cyb and Lios, the pair frozen stiff as they listen carefully to a strange noise, like choking . . . or gagging . . .

"Oh my god," Cyb breathes. The realization dawns on us all simultaneously, but she's the one who speaks first. "MEROPE!"

We whirl in unison, facing the space twenty yards to my left where Merope was once standing, but is now folded over herself, gasping frantically for breath.

It's common knowledge that, as an Empath, Merope will detect the Muted from afar. What we knew, but are startled to see for the first time, is how this detection manifests. Apparently it's like being locked in a Mute's body—breathing through the phlegm clotting its lungs, spitting up bile, heaving shrieks . . .

Merope falls into the snow, convulsing. Cyb's at her side in a flash, trying to soothe her. "How long?" she asks me. "Do you know how long!?"

"It's different for everybody!" I mutter in reference to the time it takes for an Empath to acclimate. Their first encounter with a Mute's frequency is shocking, but after a little while, they acclimate, becoming capable of handling it.

I yank out my pistol, eyes widening against the dark.

Where are they, where are they, where are they . . .

"Keep her calm," I say to Cyb. "I'll cover for—"

The words aren't even off my lips before the forest explodes with noise: the snapping of twigs, the crunch of yellowed tufts of grass being walked over. *An approach.*

I skitter backward a few steps and run directly into the dense trunk of a tree just as I hear Cyb scream, "BEHIND YOU!"

I don't have to look around to realize what I'm standing up against *isn't a tree*—because trees don't have fingers, clawing and sticky, with nails hanging loose, halfway ripped off.

Whirling, it's clear the dense thing I've just backed into is none other than a real, living Mute.

I pitch forward, rolling out of the Mute's grasp—easy to do, given the Mute is still as a stone statue. Cyb, having seen what's happening before I even did, is Persuading it to stay motionless.

Getting to my feet, I spin, looking it in the face.

I lose feeling in my hands, my legs.

It's . . . it's horrifying.

This one has its left cheek stripped off, exposing blood-red tendons flexing and pulling, tugging its jaw wide so it may shriek a sour, wet breath directly in my face.

A scream rips through my throat as fast as the bullets fired from my pistol. I peg the beast with five shots, all directly in the chest, and yet it's still alive.

The Mute's body is haggard, a skeleton in a bruise-colored casing that is thick as hide. Strands of graying hair dangle from its scalp—scarce, wiry.

And what's worse, it doesn't have eyes—just two carved-out sockets, hollowed and pitted, oozing tears of puss. Its eyelids are useless flaps of skin, reminiscent of an ancient Egyptian mummy.

Just as I'm about to puke, the scent claws forth.

The Mute smells stale and decayed, like cracking open the mouth of a corpse and inhaling. It's so sickening, I practically lose myself completely.

I aim again, palms sweaty, and fire. This time I aim for the gap between its empty eyes. I know immediately after pulling the trigger that I've managed to kill it. Seconds later, I leave it heaped messily in the snow.

But that's only one dead Mute out of hundreds more, all of which perpetually shriek and cry, bringing the sleepy midnight forest to life. To chaos.

Merope and Cyb are gone now, completely out of sight.

All I can see are the Muted.

I stop, pressing up against a tree—a *real* tree this time—and catch my breath. The forest is alive with movement. Every gap between trees filled, every pocket of shadow twisting vociferously with life.

I move through the forest like I'm lost in a fog—not really thinking at all, just acting and reacting—my pistol bucking in my palms, popping bullets through Mute skulls.

This is not the glory I envisioned. This is not the exciting adventure, the thrilling risk. *This is nothing like my dream . . . This is a nightmare!*

All around me, I hear the Muted's ragged shrieking.

Their breath is on my neck, their sticky fingers grabbing for my clothes; their stale, bloody odor as thick as a cloud rolling out over the landscape.

They have descended upon us like locusts.

I turn a corner too quickly, skidding and falling. The snow explodes in my face like a feather-filled pillow cut open, and for a few foggy seconds, I can't see. The ice melts. I blink.

Lios stands before me—so does Apollo, both fighting with knives now, presumably out of bullets. Just as I heave myself up, I spot a Mute approaching Apollo.

"Apollo!" I say, shouting the warning.

He turns, but isn't fast enough. The Mute is there, heaving plumes of steaming breath, a bull ready to charge. But somebody stops it before it gets any further.

Lios.

He throws a knife, planting it in the Mute's throat.

Apollo lunges forward and rips the knife free of the beast's esophagus, lancing it elegantly through its empty eye-socket. The blade sinks into brain.

The Mute falls, only for another to approach.

Another nobody sees.

It's big. Bigger than all the others. And it would be coming straight at me if it weren't for Apollo standing between us, acting yet again obliviously inattentive.

Lios sees the Mute going for Apollo just as I do. He dives between the pair, shoving Apollo away from the Mute's readying lunge, and takes the blow himself.

Apollo panics, trying to fire his gun—it's empty—and when he goes looking for Lios's knife, we both realize he's left it in the eye-socket of the last Mute.

I try firing my gun, knowing already it'll be empty.

I've shot over ten rounds already—all on one Mute—and when my hand dives into my pocket for the magazine I'd packed there earlier, I realize it's missing. *It's missing.*

The Mute fights Lios like a wolf, jaws hooked on the front of his jacket, thrashing. In seconds, Lios is thrown prostrate on the ground and attacked by a host of the Muted, all diving in to have their share of him.

I am screaming.

I am screaming like a madwoman.

Blood blossoms out from under Lios's body as he kicks his legs and throws fists, but the beasts upon him aren't deterred in the slightest—their hunger overshadowing all else.

All the while, I'm trying and failing to get the knife out of my new boot, but my hands are shaking and numb, and I can't get a firm grip on its hilt.

Finally, I rip off my boot in full. I sprint forward, met head-on by another Mute. I punch the blade just as Apollo did before, right in its empty eye-socket, but another is swarming me, and another, and another . . .

Apollo screams in the distance. I lose my knife, stuck in the belly of a Mute. I dip and dodge, trying to find my path back to Lios, screaming uncontrollably, unashamed.

By the time I've gotten to Lios, Cyb and Merope are there, firing rounds wildly at the group of the Muted.

I hear their guns click.

"RELOAD," Cyb demands frantically. "RELOAD!"

But there isn't enough time. One Mute remains, looming overtop Lios, its cruel maw glistening with his blood. The sight is like getting kicked in the stomach, and without thinking or strategizing or considering, I find myself on the ground, raking my hands through the snow.

I withdraw a rock—jagged and sharp, its surface pitted like the moon's lumpy, cratered flesh—fingers gripping it in my fist as I roar, launching myself at the Mute mauling Lios.

Plunging a heavy boot into the beast's spine, I successfully knock it off balance. Apollo sees what I'm doing and leaps forward, pinning the Mute on the ground.

Falling to my knees beside the Mute, I elevate the rock over my head, recruiting the vigor of gravity. And I throw it down as hard as I possibly can, breaking it against the Mute's skull. *Again and again and again.* I don't stop until I see its brains spilling in a messy halo around its ugly, hellish face.

Silence. Total silence.

Apollo gasps, gripping my arm. He gives a shaky nod.

Good job.

Except we got here too late. Lios is groaning in agony at my side, so pained he can't move. I drag myself closer, suddenly feeling heavy and exhausted. My bootless foot freezes in the snow.

"Lios," I gasp, tears hot and sour in my eyes.

"How bad is it?" Cyb begs, staying away—as though it's too much for her to handle seeing herself. "HOW BAD?"

I glance at Merope, who's still pallid, but is at least standing on her own, having acclimated at last. She looks back with a raw and terrible grief in her violet eyes.

"There are others," I growl, trying to shield Lios's shredded body with my own, addressing Merope. "You done reloading?"

"We'll cover for you," she says vacantly, tugging Cyb's sleeve in her fist, urging her to go along. "Get . . . get Lios together."

"I will," I say, voice cracking.

The pair trudge off through the snow, leaving Apollo and I alone with Lios. The night sings with gunfire. Every single part of me wants to collapse, but I keep myself together as I peel off the front of his ripped jacket and examine his wounds.

His chest is completely ripped open, skin hanging like a flap over his ribcage. The Mute went after his heart. I gulp back the sick rolling up from my stomach, telling myself that if we find help soon enough, he's fixable. He's savable.

But is he?

I run fingers through his hair. "You're okay," I cry, barely able to speak, as I tear off my jacket and place it over his body.

Apollo is at my side, whispering something I'm not paying any attention to. I feel his hands slide down my forearms in an effort of comforting me, but I shrug him off.

"This," I snarl, glaring at him, "is *your* fault."

"I—I'm so sorry."

"That isn't good enough," I cry, breaking. "You weren't paying attention! You cocky, self-satisfied bastard—out there like you're *invincible*, like you're *too good*—"

"I said, I'm sorry!" Apollo yells.

"Just get away from me—from *us*," I spit, shoving him hard in the ribcage. He stares back at me with the audacity of having hurt in his eyes before getting up, walking off.

I gladly return my attention to Lios, stroking his hair out of his sweaty face, trying to ignore the sickening way his blood spills in distinct pulses, bleeding out with every beat of his heart.

"It's okay," I lie. "You're fine."

"Eos," he whispers, sapphire eyes locking on mine: tearful but so utterly brave, so coherent.

Lios reaches for me. I take his hand—too cold, far too cold to be okay—and press it against my cheek as I whisper, "Just rest for now. Save your energy."

But Lios's hand grips mine tighter, and I know he's asking me to come closer—to listen.

"What is it?" I ask quietly. I lean in, ear to his lips, not at all prepared for the raw certainty in the words that follow.

"I'm dying, aren't I?"

10

"YOU'RE NOT DYING."

I sit on my heels, sniffing back tears. Lios's hand goes limp in my own, but I don't release it.

"Stop being a wimp," I add. "You're going to be fine."

A final gunshot sounds and everything is quiet at last, the rest of the Muted either bored, scared off, or dead. Merope and Cyb return red-faced and sprinting, the torch I'd thought we lost held high in Merope's hand.

Cyb stops about twenty feet away, as though she's tethered to the spot and can't come any closer.

"How is he?" she asks breathily, quelling a cry.

To the emotionally stable onlooker, it would seem bizarre that she wouldn't run to Lios's side—but Cyb's always been this psychologically guarded, *especially* when it comes to Lios.

What she'd do if she found out he's . . .

That he could actually . . .

"He's fine," I lie again. "If we can find help."

"Help," she echoes distantly, a very real edge to her voice now as she pins me with those silver-gray eyes. "Help? Out here, in the middle of the forest? After midnight?"

"Cyb," I warn.

"Who's going to help him?" she asks shrilly, her emotional well overflowing. "Who, out here, could *possibly*—"

Merope steps closer, the torch casting a dim, flickering light over Lios's bloody scene.

"Actually," she whispers, "help might find us yet."

"Native-borns?" Cyb asks disbelievingly.

"I'm sensing three. They're coming this way."

"Now?" I say, shooting up to my feet.

"Yes, right now."

"From which direction?" I pull out the compass.

"North." Merope chews her lip. "I can't say for sure, but it seems like they're coming from Mabel's quarantine. If they are, we have to stay on guard."

"Let's go find them," Apollo says, addressing me. I twitch at his sudden emergence at my side. "You and me. We'll meet them directly, head-on. We'll convince them to help Lios."

For a moment I regard him curiously, those startling eyes searching my own—uncharacteristically vulnerable. It's as though the shield he wears has fallen.

I look to Merope. "We'll be back in fifteen—tops."

"And what if you're not?"

"Then run," I say firmly.

Apollo loads a handgun, forking it over. I holster it without thinking and we go, leaving Merope to look over a too-quiet Lios and a tearful Cyb.

Before I dip into the woods, I find Merope's eyes. We make a brief exchange, wordless but meaningful, that feels a lot like a secret language we've developed together over the years.

Merope's eyes tell me, *You know I'm not running. If you're gone too long or if I hear a single scream from the north, I'm coming.*

I give her a stale glare. *Love you.*

She returns it. *Love you too.*

Apollo and I traipse northward, my bootless foot screaming against the frigid snow. I almost didn't realize I'd lost it, in the chaos of almost losing Lios to a pack of the Muted.

"Look—up ahead," Apollo whispers, nodding to an orb of golden light bobbing in the dark. Then he shouts, "Who's there?"

The light stops, hovering in the air.

I tug Apollo's sleeve. "Keep going—I'll play backup."

"Backup?"

"I'll go west," I urge, leaving before he can argue. I put fifty yards between us, but stay parallel to his position and keep myself well within sight.

From afar, I hear him yell, "Who's there? Answer me!"

And yet again, they don't give a reply.

Apollo quickens his pace, rifle raised as a precaution, his stride fast and sure-footed. Something wiggles uncomfortably at the pit of my stomach. Why aren't they responding?

I crest the edge of a clearing just as Apollo penetrates it.

Standing at the center is a boy Apollo's age. He's smoking a cigarette, a torch tamped into the snow at his feet. When Apollo bursts into the clearing, he raises a rifle. "Stand down!"

Apollo raises his hands in submission. "We aren't here to pose a threat. We . . . we've got a friend who's injured, attacked moments ago by a Mute."

Cigarette Boy's eyes rake through the dark forest.

He asks, stiffly, "Why would I care?"

"Help us," Apollo begs.

"Give me your rifle."

"Fine. It's yours."

"Very nice." Cigarette Boy tosses the rifle over his shoulder after a brief examination of it, making no move to help Lios or do anything at all, really.

"Are you going to help us or not?" Apollo prompts.

"Of course we'll help." This time, it's somebody else that's speaking. This boy, similar in age to the first, has ash-blond hair and pale eyes. He's slender—gangly in the way a person that's malnourished often is, all angles and dirt smudges.

Apollo glares at the speaker. "Who are you?"

"I'm Silas," the ash-blond boy says. Instantly, his eyes begin roving the clearing's perimeter. "That guy, over there," he adds a little too loudly, nodding at Cigarette Boy, "is Jac."

"One's down," Jac relays as Silas pats Apollo down, looking for additional weapons. "Doesn't look good. They want help."

Silas operates quietly, patting Apollo down longer than he probably needs to—stalling.

"Let's get Rion," Silas says at last. "Where is he?"

"Dude, who even knows?"

"I'm over here." The voice is at my back, but before I can turn to face its owner, I'm enveloped in a set of strong arms that pin me down like a folded umbrella.

But Rion's going to have to do better than that.

I throw my head backwards, aiming for his chin, but only getting his chest—he's taller than I initially guessed—managing to throw him off balance ever so slightly.

That's all I need: a blip, a split-second's advantage.

I rip free, pitching forward, but he's on me again in only a few seconds flat, grabbing me by the waist and tackling me into the snow. We engage in what becomes a one-sided fight where I'm throwing punches and he's throwing blocks.

Why aren't you fighting back, Rion?

I fake a punch—he doesn't fall for it, snatching my wrist midair and forcing it away. I throw a left hook, which he dodges the first time around, but not the second. Maybe he doesn't take me for a girl who's capable of a vicious backhand—either way, I catch him hard across his perfect mouth.

Fire ignites in his eyes—he's done playing—and in a flash he's lifted me up out of the snow, thrown me around, and shoved me back down with merciless strength. Flurries and whorls of snow twirl in my periphery, as I lay prostrate on my back.

Rion's got me trapped beneath him and I'm left privately cursing myself for underestimating a person with such a lithe, muscular build.

I should've known he was a fighter based off that alone.

He leans forward, looking down at me through hair that's grown out of its cut: dark and slightly curly, framing bronze cheeks and heavily lashed eyes.

I dive a hand to the gun Apollo gave me—located on my upper thigh—and realize he's basically sitting right on top of the damn thing. But a guy's private area isn't going to stop me from reclaiming my gun and shooting him with it.

I reach again, angry with myself for pausing long enough to make eye contact with Rion, who feigns modesty. I can almost hear him say, *Now? In the woods? I would never!*

"Don't even flatter yourself," I spit, reaching between his thighs fearlessly and taking ahold of my pistol. I raise it up so the barrel faces my assailant's pretty face, surprised that he didn't bother to take it from me first.

Why do I get the feeling he . . . let me take it?

I loose a smile. Rion's head tilts, gazing back at me with his full lips climbing into to a smirk, and doesn't so much as flinch at the gun I've got pointing between his eyes.

I aim the gun right over his shoulder, and fire a warning.

But *click.* It's empty.

Rion runs a thumb over his bloody lip, wiping it clean as he expels a laugh—though light, it sends a plume of white vapor colliding against my face.

"I know the look of a killer. You don't have it."

Rion grabs the pistol, revoking it from my custody as easily as an adult stealing a child's plaything. I don't fight for it, still too shocked to find it was empty, watching soundlessly as he stuffs it into the waistband of his pants.

Then he stares at me, pinned beneath him, shrouded in a cloak of ice and snow. There is something so odd about the way he looks me over, as though drinking me in. His face is youthful and soft, despite the damage he's clearly capable of inflicting.

There's something about him—like his eyes, themselves, are some kind of a bizarre weapon, a net with which he's capable of ensnaring prey.

I shove him. Hard. But my effort is in vain; it's like trying to roll a fallen tree off my legs.

Rion scoffs again, laughing a little at my futile efforts, as he tilts his head back and surveys the cloudy sky. When he looks at me again, he's all business.

"There are five of you," he says. Not a question.

"Yes," I croak.

He gives a distant nod, eyes leaving mine. Then, without a second's warning, he grips the collar of my jacket and drags me up to a standing position.

I consider putting up a fight—or arguing, at least—but then

again, we're at his mercy. We need his help for Lios.

I'll stay in line for that reason alone.

When we make it to the clearing, Rion pushes me down to my knees in the snow, beside Apollo.

"Found this one. She's a spy," he says, instigating identical reactions of surprise from Jac and Silas.

"How many?" Silas asks.

"Five," Rion echoes.

Meanwhile, I glare at Apollo. *You idiot . . . You complete and total idiot, handing me an unloaded gun!*

What's wrong with you?

I shift my focus to the three natives. *Are they Mabel's people?*

Couldn't be. Three skillset-less guys, taking down four leagues like ours, two back-to-back? Impossible. They must be seconds, or back ups, or maybe they're just in the wrong place at the wrong time . . .

And yet, as it stands, I'm the one kneeling to them.

Rion nods at Silas. "Go twenty yards southeast and you'll find the others. I can confirm three, one of which looks like he was just mauled by a Mute."

"Aye-aye," Silas replies, jogging off into the dark. Jac keeps his gun trained on Apollo and me, cigarette limp between his lips, glowing a dull, dying red with each inhale.

I put my pride aside, snagging Rion's sleeve as he goes to walk by my side. "Do you think you can help him?"

Rion pins me with a stare. He's got Apollo's rifle propped over his shoulder. He pulls his sleeve away from my grip, his gaze unyielding, analyzing me openly.

"Help him—or help you?" he inquires before walking off, leaving me to stare speechlessly, gawking, in his wake.

Jac prods me in the back with a gun's cold snout, urging me

to move forward. Apollo eyes me warily. The three of us move wordlessly at Rion's back, the hush disrupted by Jac's random humming and spattering of questions.

"What's your name?" he asks to nobody in particular.

"Which of us are you speaking to?" Apollo asks.

"Both of you." Again, he prods the gun uncomfortably into my spine. "Starting with her."

I swallow. If they are Mabel's people, then they're a part of a community we've got to gain access to—and thus, they cannot know who we really are.

"I'm Elizabeth," I reply coolly.

"Elizabeth," Jac says, feeling the name out. "Old name."

"My parents liked that stuff . . ."

"Old stuff, yeah?"

"They liked history," I reply convincingly.

"Well," Jac proceeds, showing no indication whatsoever of suspicion or reluctance towards me, "*Elizabeth,* what should I call you for short? Eliza? Liz? Beth?"

"Abe," I quip. Apollo stifles a laugh. "I prefer Abe."

Jac stares at me, not quite catching my sarcasm, itching a stubbled chin before yanking the limp cigarette out from his lips and tossing it aside, where it fizzles in the snow.

"I'm Jac," he carries on, "and you're free to call me Jac."

"And I am David," Apollo adds, unsolicited.

"He prefers to be called *Davy,*" I say, much to Apollo's overt displeasure, which worsens only as conversation continues and he's repeatedly called Davy.

Eventually he turns to Jac and says, "Are you a member of that large quarantine nearby? Mabel's, is it?"

"Yep," Jac says simply. He doesn't elaborate, and I wonder if that's because it isn't a big deal to say so, or if it's because he's got something to hide.

We make it back to Lios, who reeks of the metallic odor of spilled blood, and is moaning in abject agony. I feel a cold sweat break over me, rolling sickeningly like a bout of the stomach flu.

Cyb's at Lios's side. *Finally*, though she refuses to look at his wounds when Silas peels my jacket off his chest. He cringes at the sight of it, going pale.

"Signature," Jac says, looking at Rion. "Definitely a Mute."

"Twelve inches, at least." Silas hovers a finger over the long laceration cleaving Lios's muscled chest. "He'll need stitches and a large dose of antibiotics, at least."

Cyb croaks, "Do people . . . Can . . . Is this *survivable?*"

Nobody replies.

The forest goes quiet, filled only by Lios's whispering, his incoherent gibberish: the language of severe blood loss. That's the biggest downfall—and *irony*—of Lios's skillset.

He can heal other people, but he can't heal himself.

Silas's pale brows rise, looking at Rion. "Your call."

Rion nods. "Take him."

Cyb's eyes brim with tears. "You . . . you're going to help?"

Silas, Rion, and Jac kneel beside Lios, preparing to lift him to his unsteady feet. Apollo leaps in at the last minute, and they heave Lios's large frame upright.

Silas breathes heavily, straining under Lios's weight as the four of them act as his crutches. "We'll do what we can," he says as they pass by, leaving.

Cyb stays on her knees in the snow and doesn't move. Her eyes fixate on her bare hands, gloved in a thick film of sticky, half-dried blood. *Lios's blood.*

I drop to my knees. "It's okay, Cyb."

Her eyes—tearful, pink, and puffy—find mine. "Be honest with me, Eos," she gasps fragilely. "Will he die?"

I sit silently for a while, drinking in the weakest side of my oldest sister I've ever seen—a side that is, despite it all, far more beautiful than the mask she usually wears.

"Not today," I say, extending a hand, which she takes. I lift her up, and we walk together, lingering at the back. The snow falls in a white veil, drifting hauntingly through a night that feels like it'll never end.

Everybody is quiet except for Lios, who heaves dry, piercing sobs for hours—until eventually he doesn't anymore, and the ensuing silence is so, so much worse.

AN HOUR LATER, WE arrive at the quarantine.

I swear my foot is frostbitten. We never did find my other boot and after trekking five miles through dense snowfall and endless gusts of cheek-chapping winds, I'll be surprised if by the end of this, my whole foot isn't blackened with frostbite.

Up ahead there is a glow of smoke in the air.

The quarantine.

We approach a wall of logs: a two-story, fenced perimeter with sharp, fang-like tips. Rion identifies a door that's invisible to the rest of us, blending in with the rest of the fence. He jams a key into four padlocks, unlocking it. Then he backs up, generates a burst of momentum, and rams his shoulder into the warped wooden door.

It gives way, swaying open.

There's an immediate rush of heat that follows, and a burst

of flickering firelight. A bonfire sits before us, spitting glowing embers into the inky midnight sky.

We shuffle inside. They lay Lios down by the fire. His skin has gone so pallid it's almost translucent, and his injuries are still bleeding heavily, emitting a strong metallic odor. I try closing my mouth against the smell, so pungent as to inspire a flavor, and yet again, I feel my face drain to a light gray-green.

I look away. The quarantine is not at all like I'd imagined it would be—not a large warehouse of a building, with one massive communal room, but a *community*.

The center of the quarantine is marked by the bonfire. All else is wrapped around it. Staggered slightly, like rose petals, row after row of huts made up of saplings sealed together with clay and insulated by stripped bark and dry leaves.

I notice each hut has a chimney burping wisps of smoke into the night sky. A few huts even have hides draped over their doors for additional insulation, furs I can identify as belonging to white-tailed deer.

Something moves at my periphery, drawing my attention.

A girl is approaching from across the way. I'd guess she's no older than I am, with smooth skin, a complexion of coffee with cream, and a veil of black hair framing startlingly bright eyes.

Jac looks up from Lios and shouts, "Mia, *hurry up*. This isn't a walk in the fucking park."

Mia's jaw tightens, but she picks up her pace. When her eyes find Lios, they flare wide with concern. "Holy shit."

"The Muted," Silas confirms.

"Where's Mabel? Is she on the compound?"

"No," Silas confirms grimly. "She's spending a couple days in the city, helping with—" To my chagrin, Silas pauses, eyes clicking to mine. "She'll be back in a few days."

Damn it. He was so close to slipping up . . .

"All right, it's up to us, then." Mia stands, brushing her hands off on her pants. "Let's get to work on him, shall we?"

"You're taking him away?" Cyb asks. "Where?"

"To Mabel's cabin. She's our quarantine's founder and has access to all of the medical supplies." Mia shakes her head, eyes glued to Lios's injury. "Your friend is going to need a lot of help."

"Can I go?" Cyb practically begs.

Mia glances at Rion, as though looking for permission and after a moment's pause, he gives her a fraction of a nod.

"Yes," she concedes. "But we've got to hurry."

The boys gather around, readying to lift Lios again. I wiggle my way in between them, finding Lios's hand and holding it in my own. It's sweaty, clammy. Everybody stops, expecting me to say my goodbyes.

But I am not here for that.

Say what you will, but I can't say goodbye. The word isn't part of my vocabulary. I sometimes wonder if this is the softest part of me as a person: my inability to say farewell.

I look to Cyb, who's watching with sad eyes. Merope gives me a quiet nod of encouragement. I pull Lios's mushroom hat off his head and clutch it against my chest, like it's some kind of a talisman, and face him as I calmly say, "Goodnight. I'll see you in the morning."

The corner of my eye picks up the native-borns exchanging skeptical glances, as though to say, *Wait, did she just tell him what I think she just told him? Goodnight instead of goodbye?*

But I don't give a damn what they think.

I watch as they, *strangers*, carry him away.

Before Cyb follows, she casts us one last glance, eyes wary and panicked—distraught. I'm glad they're letting her go. It's a mercy, a kindness, we haven't yet earned.

These people are tough. But they are good.

They fade into the darkness of an unlit path, finding their way based off memory alone. Merope and Apollo inch in close beside me, masked in the golden light of the bonfire.

"So," Apollo says as soon as they're out of earshot. "I hear that our target isn't currently present."

I echo Silas. "A few days, and she'll return."

"We'll need this time, anyway," Merope declares. "We've got to earn their trust, gain membership. And now, with Lios in their care, we really can't leave."

11

WHEN RION AND SILAS return, it's without anybody else.

Silas is holding a key, which he twirls in his fingers. He juts out a pale, lightly stubbled chin, nodding at Merope and Apollo as he begins barking orders. "You two. This way."

"We're not splitting up," Apollo says curtly.

Merope pins Apollo with a lethal stare. "They're helping save our friend's life. We'll do whatever they ask of us, whatever makes them the most comfortable."

"You're strangers to us," Silas defends, shrugging. "We don't know if you can be trusted, and until we're sure, you're going to be split up individually and supervised."

"Who is going where, then?" Apollo demands to know.

"You two are going with me. I'm supervising Mary, and Jac is going to supervise you." Silas drops his hand down to his side, palm resting threateningly on the handle of his gun. "Do we understand each other?"

Apollo's posture stiffens visibly. "What about Elizabeth?"

Silas falters, casting a nervous glance at Rion. "We weren't expecting so many. We're, uh . . . well, we're still looking for a volunteer for her."

"It's fine. I'll take her," Rion says.

"No. Dude." Silas drops his voice to a whisper. "I know how much you hate playing babysitter. I'll take them both myself, or we can always wake up Fallon—"

"Fallon is an asshole if he doesn't get his sleep." Rion gives his comrade a tired smile. "It's fine. Really."

"All right. Well, that's great, then," Silas says, turning his attention back to our group. "Your friend Lucas is doing better after getting stitches, antibiotics, and painkillers, but he still isn't even close to being out of the woods yet. We're keeping him and that other girl—Cindy?—together, supervised by Mia."

I expel a sigh of euphoric relief.

Lios is doing okay. He's strong. He'll make it.

Silas goes to walk off, saying, "We'll keep you posted on his progress," but is stopped abruptly by Merope, who has caught ahold of his wrist.

Silas's eyes take on a hysterical sheen. "Don't *touch* me."

Merope looks gob smacked. "I—I was jut going to thank you for everything—"

"Use your words next time," he snarls, stomping off toward a darkened, unlit path. "Never touch me again."

I feel myself go red in the face. I'm so absolutely furious, the urge to claw out Silas's eyes pipes into my mind. Instead, I turn to their ringleader, Rion.

"Your friend is rather rude," I growl.

Rion nods, lips tightening. He glares down the path. Silas is waiting there, unable to leave without his hostages.

Rion nods at me, indicating I should follow. When I don't go as ordered, I feel his hand grip mine, tugging me along. From the corner of his mouth, he says, "Rude is an understatement."

When I look back, Merope and Apollo are following Silas into the night's syrupy darkness. Just before I look away, Apollo's eyes catch mine.

I mouth, *Take care of her.*

Then, mouthing back, he says, *Take care of yourself.*

I discover shortly afterward that Rion's dropped my hand and has started walking off without me, perhaps expecting for me to follow orders like all his other little minions without being asked twice.

I just put a gun in his face.

He's got gall, turning his back on me.

"Are you going somewhere?" I ask as he's almost entirely out of sight in the dark. "Or are you expecting me to plod along at your ankles, like some kind of a lapdog?"

Rion turns slowly, shoulders swaying under the rifle he's thrown over them. I prepare for the worst, but don't get it.

He throws his head back and laughs.

I squint. "Is something funny?"

"Stay outside, if that's what you'd prefer," he shouts through the post-midnight black. "I don't have to supervise you. You're no threat to anybody."

My blood boils, eye twitching. "No threat, you say?"

"None," I hear from a distance as he turns around and goes deeper into the night's moonless dark—and with every step he takes, he'll be harder and harder to find again.

I hiss through my teeth. "I'd rather sleep outside in the snow than rely on you," I snarl, pointing to my foot, which is still cold and bootless. "But because of *this,* I've got no choice."

"You've always got a choice, Elizabeth," Rion says as I catch up to him in the dark. He turns to walk backward in front of me for a few steps, cheekily adding, "Or should I call you Abe?"

The nerve . . .

Who does he think he is?

At every turn, every fork in the path, we take whichever one has the least amount of light and heat. We walk so far, I start getting nervous. *What if he's taking me all the way out here, where nobody can hear me scream, to kill me?*

Just as I'm about to voice this concern, we dip down a final twist in the irregular serpentine path we've been following, and face a stretch of empty space—and at the very end, a single hut.

Unlike the previous enfilade of huts, Rion's stands in total solitude and loneliness. Firelight sets its small, crooked square window aglow, and my bones ache in anticipation of warmth.

Now that we're upon it, I realize it's stationed flush against the quarantine's toothy perimeter—quite literally situated the farthest away from anybody else as possible.

Rion's face is lit up in gold. He unlocks the door, peeling it open, and a rush of heat flows outside. There's a fire built inside, small but hot. In my haste to get closer to warmth, I practically mow Rion over as I stampede inside.

"Woah, there," he says, closing the door. "I've never before had such an eager houseguest."

"I thought I was a hostage," I say, "not a houseguest."

"Note to self: the girl's good at spotting lies."

"Note to self: the boy lies a lot," I add, refusing to leave the halo of heat cast off by the fire. I pin him with a glare. "You've lied to me twice since we've walked in here."

Rion stares me down. "Twice? No I haven't."

I smile, eyes pointing to his bed—where a lacy, pink bra lies tangled up innocently in the blankets. Rion's jaw drops a little, the ghost of a smile itching at his lips.

"No eager houseguests, indeed," I say, smirking.

"Eager, just not as eager as you," he counters.

"Oh, I see." Silence washes in, filling the gap of our porous conversation, and I take the opportunity to look at things other than the fire and Rion's bright, mischievous eyes.

The hut sags slightly, like it's wilting under the weight of a heavy burden. The walls have been all but wallpapered in a spate of wrinkled, half-tattered maps of the world. Everything smells like cedar and tree sap, fresh soap.

And distinctly . . . *boy.*

I run my fingertip over the crease of a map.

Rion mutters, "It's not much, but it's all I've got."

I turn my focus back to him just in time to see him seizing the pink bra and readying to stuff it in his drawer. Noticing me looking, he freezes. "What?"

"You—" I pause, squinting. "Is that your girlfriend's bra?"

Rion laughs, shaking his head in a way that says, *You've got some nerve.* "That's a very personal question you're asking—and to somebody you don't even know."

"Well, is it?"

"Nah."

"How eloquently put," I remark.

"Are we really having this discussion?" He shakes his head with a slightly crooked smile and slingshots the bra into a pile of clothes beside his doorway.

I drop down to the floor, rolling off my soaked-all-the-way-through sock. Rion's eyes take this in, studying me. He shrugs out of his jacket and steps closer.

"Checking for frostbite?" he deduces.

"More like confirming the frostbite I know I have." I pinch the tips of my toes, which are totally numb. "After five miles in the snow and ice—*bootless*—I'm pretty sure I'm doomed."

"Stop crying about it. You'll be fine."

"So inconsiderate," I rebuke. "This is a sensitive subject."

"Take off the sock already," he whines, crouching down at my side to get a closer look. A wry smile later, and he's already making bets. "Five squirrels says you don't have frostbite."

I regard him, overtly scandalized. "Only five?"

"Get on with it," he says, and before I can stop him, he has stripped off my sock on my behalf.

I'm about to reprimand him when I realize I've still got all my toes intact—flesh-colored and completely healthy.

"Told you," he says, giving me a lazy smile.

"Well, this is something I'm happy to be wrong about."

He sits back, shaking a lock of his hair out of his eyes—lit up by flame so brightly it's as though he's gilded. There's a scar that falls in an arc through his full lower lip, and I wonder how it got there and who—or *what*—gave it to him.

I realize I'm kind of staring and force my gaze away.

Rion asks, "How did you lose your boot?"

I feel my every muscle stiffen.

He doesn't realize what he's done. He doesn't realize what question he's asked . . . what it means, what memories flood forth in the wake of it. I feel my skin tighten, armoring itself.

His whole demeanor shifts when I don't reply.

He's realized.

Note to self: boy is observant.

"I ran out of bullets," I say before he can stop me—because for some absurd, inexplicable reason, I want to tell him. "Needed a weapon. Went for it but . . . somehow I lost my boot and the knife with it . . . and I was out of time, so I just . . ."

I drop my eyes, picking absently at a fingernail, its crescent filled with dried blood. Rion's hand—bronzed, soft—enters my vision from the side, pointing at my clothes, at the spattering of blood all over them.

"Was this before or after?" he inquires softly.

"Before," I say.

"So you did find something, a weapon?"

"A rock. But I was too late."

"For Lucas?" he asks quietly, and I give him a nod, unable and unwilling to discuss it further. "You're wrong."

"What?" I say, barely breathing.

"You're wrong. It's not too late." He gets up, wanders to a series of shelves, takes a pair of drawstring pants and a dingy, but clean, white shirt. "Knife or rock, you're the reason he's alive."

He tosses me the clothes, and I look up.

"And you're going to keep him that way, right?" I hold the clothes tight against my chest. I hate the way my tone has shifted to that of a beg.

Rion rolls out of his sweatshirt. It tugs at his shirt, lifting it ever so slightly, exposing tanned skin as smooth and sun-kissed as a summer day. Then he grabs a pistol, slides down the length of the wall at his back, and sits.

"Of course I will," he whispers. For a moment we stare at one another speechlessly, making a cryptic exchange.

My eyes fall on his gun. "I thought I wasn't a threat?"

Rion's lips hitch a crooked smile as he drags the slide back on his pistol and says, "I thought you were good at spotting a lie."

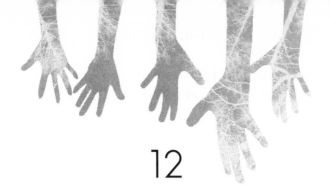

12

A FEW HOURS PASS, and already dawn is rising. A dreary, blue-gray light seeps in through the hut's web of cracks.

My eyelids snap open. I peer at the wilted ceiling, my breath a white vapor, and for a long while don't remember anything: not where I am, or how I've gotten here, or why there's a sour flavor in my mouth and an ache clawing at my core.

Then, without warning, it all floods in.

Lios.

My heart throws itself into such a frenzy, I gasp and lay a palm against it, thinking feverishly about how it's beating so hard it's probably tearing itself to pieces.

I'm coiled in a chrysalis of blankets, entangled so tightly, it feels as though I'm in a straightjacket. I kick and flail until they're off my body, and I'm free, breathing heavily.

Across from me, Rion's sitting—half asleep, the pistol still in his hand—up against the wall. He blinks, pushing the heel of his palm into his eyes, rubbing coherency into them.

"It's a good thing I don't like a lot of sleep," he grunts.

I'm already up, pulling on a jacket. "You're going to take me to Mabel's cabin. *Now.*"

He stares distantly at the fire dying slowly, just a heap of semi-golden coals hissing smoke.

"Rion," I prompt wildly, but he doesn't reply. His eyes flash away from the fire, meeting mine—soft and edged all at once, beholding a look I interpret as something akin to a warning.

"Are you sure?" he asks.

"I . . ." I say, speaking nearly inaudibly. "I've got to know."

"All right, then. We'll go."

"Thank you." I watch him stuff his pistol back inside the waistband of his jeans, rolling into the same blood-spattered hoodie he wore the day before.

Just as he's almost ready, there's a knock at the door.

Rion's eyes leap to the door so fast, it's as though he doesn't trust a single soul in the whole compound. "Who is it?"

"Dude, it's Jac." A pause, muffled only by a scoff emitted from the other side of the door. "Who else would it be?"

Rion's fists clench, his eyes locked elsewhere—as though he's lost in a memory. I step a little closer, and he snaps out of it in an instant—but that's still not fast enough.

"Yeah," I whisper, staring at him knowingly. "Who else?"

Rion stares coldly in reply. Then he's off to open the door of his hut. It cracks, spraying shards of ice as it breaks open and emits the lethally cold breath of winter.

Jac's been cleaned up: fresh, bloodless clothes; new boots; a just-washed face. The stubble along his chin is still there, though, and dark semi-circles cup his tired eyes.

"How is he?" I ask worriedly.

Jac's nose and cheeks are a shiny, wind-burnt red. His tired eyes glance sidelong. I realize it's lightly snowing outside, just a flurry falling, but flakes have caught in his lashes and he doesn't blink them away.

"He's alive," he says bluntly. I heave a near-euphoric sigh of relief and sit back down on Rion's bed. "For now."

I look to Rion. "I've got to go."

Rion gives me a quiet nod, eyes unfocused as they drop to look at his hands. Again, I get the feeling he isn't really with us, but before I can say anything a pair of boots float into my vision.

Jac thrusts them forward. "You look like you're about the same size as Mia," he says as I accept them. "Try them on, see if they fit. She thinks they'll work—"

"How did she find out Elizabeth was here?" Rion interjects.

"I—I told her," Jac replies. I'm not sure why he stutters, or why there's a crease cleaving the center of Rion's brows, but there is something that I clearly don't—

The bra.

I'd laugh if I were in a laughing mood.

Rion wipes his palms on his pants nervously. "Is she . . . ?"

"She's fine, man." Jac smirks. "Said she's never slept better."

"Do me a favor . . ." Rion angrily grabs the pink bra from the pile of clothes and throws it right into Jac's face. "Give this back to her, will you? I don't need it here."

Jac slaps the bra out of the air, staring strangely at it lying awkwardly on the floor. "Somebody tell me how we're living in mud huts, but Mia's got lingerie."

Meanwhile I'm dragging on Mia's boots without socks and actively not giving a damn. When you've grown up with an older brother, lingerie-talk very quickly loses its novelty. I stuff my foot into the left boot and it hits something hard and cold.

A knife. She must've forgot it was in here.

While the boys heatedly debate *the unsolved mystery of the post-apocalyptic lingerie,* my chest caves in on itself, collapsing under anxiety that's like an icy encasing.

I gasp, patting my chest with a fist, trying to break through that sheet of fear so I may breathe again. I start rapping my fist a bit harder, my breath quickening, the threat of a panic attack beginning to feel very real.

When I look up, the boys are both staring. I feel my face fall into a grimace, breathing steadying.

"Can we go, already?" I sniff, taking my hat and dragging it over my head. "I've got a friend who's *'alive, for now,'* and I would appreciate a little haste."

"You're right." Jac glances at Rion. "She's right."

"Of course she's right. Let's get going." Rion rips his half-frozen door open, casting a backward glance to the bra. "Don't forget that," he tells Jac.

"Right, precious cargo." Jac snatches it up, and the three of us head out into the flurries of snow so wispy they make me think of fluffs of cotton.

The snow is knee-deep. We trudge in silence, listening to the strange moan of fresh-fallen snow underfoot. The sight of it jettisons me back in time, when Pavo *made snow* for specimens deploying last winter. It was the first time I'd seen such a thing.

As I trudge, I realize I'm in pain; it's as though every ache has been whispering for my attention, but only now that it's quiet do I hear its plea for water, food, and a few days of rest.

While I walk behind Rion, stepping in his tracks, Jac forges his own path parallel to me.

"So," he begins, clapping his hands. "What's your story?"

I spout off a premeditated lie. "I've been migrating through abandoned neighborhoods. Eventually I met up with Mary, and later we met Cindy and Lucas. For years, it was just us."

"When did Davy show up?" Jac prods, eyes glinting.

"A week ago." This, at least, isn't really a lie.

"What do you think of him?"

"He's . . . okay," I surmise.

"He doesn't strike me as trustworthy," Jac says, giving me an opinion I didn't ask for. His soft, light-brown eyes find mine in an unreadable stare, and I wonder, *What if these people really are the enemy? What if they somehow really did take the last four leagues?*

Are those leagues still alive? Are they as well off as we are?

If they are, then surely the native-borns here are already well aware of our skillsets. Are they buying our lies?

Willingly . . . willingly going . . .

The word is like a jab to the throat. Isn't that exactly what my league is doing? Going *willingly* with these people? And yet our microchips are intact. We're still alive. That's not flush with the last four leagues' experience—though, to be fair, we don't exactly *know* how it all went for them.

Maybe these people—Rion, Silas, and Jac—were just in the wrong place at the wrong time? Maybe they don't know anything about Mabel, or what's really going on here?

I've got to get to my league. I've got to talk to Merope, Cyb, and even Apollo. We've got to strategize—something we haven't had the chance to do at all since getting attacked by the Muted.

The snow begins falling harder, flakes as big as quarters.

We weave our way through the quarantine, passing by the roaring bonfire, circled by a ring of people with outstretched hands and red faces.

The smell of breakfast—a clumpy, pasty-white substance that jiggles on plates like overcooked porridge—floats on the icy, winter air. Faces young and old turn, staring as we pass: cheeks smudged and sooty, jaws angular and sallow, skin leathery and weathered. They wear their hardships in their faces, cynical and cold, innately untrusting. The A-42's damage is clear. It's taken everything. Maybe even their humanity.

We turn the corner, entering a cul-de-sac. There's a cabin at the end, windows lit up with the glow of firelight. It's the only actual house on the compound: single-story, but it's large, with a lovely stone pathway leading up to its broad wooden door.

"Who's on shovel duty?" Jac asks, walking up the pathway cleared of snow. He raps his knuckles against the front door, muffled slightly by gloves. "Sucks to be them."

The door opens, exposing Mia. "What sucks?"

Her light eyes are a strange muddled color of gray, yellow, and blue. She's more stunning in daylight, even with her eyes looking so tired and her perpetually haunted expression.

"Shovel duty," Jac says before handing her a fistful of bra while he walks past her into the cabin. "You forgot this."

"Wha—" Mia's jaw drops. "God, you're a prick."

"A prick? Really?" Jac pushes inside. "Isn't doing you a favor a very non-prickish thing to do?"

"I wasn't talking about you," Mia says curtly, casting an icy glare in Rion's direction. He walks past her without even meeting her eyes, and I feel the twang of tension ring in the air.

Mabel's cabin is full of mismatched furniture: wicker and lumpy old couches, love seats draining stuffing from a series of holes, and a unique copper end-table with a turquoise patina.

Weirdest of all, a chicken walks by, clucking cheerfully.

I stop, totally frozen, mid stride. "What . . . is that . . . ?"

"She's an indoor chicken." Rion heaves a sigh, as one might

after losing too many battles to the same war. It seems likely he, among others, protested this in vain. "Mabel's pet hen, Gloria."

Gloria's red-eyed stare ignites a strange phobic kind of fear in my chest that not even a Mute could inspire. I start walking as fast as I can without looking ridiculous, but wherever I go it's as though Gloria purposefully follows.

Until now, I've never seen an animal before.

I look at Rion. "Get her away."

Jac's lips itch to smile. "Awe!" He kneels swiftly to pick her up, following behind me a little faster as my cowardice takes hold and spurs me across the living room. "But she likes you, Abe!"

Gloria's red-eyed stare indicates the opposite.

I sidestep Jac. "Get her *away,* I said!"

"Fine—but no scrambled eggs for you later." Jac gives me a playful wink, setting the hen on the headrest of a love seat, where she perches and fluffs her feathers, preening.

I cast Rion a cold stare. "Can we go?"

"*You* can," a voice says—a voice that's Mia's. "Lucas is in the last room at the end of the hallway." She pets Gloria's head, the hen's eyes closing happily. "Everyone's there waiting for you."

Rion looks at me. "I'll take you."

"No." Mia's starry eyes widen. "Can we talk?"

"I'll be fine," I assure Rion before heading down the gloomy hallway, stopping at the end. Voices murmur inside. I palm the warped wooden door and find myself thinking of Rion's words to me this morning. *"Are you sure?"*

I look back at him without thinking. Mia speaks to him in shy whispers, reaching a finger forward and hooking it around the belt loop of his jeans, tugging him closer.

His hips sway, giving in, and—

I look back at the door.

What am I doing?

Before they realize I've hesitated, I burst through the door and am greeted by the taut, worried faces of my league. I wonder if my face looks similarly—all angles and hollows, shaped by a fear that won't relent until Lios is well again.

If he's ever well again.

My eyes land on Cyb's, of all people's. She looks through a lens of unspilled tears.

"Finally," she says.

Lios is lying in a twin-sized bed, flanked by Merope on one side and a tearful Cyb on the other. Apollo stands, wraith-like, in the far corner of the small room.

Lios has been bandaged in white cloth. A series of dirty, blood-stained rags fill a bucket at the end of the bed, emitting that same foul, metallic odor. He looks pale, his hair falling in finger-thick locks that tickle the back of his eyelids.

I don't know what I expected—not that he'd be awake and cheerful and alive, but certainly not this.

"How is he?" I croak.

"He's alive," Cyb says, echoing Jac's earlier sentiments, but with a far darker delivery. "Heavily medicated. Has a few cracked ribs, chance of an infection, and a ton of bruises, but he's doing okay for somebody who nearly died of exsanguination."

I sit at the edge of the bed. Its coiled springs strain, and for a split second, I worry I've just disturbed him, but Cyb's right.

He's completely out.

The door creaks open, emitting Jac and Rion. The room is so small they brush up against me, smelling strongly of pine sap and in Jac's case, the earthy, stale smell of cigarette smoke.

"What medication is Lucas taking?" I ask.

"Heroin," Jac replies simply. "Pain killers are impossible to come by, as you know. The pharmaceutical companies having gone down, oh, what was it? Twenty-seven years ago?" He stuffs his hands in his pockets. "But *drugs,* man—hard drugs will always exist. People will always find ways to keep them alive."

For a moment we stare at Lios; he's so still, he could pass as a cadaver. Now that I'm looking for it, I notice the track marks spotting his bruised inner elbow.

"Where do you get it from?" I ask offhandedly. "Heroin?"

"Another quarantine," Rion replies. He takes a step to his right so he's hovering over my shoulder, so close he brushes against me. "Our quarantine is the biggest. With that comes the ability to gather more supplies—which we trade for heroin."

"Speaking of," Jac interjects abruptly, "there's a supply drop three days from today, man. Mabel's asked us to take first run."

Rion's posture goes rigid beside me. "Shit."

"Yeah—it's winter, after all." Jac fidgets, his fingers flexing at his side. "I'm going out for a cigarette," he adds. "We'll hash out the details later, man."

"You got it," Rion answers distantly. Jac leaves, navigating through the cramped room and bumping Apollo accidentally as he does so before exiting.

Apollo grimaces, scandalized. "A little privacy," he growls as his dark eyes regard Rion, "would be appreciated right now."

"He's not going to leave us alone—*here*," Cyb hisses, glaring at Apollo intensely. "With precious medical supplies? With all the medication?"

Rion shifts his weight as though to say, *Not happening.*

"Fine." Apollo's nostrils flare, accepting defeat. "I forgot we're in a hostage situation. Thought for a second we were being treated like human beings."

"We *are*," Merope snaps angrily. "They saved Lucas's life!"

"Just shut up, Apollo," Cyb adds in a raw bark.

"Stop arguing," I order, resting a hand over Lios's. It's cold and stiff as something that's been long-dead, and I feel a fissure break my stoicism like a pickax chipping ice.

He's all stitched up, scabbed and still bloody—blooms of it seeping through his bandages and into the blankets. It's cold in this room when it should be warm. Supplies are limited, and he's forced into taking heroin . . .

And after all this, a simple *infection* could kill him?

All so we can complete our stupid Purpose?

The supplies and medication Lios needs are plentiful on our ship in space. Are we really going to stay here and watch him die when there's a way to save his life?

To hell with our Purpose. I want him to live.

"Why aren't we taking him back?" I whisper. Everybody stills in response—my league, especially.

Cyb's bloodshot eyes flare, shooting an indicative glance at the space over my shoulder—at Rion. "You know that is not an option for us," she spits.

My breathing quickens aggressively. "We could *save* him."

"You're delusional." It's Apollo speaking, of course. "I think it's best if you step outside—get some air. I'll go with you."

"I'm not leaving Lucas," I snarl, but Apollo isn't finished with me yet. He steps sideways, gripping my arm feverishly, and yanks me up to my feet.

Rion's arm rises in my periphery, but then he stops, likely thinking better of shoving Apollo off me.

Apollo smirks, his upper lip curling at Rion. They're inches away from each other. Briefly, I forget my argument with Apollo and worry they'll get in a fight—right *here,* in this cramped room.

"Going to hit me?" Apollo challenges.

"I think I'll leave before I do just that," Rion says with a breed of such lethal calm—so pure, so genuine—there's no need for a raised voice. It's clear, without question, he'd love to throw a punch or two into Apollo's face.

Apollo doesn't speak, waiting until Rion leaves to clamp a hand on my shoulder. His fingers dig into my skin like a hawk's cruel talons, and along with them I feel the zip of his energy, the pull of his strange, beautiful skillset.

He presses his cool lips to my ear. "You're aware of what's at stake here, aren't you?"

"Get off her," Merope warns, but Apollo isn't done.

"You're aware of what we have to lose?" he raves on, his grip on my shoulder tightening. "You're blowing our cover! If you ruin this for us, I swear I'll kill you myse—"

"That's funny, Apollo," Cyb scoffs, rolling her eyes. "Didn't she beat you in sparring less than a month ago?"

I stare blankly for a second. I don't think Cyb's ever paid me a better compliment—or *any* compliment for that matter—in all the eighteen years I've been alive.

"And if you did touch her," she goes on, "Merope would kill you faster than a guillotine."

Merope smirks, as though enjoying the mental image.

"What's wrong with you idiots?" Apollo yells. "Have all of you forgotten why we're here?"

"We get it," Merope says, sobered. "But issuing threats—"

"Eos nearly blew our cover," Apollo crows, pointing a finger rigidly at the door. "We're in enemy territory! If Rion has a brain in his head, he's already figured out we aren't from—"

"Don't you think Lios's life is worth more than completing this cursed mission?" My jaw is actually sore from clenching my teeth in an effort to hold myself back.

"It's not a *mission,* it's our Purpose!" Apollo speaks quietly but looks hysterical—a glint of severity in his eyes I've never really seen in anybody else. "It means *everything* for us—"

"For *you,*" I breathe, swallowing hard, unable to get Nova's final words out of my mind. *It's all up to you. Tell your league. Once they get to Earth, they must betray the Project . . .*

What if she's right? What if we're fighting for something that isn't actually worth fighting for because we're too busy with following orders, with falling for false promises?

And what if Lios dies for it?

I get up, glaring at Apollo. "This is all *your* fault," I seethe, sloughing him off with a fast jerk of my arm after he tries, yet again, to rein me in. "Lios was trying to save *your* life!"

Apollo stares, shocked. "You're taking it there?"

I inch closer, putting my face in his. "I'd sooner die than have somebody else die on my behalf."

"Ah, that's ironic!" he chuckles mirthlessly, his face so close to mine we're almost touching foreheads. *"Coming from you."*

"Apollo," Cyb barks in warning.

"Failing your Psych Eval," Apollo recites. "Not having any particular . . . skills," he adds with an indignant sniff that tempts me to claw out his eyes. "Onyx was right about you."

"I don't *care,*" I yell riotously, "about *Onyx.*"

"She tried to keep you away from us, knowing you'd only

weigh us down like an anchor," he says, breathing each word in my face, his lips taut. "Why don't you *stay* here. Why don't you go back to doing what you're *good* at: tending the gardens?"

That's it.

I throw a knee into his stomach. He pitches forward with an audible, pained grunt. *But it doesn't feel good enough.* I'm on fire and I'm seeing red and I've already *gone there.*

I ship a fist to his jaw, bashing him into the bedroom's wall.

Merope shoots up. "Apollo! Go for a walk."

Apollo rubs his jaw and leaves, plowing angrily through the room's exit. We hear the front door slam behind him and even though he's gone, nobody dares to speak.

What is there left to say?

He's right. He's right about *everything.*

I almost blew it. I am deadweight.

My fury fizzles and despair funnels in. I don't even dare to look Cyb and Merope in the face. I know they're looking at me, waiting to see what I'll do next after facing the undeniable truth.

Maybe they didn't want me to join their league . . . Maybe they were happy that I wasn't going to deploy, are disappointed I have . . .

I exhale sharply, moving to leave.

Cyb catches my elbow. "Stay," she begs. "Please."

"No."

I move so quickly—so *blindly*—it's almost as though I've teleported to the cabin's front door. I slam it shut behind me and drag in a breath of the cold, snow-smelling air.

And see Apollo is standing right in front of me.

"You think you can just hit me like that?" he says, coming closer, but moving slowly—*dangerously.* "You should be thanking me for keeping you in check."

I don't know why I say it. "Give me your hand."

"Why?" Apollo's lips lift into a sly smile.

"You know exactly why." I snatch his hand in mine and am surprised to see he isn't resisting me.

Apollo stands perfectly still, his bare palm facing skyward in my own, allowing the thrum—*so unlike Onyx's!*—to beat through his skin and drip into my own.

I feel my breath catch pleasantly as I'm swept up and away in the intoxicating whirl of this mysterious energy. Nobody has ever felt the way Apollo does—like melting, collapsing blissfully into the beat of a song.

"You should probably let go," he whispers.

"No," I breathe.

"Let go of me, Eos."

I can't and I won't. It's like I've lost full control, and even as he begins pulling away, my hold doesn't loosen. I feel the energy transform, manifesting into something new—*something else.*

Images flash in my mind's eye.

"Who are you?" I ask—no, I *beg.*

Apollo's eyes dance over my own, and when he replies it's as though we're standing at a distance and shouting over the rush of a strong wind. "I thought you'd remember."

I do remember.

Years and years and years ago. I was baby. You were a toddler.

In my room. Playing.

Onyx caught you there when you weren't allowed to be. You held out a finger and my whole hand wrapped around it. Then something happened and there was screaming. Onyx punished you for months for going against orders and disobeying her.

It's as though Apollo sees the memory—as though we are, at

the same time, *together*, looking through an identical lens. The edges of his lips twitch.

"You do remember," he breathes.

"What—" I lift my eyes to his, my hand still tight around his open palm. "What's happening?"

There's a shift in his energy, an increase, and he notices it at the same time I do, his eyes widening.

"Stop," he begs. "Eos, STOP."

But it's too late.

Visions flower in front of my eyes, colors drizzling to shape the image of a dirty, unventilated house. I'm looking through the eyes of somebody else.

This isn't an image. It's a memory, and I'm reliving it.

A silver vase is shattered on the floor. I stop before a large shard of it and see my reflection: *I'm a boy—just a little boy—with a mop of black hair and eyes, and porcelain skin.*

Apollo. This is Apollo's memory.

Alongside the broken vase are bodies. Four of them are the corpses of people, and twelve are the Muted. The living room window is broken, exposing a ridge of purple mountains and a soft, cerulean sky.

My chest tightens. *No . . . There's no way.*

The boy was drawn out of his hiding place by the sounds of approaching footsteps—distinctly alive, uninfected ones, which he was hoping would help him.

His parents are among the corpses strewn on the ground, as well as his older brother. He's alone, now—and he hasn't seen a living thing that wasn't a Mute in days.

The people enter the house.

The first thing I see is a pair of bulbous, pitch-black eyes.

Onyx.

And walking beside her, *Pavo.*

"The boy was present for the attack," Pavo says, stepping lithely over shattered glass. "He stood alongside his family as they were slaughtered by the Muted—yet he's still alive."

"How is that, Brother?" Onyx inquires.

"The Muted didn't see him . . . He's a very special boy, a very special threat." For a moment the siblings study each other with their matching black eyes—a silent exchange. "You're aware, I'm sure, of the two options facing us?"

Onyx's lips tighten.

"We're not leaving without this boy, Sister."

"We can't *take* him."

"We must."

"We can't just pick native-borns up off the streets and bring them into the lives we've lived for so long—the lives we've lived in space, orbiting Earth!"

Native-borns.

Apollo isn't a specimen like us. He's a native-born!

From the shallower levels of my consciousness, I think his hand twitches, trying to skitter away. I hold it tighter.

Today, I solve the mystery that is Apollo Lux.

Pavo replies to his sister, dragging me back into the dark memory for the three of them in a dirty, fetid house. "This boy is either our greatest advantage, or our most powerful enemy," he says in a dire whisper. "If he stays—he dies."

"You just said the Muted won't hurt him."

"Sister, Sister," Pavo says, *tisking.* "If he stays behind, he's at risk of falling into enemy hands, and we wouldn't want that, now would we?"

Onyx's face blanches. "You're not saying . . ."

"That's *exactly* what I'm saying." Pavo raises a palm, splaying his fingers only to clench them back into a fist. I think I see a dull glow beneath his skin.

"If we do not take the boy today," he adds malevolently, eyes fixed on his disapproving sister, "then he's going to die—not by the Muted, but at my own hand."

13

THE MEMORY FADES, REPLACED by a painful choking sensation.

I writhe, my awareness reemerging. Apollo has me pinned up against the wall. My feet dangle off the ground, and my throat burns, crushed under his strong, two-handed clasp.

I can't breathe!

I raise my legs, kicking his stomach. He drops me but is fast to recover, slamming me with a heavy backhand to the face. I'm thrown into the cabin's wooden wall, my cheek banging viciously into its splintered logs; my lip burns, split open.

I lunge after him—but am stopped by somebody else.

I'm pulled into strong arms, a broad chest. I realize who it is based off smell alone. *Cigarette smoke.*

Jac.

Rion approaches fast, holding his pistol so it's cocked and poised at Apollo's chest.

I feel my blood rush back in place, and my vision sharpens.

Apollo knows that I know. Whatever he's just shown me was an accident, a secret he didn't want divulged—and now that it has been, he's willing to kill me to keep it quiet.

Apollo isn't a specimen. He's a native-born . . .

Apollo's dark eyes regard Rion, lip curling wolfishly. "This just made your day, didn't it?" He speaks cockily, but is holding perfectly still. "Are you going to shoot me now?"

Rion walks forward, close enough to thrust the gun's snout under Apollo's jawline—right at his throat. "Are you going to give me a reason to?"

"Maybe another day," Apollo concedes as he turns his back toward Rion, holding his wrists together like he's being arrested and handcuffed. "Take me away, or whatever it is you do."

Rion's lips lift slightly. "Turn around, *Davy*."

Apollo looks over his shoulder, skeptically at first, then he drops his wrists, swiveling back around. "Well, I'm glad to see that you're willing to act with civili—"

Rion throws the pistol across Apollo's jaw, a blow so utterly ferocious I'm afraid he's just killed him.

It knocks Apollo completely off balance. He leans forward with blood dripping off his lips, gasping heavily as he teeters and nearly face-plants in the snow but recovers just in time.

Apollo lifts his face, exposing a horrific sight. Two of his teeth are shattered completely. He gives Rion an eerie, bloody smile as he slurs, "Should've expected that from—"

In a flash, Rion rains a fist hard against Apollo's temple.

This time, Apollo's knocked out. He teeters precariously before crumpling over himself, falling with a sickening thud in the snow, and begins snoring loudly as he unconsciously breathes.

I look away, noticing for the first time that Merope, Cyb, and Mia are all present. I hear a shout from afar and realize that farther down the road is a familiar, sickly looking guy.

"What's going on over there?" Silas shouts repeatedly, not getting an answer. Jac looks at Rion for permission to answer but doesn't get a reply besides a tired shake of his head.

"Take him to the barn," Rion says, pointing at Apollo with his pistol, breathing heavily.

Jac hesitates. "The barn?"

Rion gives him a look that clearly says, *Do it—now.*

Jac nods. He calls out for Silas, who comes running through the snow to provide assistance. Just as they arrive, Apollo slowly starts waking back up, face paler than usual, gasping for breath.

My focus falls back on Rion. He's raking a hand through his dark hair, a hand that's trembling slightly. He meets my gaze and his whole expression softens. White flakes of snow cling to his eyelashes. He starts walking over, his lips poised to—

"Why don't we go inside?" Mia's slim, cold fingers glide up my arm comfortingly. "It's freezing out here, and we have some dried mint and lemongrass left in our reserves. I'll brew us a pot of tea or something. That sound good?"

I keep my eyes on Rion, inexplicably eager to know what he was about to say. He stops, seeing Mia beside me, and after a subtle nod, he walks away.

Where he's going, I don't know.

But I have the strangest desire to follow.

WE FILE BACK INSIDE, Merope and Cyb following. Mia leads us to another small, perfectly rectangular room that's both a kitchenette and dining area. The pantry is ready to explode with packaged, freeze-dried, and canned foods. She takes a bag full of dried leaves and starts getting to work.

A fire is pre-built in a soot-coated hearth, a host of kindling and dry pine needles assembled in a teepee shape, ready to be lit.

"Can we help at all?" Merope asks Mia, who's rummaging through cupboards in the kitchenette.

She glances up, smiling. "There's a book of matches by the fireplace over there. Start that fire up for me?"

Merope nods, doing as she's told, and for a while everybody works silently. A warped, slightly tilted table is surrounded by rickety chairs, which Cyb and I occupy, keeping our eyes trained absently on the ground.

Eventually, I hear her whisper, "I tried."

I look up. "You tried . . . to do what?"

"Stop him," she mutters, so quietly nobody can overhear her speaking. "I've never tried it on him before. But when I saw him choking you . . . I tried to Persuade him to get off."

I stare, brows cinched. "And?"

"It didn't work." Cyb's eyes lift sharply to mine. "My skillset is strong enough to work against Pavo, but it won't work against a specimen in my own league, at my own level?"

"I know why," I reply icily. Merope stops messing with the ignited fire—which crackles wildly, sap popping like firecrackers as the flames roar to life—turning to look over her shoulder.

Cyb's lips tighten as she says, "Tell us."

"Apollo isn't like us." I gulp back a choked breath, throat still raw from the bruises he's pressed in my neck. "He's a native."

Total silence ensues. Cyb and Merope's eyes interlock in a question mutually shared: *What? How? That's impossible.*

"He showed me with his skillset—just now," I add.

"He showed you?" Merope echoes.

"That's why he reacted so strongly. He didn't want me to know the truth about him, about why Onyx has kept him away from us all these years."

Merope delicately adds, "But natives don't have skillsets."

"He does," I say with certainty, thinking of the thrilling feel of his touch—the heavy, wild song it sings. "He's different."

I tell them everything: the way he felt to touch, the way that feeling intensified as I dipped into his memories and saw him when he was just a boy.

Just a native, orphaned and alone, and rescued by a pair of strangers from space. Rescued because he had some kind of a special ability, making it so the Muted couldn't see—

I stop.

But a Mute *did* go after him, though. If it hadn't have gone after him, Lios wouldn't have had to save his life. I saw it all right before my eyes: Apollo was reloading, casually, like he . . .

Like he *knew* he wasn't in danger.

My blood runs cold.

The Mute wasn't charging for Apollo. It was charging after a different target, one behind Apollo. It was coming after—

"Eos?" Cyb prompts. "You were saying?"

I feel like I've just had a horse kick me in the chest. "There's something special about Apollo."

"Yeah, you said that. But what is it?" Cyb asks.

"He's immune to the Muted in ways we aren't. We can't *catch* the A-42, but they still *see us*. I don't know how this works, but they don't see Apollo. It's like he's invisible to them."

I lean forward, face in my hands. "The Project could benefit hugely from that research. If they could genetically program new specimens with whatever Apollo's got naturally, we'd be—"

"Invincible," Cyb mutters, almost greedily.

"That kind of knowledge could save the world. It could end the plague, altogether, couldn't it?" Merope adds, the fire at her back picking up. Somewhere in the kitchen, I smell the essence of bittersweet lemongrass brewing.

"When we landed," I go on, face still hidden in my sweaty palms, "Apollo was reloading—*calmly,* because he knew he wasn't in any danger. But Lios and I saw a Mute coming for him and we thought he was going to get attacked."

I look up, destroyed inside. "But the Mute wasn't charging after Apollo. It didn't even see him standing there. It was going for a target standing behind him."

Merope whispers, "Eos . . ."

"The Mute was coming for me," I choke. "It's not Apollo's fault that Lios is . . . It's *my* fault."

Cyb waves a hand. "Stop pity-partying. It isn't your fault that Lios is where he is now, Eos. It's Apollo's. He didn't tell us about his ability."

"Speaking of," Merope adds in a whisper, "this still doesn't explain Apollo's supposed skillset. What is it anyway?"

"I think it's like Onyx's," I reply.

Cyb pinches the bridge of her nose, frustrated. "Skillsets are programmed into our DNA when we're still in embryo, and that is why a native couldn't possibly have one."

"I don't get it either," I sigh.

"That explains a lot, though, Eos." Merope turns back to face the small fire. "Why our skillsets don't work on him—the way they can't work against native-borns in general. I'd always kind of wondered why I didn't pick up on him."

I nod and everybody goes quiet again. Now is the perfect time to tell them about Nova, yet I find myself hesitating. I don't know if anything she said was trustworthy. Onyx did say she was ordered to be terminated, that she wasn't mentally sound . . .

Whether I believe Nova's claims or not, to tell the others what she said is speaking treasonously . . .

No, I won't endanger them. Not now—not yet, at least.

WE SPEND THE WHOLE day in Mabel's cabin.

Mia brews tea. It tastes a little stale, but the water is hot and soothing against my sore throat. Snow keeps falling. We watch it drift in flurries and spindrifts as the sky darkens to a gray dusk and the trees collapse in on themselves, leeched of color, a series of empty silhouettes.

With Mia's supervision, we can't properly snoop around the cabin the way we'd like. Gathering evidence will have to wait until later, after we've gained their—and Mabel's—trust. Then we can do all the snooping we'd like.

If all goes according to plan, that is.

After our mugs are dry and empty, and our stomachs begin to grumble in earnest, Mia stands up. "I guess it's time for a little dinner, don't you think?"

"Finally," Cyb says with a hint of a smile. "Your wooden furniture was starting to look good."

"Dinner won't taste much better—it's Pudge night."

"*Pudge* night? Dare I ask?" I say.

"Once a month," Mia says, beginning her spiel, "all the leftover, perishable foods are collected and heaped together in what's not-so-fondly referred to as Pudge."

"Sounds lovely," I say with a grimace.

"Don't get me wrong, not a spoonful will be left uneaten."

"I'd eat cardboard if I had to," Merope confesses. "When is dinner served tonight, Mia?"

Mia glances at the clock, which reads 5:34 PM.

She sighs. "*Now,* actually." But she doesn't move to follow us as we gather at the cabin's front door. Instead she waves us away, heading down the hallway. "It's time for Lios's pain meds."

"We'll meet you there, then?" Merope offers.

"Probably not. I've got a few things here I've got access to that nobody else does." Mia winks. "Enjoy your Pudge. I'll see you all tomorrow."

I glance askance at Merope, who shrugs. "Well, guess we're on our way—unchaperoned and all."

We traipse through the snow carpeting the whole of the large compound, heading for the bonfire. It seems to be where all of the main events are held, and it's where the flow of traffic is leading us, so we follow awkwardly along.

People eye us suspiciously, not caring to hide their sneers.

"Friendly place," Cyb mutters derisively.

"*What,*" Merope interjects, "is that god-awful smell?"

The already-angry people around us go still, affronted by her remark, but I'm too distracted by the stench rolling forth to care about their open hostility.

It *reeks.*

Like eggs and fish, and maybe . . . dirty socks?

"That has to be the Pudge," I say, cringing as we turn along an elbow-tight twist in the path and see before us an impressively long line set in front of a large caldron-like cooking pot.

The bonfire roars vivaciously, singeing the influx of falling snow tumbling from the sky.

We join the line, and as soon as we do the angry looks we got earlier transform into furious grumbling.

Then, suddenly, a dirty woman grips Cyb's arm—*a serious*

mistake to make. With steel-cold eyes, Cyb throws the woman off her with such ease it looks choreographed.

"Cindy!" Merope hisses. I join Merope, holding Cyb back.

The dirty woman looks surprisingly unfazed, her lips thin and cracked, forming a wicked snarl. "Leave! There isn't enough for us to share with you."

"Looks like there's plenty for all of us," Cyb spits, nodding at the large cauldron of Pudge. "And if you *ever* touch me again like that, lady, I'll—"

"Cindy, calm yourself," Merope says, tightening her grip.

"None of you have been initiated yet," a man chimes in, his eyebrows thick as collarbones. "If you're not an initiated member, then you can't eat our rations!"

"Do you know what I've had to do?" the dirty woman rages on irrepressibly. "The sins that I committed to get here? I'll be damned to hell for it all, to be sure—but for now, while I'm alive, the benefits are mine to reap, not yours!"

The man encroaches. "I've killed people," he says with a spray of spittle. "I've killed people for less than standing in the way of my dinner—and that's what you're doing now!"

The whole crowd watches us now, their mouths full of sharp, rotten teeth, their glares honed and chiseled by corruption and malice and a fierce, undying hatred.

I've faced a lot in my life, but never anything like this.

Even Cyb is sobered by the severity of the fact that we are currently surrounded by killers—and just as I sense their ranks tightening around us, I hear a voice somewhere at my back.

"Okay, okay!" Jac shouts, clapping his hands as he pushes his way into the angry crowd. "Lucia, Tex—that's enough, okay?"

"Enough?" Lucia decries wildly. "Surely you're not going to

stick up for these freeloaders, Jac?"

"They will be initiated soon enough." I feel Jac's cold palm rest at the nape of my neck as he, like a mother hen, ushers the three of us away.

As we walk off, the crowd erupts.

Tex growls, "Better fight hard, *little girls,*" as he hocks spit in our direction with such venom I feel sickened by the sight. To add insult to injury, he lifts two fingers, forming a V, and sticks his tongue between them crudely.

"Got my eye on the brunette," he laughs, leering at Merope in a truly nauseating appraisal of her whole body. "Where's she sleeping tonight, Jac? With you? Let me get her when you're—"

I roll out of Jac's grip effortlessly, feeling rage beat through my blood in waves of fire.

"Pig," I seethe, hungry and tired and sick of feeling upset all the time over everything. I rip my boot off to gain access to the knife I've stashed there, raising it at Tex. "How about I kill you so there's enough food for me, eh?"

"I'd love to see you try," Tex says, though he looks shaken.

"You will, I'll—"

But for the second time today, I'm held back by strong arms pulling me against a broad chest—but this time the grip doesn't smell like stale cigarettes.

It smells like sap and freshly cut cedar . . . a campfire.

It smells like winter.

Rion lifts me off my feet effortlessly, tossing me over his shoulder while simultaneously dipping down to grab my boot as we leave the bonfire area. Cyb, Merope, and Jac walk hurriedly ahead of us, Jac's arms rested flirtatiously over their shoulders.

I struggle against Rion. "I want no part of this quarantine if those are the sorts of people that reside here!" I declare, pivoting to glare at Tex—but he's gone.

"Are you going to run off if I put you down?"

"No," I say unconvincingly, but Rion lowers me back onto the snowy ground. I grip his jacket for balance as he hands me my other boot to wiggle back on.

"That your signature move or something?" he asks, his lips forming a smirk. "The boot thing?"

"Yeah, well, it's harder to get a knife out than you'd think."

"A knife?" He cocks a brow, holding out a hand.

"You're not serious?" I ask and he gives me what's become a very Rion-ish smile: lazy, but genuine. "Well fine, but I'll only find another," I avow, holding out the knife for him to take.

But instead of taking it, Rion grabs its hilt and my hand all at once, pulling me close. I'm flush against his chest, breathing in the distinctive campfire scent of him as I stand—shocked—my hand trapped in the constraints of his warm, calloused one.

"What," I gasp, yanking away, "*the hell* are you doing?"

"Trying something," he replies cryptically, stuffing the knife in his pocket and trudging in front of me. "Trying something on the girl who can't stop fighting."

The sky is darkening quickly, fading to dusk. A member of the quarantine walks with a burning torch, lighting up a series of tall-standing cressets lining the paths.

After a beat of speechlessness, I say, "Trying *what*, Rion?"

But he doesn't answer—doesn't say a word—going silently through the snow, rubbing a thumb over the blade of the knife he just took from me. Mia's knife.

I'm about to stop following when we reach a path that isn't lit up by cressets—a path I recognize as the one leading directly to the quarantine's eastern perimeter.

The path to his hut.

Then he turns and says, "Eat with me?"

"Eat with you?" I echo stupidly. "What, *just* with—"

"She will," a voice blurts from my back. I glance over my shoulder and realize it's Merope speaking. "But only if we can eat with you too."

"We?" Rion asks brusquely.

"The three of us," Jac replies, filtering out of the darkness with a slightly happier looking Cyb beside him. "What's on the menu tonight, buddy?"

Rion laughs, shaking his head, and starts walking off.

Jac looks at me. "Guess that's a *yes.*"

I hang back with Merope and Cyb, looping arms between the pair of them, and we walk linked together.

Cyb fixes Jac with an ironclad glare and launches back into a conversation they were already having. "Just give us a task and we'll take care of it. We're ready."

"Ladies, I've told you, it's not up to me. It's up to Mabel."

"And you can't talk to Mabel for us?"

"You'll get your initiation," Jac reassures confidently, resting an arm over Merope's shoulder now too. She rolls her eyes in a flirtatious way. "Just relax. Now is the fun part."

"And where's the fun exactly?" Merope asks.

"Well, right now," he says, nodding as Rion rips his hut open up ahead and like before, a flood of firelight breaks through the night's liquid dark, "the *eating-food-that's-not-Pudge* part."

Jac lifts his arms off Merope and Cyb's shoulders, dashing off toward Rion's hut excitedly, leaving us behind. Cyb gives me the happiest look she's had yet.

"Almost there," she says, voraciously. "We're so close."

"I hear we're getting initiated?" I say.

"Yes—and *soon*, if all goes according to plan." Cyb's voice drops to a whisper. "Jac has been *cake* to manipulate into trusting our group; a little flirtation, and he's rooting for us already."

"But Rion," Merope adds, eyeing him from afar as he sets up a small campfire outside of his hut. "We suspect he's going to be a little harder to sway."

"Jac says Rion has the highest standing with Mabel, and so my guess is if we get his backing, we're in," Cyb raves, grabbing my hand and tugging me closer. Her silver-gray eyes are bright with hope. Her breath is a swirl of pale vapor. "Last night . . . did you guys talk?"

"Kind of, I guess," I say, shrugging.

"Do you think you can win him over?"

My gaze shifts back to Rion. Coincidentally, he looks up at me at the same time, giving me a subtle nod indicating I should join him and Jac by the fire.

"Yeah," I breathe to Cyb and Merope. "I've got him."

"That's right." Cyb walks ahead, pausing briefly before she turns around and quietly adds, "But don't forget about the last part of our Purpose."

I glance sidelong at Merope. "What part?"

I'm startled to see the pair equally hesitant to reply.

Merope glares at Cyb. "Go on. Tell her."

Cyb sighs, traipsing back to my side, her cold hand clasping tight around my elbow, piloting me toward the campfire as she gives me the final details on our Purpose.

"We don't know what Mabel's told them—if anything."

"They act like they know nothing," I say.

"Doesn't matter," Cyb says with a cruel sterility. "The only way to keep the Project's secrets safe is to make sure we leave this place without a single end left untied."

I feel myself go numb. "And?"

"And to do that, it's our job to terminate the whole place."

"Every member," Merope elaborates, eyes glistening. "If we fail to do so, our chances at making the Elite are revoked because we won't have followed the rules."

"You're . . . We can't . . ." *I feel ill.* "All of them?"

"All of them," Cyb confirms unfeelingly, and then trudges off toward the campfire without looking back. Merope lingers at my side silently for a while, turning only after she's sure we can't be overheard, even by Cyb.

"Get close to him," she warns me, voice desperate and lost in ways I didn't think her capable of, "but not too close."

14

CYB, MEROPE, AND I sit with the boys in a series of brightly-colored, mismatched lawn chairs—the exact kind that might've perched beside a pool on a summer day, lifetimes ago.

But instead of a pool, it's mid-winter, and we're roasting a bucket of plucked doves over a small campfire.

That's life on Earth these days.

The sky is especially dark because it's a new moon. Stars as bright as jewels occasionally peek out from the clouds knotted and straining overhead, but otherwise it's overcast outside.

Snow falls, so light it looks like glittering dust.

Beside me, Jac rolls a cigarette. "So, ladies," he says, sealing the paper with a lick. "You're quiet tonight. What's up?"

"Today sucked, that's what," Cyb snorts. "Our best friend is in critical condition. Davy and Elizabeth got in a fight. We had a crude man yell at us over trying to get Pudge . . ."

"Speaking of," Silas speaks up, eyeing Rion cryptically, "Mia should know better than—"

"I know." Rion tosses the knife at Silas's feet, where it thuds in the deep, wet snow. "Mia gave Elizabeth a pair of boots—and guess what was left inside?"

"No way," Silas laughs disbelievingly, holding up the knife.

"That conniving little brat." Jac lights a plump, freshly rolled cigarette and inhales, breathing deeply. "I bet she would've loved it if nobody had stopped Elizabeth from stabbing Tex to death."

Cyb's brows tighten. "Why would she have wanted that?"

Silas rolls the spit of plucked doves browning perfectly over the small fire. It fizzles as oil and juice rolls in flavorful beads off the skin of the birds. I imagine what it would've been like to share this meal with Rion alone—the way he'd wanted.

"Mia doesn't like outsiders," Jac says, shrugging. "And aside from good ol' Davy, Elizabeth is the biggest hothead out of your whole group. Mia probably wanted her to do something so bad you would be denied a chance at initiating."

"Like killing a quarantine member?" Cyb guesses.

"She *might've* too," Jac adds, clearly amused, "if Rion hadn't have stopped her."

"Not kill—castrate," I interject jokingly, but heat rises in my cheeks despite my best efforts, suddenly painfully aware of how absurd I've been acting.

Fighting with total strangers and friends alike?

Enough, Eos. Enough of this.

Thankfully the topic shifts to food as Silas removes the birds from the spit, none of which are very large, and I'm glad to see we don't have to share.

"Who shot these?" Merope asks, biting into her bird. Juice rolls over her lips, glistening in the firelight.

I bite into mine too. It's plump and flavorful, spiced lightly with dried rosemary and sage Silas took from the kitchens. *I've never had anything so delicious in my life.* The Ora's rations were always limited: freeze-dried, chewy, and consistently flavorless.

"Rion, of course," Jac praises.

"Well," she says through a mouthful of meat, "thank you."

For a while nobody speaks. The night fills, instead, with the sound of cracking bone as wings are dislocated and chest cavities picked completely clean.

When we're finished, and our plates are left with only a pile of delicate bones, discussion ramps back up.

"So, Mabel gets back soon," Silas announces suddenly.

"Really?" Cyb leans closer, intrigued. "Will she be seeing to our initiations soon?"

"I don't know if, for you guys, it'll be like that."

"What's that supposed to mean?" Cyb eyes Silas, who looks away from her—her gaze leaps to Jac and Rion. "What are we supposed to expect from initiation, anyway?"

A coarse hush falls upon us.

It's obvious, suddenly, that this isn't a welcome discussion.

Rion clears his throat. "It's different for everybody."

"How?" Cyb probes, either ignoring or not catching the stiff faces of our company. "What about *your* experiences—examples?"

I curl into the chrysalis of my jacket awkwardly, trying to keep my eyes on the fire. I hate prying, but we've got to get into this quarantine or risk failing our Purpose.

Do you care anymore, Eos? a voice begs in my mind, a voice that sounds eerily like Nova's. *Do you even want to fulfill a mission so gruesome? Could you ever, really, live happily in the Elite knowing it came at the cost of hundreds of lives?*

"Mine was a test," Silas divulges unexpectedly, whispering.

Both Jac and Rion's eyes flash, giving me reason to believe that not even *they*, Silas's friends, knew about this.

Again, a heavy silence falls, but this time it's rife with the electric buzz of anticipation—of suspense.

Cyb leans forward, elbows resting on her knees. "What kind of a test did you take, Silas?"

Silas shakes his head, as though he's disinterested in saying anything more, but goes on regardless. "There were four others."

"Ah," Cyb says. "A competition, was it?"

Silas gives her a slow nod. "We were released together, right outside this compound, near a large nest of the Muted. We were told whoever killed the most would win."

"And you won," Cyb finishes gleefully.

"No. I won by default," he says. "There was a guy, he was bigger than me. Killed twelve of the Muted in ten minutes. He was the one who really won, but he died."

"How?" Merope asks breathlessly.

"I killed him." Silas's pale gray eyes are dead. "I'd been all by myself for nearly four months—my family gone, my friends all killed off, my resources used up."

Silas dives his face into the cover of his hands, miserable, as the rest of us wait in shocked silence.

"*I* should've died that day—not that guy," he croaks.

"You're wrong, Si," Jac says, speaking softly, his cigarette all but forgotten, burning low in his hand. "You've done so much for all of us, for this quarantine . . ."

Silas's mutters, "I'll never forgive myself."

"We've all," Rion interjects, speaking low, "done things we regret in the name of staying alive—things we wish we could take back but can't. You're not alone, Si."

"Nothing is worse than what I've done." Silas grips his pale, straw-colored hair, ripping out a fistful of wispy strands. "I didn't kill to survive. I killed out of cowardice."

My eyes find Rion, who's staring intensely at the flickering flames of the campfire. He looks on edge.

Just as I register as much, he grabs a bucket of water at his side and throws it at the fire. It hisses, coils of steam rising up from hellish coals.

We'd be left in total darkness if it weren't for the fire raging in the hearth of Rion's hut. Its light filters dimly out through a small window, highlighting our grim faces.

"You're not a coward," Rion says, angrily kicking the empty bucket aside as he strides to his hut's door, rips it open—spraying ice everywhere—and slams it shut behind him.

We're left startled, silent. The empty bucket sways noisily back and forth, scratching the icy surface of the snow. I hear the shuffle of chairs moving. Jac takes the plates, piled high with bird bones, and swipes their contents into another bucket.

Nobody speaks. Nobody does anything.

Not until a jagged cry pierces the night's quiet like the slow rip of fabric being torn. It's the strangest noise: a scream that's raw and phlegm-filled and strikingly inhuman.

The Muted.

Jac groans, chucking his cigarette. "Ah, *shit.*"

Beside me I hear Merope begin to gasp for breath, her hand cold and clammy, gripping mine.

"Cyb," I bark, and in an instant her silver-gray eyes find mine in the darkness. "What do we do?"

Jac mistakes my question for him, and says, "You're aware of how the Muted are drawn to groups? Quarantines often become targets for that reason. We've got to go fight them off."

"Or better yet," Silas says, "draw them away."

"It's not bad enough for—" Jac's cut off by a host of shrieking tolling through the night in chilling waves. It's clear to us all that this really could be *bad enough.*

"We're leading them away," Silas ratifies. "If we don't get them out of here, they'll take over the compound again."

"Again?" Cyb snaps.

"Don't worry, you won't be coming." Jac pounds a gloved fist against Rion's door. "That mistake isn't one we're ever going to make again."

But before I can ask for details, Rion's door opens. A rifle is tossed out, which Jac catches. A second follows, which is passed quickly on to Silas.

"I heard" is all Rion says as he cocks his rifle with one hand and holds a lit torch aloft in his other. "They are always hungrier in winter, aren't they?"

"Where are all of you going?" I ask as they walk by, my tone high-pitched, imploring. "Take us with you. We'll *help.* It could be our initiation!"

Rion passes the torch to Silas, trudging back down the path toward the three of us. A moment later, he's so close to me he doesn't have to speak louder than a whisper.

"The three of you stay inside," he says, pressing his rifle into my arms, nodding at his hut glowing beside us. "We'll be back in a few hours—maybe dawn."

"I can help you," I repeat, stopping only because Rion's put his face so close to mine we're sharing breath.

"No," he says. "You can't."

And then he's turning back to Jac and Silas, issuing rounds of orders and coded warnings: "Tell Mia we're performing what we think is a Grade 10 pushback—and get the keys to the truck at the entry perimeter while you're at it."

"Who else are we bringing?" Jac asks.

"Mabel's council will insist on being involved . . ." Rion starts to say as the three walk up the path, their torch a golden ball of light bobbing as they go. A chorus of shrieking fills the night yet again, pointing out the Muted's alarmingly close proximity like an arrow.

"Hurry," Rion says as the shrieking continues to fill the night full of panic, voices of those awoken by the chaos—hasty and terrified—adding to the mix.

His eyes find mine once more, holding my gaze. Without another word, he leaves, disappearing into the night's pitch-black to fight the Muted without us.

AT CYB'S INSISTENCE, WE follow Rion's orders, hunkering down in his fire-warmed hut for hours, yet as the Muted's cries begin to reach higher and shriller, our doubts intensify.

When it's clear the Muted have reached the perimeter, their claws raking violently against the wall, I feel my resolve to stand back and wait unravel altogether.

Cyb picks nervously at a dirty fingernail. "We can't give him a reason to kick us out, Eos. Disobey his direct orders, and we're as good as done here."

I grip the rifle Rion gave me, knuckles white.

Merope's pale, sweaty face lifts. "There are hundreds, if not a thousand, coming tonight." Her violet eyes pin Cyb in place as she speaks. "Do you actually believe these native-borns will come back in one piece—alive?"

Cyb purses her lips and doesn't answer, throwing another log into the flames. Outside, the wall booms thunderously under the fists of the Muted trying to gain access to the compound.

"You said so yourself," I argue wildly. "We need their trust to get into the quarantine. We can't fulfill our Purpose without their blessing. How will we get that if they're all dead?"

Cyb sighs, a hiss. "How will the three of us make any damn difference? You don't even have a skillset! And Merope's barely acclimated as it—"

"We've got to get Apollo."

"Eos," Merope says, disbelievingly, straightening up. As she stands, so does Cyb. "He isn't a specimen."

The walls of the hut rattle from outside as the Muted rile up against it, clawing and kicking and biting. Something falls off a shelf on the other side of the room.

I pick it up to replace it and realize it's . . . a necklace?
No, dog tags. Military.

XII VII IV XIII XXI
PILOT

"What's that?" Merope asks. I'm spared answering when a bout of shrieking issues so loudly from outside, I'm afraid we're in real danger of the wall falling.

"Nothing," I say hastily, tossing it back on the shelf and, in a swift motion, cocking my rifle. "Apollo's in the barn—beside the bonfire. He's invisible to the Muted. We can use him."

I rip open the hut's door, glancing back at the pair.

"Are you with me?" I ask.

"Obviously." Merope is still unsteady, but that doesn't stop her from joining me at the door. Cyb eyes us both from the fire, a war waging within.

"All right," she says at last. "But I better not regret this."

15

THE SECOND WE LEAVE the safety and seclusion of Rion's hut, we realize the whole quarantine is in chaos.

People run screaming, hordes of them pressing their backs to the walls, straining against the push of the Muted. The smell of decay is as thick as the panic in the air, leaving the hair on my arms perpetually raised.

"The barn," Cyb notes sharply. "Straight ahead."

"We can't find the others until we've secured the perimeter on this side," I say as we jostle through groups of wild-looking people, yelling and crying in horror. "Why," I add on, "are these idiots not fighting?"

"Are you joking? I wouldn't trust a single one of these fools with a gun," Cyb barks as we approach the barn—a three-story tall building looming behind the bonfire. "That has to be it."

I follow her gaze, finding a single door roped in chains with a series of padlocks dangling—

"The locks are open!" I declare. A closer look confirms my discovery, each padlock's mouth gaping wide. "Where did they take him? This is the only barn . . ."

Just then a loud *crack!* calls for our attention.

We whirl around, facing utter chaos: a large log in the wall has snapped in half. Instantly, the Muted take advantage—a set of strong, sinewy arms reach in and begin grabbing wildly.

A man shoves his teenage son aside, getting himself taken by the Muted in the process. He screams viscerally as he's pulled through the gap, the wood's splinters raking into his skin, and his ribs snapping loudly as he's yanked violently through.

The Muted practically sing, tearing into the man like a pack of starving, rabid dogs.

"Oh, to hell with Apollo," I say, dropping the chain. "We've got to secure the perimeter—*now.*"

"One step ahead of you," Merope says, still pale and sweaty in the face, but otherwise balanced as she walks out from inside the barn's shadowy depths—carrying guns.

Cyb takes a loaded rifle. "There are *guns* in there?"

"With prisoners?" I say, finishing her thought, but there's no time to think on the logistics of it. The wall's logs are strong, but not strong enough. They can't withstand the Muted's charge for much longer, especially without reinforcements.

I try not to think about what will happen if the wall falls.

"Okay," I say. "Here goes nothing."

We walk in tandem toward the gap in the wall, stepping in sync with one another. My periphery is dominated by the whites of eyes and crooked teeth, bared, mid-scream.

Nobody tries to stop us.

"Persuade whichever Mute's in the gap," I order as we get close enough to fire, members of the quarantine parting with a surprising degree of cooperation before us.

Cyb nods, totally focused.

"Stand back!" I yell. The last few people do, revealing a gap much bigger than I'd originally thought—so big, it's capable of birthing a whole, man-sized Mute.

"Got him," Cyb grunts as the first Mute's face appears in the gap of the wall; it's instantly frozen, twitching wildly, as if it's aware of its own paralysis.

I raise my rifle and fire a single round. It pegs the Mute in between its gouged-out eyes, ripping a hole through its skull like a dart through paper.

The next Mute presents itself. We do it again.

With every one killed, we take a few steps closer, until we're positioned right in front of the gap. Merope waves over the few members with their wits still intact, and they begin patching the wall with thick saplings.

Cyb's gotten the hang of Persuading each Mute so well, she is doing everything on her own: keeping them still and shooting them dead, one by one.

Merope and I scout farther down the wall, finding ourselves back at the barn. It's full of weapons, supplies. I trail my fingers along the wall, feeling my way in the dark.

"Sense anything?" I ask her. "Empathetically?"

"Whatever Rion's crew is doing, it's working," she says in a voice so breathy, it worries me. I hear the clinking of things falling from the wall when she leans up against it. "They're being lead away from the compound."

I rush to her side, picking up the things that've dropped off the wall behind her. "But how? If the Muted are drawn to groups of people, why would they follow just the handful of them?"

My fingertips brush against something cold and edgy on the ground. I pick it up: a ring of keys.

"We've got to get to them," I whisper, holding the keys up in the firelight. "When Cyb's got the wall patched, we'll steal this vehicle—we'll go out there and find them."

"Find them?" she croaks.

"You'll sense them with your skillset," I say, dropping my unloaded rifle in favor of another—already preloaded, hanging on the wall with others.

I take Merope's rifle and give her another, along with a slew of glistening knives.

I grip her arm, eyeing her severely: her lips are chapped and peeling, dark circles cupping her pretty eyes. It occurs to me that I'm risking her life. *By asking her and Cyb to follow me, I'm risking their lives . . .*

I'm brash . . . hotheaded . . .

Just like my Psych Eval reflected.

Merope's posture shifts. "You're second-guessing yourself."

"Stay with Cyb," I say suddenly. "Guard the wall."

"And let you go alone?"

"This is my idea. I'll go, get it done by—"

"Shut up, Eos," Merope says, marching out of the barn with her black hair swaying at her back. "I said *I'm with you,* or have you forgotten that already?"

"I'm asking you to risk—"

"You're asking me to do what's right," she interjects, violet eyes glistening as she takes my wrist and drags me along. "You're right about this. What better way to gain somebody's loyalty than to risk your life saving theirs?"

We hear footsteps approaching rapidly, turning just in time to see Cyb round the corner, gasping for breath. "The wall is up, the wall is back up!"

I throw her a fresh rifle. "I've found something."

"What?" she says, skidding to a halt before us. I hold up the ring of keys for her to behold. "Car keys," she adds, nodding with a genuine smile. "Where do we find their vehicles?"

"Entry perimeter," I say, recalling Rion's orders to his group before he left. *Don't forget to get the keys to the truck at the entry perimeter while you're at it.*

I sheath a knife in the belt loop of my pants. "Ready?"

"More than ready," Cyb growls as we begin to jog toward the entryway. The padlocks locking the large, swinging door have been left locked, but Cyb uses a metal-cutter to destroy them.

The Muted haven't caught on to this entrance. They aren't at the entryway in full force, but scattered. The night echoes with their cries, so shrill they settle and ring chillingly under my skin.

I look to Merope and Cyb, my chest swelling.

"We can do this," I assert. "For Lios."

"For Lios." Cyb's lip trembles, eyes bright as moonlight.

"For Lios," Merope adds, cocking her rifle. And for a brief stretch of time, we stand together—*truly together*—aware of the fact that we could be facing death.

And choosing to face it anyway.

Together.

Cyb smiles wolfishly. "Let's do this."

I kick open the entry door, which groans as it swings wide to release us. Merope clicks new padlocks over the ones we've just destroyed behind us, and Cyb sets the metal-cutter aside, stashing it by a nearby tree for when we come back.

If we come back.

"They headed southeast!" Merope yells as we turn around the corner, looking frantically for the trucks, which are—almost too conveniently—at the exact spot Rion said they'd be.

"It's the Chevy," I say, referencing the keys as we approach the only truck—pale yellow, ringed with circles of rust—of that particular brand.

We pile in, surprised by the luck of having picked the right key on the first try. None of us have driven before, but learning the basics of native-born transportation was a requirement for our studies, and given that traffic laws no longer exist . . .

I take the driver's seat and rev the engine, which booms to life in an echoing, thunderous roar. We take off, spinning out of the parking spot and onto a dirt road rolling along the perimeter of the whole quarantine.

Cyb grips my shoulder. "Let's check the east side again."

I nod with a smile, enjoying the thrill of driving—the air washing in through the window, the way speeding through the moonless night both tightens my chest and shakes something in it loose, releasing it.

Merope shouts over the engine, "More up ahead!"

I jerk the steering wheel, making a hairpin turn, and we're back at the eastern perimeter. The Muted continue to claw and rile against the wall, moving with a startling agility.

"Fire at will," I say, revving the engine again in preparation to mow over the Muted still remaining. Cyb and Merope raise their rifles through the passenger side window, aiming to take out the ones crawling up the wall.

I slam my foot against the gas pedal.

Everything is in shadow, exposed only if it's directly in front of our truck's headlights. The golden glow from the quarantine's always-burning bonfire lights up the wall's cracks, illuminating the Muted scaling the logs.

Cyb and Merope shoot off rounds; I can't see the Muted die as much as I hear the echoing blast of gunfire followed quickly by the thud of falling corpses tumbling off their place on the wall. I gun the engine, clipping the Muted that barely dodge the truck as it passes by.

"Look!" Cyb says, pointing at a ridge in the dirt road, where tracks visibly veered off to the left. "They went that way!"

We fly to the left as I yank the steering wheel, peeling out of the path we were following and head into the moonless, pitch-black dark, trailing the tracks left for us but having close to no visual warning before abrupt twists in the path.

The Muted are everywhere, thicker with every stretch we take deeper into the forest. My heart pounds like a fist against my sternum—alive and thrilled and terrified at once—as we do what we were specifically created for.

Kill the Muted.

Cyb laughs maniacally after Persuading a Mute to lie down in front of our truck as we blaze by, crushing its skull like a small watermelon. Her euphoria is interrupted by a searing light exploding in the night sky, hissing smoke.

"A flare," Merope identifies wisely. "For backup, I bet."

"Why do you say that?" I ask.

"Too many," she wheezes, pounding a fist against her chest as though in the effort of clearing it. "Too *many*. We're almost there, now—they're *everywhere*."

"Look!" Cyb says, nodding ahead of us. Several lights blaze through the night's dark. "Torches! We've made it!"

Merope takes our rifles and begins stuffing clips into their magazines frantically, reloading in preparation for a scene we are in no way mentally ready to face.

The Muted. Everywhere.

They are chasing a truck that's going full speed over the hills and dips of the clearing. In the truck-bed is a large Mute lying flat on its back, strapped in. The Mute is the largest I've ever seen before, exceedingly larger than a man is physically capable of being naturally . . .

Ten feet tall, at least. Muscular. Teeth falling over its lipless mouth in bloody, hooked fangs. And a roar that echoes over the landscape in haunting waves of undiluted fury.

It doesn't look like a man infected by the plague.

It looks like a monster.

"Is that, like, the queen bee?" Cyb asks, eyes narrowed.

"Actually they—" Merope's arrested mid-sentence by a second flare issued sky-high, and a series of yelling. The light of the flare reveals Rion steering the truck with the Mute strapped in the bed, Jac and Silas sitting beside it.

A spread of armed men scatter in the blazing red light, all on foot, facing the Muted head-on. This side of the forest is not only alive with shrieks of those infected by the A-42, but by those not infected at all—screaming as they're taken down.

Devoured.

"No," Merope breathes, averting her eyes to the gruesome scene of a man running out of bullets, crab-walking backward as he's pursued by three of the Muted. Their maws drip with blood and saliva and phlegm, vocal cords clicking with excitement as they corner their prey.

Merope glances at Cyb. "Do something!"

"That's Tex," she replies with disgust, a hint of satisfaction in her expression as he screams shrilly. "Let's just let him—"

"We can't," I groan. "As much as I'd love to let him die, he's one of us if we get into the quarantine."

Rion's truck explodes in a spate of bubbling, choking noises as it putters, then stops.

Jac launches himself out of the truck—Silas springing wildly out behind him—the pair shouting in unison, "NO FUEL! WE ARE OUT OF FUEL!"

"Who do we save, Eos?" Cyb asks, turning to me with those sparkling, overcast eyes—always sharp with challenge. "Do we save that asshole, Tex, or do we save Rion?"

I swallow. Across the way, the truck chugs forward a few feet only to stop seconds later. Its fuel has run dry. Additional flares fly, whizzing and tearing through the black night sky, but we all know help isn't coming.

We're the only backup they've got.

I look back at Cyb. "We save both of them," I say and drop my foot on the gas pedal once more. "Starting with that undeserving prick, Tex."

We blaze through the clearing, gleaning the attention of all those still fighting—they pause, squinting in the dark, trying to identify the three girls who came to save their asses.

Our truck peels out, skidding to a halt in front of the tree that Tex now leans against. The Muted close in tight and unforgiving around him.

"DRIVE," I tell Merope, spilling out of the truck to head the rest of the way on foot. "Cyb—back me up!"

Merope drives the rest of the way across the clearing, engine growling low and booming, to help the others.

Cyb presses a fingertip casually to her temple, Persuading the first Mute in front of Tex to freeze. In mere seconds, we've taken all three of them out, their foreheads gaping with bullet holes so flawlessly aimed they look like third eyes.

Tex staggers, straightening up. "You—*you!*"

"Yes, us," Cyb replies dully.

"Fight hard, *big man*," I add sardonically, tossing him one of the knives I've stolen; it lands right between his feet. "You're on your own now."

Cyb and I take off, plunging into the clearing. Merope has both Jac and Silas in her truck, trailing behind Rion's as it keeps sputtering forward, only to stop shortly after.

The Muted are closing in.

"They want that bigger Mute," I observe curiously, lunging through the thick, tall-standing shrubs poking through the layer of snow carpeting the clearing.

Cyb raises her rifle's scope for a better look. "Rion's getting out of his truck. It's completely empty now."

"Where is he going?"

"Oh . . ."

"What?" I say, ducking into the shrubs, trying to stay out of sight from a swarm of the Muted still buzzing around us, shrieking and dodging in the shadows.

They seem . . . riled up, distracted.

"That Mute—the big one—it's getting free," Cyb relays in a deathly whisper, and sure enough I see the scene unfold through the scope of my rifle.

Rion leaps out of the truck at the *worst possible time.*

The smaller members of the Muted chase the big one while it's going right after Rion. The larger Mute's strides are three times as long as its smaller counterparts, gaining on Rion fast and effortlessly.

I throw myself into a sprint.

Cyb's footsteps pound behind me. "You're insane!" she says, voice breathy, as she runs. "We can't stop that Mute with rifles and a few knives, Eos!"

"Exactly," I shout over my shoulder. "It's a good thing we've got more than that."

"What're—"

"Follow my lead," I yell, diving into the chaos—a torrential storm of snarling Mute faces and teeth. Distantly, I hear Merope and Cyb shouting—maybe even Jac and Silas.

I don't care. I'm right. I can solve this.

Trust yourself, Eos.

Rion's completely surrounded. The Muted disinterested in the bigger one shrink their ranks around him, closing in like the tightening of a noose.

Farther off, the big, lumbering Mute approaches.

Another flare blazes through the sky.

A call that won't be answered.

I skid to an abrupt stop, spraying snow and ice with the heel of my boot as I do so. I turn to Cyb, who's right behind me, and nod at the big Mute.

"Lead it away. The others will follow," I breathe.

"Persuade that big guy?" she asks disbelievingly, her temples glittering with a band of cold sweat. "Eos, it's hard enough to tell the others what to do, *let alone*—"

"You can do it." I grab a fistful of her jacket, dragging her so we're eye-to-eye, and growl, "You've *got* to do it."

Cyb gives me a stiff nod and darts off, dipping behind the cover of trees to get closer, leaving me to spin on my heel and drive myself deeper into the whirling chaos ahead.

Without a skillset. Without an advantage.

With only my steeled nerves.

Merope drives the truck around the clearing. Jac and Silas grab the hands of members, dragging everybody aboard, sitting them in the truck bed. *Okay. Easy . . . All Rion and I have to do is stay alive long enough for them to make their way over to us.*

The Muted envelope me instantly. Up ahead, Rion fires the remaining rounds he's got in a pistol. He's a great shot, making every mark perfectly, staying ducked beside the immobile truck to keep his back covered.

But for every Mute he kills, another five emerge.

There are just too damn many.

In all the screaming—and the engine of Merope's truck rumbling—he doesn't hear my gun firing off rounds at less than twenty feet away, pegging all the Muted he misses, plus some.

I keep my breathing steady. I stay focused.

Until I hear the gut-wrenching *click!* of his pistol as it runs out of bullets, leaving him vulnerable. Even in all the noise, I'm able to hear him swear viciously, eyes scanning the clearing for any backup—for the truck, which is still so far off, they haven't even noticed we're in trouble over here.

And then, his eyes find mine, their scanning halted almost instantly as they register who I am, trying to figure out how I've gotten here, *why* I'm here.

Briefly, it's as though the chaos surrounding us has faded to a dull roar, ticking by slowly—delayed.

I give him a quiet nod and throw my rifle, which glides in total elegance over the ice-coated snow, caught perfectly under the tip of his boot.

Just then, I hear the big Mute roaring loudly, stomping off in a direction leading away from the quarantine. I catch sight of a figure huddled in the woods, fingertip pressed avidly to her pale temple as she strains, controlling the Mute's every stride.

As it goes, it swipes avidly at the smaller members of the

infected, knocking them aside and killing a few too.

Way to go, Cyb.

I feel a rush of pride and adoration for her warm the coldest parts of myself—pockets of my heart I didn't think she'd ever have access to—and now, somehow, throughout this insane moment in our lives, she's found her way in.

And then, I see it.

A group of the Muted slink up behind her, swaying slightly on their feet—unsteady, as though drugged.

Their lips drip fresh blood. Behind them, I see a corpse of somebody I can't identify—a corpse they've just feasted on to the point of leaving its face beyond recognition.

And now they're heading for Cyb.

No, no, no!

I don't spare Rion a backward glance—he's got a rifle, he's got a chance. Cyb's defenseless, and the second she lifts her focus off controlling the big Mute, it will reign supreme.

I throw myself into a full-blown sprint, legs pedaling so fast beneath me, I almost trip over myself as I rip through the center of the clearing. My mind is absorbed by the snow hardened by ice underfoot and the red glow of lit flares lighting my way, the cold hilt of a dagger in my palm . . .

That's all I've got now—a dagger.

I tell myself it's all I need.

I'm feet away when all of a sudden, I'm knocked breathless and into the air, flying high and falling hard, head whiplashed by the unexpected impact.

Dizzily, I roll to my side, getting back to my feet.

I've been targeted by my own group of the Muted—three, all with their eyeless faces lifted, sniffing through noses worn free of cartilage, set over lipless, vicious mouths.

They, too, look drunk—moving swiftly, with more agility than ever, and yet with a strange intoxication in the way they delicately approach. *No longer out of need, but out of want.*

I raise my dagger but am spared the need. A figure darts out from behind me in a manic dash. The figure wields a machete in high, vicious arcs, hacking the Muted into slabs of still-twitching flesh and cracked bone, clearing my path.

Without wasting a second, I sprint off, only sparing a brief glance over my shoulder to the figure who's possibly, by helping me get free, saved Cyb's life.

And when I do, I feel my throat seize up.

Apollo's lips are elevated in a self-satisfied smirk—a sheen to his black eyes that is startlingly like Pavo's.

How did he get here? Did they . . . invite him, ask him for help?

I turn my back on him, heading straight for Cyb, who's now a plaything to the Muted pursuing her. They slap her around in a catlike way, and though I hear her yell in frustration, scuttling off to distance herself, she doesn't break focus.

"HEY," I shout at the Muted, trying to get their attention off her and on me instead. "OVER HERE."

They lift their ugly faces, delighted to spot new prey.

I skid, stopping as I did before in a spray of snow, falling to my hip as I do so. They slink closer. I get back up and dive for the closest Mute, plunging a dagger into its heart.

The Mute folds over itself—*dead.*

Suddenly it's not a game for the Muted anymore. They hiss and spit and shriek—voices clicking, ragged—as the rest of them blitz for me simultaneously.

I plunge my dagger into a Mute's empty eye socket, rip it

out fast, and slice it gracefully through its throat, just in time to thrust it backward, dragging it up through the guts of another behind me, eviscerating it.

Another Mute tackles me to the snow, lowering its hideous, gaping jaws to my throat. I slash a dagger and snag the flesh of its cheek, ripping it open. The Mute shrieks, parrot-like, before trying to tear my arm off my body. It yanks wildly, its grip like a vice on my left wrist, before I hear a loud *pop!* and realize it's just dislocated my shoulder.

I loose a cry, unable to hold it back.

A few feet away, Cyb twitches with concern.

"I'm fine!" I assure her, freeing my right hand just in time to throw my dagger into its chest. It heaves, shrieking. I realize that despite my proximity, I haven't hit its heart.

The Mute flails, making it impossible to retrieve my dagger.

It lowers its face to mine, expelling a vicious, hot-breathed shriek inches from my own, and before I can even *think* to be afraid—before I can realize that my life's actually in danger—its jaws clamp down on my left shoulder.

Its teeth sink deep, grinding against cartilage and bone.

Pain. A wave of scalding heat, licking my insides, rolls in an unbearable upsurge through my body—so great, I can't find any breath with which to scream, every shred of my focus snagged on one repetitive phrase: *You failed, you failed, you failed.*

And then, another—emitted from a place so deep, it doesn't sound like my own when it voices itself to me, barking the command confidently. *You haven't failed yet, Eos. Not yet. Keep going.*

In a flash, the Mute's lowering its jaws again. My right hand glides over the ground, feeling snow—and, as though left there for me, a broken sapling.

A spear.

The Mute and I race to kill each other first—my makeshift spear lancing forward, its jaws dropping unnaturally wide as they sail closer, targeting my neck.

Then, gunfire—loud and close.

The thudding of flesh. The spray of hot blood.

The Mute falls, crashing lifelessly over me, nearly crushing me to death with its weight alone.

I hear voices. The grumble of a truck's engine. The enfilade of additional automatic gunfire. The hiss of a final flare blasting through the sky, blinding my eyes in its luster.

The Mute is heaved off me, tossed aside where it flops into the snow like a boneless heap of flesh. I can breathe. The spear is still in my hand. I roll sideways, plunging it into the Mute's gut for no reason aside from my own blatant hostility.

Rion emerges—covered in blood, clothes torn, dirt smudged over his face like war paint—holding the rifle I left him, which he'd just used to kill my assailant. He lowers a hand to help me up. I give him my good arm, and like earlier, he pulls me so close we're nearly chest-to-chest.

"Are you insane?" he asks, releasing me.

"I *am*, actually," I wheeze, thinking of my Psych Eval.

Rion's eyes dance off mine analytically, as though I'm a face he recognizes but can't pin a name to. The truck roars as it skids up to us, ready to be boarded—the Muted still a churning force, despite trickling off steadily away from the compound, following the large Mute controlled by Cyb.

"Come on." Rion swallows, taking my right arm and tossing it over his shoulder to support me. "Let's go home."

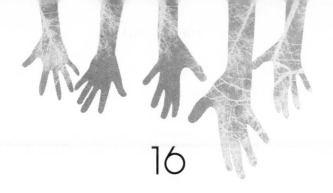

16

"THIS IS GOING TO hurt."

Mia traces her cold fingertips over my arm, finding the best place to forge a grip. We're in Mabel's cabin—a burgeoning mass of others waiting noisily in the living room, bruised and bloody, for their turn in the examination dock.

Which really is more like a glorified closet.

No—not a closet, a *refrigerator.*

It's freezing in here.

"By all means, take your time," I say, shivering against the steel table I'm lying on. It doesn't help that my shirt's halfway off so she can gain access to my dislocated shoulder.

Mia eyes me irritably. Behind her, Merope and Cyb bounce on their toes, shivering just as fiercely as I am. They, somehow, came out of tonight's mayhem unscathed.

Cyb hasn't been able to shake the sickly sheen she's adopted since Persuading the large Mute earlier, though. Her face is more pallid than ever before, lips milky.

"Go to bed," I tell her, glaring. "At this glacial pace, my arm won't be fixed before—"

Mia yanks my arm. Hard.

I feel the tendons strain painfully, hear cartilage crunch as my shoulder is pulled straight then replaced, snapped back into the socket it shouldn't have ever left.

I don't yell.

I *flail*, seizing like I'm possessed. A few excruciating seconds pass before I can even breathe—and to my chagrin, before I've had a chance to compose myself fully, the door swings open.

Rion walks in with Jac and Silas, the three of them looking startlingly disheveled in the fluorescent lighting.

"Finished?" he asks, addressing me. I look away, averting my eyes to hide the fact that they're still burning with tears. "What about that cut on her shoulder, Mia?"

That bite, you mean.

I reach up hesitantly and dab a fingertip along the ridges of the puncture marks. It stings, still bleeding.

Mia digs through a drawer and pulls out a clean cloth and a jug of clear liquid. *Vodka.*

Rion squints with disbelief. "No hydrogen peroxide?"

"Nope." Mia shrugs innocently, a truly evil glint to those slate-colored eyes. "This will hurt like the devil, but it'll get the job done in terms of disinfecting the wound."

I'm off the table before she can lay another finger on me.

"Passing on that one, Mia," I grunt angrily.

"Passing?" she asks as I traipse by, making a beeline for the exit across the room. When she speaks again, her tone is rich in barely concealed, mock-worry. "But you'll get an *infection*, which, if left without treatment, can *kill you*, Elizabeth. Surely you don't want that?"

"Oh, I don't, but I'm sure you'd *love* it." I sniff, casting her a glower as promising as a verbally spoken threat.

Mia opens her mouth to retaliate, but she's distracted when

the jug of vodka is stolen swiftly from her custody.

"I'll take care of it later," Rion says, eying her critically.

Mia's brows lift, but ultimately she stays quiet—leaving me to give crippled side-hugs to Merope and Cyb, vowing to see them in a few hours at breakfast, and go.

Merope follows Jac, and Cyb follows Silas, the four bravely facing the hordes of people awaiting Mia's medical help, taking the primary exit from Mabel's cabin.

Rion takes me elsewhere. We navigate the cabin's twisted innards and end up in a distant back room, left as a large storage space. Rows of locked cabinets linked along the far wall contain paperwork with origins that are difficult to fathom.

After a good shove on Rion's end, we break through a door concealed by supplies and are back outside, spat out into the smear of endless snow flurries, shivering, and dark.

We make our way back to the eastern perimeter, turning by the large bonfire. My arm aches tremendously. I keep it clutched across my chest as we walk, my sole focus occupied on keeping my breathing steady until I hear something.

Wailing. Sobbing. Weeping.

The echoed cries draw my attention like a sharp tap on the shoulder, and I can't help but look.

Bodies. Everywhere.

Draped in dingy, white sheets. A feathery layer of snow has settled overtop, softening the severity of it.

Though there are places of blood blossoming through the white fabric, like scarlet flowers budding, the scene strikes me as strangely peaceful: the slow falling of spiraling snow, and the dim wash of golden firelight—songs sang, issued in voices burdened by gravel, by a ring of grievers encircling the dead.

A mother sits beside her adult daughter, invited to mourn at the center of the circle while the others sing beautifully, pitched plangently in expression of the gravity of their loss.

Of *our* loss.

The daughter is a corpse, her tanned fingers scaled with dry blood, stiff with rigor mortis, and blackening at the tips. Her hair is a mop of black tightly-coiled spirals, eyes big and dark, just like her mother's.

Rion's hand finds the small of my back. "Let's go."

Just as he speaks, the singers—the mother, kneeling beside her dead daughter—notice I'm watching. My breath catches like a shard of glass in my throat as I search frantically for something to say, something to convey, to express how . . .

How, what?

Sorry I am for her loss—a loss I can't fathom?

I gasp, feeling ill, and look to Rion. "How did this happen?"

"A breach," he relays quietly.

"Where—how many?"

"The only perimeter that held was the eastern." Rion's push on my back strengthens, but instead of pushing me away, he's pulling me in. "Thanks to you."

I feel the hardest part of myself shatter—like my spine, my every vertebrae, crumbling to dust.

"I should've stayed," I say, sick over my culpability, resting my hands flush over his chest—and without realizing why or how or when, I've rested my cheek along with them.

Physical touch isn't something most specimens are prone to engaging in. It has nothing to do with survival, and so we aren't taught how to do it properly. We aren't ever *shown*.

But that doesn't stop it from feeling natural, feeling like a bit of home in a foreign place.

And so I press myself up against Rion, even though he's a total stranger, and let myself feel comforted by it—by his fresh cedar, campfire smell, and by the way he finally gives in and falls into me in return.

After a while, it's not me leaning on him, but us leaning on each other.

When he speaks again, I feel his lips brush my temple.

"This isn't your fault, it's mine," he says, speaking in a rush that carries his guilt. "They are *my* people, *my* responsibility, and still I didn't—"

"We did everything we could," I interject.

"We," he echoes. "When did we become a team?"

"When you decided to save Lucas's life." I pat his chest, my mouth dry, pulling away. *Lies, Eos. You're lying. You helped to help yourself—to fulfill this despicable Purpose, to support a Project you've begun to lose faith in . . .*

I turn my back on Rion, trying to quiet the voice roaring on the inside, but it only shrieks louder. *Don't forget about me. Don't forget about what I told you.*

Run away, as fast as you can, and never look back.

THE NEXT WEEK PASSES in a fog.

We learn, later, that Tex was one of the many who died in the breach, even after Cyb and I saved his life. Lucia was at the opposite perimeter—the western—and was killed after a leak of the Muted scaled the fence.

The final body count was fifty people, even. We piled their corpses together on a wooden platform built three miles away from the quarantine's compound and burned their remains.

I'll never forget it—the column of black smoke rising into the pale sky, the way it made my gut churn. I'll never forget the pungent odor of burning flesh or the way ash got whisked up in the breeze, settling in my hair, a dry wisp of somebody else.

I had stood by myself, absorbing that moment, every shred of its hideousness, when Jac arrived. With a lit cigarette bouncing between his chapped lips, he told me about the Muted. There are different kinds, different "classes."

"Not a lot of people know about the Haunt," he'd said with his jaw set grimly, a band of sweat collecting on his lip, despite the cold weather. "Don't tell anyone."

I'd raised my brows, unfamiliar with the term. "I won't."

"If the infected live long enough, they eventually transform into a different class of Mute—a Haunt, we call them, because they no longer need physical sustenance to live." He'd thrown his cigarette into the snow, bitterly. "They suck the souls right out of the living. I've seen it myself, seen the way they *reap* a life and get stronger from it."

"How?" I'd asked disbelievingly.

"Nobody knows." Jac, being who he is, laughed fully and genuinely at the absurdity of it all, tilting his neck back and forth, giving it a crude popping. "But the others infected—the smaller, second-class ones—are fucking obsessed with them."

"Obsessed?" I'd asked as he started walking off, no longer interested in the conversation.

Jac's eyes had glinted malevolently. "They will die trying to devour a Haunt—that's why we caught one and used it to lead all the others away."

At that point in time, Silas arrived, jabbing an elbow into my side as he passed. "Didn't you figure that out already?"

To this day, a week later, Mabel hasn't returned and nobody has really been the same—especially Rion, who disappears where nobody can find him, not even Jac or Silas.

And when he "supervises" me at night, we barely talk.

So far, it appears they don't know anything about who we really are or where we've come from—and I wonder if that's the only reason we're still alive.

Will it be this easy to fool Mabel?

This afternoon, I help Merope clean guns—an order issued by Silas, who's impressively managed to keep his head straight since the breach last week.

We sit outside of the barn, running dirty rags over the guns set aside for us, watching grievers wandering the compound with bouquets of sage smoking in their hands. They mutter prayers and sing sad songs, a terrifying lethargy wrought into their bleak and hollowed eyes.

I've been thinking a lot about Nova. More and more, I get the feeling she was just crazy—just *crazy*, like I was *desperate* and *angry*, resentful toward the Project.

I couldn't handle everybody else getting to deploy, and my being held back—so I found reasons to trash the Project even if it meant believing in a sick girl with treasonous claims.

Foolish, Eos . . . Stupid.

I polish another pistol, snapping its pieces back together and closing its slide. The grievers wander by, hanging chips of crystal and dirty, uncut gemstones along the wall.

Merope clears her throat. "Something," she whispers, eyeing the grievers as they pass, "is off about this place."

"Fifty of their people died a week ago. They're mourning."

"Where is Mabel?" Merope leans forward, elbows resting on her knees as she adds in a whisper, "Fifty of her people have died and she still isn't here? And nobody has a way of reaching her?"

Just then, the barn's door whines, slamming shut.

Rion walks out, gripping a bottle of vodka. He stumbles off in the direction of his hut, garnering startled glances from those he shoulders roughly through on his way.

I sigh, setting aside the pistol.

"That's my cue," I say, getting up to go.

"Wait—where are you going?"

"To get some answers."

"You're leaving me to clean all these alone?"

"I'll be back in a second. Don't worry," I say, giving her a playful wink she doesn't return before jetting off in the direction of Rion's hut.

It isn't long before I've caught up with him; his pace is off balance, slow. He keeps pausing to drink deeply from the jug of vodka dangling in his hands before shoving his way through a throng of people also walking the path.

By the time he's ripping his hut's door open, I'm standing directly at his back.

"Hey," I say, announcing myself. His eyes drift sidelong to behold me blearily. "Mind if I join you?"

He follows my gaze, resting on the vodka.

Then, sighing, he hands it over. I'm startled to see that it's nearly half gone.

"Probably best if you cut me off, anyway," he says.

I follow gingerly at his back. The hut's curtains are drawn and the fire's gone out, leaving it gloomy inside. He collapses on his unmade bed, pressing his palms to his eyes, and groans.

He clumsily rips off a hat, his almost-black hair awry, a mop of wild strands dipping into his eyes.

Leaning up against a map of Asia, I casually uncap the jug of vodka and lift it to my lips. The taste is unlike anything I've ever sampled before, and I try not to gag.

I've never had alcohol before.

"So," I begin. "What's the occasion?"

"Elizabeth," he scoffs lazily. "The world is ending—that's the only occasion there is."

"You're drinking because the world's ending?"

"No," he says—thoughtful, quiet.

"Can I ask you a question?" I slink down the wall, sitting on the floor with my back up against it. At my side is a shelf. I run my finger along it.

Rion's head lolls back, his eyes staring at the ceiling.

"Go for it," he says.

"What," I say, holding up the military tags, "are these?"

"They're military tags."

"Obviously, but where did you get them?"

"I—" He pauses, exhaling. "My dad was a great man, back when he was alive."

This takes me completely off guard. "These were . . . ?"

"My dad's, yeah."

"He was a pilot?"

"The best."

"Tell me more," I say, relocating to his bed. I sit perched on the edge, right beside him. "Why did he join the air force?"

"My little sister, Lindall, caught the A-42." Rion's voice is all of a sudden very angry. "Have you ever seen anybody with the plague flip before?"

I shake my head—a small, fractional movement.

He smiles cynically. "You're lucky."

"What happened?"

"Right before she flipped, my dad killed her—it was what was best for her, the merciful thing to do." Rion drops his dark eyes to his open palms. "My mom got the A-42 too, less than a month later, but we waited too long."

"She . . . flipped?" I breathe.

"Dad was really brave about the whole thing."

"I'm sure he was," I say, handing over the tags. He grips them so tight, they nearly cut into his calloused palm.

"You think that's brave?" he asks contradictorily, his focus waxing and waning. "Killing your family? Would *you* have?"

I rest a hand on his forearm. "You can't kill somebody who is already dead, Rion."

"Would you have done it?"

"Of course," I say softly, shocked by how imploringly he's looking back at me—a void gaping wide behind his eyes, stirring and dilated, ringed in maple. "Your father was brave enough to give them the one thing they really wanted before dying."

"And what was that?"

"Dignity," I say, and for a long while Rion's quiet.

Then, all of a sudden, he's clasped his hand over my own, and is pulling me close—a delicate tug, an invitation, which I'm startled to be so willing to follow. I collapse sideways, lying flush against him in his bed, the two of us operating wordlessly—and I don't know what I'm doing or why, just that I am.

We lie together quietly, only our sides touching but our eyes locked on each other—a smile rising on Rion's full lips like dawn.

"Your parents," he asks. "What were they like?"

"They . . ." I wet my lips, stalling. *My parents are long dead and never knew each other—they are DNA samples thrown together in a genetic log without names, without faces, without memory . . .*

I don't really have parents.

My eyes fall to the thin scar along my inner wrist—it arcs flawlessly, almost invisible. "My mom always inspired me to try harder, to be better. For a long time, the only thing I cared about was earning her approval, her respect."

"Did you?" he surprises me by asking. I can't believe the way my throat tightens in response.

"No," I breathe—and I don't know why, but it feels less like a lie and more like a confession. "I never did."

Rion's eyes float to the ceiling—bleary still, and sad—and I feel his hand lift a fraction, resting itself on mine.

"You should've stayed," he whispers. His hand clasps mine a little tighter, a warmth blooming through me like the spill of summer sunlight.

"What?" I gasp.

"You should've stayed."

"I didn't want to," I hear myself say. My voice sounds like a shout stifled by a gust of wind—far away and unfamiliar, even to my own ears.

"Why didn't you?" Rion rolls over, cupping my cheek in his hand now, the feel of his touch like an open flame. "You've got to get out of here. It isn't safe for you."

I gasp, suddenly euphoric and blissful and high—a tickling warmth pooling at my center, filling me up as the beat of a song thunders rhythmically through my veins.

It shakes my heart in a way I've only felt once before.

Only this is deeper, clawing at my roots.

And abruptly, without warning, I'm sinking into Rion's eyes the way I would if diving into the ocean—a terrifying, blind fall that is as exhilarating as it is stupid.

I hold my breath, squeezing my eyes shut—and when they reopen again, I'm not looking back at Rion. I'm looking through his eyes, from sometime in the past.

And somehow, I know everything about him.

I know what he knows.

He's twenty. Injured severely. Vision blurry, unfixed, as he peers up at a dilapidated sign looming over him—a stark green that has dented and faded over time.

It reads:

KIPLING, COLORADO

He's on the side of an old highway, his wrists pumping out blood to the beat of his heart. Across the road, having flown over a guardrail and into a rock wall, a car hisses with steam, its hood folded and crumpled like an accordion.

The driver is facedown against the steering wheel.

Dead.

I feel my breath quicken, readying to scream, when Rion's hand slips out of my own and the connection's lost.

I'm back at the quarantine, lying beside him, feeling high and happy, pleasure as rife in my veins as the rush of adrenaline whistling and wild with every beat of my heart.

And all I want to do is touch him, to put my hands all over his body and drink—

Reality falls slowly, a net enveloping me, triggered by the untrusting look in Rion's beautiful eyes.

"I'm sorry," I gasp, the dawning of comprehension as fast and unpleasant as getting whiplashed. *I saw Rion's past. A fatal car crash, which he survived, in Kipling, Colorado. Not far from here . . .*

I saw it all, but how?

My chest feels as though it's caved in on itself.

I whisper again, "I'm so sorry," and get up, feeling unsteady on my feet and dangerously close to throwing up. "I don't know what happened—"

I lean against the wall, heaving. As fast as I've stood up, so has Rion, who pilots me to a chair beside his unlit hearth—all of a sudden very serious, very sobered.

As I sit, I grab his wrist and pull it out for inspection.

He's a specimen, I think frantically, seeing a trail of knotted scars along it—exactly like a butchered extraction might look if a professional didn't take out his microchips.

I glare at him. "*What* is—"

Rion jerks back his hand. "Be quiet," he hisses, eyes leaping to the door anxiously. "We can't let anybody know you're hearing what I'm about to tell you, Eos."

"You," I breathe, feeling ill again. "You know my . . . !?"

"Be quiet. It's *okay.*"

"No, it's not!"

"I'm not like you," Rion reiterates, speaking so quietly he's almost completely inaudible. "I'm not like your league, or any of the other leagues that've come off the Ora."

"But your *wrist,*" I insist hysterically.

"You just saw where that came from!" he says, spitting the words through gritted teeth—angry and ashamed. I think of the blood pulsing out of his wrists and realize that maybe these scars didn't come from the car wreck—but from something else.

I'm not like your league . . .

Or any of the other leagues that've come off the Ora.

The room is netted in heavy silence, letting my thoughts buzz in full measure. *So all along, he's known . . . but what about everybody else? If they know who we truly are, why have they yet to capture us the way the other leagues were?*

I change the subject as well as I can: "Those scars weren't from the car wreck."

Rion exhales, raking his fingers through his unkempt hair.

Then, as though he's afraid waiting any longer might risk the possibility of him losing his nerve, he rolls up his sleeves and shows me both wrists in full.

"I . . ." He stops, shaking his head. "I tried . . ."

Each wrist wears an ugly, knotted bracelet of scars. One of his forearms is marred as well, a vertical slice that meets the band around his inner-wrist with gruesome precision.

The other forearm is untouched. I bet he lost consciousness before he could get to it.

After I've seen enough, he rolls up his sleeves. A stark quiet ensues during which I wonder if he'll ever speak to me again after what I've seen—*scars,* yes, but also a piece of himself, of his soul.

Eventually he scoffs, head shaking. "*Weak.*"

"Don't be stupid." I get up, still uneasy, approaching only to have him turn his back on me. "You're not *weak,* Rion."

"Stop," he says, turning to face me. "I don't need sympathy from anybody, Eos."

"I wasn't giving you *sympathy.*"

"Just go, okay?"

"I'm not going anywhere until I've got what I came for."

"Which is ... what? To kill—"

We both freeze, startled by shouting. Rion's up and tearing open his hut's door before I can say another word, looking for the source of the yelling.

A second later, he's looking back at me—and I find myself unable to look at those lovely, stirring maple eyes in the same way anymore, and wonder if I ever will.

"It's Merope," he says, using her real name.

"What's going on?" I bolt to the door, standing halfway in the hut and halfway out. The snow falls heavily in the creeping shadow of dusk, and I shout out for her. "I'm over here!"

Merope gallops up, her cheeks reddened and her face pale in a sickly, terrified way. "It's Lucas," she gasps.

She doesn't have to say a word more.

I run.

17

I PLUNGE INTO THE darkening day, flecks of snow slapping my cheeks as I push into a sprint.

Rion follows, not even caring to put on a jacket.

Merope updates me as we run. "He's awake, but he's in a lot of pain without his meds."

"Mia's holding off on his pain killers?" Rion asks as we turn the corner, getting to a more populated area—cressets fiery, laid alongside the path.

We swing past the bonfire and barn, ignoring the curious faces of onlookers queued up for dinner. Just like Pudge night, a line has formed in front of a large cauldron-like pot bubbling on top of a fire; inside there's an off-white, pasty substance.

Replying to Rion, Merope says, "Mia's trying to keep him awake for a while; he's been unconscious for too long."

"He's going to be in bad shape," Rion says.

"Yeah, he is."

"How long has he been awake?" I ask.

"Ten minutes, tops." Merope breathes heavily as we walk up the stone walkway to the cabin. Firelight glows through the dirty windows, emphasizing the falling snow.

"Let's go," Rion offers, nodding at Merope. "You first."

"Cyb's already here—" Merope's voice is cut off as the door slams behind her. I'm unable to follow, anchored by a gentle tug on the back of my jacket's hood.

Rion's towing me back.

"Stop," I say, trying to yank away. "What're you doing?"

"Hey, listen," Rion exhales, speaking tentatively. "He's not going to be himself in there, okay?"

"I *know* that," I seethe.

"Just prepare yourself, that's all I'm saying."

He drops my hood and I leave, frazzled by the fact that my whole sense of reality has been upset. *Who is Rion, anyway? How much does he really know? Can he be trusted?*

In a daze, I fly through the cabin's front door and navigate the familiar labyrinth of dark hallways, my every step followed by the shadow of Rion clinging to my heels.

Before I've left the living room, I hear sobbing from Lios's bedroom—a horrible, visceral sound that leaves my heart beating a little faster and my palms sweaty.

I've never been good with sick people. Or emotional people.

It makes me nervous.

For the second time upon reaching Lios's door, I can't get myself to enter immediately. After running all the way here, and caring so deeply . . . I'm still somehow stopped cold by the sound of his sobbing.

Behind me, Rion leans against the opposing wall. He holds my gaze with the steady grip of familiarity—the way somebody might with a best friend, with family. Unflinching and soft.

He whispers, "You're okay."

"Am I?" I whisper back—feeling suddenly weak and afraid and unsteady on my feet. Rion gets off the wall, taking a couple steps closer to me. Now he really is like a shadow.

"Yes, for as long as he needs you to be."

"And when he doesn't?"

There's a pause, during which Rion stuffs his fists into his pockets and shrugs. "I'm here."

"All right," I say, studying him. "I'm ready."

"I'll be right behind you," he adds, throwing an arm out in front of me and pushing open the door.

The room is packed. Mia, Silas, and Jac crowd one end of the room while Merope, Cyb and Apollo gather in the other. A series of others—whom I've never met—stand with restraints and one holds a syringe full of amber liquid at the ready.

Mia's eyes jump off me, skittering to Rion, her expression strangely suspicious. Then, *click,* and she's back to being cryptic and enigmatic and unreadable—as always.

"He's been asking for you."

"Sorry," I say hoarsely, walking in. Instantly, I know Rion was right to warn me. Lios isn't himself at all—a pale husk of who he once was, ill and empty and mirthless.

Cyb kneels beside his bed, whispering soothingly. He won't hold her hand. I can tell she's trying hard not to lose it altogether and burst into tears—just like me.

"Hey," I say, sitting at the end of his bed, patting his foot through the covers lovingly. "What's wrong?"

Lios's foggy, incoherent eyes regard mine with a hostility they have never expressed before. To anybody. Ever.

"You—*you'll* help me," he growls. "Won't you, Eos?"

"Of course." I look to Rion questioningly. He shakes his head a fraction of an inch, a gesture that I interpret to mean, *The others don't know your real names. They don't know the truth about who you really are . . . We've got to keep it secret.*

"Eos, please, tell them—"

"My name is *Elizabeth*, Lucas," I add resolutely.

"You too?" Lios's voice cracks hysterically, his eyes red and bloodshot, flitting around the room. "All of you? Really?"

"Shh," I soothe.

"Where are we? Where's Onyx!?"

"Lucas, just try to breathe deeply and relax—"

"No, get me out of here!" Lios thrusts a heavy arm directly at Cyb's chest, shoving her out of the way. He sits up, so fast his stitches tear with a sickening *rip!*

I launch to his side, helping Cyb and Merope pin him back down in bed. Even Apollo finds a way to help, whispering firmly and hastily, begging our friend to calm himself.

But Lios raves on. "Who are they?" he asks, sneering at the hordes of other people standing stagnant in the room. "Get your hands off me! Let me go, I'm leaving this place!"

"You're hurting yourself," I say, surprised to hear my voice escalate to a yell. "Stop moving *right now*, or they are going to sedate you, and we won't see you again for another week!"

But he's absolutely out of his mind—thrashing, far stronger than the rest of us combined. I see spots of blood bloom through his white hospital gown, and feel myself officially panic.

He's not just hurting himself . . .

He's killing himself.

"LET ME GO," he screams, flailing.

"STOP." I grab his jaw, forcing him to face me, forcing his eyes to look at mine. "Stop *right now*, Lucas!"

"THAT IS NOT MY NAME."

"LIOS!" I cry, voice quaking. I breathe heavily, watching his sapphire eyes fill with tears. "It's okay, Lios. We're here."

He breaks, crying in earnest now. I pull his face onto my chest and rock him back and forth, feeling tears burn along the edge of my eyelids threateningly.

"Eos," he weeps. "Eos, I knew . . . I knew you'd . . ."

"You're going to be okay, Lios."

"Promise?" Lios's dry lips brush against my chest.

"Do you trust me?" I ask him, but find myself peering at the other side of the room—at Rion. "You do, don't you?"

"Yeah. I do."

"I'm going to help you feel better, okay?" My eyes shift to look at Mia now. One step ahead of me, she collects the syringe from an apprentice and starts closing in.

Cyb and Merope nod at me, their grip on Lios tightening.

"I don't want to go back to sleep," he begs. "You wouldn't do that to me, would you?"

"Never," I lie.

"Tell her to go away," he snarls, glaring at Mia, but she pins his arm down with the alacrity of an experienced professional, swiftly injecting the amber liquid.

Lios wilts. "Why?" he asks, looking at me. "Why did . . . ?"

My jaw feels jammed shut, unable to say another word, to utter another lie—even if it's a helpful one. Lios regards me with open betrayal as he fades, slipping back into himself. I feel him wither in my arms as he falls asleep.

I rest Lios back on his bed, feeling weirdly compelled to rid myself of this strange, unfamiliar side of him—a side I don't like and am pathetically afraid of.

Mia pulls up his hospital gown, identifying several stitches that have torn. "Damn . . . We need more rags, hot water, and another strong dose of antibiotics," she remits. The others bustle off, gathering her requested supplies hastily.

Cyb nudges my side, standing. "Let's get out of their way."

Merope and I follow her out of the room, the three of us left utterly speechless. Apollo files out after us, shaking his head with grim defeat as he passes, exiting the cabin without anyone there to escort or supervise him.

"Why is *he* allowed free rein?" Cyb asks, her eyes still puffy and red from crying.

I shrug. My energy is gone. I can't shake the look on Lios's face when he registered that I'd lied to him—that I'd helped put him back to sleep, even though he begged me not to.

It was for his own good, Eos.

You didn't have a choice.

Jac and Silas wander into the living room, badgering Rion with a series of whispered questions. Rion raises his eyes to find mine, though, apparently ignoring them both.

"Can I talk to you?" he asks, tearing way from Jac and Silas, who stare irritably at me—as do Merope and Cyb, though maybe it's tonight's experience that's warped their expressions.

"Yeah," I say, nodding a hollow goodbye to my friends, both pale and emotionally beat. I exit Mabel's cabin alongside Rion, bursting into the starless night.

It's snowing really heavily, now—so heavily, it's like getting caught in a wedding veil. The world takes on that unique, stifled silence that it only adopts when it snows.

"I see Apollo isn't being supervised," I note. "Am I still?"

"Not anymore."

"Is that what you wanted to talk about?" I ask and he gives me a subtle nod, his hair collecting snow. "You aren't supervising me anymore? Really?"

Smiling slyly, he adds, "Not unless you want me to."

"Stop." I scoff, grinning despite myself, and trudge through the knee-deep snow into the dark.

THE NIGHT BLANCHES A shade lighter.

I can't sleep. I lie awake, eyes glued to the sagging ceiling.

In these early, solitary hours, I can feel Earth's sharp edges carving into my soul, eroding everything I was before all this and reforming me into somebody different.

The people living today aren't like the people that lived here generations ago. They have been reduced to varieties of despair, strength, and ceaseless, blind fighting.

They are Silas—*killers, out of necessity.*

And now I'm becoming just like them, day by day.

I glance sideways at Rion. His hair is still stuffed inside the warm carapace of his hat—eyes rimmed in a fan of black lashes, his chest rising and falling peacefully with sleep. I get the oddest desire to rest my palm flush against it, to feel his breath and the warmth of his body, to—

His eyes are open.

"Do you watch me sleep *every* night?" he asks, groaning as he stretches, the vodka fully worn off in favor of what's likely to become a brutal hangover.

"This is the first time I've really *seen* you sleep." I roll over so my back's facing him, keeping the blooming blush in my cheeks to myself as I look at the opposite wall dancing with shadow and firelight. "You were talking."

After getting sick of arguing nightly over who had to sleep on the cold dirt floor, with a threadbare blanket and a pillow that failed miserably to offset the discomfort, we began sharing a bed.

And every night, if he slept at all, he'd sleep-talk.

"I was talking in my sleep again?"

"Yeah."

"What did I say?"

"You were spouting off numbers, as usual." I drag the covers over my shoulder, readjusting myself. I can feel the heat of his body beat through the layers. "Aren't you going to tell me what you're dreaming about?"

"I don't remember anything."

"Liar," I say, yawning. "Let's go back to sleep, then."

"It's dawn already," he says, throwing the covers off him so he can get up. I roll back over on my side, facing him as he pulls on a clean, white shirt. His body is smooth and supple, skin as bronze as a summer holiday, utter perfection until my eyes get to his wrists and forearms, scarred beyond belief.

My chest aches every time I see them.

Yet again, he catches me looking. With a laugh, he tosses me a fresh shirt. "Your turn to change—my turn to stare."

"I don't think so." I snatch the shirt midair and dive under the privacy of the bedcovers, changing. When I pop back up a few minutes later, he's dragging on boots, grimacing.

"What's wrong?" I ask.

"I'm never drinking again," he grunts.

"You never really told me why you were in the first place."

"Does it matter?"

"To me, it does," I say, and Rion's eyes find mine, looking up through the hair falling in his eyes.

"Everything." He gets up, rummaging through a pantry for a

bit before pulling out the last of his water bottles. He thrusts it toward me and asks, "You want any?"

"It's okay," I say softly. "You need it more than I do."

"I would agree," he replies before downing all of it in a few deep swigs, his complexion improving. "I was drinking yesterday because I failed Mabel."

My mouth goes dry. "What do you *know* about us, Rion?"

Rion tosses the empty water bottle away, grabbing his pistol to check if it's loaded. He removes the magazine, stuffing a few additional rounds in its empty well, staying thoughtfully quiet.

After a minute, he looks up. "I was drunk yesterday, Eos."

I sneer. "So what?"

Rion sits against the wall, under the map of Europe, with a flexed jaw and a deep look of introspection. "So I shouldn't have said anything—that's *what.*"

I stay perched on the edge of the bed. A sense of foreboding washes up, acerbic and sharp, as I consider telling Rion the one thing I haven't even told my own league.

"Somebody, a specimen, told me not to trust the Project."

"Really?" Rion asks, voice pitched low.

"Tell me she was wrong." My voice quakes as I ask—for the first time, truly, *openly* questioning my Purpose. "Tell you you know for a fact she is a liar, that she's crazy."

"I don't know that," he says, rubbing his jaw. "But what I do know is you've been—you're *being*—lied to."

"By who?"

"Your people," he says, nodding up at the sky. "How else do you think we know your names? There's somebody aboard your ship, a traitor. They give us a list with everything we need to know about every league that deploys." He sighs, chest rising and falling, his gaze fixed through the window to his left. "Apollo helped us during the pushback because of his records—we know he's human. We also know he's invisible to the Muted. We just couldn't pass up his help, even though I wanted to."

Reflexively, my hand finds my throat—the bruises from his choking me have faded with time, but apparently Rion's fury for what Apollo did to me hasn't.

"We've had specimens help before, during pushbacks, but without loyalty to us, they'd usually escape—that's why we didn't invite you to help," he adds, and it all makes sense.

"What—what else do you know?" I inquire unsteadily.

"Deployment coordinates, so we can be nearby the second leagues land and harvest them."

"Harvest?" I say, standing, suddenly feeling hostile.

"We get their names, ages . . . stats," he goes on, eyeing me in a strangely fervent way. "Skillsets."

"And what did this list say about me?"

"Nothing," he says, taking a single step and bridging the gap between us swiftly. "We were told this league would contain four specimens—and yet we got five. Why?"

"I don't know," I lie.

"The traitor aboard your ship gave us permission to harvest every deployed specimen, with the exception of one: an eighteen year old girl with a skillset dangerous enough to rip the war we're trying to wage in half."

"War?" I echo, suffocating. "What kind of skillset?"

"The girl belonged to your league, Eos." Rion's hand finds mine and pulls it up, tracing a finger along the microchip scar lining the inner side of it. "I think you're that girl."

"Impossible," I say breathily, pulling my wrist away, trying and failing to form a single coherent thought. "I don't even *have* a skillset, let alone a *powerful* one."

Rion's eyes rove over mine, as though now that he's spilled his soul, there's no holding him back. He wets his lips and comes closer, holding out a hand.

"Not one you know about," he whispers, cupping my cheek in his palm. Instantly I feel that distinct flare of warmth I've felt before, with him and with Apollo.

I think about how every skillset feels differently. Making skin-to-skin contact with Apollo felt like a rhythm, a shrill song that I didn't know the words to. With Rion, it's deeper, wilder, and less a rhythm—more breathless, unpredictable.

Like falling.

I buckle under the influx of energy, gasping.

Rion retracts his hand. The feeling dies instantly, and just like before, I'm left desperate and hungry, my desire to touch him once more as crazed and irrepressible as addiction.

"All along, you thought it was Apollo's skillset ability you felt when you touched him," Rion divulges quietly. "But it wasn't his ability, it was your own you were feeling."

"Apollo said it was—"

"His, yes," Rion interjects. "Trying to throw you off."

"Why would he do that?"

"Because he's trying to keep you out of—" But he's stopped midsentence. There is a knocking at the door, a muffled voice added to it moments later—*shouting.*

Exhaling sharply, he studies the door, as though deciding if he's going to open or it or not. It continues to rattle under the fists of whoever is trying to gain entry.

"Harvesting us," I say, nostrils flared, "for what?"

"For war."

"Rion, please," I gasp wildly, shaking. "Tell me everything."

"When we're alone," he whispers huskily and jerks open the hut's door with a heave, exposing Jac shivering outside with a tall shadow at his back. A tall, *smirking* shadow.

Apollo.

Rion snorts, throwing the door shut in their faces. But it's reopened a second later, hesitantly, by Jac. "Listen, man, I know you're still pissed—"

Rion glares lethally at Apollo. "Leave."

Apollo slinks in, eyeing the pistol on Rion's shelf. "Hate to tell you, but you're no longer in charge. Mabel's back and she's personally sent—"

"Back?" Rion interjects, glaring accusatorily at Jac who, as a fairly large guy, surprises me by looking terrified. "Why didn't you come tell me immediately?"

"I know I should've, man, I'm sorry."

"What stopped you?" Rion approaches, fierce and predatory, so furious I feel myself tense, readying to break up a fight.

Jac shakes his head, lips twitching. "I was only looking out for you, man." His eyes widen, fierce in their own right. "But you got super drunk yesterday, and Mabel hates—"

Rion finds his pistol, and for a heart-pounding second I'm afraid he's actually going to pull it. Instead, he sheathes it in the waistband of his pants, grabs a jacket, and goes to leave.

But just as he rips open the door again, two more people are standing there: Mia and Silas.

"You can't see her right now, Rion," Mia declares, splaying her fingers over his chest. "She's meeting with an ally, an ally we really need to—"

"When can I see her?"

"Today," Silas interjects, swallowing. He looks to Jac in an imploring kind of way. "After the supply drop."

Rion's deathly quiet for too long. Everybody tenses.

At last, he says, "The drop?" His tone indicates he, like all the rest of us, completely forgot about it.

Mia replies by way of holding out a calendar. "Today marks the start of a new quarter. The drop isn't scheduled to land for a few hours, but it's probably best if—"

"First run?" Rion says coldly.

"We're heading into midwinter. We're going to need all the supplies we can carry." Mia leans in, gripping Rion's bicep in her thin fingers, and whispers, "Mabel won't see them until the job is done, Rion."

"Fine," he says, turning to the others. "Who's coming?"

"Jac will be, of course," Mia replies, even though Rion didn't ask her. "Six is usually the best number, given the capacity of our truck and the room we'll need for supplies."

"Who else, Mia?" Rion growls.

"Us." I'm surprised to hear it's Apollo speaking. "The four people in my group. Mabel's made the generous offer of allowing this job to serve as our initiation."

I feel my limbs freeze. If they're harvesting us—planning to use us for a war, of some kind—why would they waste the time acting like there's a point to this initiation? *Should I defy Rion's advice and tell the others? Should we run?*

"And of course if your group decides not to initiate, that is perfectly acceptable," Mia proceeds, eyeing me. "But please know we don't spare medical supplies for anybody who isn't a member of the quarantine."

An open threat, then. *Do it, or Lios dies.*

"We're in," I blurt out.

"Excellent." Mia starts walking off, waving for the others to follow as she heads up the path. "Why don't you two join us for a quick breakfast? You'll need the energy before you go."

"I'm sure we will," I mutter and go.

THE BONFIRE IS STILL burning. It's always burning.

Sputtering to life is a small cooking fire, positioned under the vaulted ceilings of the three-story barn, nestled in what looks like a massive steel trashcan lid.

A malnourished individual I recognize as Silas crushes eggs in his fist, dropping the slippery contents onto a cast-iron skillet over an open flame.

Everybody is very quiet.

Rion drags up a pair of chairs, which scrape against a series of dry floorboards and a fluffy carpet of sawdust, before setting them to rest at the fire's side.

I'm just taking my seat when I see Merope and Cyb coming.

The three of us exchange looks of warning—my glance an altogether different variety.

How will I ever get them to believe what I've learned?

Silas clears his throat, plopping a barely-cooked egg on what was once a kid's plate: ridged and divided into seconds, a picture at the bottom that's lost its color.

"I assume we should go over the game plan?" he suggests.

"Oh, that's easy," Jac chortles mirthlessly, snagging the plate before Apollo can snatch it first. "Grab as many supplies as you can carry and proceed to run for your life."

"Two steps, eh?" Apollo eyes the food irritably.

"Well, that's the simplified version, obviously," Jac says with a mouthful of egg. "Outrunning starving Skims and the Muted at the same time is essentially my worst nightmare."

Silas claps Jac on the shoulder. "A nightmare you're forced to relive every quarter."

"Poor baby," Mia chimes in.

"Hey—I don't see *you* helping, Mia," Jac says, ripping off a glove to expose his hand, which is missing the first three fingers and most of his palm.

"God, put that *away,* we're eating!" Silas begs, making a big show of hiding his eyes.

"Fuck yourself, Si," Jac replies coolly, stuffing his fingerless hand back in his glove, as commanded. "Got this little souvenir on my first drop, four years ago. The Skims shot me right in the kneecap, so I couldn't outrun a Mute."

"Skims?" Merope asks, steepling her fingers—exposing her wrists on accident, which are encircled by a haze of yellow and purple bruises wrapped like bracelets.

I stare at her, openly concerned. Merope's eyes snag mine, but are fast to look away—an edge of anger, of *accusation,* buried deep within her violet irises.

Jac tosses his plate back to Silas. "Skims are the people left without a quarantine. They fight for their own supplies, kill for their dinner, and are as ruthless as the Muted."

"The Muted—*with guns,*" Silas adds gravely.

"So, we're fighting them?" Cyb asks. I realize she's fast to avoid my eyes too. "How does this all work?"

"A supply drop is made in a general location for the whole city to fight over. The supplies are usually scavenged in about three hours. The first hour is the most dangerous, because there are more people present to fight."

"First run," Silas interjects wisely, raising a spatula.

"Right—that's first run." Jac fumbles for a cigarette behind his ear, as though getting subconsciously worked up just *talking* about the chaos awaiting us.

Cyb's lips purse. "So, first run means fighting?"

A beat of silence follows in the wake of her question, heavy as a black cloud bursting with rain. Rion surprises us by speaking up for the first time.

"No," he says, accepting an egg. "First run means killing."

18

EVERYTHING MOVES QUICKLY.

Silas starts cooking for the other quarantine members while the rest of us raid the barn, stocking up on supplies: weapons of all kinds, bullets, and jugs of water.

Apparently Jac and Rion have their own lockers, which they unlock and begin digging through, leaving Cyb, Merope, and I alone—all three of us together—for the first time in days.

"So," I begin, loading a pistol. "What the hell is going on?"

"What do you mean?" Cyb barks too quickly, her fingers tangled up in Merope's long hair, braiding it.

"What's up with those bruises?" I point out, nodding at the bracelets of yellow and purple Merope's wearing. "And what's up with all the death glaring?"

Neither reply. Cyb fastens a rubber band at the base of the braid she's just made down Merope's scalp. I feel anger creep up my spine—a blooming, black heat.

I take a fast step to the right and grip Cyb's arm, twisting it so she's forced to face me. "Do we have a problem?"

"Maybe we do," she says, jerking her hand out of my grasp.

"May I ask why?"

"You shouldn't have to ask why," Merope says, turning on her stool to face me, violet eyes edged like razors. "Maybe if you were around more, you wouldn't have to."

"Around more?" I crow.

"While you spend every night with *Rion*," Cyb says, sniffing her way through Rion's name, "Merope and I are staying up all night helping Lios recover!"

It feels like I'm choking on barbed wire. "You are?"

Merope examines her wrists. "Lios wasn't himself when he gave me these bruises."

Cyb finishes cleaning a gun and tosses the dirty rag angrily across the barn, where it falls in a heap of sawdust. "What really pisses me off is he asks for you—*a lot.*"

"But you're never there," Merope adds bitterly.

"Look, I didn't know any of this," I say, genuinely upset with myself, but apparently it isn't enough of an apology.

Merope stands, brushing herself off.

Cyb offers her a gun. "Let's just stay away from each other for a while, okay?"

"Great—can't wait for the ride over," I grumble as they walk away from where I am, sequestered in the far off corner. When I see Apollo slowly approach, I cringe.

Not him. Not now.

As usual, his lips are twisted in a smirk.

"It can't be! The Three Musketeers, broken up!?"

"Get out of here, Apollo," I hiss, lifting my gun so it's aimed right at his genitals. "Or I fear I'll be tempted to engage in a little friendly fire."

"You wouldn't dare ruin a thing of such beauty!"

"You're disgusting." I roll my eyes, grabbing my packed bag and a pistol, and begin trekking away—but he rounds on me, his expression altogether different.

Not smirking. *Serious.*

He grabs my arm, piloting me back to the corner. "But in all seriousness, Eos—we've got to talk."

"Start talking, then," I say.

"Have you told Rion anything?"

"Never," I lie, pinned between his arms and the barn's splintering wall. My eyes flit over his shoulder, where from across the room, Rion eyes us suspiciously.

Apollo's nostrils flare. "He—he hasn't told you?"

"Told me what?"

"Nothing." Apollo exhales with relief, arms dropping. "You two just seem to talk a lot. I was left to consider—no, it doesn't matter, if he hasn't said anything."

"Apollo," I whisper, feeling suddenly fierce. "What are you babbling on about?"

"I'm just impressed," he says, dragging a hand through his pitch-black hair absentmindedly. "Impressed the soldier didn't say anything. Though, I'm sure the opportunity has presented itself to him, and yet he—"

I grip Apollo's throat in my hand.

He holds perfectly still.

"Why did you just call Rion a soldier?" I growl, feeling the beat of his energy bleed over my palm like the pulse and swell of spilling blood—a skillset ability being called to action.

A skillset that's *my* skillset.

Impossible, I still think to myself, despite the flare of energy exploding through my fingertips like bolts of lightning and the thrill of sputtering static. Apollo's song sings—vastly different than Rion's sensation, which is like that of a free fall.

The whites of Apollo's eyes glow in the shadowed corner.

Gasping, he says, "Eos, stop what you're doing—*now*."

I rise up on my toes to look at his eyes. "Why did you just call Rion a soldier?" I echo, grip tightening wildly. "And why would you lie to me about my skillset?"

"Eos," Apollo begs—a warning.

"Answer my questions, Apollo, or I'll siphon them from—"

"Children, children!" I hear somebody say. I release my hold on Apollo's throat immediately, turning to see Jac walking forth with a shotgun slung over his shoulder.

I step away from Apollo.

Jac taps an invisible watch on his wrist. "We're on a tight schedule, I'm afraid. Let's get going."

A few steps away, Rion holds the barn door open, allowing both Cyb and Merope to file out. He keeps his gaze trained on me and Apollo, though.

"Of course." I grab my backpack and trudge off, my fingers itching to pull my pistol. What does Apollo know? What else does Rion know?

All along, I've had a skillset. The reality of it strikes harder and fiercer every time it swings, pendulum-like, in my wild thoughts—and yet Apollo and Onyx kept it from me?

I dip under Rion's arm, holding the door open, bursting out of the barn and into a day draped in a silver sky—heavy and pale with ready-to-fall snow.

"What was all that about?" Rion inquires dryly.

"Nothing." I grit my teeth, facing him. "*Soldier*."

Rion's brows raise in question.

"Ask *him*," I bark and traipse off, rubbing my arms in the attempt to keep warm. It's absolutely frigid out here. I stand by my league. None of them speak to me.

Stay calm, Eos, I beg myself, palm resting on the freezing handle of my pistol. *Don't do anything brash.*

"This way," Jac says with a smile, a freshly-rolled cigarette pinned behind his ear. He indicates the quarantine's primary entryway, a mouth that spits us into Mute territory.

My body feels stiff and robotic as I stray through the door and slip back into unregulated lands. Gunfire sounds from a few miles off, and Jac says, "We've expanded the perimeter and kept it secure. A handful of volunteers are staving off the Muted until we have fully left the compound."

More gunfire, a rapid enfilade this time.

"Let's keep up the pace," Rion suggests, walking ahead of the group, a rifle hanging by a strap on his shoulder. I see a pistol in his waistband and a machete glinting from its sheath somewhere on his back. *These weapons . . . are they for the Muted, or are they for other people, for the Skims?*

There's a biting chill in the air carrying the scent of danger.

My league walks quickly, trying to catch up to Rion and Jac at the head of the line—but before Merope can join them, I find myself tugging her sleeve hard, holding her back.

She whirls, violet eyes hostile. "Yes?"

"Did you know?" I'm shocked by the hostility laced in my own demeanor, a hostility challenging hers. "If you've ever loved me like a sister, tell me the truth."

"Know what?"

"That I've got a skillset." The words tumble off the edge of my tongue like an accident—a trip, a fall. "That all along I've had a skillset ability, but Onyx deliberately kept it from me."

Merope's complexion blanches.

"You—*you* did? You knew?" I feel like I've been slapped in the face without warning. Snowflakes fall, catching in Merope's chocolate hair, dangling like stars.

But her fading complexion isn't a result of my question, it's a result of what's lurking at my back.

"Get out of the way," she says, *older-sister-like*, as she shoves me aside forcefully and raises her pistol at two of the Muted staring at us with gaping, eyeless faces.

We glance ahead. The group is out of sight. We're alone.

The sight of the Muted, alone, is debilitating—their lips so worn down by perpetually fighting and feasting, there is hardly any flesh left. Their weathered faces are so startling, it's as if the mere sight of them is a physical assault—a slap that echoes its way to the marrow of my bones.

The pair charge simultaneously, just as a series of gunshots explode in the distance, accompanied by shouts to "Retreat! Tell the others—pull back!"

Merope fires, pegging each Mute in the skull.

They fall in snow, steaming heaps of flesh.

"Let's go," she barks before taking off, leaving me to sprint in her wake like a madwoman. Merope's gunfire got the attention of Jac and Apollo, who round the circular perimeter ahead of us and are visible yet again.

"Let's go, ladies!" Jac shouts, waving us over.

Merope sprints, raising her pistol perpendicular to her body as she runs, firing off rounds one-handed. I rip a large dagger out of a sheath strapped to my thigh and rake it down the chest of a nearby Mute—effectively flaying it—as we spill around the far off corner of the quarantine and find the vehicles. Rion is filling up a truck with fuel, a task I'm guessing we didn't think we'd need to rush through.

Jac fires off rounds alongside Cyb and Apollo, all guarding the truck as Rion works.

"Save your ammo!" I bark as I rush to Rion's side and yank his machete off his back for my own use—just in time to slash it through the throat of a Mute clamoring wildly over to us, having slipped through the ranks of the others.

Rion chucks the fuel can, recapping the tank. "Go!"

Jac flies, leaping into the truck, jamming the keys into the ignition and revving the engine. The engine is loud, growling like an angry beast, drawing the attention of every Mute in the forest.

Apollo launches into the truck bed, dragging aboard Cyb and Merope, calling for me—but I'm too busy firing off rounds at the influx of the Muted drawn forth by the engine's noise. I can't even follow my own advice about saving ammo. There are too many of them, all coming at once.

Fingers grip my jacket. I whirl to face my assailant, gun poised to shoot, and realize it's Rion. "What're you doing?"

"Holding them off," I bark.

Rion doesn't dignify my justification with a response, and instead tows me back to the truck. I'm piloted to the truck-bed, while he gets behind the wheel and slams the door shut, revving the engine even louder.

When I settle into place, I see Merope has wilted up against the crook of Apollo's arm, her face as white as a ghost.

Cyb's voice is hardly audible over the roar of the truck's old engine as she shouts, "How many are there!?"

Merope looks like if she opens her mouth to speak, she's at risk of projectile vomiting. "Thousands," she manages with a dry swallow, looking more and more ill by the second. "Thousands of them are coming to the supply drop."

"To the people," I interject, ignoring the petty stare I get from Cyb—who obviously is still upset with me. "The Muted are drawn to crowds, to *masses*."

"And we're heading right into it." Apollo's dark eyes flash, strikingly foreboding. He leans sideways, careful with Merope under his arm, as he fishes for his revolver. "I caution you all to remember why we're here. It's not to harm the people."

"The Skims are dangerous," Cyb notes bluntly.

"That's an understatement," Apollo retorts, jaw tight, and I think of the memory I siphoned from his thoughts: Apollo as a boy, his whole family dead, their corpses littering an abandoned house . . .

A house they didn't inhabit, but found accidentally.

A house for temporary use.

Were they Skims?

The truck gasps, choking as we crest a hill. The wind's icy fingers rake through my hair. Then, suddenly, the bumps under us are gone. We're on pavement—the *highway*, cruising toward the city where the drop's being held.

Rion slams on the acceleration, but it doesn't do much. The road is coated in a thick sheet of black-ice, causing the truck to spin wildly before catching and propelling us forward.

We speed along the highway. Totally alone.

Cyb's jaw drops, lips parted. "Wow," she breathes.

We look out over rows of crippled houses strung along the highway, rooftops sagging and drooped. Front doors left slightly ajar and eerily welcoming, as though soliciting new families to inhabit them, saying, *See? We're empty. Please, fill us.*

My chest aches. The full impact of what's happened—of the lives this world has lost, the lives it has yet to lose—really, truly hits us all, possibly for the first time.

It's one thing to see, to *know*, catastrophe has struck.

It's another thing entirely to be a part of it.

We cruise into a city full of skyscrapers and reflective glass buildings set against the white backdrop of pending snowfall in the sky and, suddenly, I feel panic take up residence in my chest.

It's as though we've stumbled across a graveyard without graves.
The death here isn't hidden, it's showcased.

Windows are broken and toothy. Buildings have succumbed to piles of bricks, wrought-iron bars sticking awry, like the bones of unraveled skeletons. Sidewalks end at the edges of cliffs, and traffic lights hang stilted and warped.

I can feel the life lost—a texture woven into the fabric of the empty landscape, a screaming echo floating residually over this town populated by ghosts.

We drive down the throat of a narrow, unlit tunnel.

Wind rushes, deafeningly loud. The roar of the engine leaps off the tunnel's walls. There's a light at the end, a pinprick that's the color of ash, a drab off-white.

Merope stiffens, her thin shoulders splaying flat.

"We're here," she discloses, panicking.

The pinprick of light swells like ripening fruit, consuming us in a swift, frigid gust of winter wind. We're in the middle of a magnificent city—dirty, broken, and wrecked.

Skyscrapers disappear into knitted clouds. Rows of clothing shops stand empty and abysmal, their mannequins left stripped bare and vandalized: positioned against one another in crude sexual stances or left as torsos without limbs.

Suddenly a blare of noise rises, setting my teeth on edge.

I can hear them, the buzz of thousands of voices mixed in

a stew of yelling and wailing, disrupted only by the infrequent shot of a gun or a Mute's earsplitting shriek.

I can also *smell* them. It's winter and bathing isn't easy.

The cloying essence of rotten teeth, oily hair, and body odor wafts densely over the landscape. It gets lodged in the back of my throat like an unwanted tickle, inspiring a gag.

Merope twists out of Apollo's embrace to look—panicked and shaking—at the scene awaiting us.

Inside the truck's cabin, I see Rion and Jac switch seats.

Jac's driving?

Rion opens the back window, looking at us. "Stay vigilant."

We nod, breathless.

"Three crates will be lowered with supplies. Don't leave the truck until you're told to," he goes on, wind scouring through his dark hair. He looks specifically at me. "You can do this."

"I know," I whisper, but he's already withdrawn back inside the depths of the truck.

We speed on, nobody speaking. My heart is a weak butterfly flapping inside a cyclone. I try sipping slow, deliberate breaths to calm myself, to *focus*.

We approach an ornate, wrought-iron gate.

People are everywhere, waves of them lapping up against the lip of the truck bed, knocking and tapping the thin aluminum shield set between us, issuing yellow-mouthed slurs.

Hanging from a rope is a long cut of pressboard, sprayed with red paint:

PIO MORSE
DROP A

I feel myself go very, very cold.

PIO Morse, did you say?

I blink a few times but the letters don't fade. What are the odds of the government using this name? The same name as the mission I've been assigned?

We drive off the paved road, still dilapidated and spotted with potholes after all the time its been left unkempt, and go through the iron gates into a clearing. It's strange to see so much space in the middle of a city.

Large trees, swaying and brittle, stand in organized rows alongside different paths. Statues of crying angels loom, chipped and eroded, their features appearing melted over time. Rows of carved stone markers are—

Holy shit.

"We're in a cemetery!" I croak wildly. If anybody ever died on the Ora, they were crudely ejected into space—the idea of a cemetery, of *keeping your dead,* has always intrigued me.

Intrigued and perturbed.

My league regards me with expressions that say *obviously.*

The people, divided into strangely recognizable groups and factions within the crowd, sport indicators such as face paint or shaved heads or tattoos to state affiliation.

Aside from the quarantine members and the Skims, what other people live here? Who else is fighting?

Is this all that's left of Earth's people?

A shout echoes from farther off, uttered by somebody deep in some kind of a ditch.

No, not a ditch—*a grave.*

The person is looting the casket—prying it open, fingering through bits of skeleton and warped hide-like skin and probably

217

even bits of wiry hair—looking for anything of value: a pocket watch, a family heirloom, a gold tooth.

Apollo clears his throat, swallowing hard. "Skims."

"How do *you* know?" Cyb barks.

"I just do."

The truck slows to a crawl. People threaten to climb aboard the slower we go, shouting and jeering as we pass, spitting at us when we don't stop for them.

What's left of Earth's people is ugly, desperate, and starved.

They are nothing like how I'd imagined they'd be.

A knobby hand claws my shoulder, and I whirl, looking at a pair of large, bloodshot eyes. The woman's face is masked in a thick layer of grime and shrouded in a mane of frizzy hair.

"Wish I had hair like yours," she whines, lips parting to show a host of greying teeth. Her sticky fingers grip a lock of my hair and start stroking it.

I jerk myself away, careening frantically into the other side of the truck, my pistol poised in a wordless threat.

"Please," she begs. "*Please,* do it."

"Stand back." I shrink away too slowly, my ankle caught as the woman launches over the lip of the truck bed and scrambles toward me, clawing at my leg.

Every touch is similar to that of a burn. Unlike the thudding rhythm of Rion or Apollo, this woman feels strange—yet oddly and inexplicably familiar—like a steady roar, a smear of static.

White noise.

This woman feels like . . . Onyx.

What is it I'm even feeling, anyway?

"Don't be angry, sweetheart," she purrs after I've slammed the heel of my boot against her bony sternum. "Oh my, you look so much like my sister when she was—"

"I don't care," I bark. "Leave!"

"No, no," she whispers, tears washing clean stripes through the grime masking her weathered face. "No, no, no . . ."

I glance at Apollo. His expression wears a worry mirroring my own, an instinctive, visceral concern. *Something is wrong.*

The woman's eyes are browning at the corners, colored in by a tearful, rheumy bloodshot. She's sweating. Her movements are suddenly mechanical and involuntary . . .

"She's infected," I gasp, realizing it the second Rion steps through the back window to investigate.

The woman sinks a hooked finger, nail jagged, deep inside her eye socket, effectively dislodging her right eye. Blood rolls down her leathery cheek in beads, meeting cracked lips and a dry tongue that sweeps it up.

Her jaw drops, projecting a ripping shriek.

She's flipping.

After extricating her left eye, the woman's bony chest heaves yet another shriek. She lunges ravenously forward, only to be stopped by Rion—who grabs a wad of her oily hair, pulls her into his arms, and slides his machete across her throat.

The woman's breath gurgles, blood bubbling at the corner of her cracked lips. She shudders, a palsy, before falling still and permanently silent.

Rion holds her in his arms, a splash of blood gloving his right hand and pooling inside the truck bed. The crowd around us is starkly quiet and eerily unfazed, as though the flipping of a person into a Mute isn't at all abnormal.

Obviously it isn't, Eos. The Muted are everywhere now . . .

They were people once, after all.

Rion tosses her limp body overboard, his eyes resting on the pistol still residually raised in my palm.

The crowd around us begins to scream, others witnessing the eyeless body bleeding into the snow. I press myself up against the back window, trying desperately to drown out their panicked wailing rising higher, higher, higher . . .

Rion sits beside me, breathing heavily, wiping the blade of his machete clean before sheathing it over his back again. I sense the heat of his unmet gaze and return it.

There's a coldness to his maple eyes I've never seen before.

"You can't hesitate."

I feel speechless and disoriented, the world a lather of ugly colors and noises I wish I could close myself off to forever.

Rion cups my chin. "Not here. Not today."

I nod and sip in the cool winter air, looking at the only place in this world that hasn't changed in the plague's wake.

The sky.

SOMETHING THUDS NOISILY, PULSING like a hummingbird's wings.

The truck lurches abruptly forward, just as my eyes catch sight of a bulky, insect-like thing flying in the sky.

The helicopter. The drops are here.

Everybody starts running frenziedly, all at once.

Jac gasses the engine. We propel forward, thrown back in our seats by the sudden momentum. The people in front of us hear the roar of the vehicle and split into halves, making a path for us as we fly, full-throttle, over sprawling hills.

The truck lifts midair, sailing over a bump and falling, only to bounce precariously over slippery, snow covered soil. We leave the others behind, who resort to sprinting. Aside from us, there are only two other trucks.

Gunshots ring like bells. The helicopter lowers its first crate slowly, ropes straining against the weight of the plywood box and its contents.

Mud sprays out from under our tires as Jac cranks the truck to the right, closing in on where the crate's going to be dropped to the ground. When we're directly under the helicopter, all I can hear is the robotic beat of its rotors, the wind as it explodes in a halo-shaped gust around us.

People in uniforms and riot helmets lower the crate down to the starving hordes, and I can't help but look up at that official and wonder, *Who are you? How did you get so lucky? Why aren't you fighting down here like the rest of us?*

I look down only to realize I've been left—Cyb, Merope and Apollo have all gone. Twenty yards away, I see Rion holding his machete high, heading for the crate.

Through the back window, Jac's looking at me, shouting something I can't hear.

Go, go, go! I think his lips say.

I leap over the lip of the truck bed, landing with a splash in an icy quagmire so deep it sinks into the fabric of my socks. My legs burn as I press forward in a sprint, gun ready, but hesitant, no matter what Rion's said. *Killing the Muted is one thing . . . they can't be saved. But killing living, breathing, uninfected people in the name of hoarding supplies?*

Apollo's right. That's not what we're here for.

And, another voice whispers, *everybody in the quarantine will die in a matter of days, anyway, if you fulfill your Purpose. They don't need the supplies.*

I dig, burying the last thought into the deepest recesses of myself and try to forget about my Purpose—and how, with every passing day, I am less inclined to fulfill it.

We're the first people to reach the crate. The other trucks roll closer, firing off rounds while kneeling behind their tailgate, just like we were. Jac spins, circling the crate, returning gunfire with more gunfire as he does so.

We've got to hurry.

Rion throws every ounce of his energy into hacking away the crate's walls. The blade of his machete bites into the wood like teeth hooking meat, and faster than I dared to hope, we've gained access to the supplies within.

Up ahead, approximately fifty yards, another crate is being dropped by the helicopter. We've got the great luck of this crate being half-rotted; its wall falls, crumbling as soon as it hits the ground, and I see a spill of multicolored toothbrushes and boxes of Band-Aids, of all things.

Inside our crate is a wealth of camping supplies: lighters, cobalt tarps, coiled rope, cast-iron skillets . . .

One crate: hygiene and medicine.

One crate: survival.

Merope dives inside the crate, handing what she gathers to Cyb, who passes it off to Apollo midway to the truck. Rion and I aren't needed in the chain of transporting supplies, so we jet off to the next crate with his machete.

Jac's shouts, barely audible over the thundering of the helicopter overhead—now lowering the third crate—but I'm able to read his lips. *Three minutes!*

Rion and I glance, in unison, at the others. Jac's excellent aim has punctured the front tires of each of the enemy trucks, leaving them immobile. They approach, like the others, on foot.

He's right. We've got three minutes, no more.

When we get to the second crate, Rion waves, urging me to pass it by in favor of the third—now lowered. The helicopter beats its way back into the sky, climbing higher.

"We don't need it. Leave it for the people who do!"

I nod in understanding. We race to the third crate, break it open fairly quickly, and discover it has been selected to carry the most precious cargo: *food and drink.*

And not just bottled water, but alcohol. Tons of it.

Rion grabs two fifths of vodka and a bottle of whisky, and gives them to me. "Take these to the truck!"

"What about the food?"

"Take them!" he badgers, turning his attention to the rest of the contents spilling out of the crate. A glance at our truck is all I need to spur me on. The others are close.

Dangerously close.

I run, glass clinking in my arms, until reaching Apollo who relieves me of my burden. "Nice!" he praises, as though we've just bought them on sale in an ordinary supermarket.

We jog back to the truck together. I help load everything.

"Get in!" Apollo says, not waiting for me to obey, shoving me inside instead. I'm tossed in the front, where Merope sits in the center seat beside Jac as he drives.

Apollo jets off, going to help Rion, who's—

My heart sputters.

Rion's so far away . . . all alone and increasingly surrounded by the others, who've reached him. They run, snarling and baring their teeth like animals, wielding guns and blades.

I realize they are all a part of a group wearing goggles and gasmasks over their faces, bandanas and bulky clothing. They have red paint—or blood—over any visible skin.

"Skims," Jac says, panicking. He readies to rev the truck forward just as we hear the tailgate clamor loudly. Cyb's just leapt in, escaping the others.

"DRIVE, JAC!" she screams savagely, kicking somebody in the chest to keep them from climbing in. The Skims seem to be focusing on nothing except commandeering the third crate.

"I'll make room for Rion," Merope says, voice edged, as she climbs through the back window and joins Cyb outside.

The truck flies closer to Rion and Apollo, but the fight to keep the supplies we've gathered is never-ending—a large chunk of the crowd doesn't appear interested in the crates at all, their sole focus on raiding those who already have.

"Fire at will," Jac breathes, unrolling his window farther as to better aim a small handgun. His shotgun rests beside his leg in the footwell.

I wish it were that easy. I lean partially out of the window on my side, seeing before anything else, a woman: dirty hair, eyes a crystal blue. She's in another truck, one which we've rendered immobile by way of destroying their irreplaceable tires.

She raises her gun, aiming at me.

I aim at her.

Neither of us shoot.

I can't do it. I won't do it.

We're supposed to be on the same side!

My eyes locked on hers, I lower my gun. I see a hint of a smile on her lips—shocked and thankful—as she lowers her own and gives me a subtle nod of mutual understanding.

A flood of heat pools at my core.

There are still good people here. They exist. There's hope.

And then—fast, so fast!—a skinny man's at her door, both of his bony hands gripping her throat as he drags her through the window and brutally into the mud.

I see the glint of a dagger, reflecting white sky.

I see the screaming spray of red blood.

I see her throat gaping wide, a second mouth, as her head swings back like it's hinged. *That wasn't a kill, it was murder—a gesture born of hate and vengeance and fury.*

The woman's body lies in the muddy water, her blood red as spilled wine, a stain.

I hear somebody cry, "AMY!?"

The man rips open their truck's door and begins ransacking it shamelessly, hoarding the supplies they collected. Without realizing what I'm doing, my finger pulls the trigger, my gun trained on his throat, and I've shot him.

I've shot him. I've shot him. I've shot him.

The man wheezes and gasps—just as Amy had—for a few sickening seconds before collapsing in the mud to die.

Killer and victim, sharing the same grave.

Amy's people turn the corner, catch sight of her body, and lose themselves completely—their wailing shrill and ferocious and unforgiving. Hysteria.

I swallow dryly, feeling ill. Just as we drive by, I look back and see two kids—skin brown with dirt and bruises—dart out from behind a copse of trees.

They're crying, "Daddy, no!"

There's a little girl with birdy, brown eyes swelling with panic and despair and a breed of undiluted rage I didn't think capable of a child.

Her little sister clings to her side. They cry, the younger sister in full grief, while the older keeps her upper lip stiff and her jaw set as she stares at me—*knowing*.

I look away, eyes burning and wet.

We stop, spraying mud, and I fling open the door so both Apollo and Rion can get aboard. They toss the supplies they gathered in the bed of the truck, where Merope and Cyb start stuffing it into our half-empty backpacks.

Just as they climb in, an enormous man with a gasmask and goggles steps forth, raising a gun.

"Take him down, Jac!" Rion yells, vaulting into the front seat beside me, Apollo climbing in after. "I'm out. Take him!"

Jac leans out of the window, moving so fast it's as though he's as adept at killing as he is breathing.

A gunshot rings loudly, but it's shot from behind. I follow the line of fire to a little girl with brown eyes, cold and distant and anguished—a little girl *avenging her father*.

Jac pitches forward, gripping his shoulder. Blood spills in rhythmic spurts, smelling strongly of copper.

He's been shot.

19

JAC'S FACE IS WHITE.

"My shoulder," he croaks, leaning on the steering wheel of the truck while gripping his arm. "My *fucking shoul*—was it shot all the way through!?"

Jac's fingerless hand dabs his shoulder blade, feeling the bloody exit wound. His face, surprisingly, lights up.

Rion reaches over me, ripping open Jac's shirt as to better look it over. "Clean shot—straight through," he confirms, pulling the shirt back down. "Now *drive*."

"Are you kidding, man? I can barely move!" Jac grunts as he wiggles out of his seat, crawling over me. As he and Rion race to switch seats, a deluge of bullets sprays, peppering the glass of our windshield.

It shatters, a drape falling.

Standing at the other end of the barrel is a Skim, face in a gasmask and eyes goggled, head cocked slightly, as though in amusement over watching us scramble.

The bullets narrowly miss us. Rion slams his foot on the gas pedal, throwing us forward—*right at the Skim.*

Merope and Cyb drop in the truck bed, the weight of them loud as they crash to their bellies, avoiding the gunfire.

The Skim turns, readying to bolt. Jac's beside me, bleeding all over my right side. Apollo's yelling words I can't understand while Rion swerves, on the tail of the Skim who runs, bulky and cumbersome, heading straight for—

A group, huddled behind hedges and statues, cloaked by the chaos twirling in a spindrift around us.

"STOP," I yell, but nobody hears. The roar of the engine, the screaming of those around us, the splash of tires spinning in mud and stagnant ice water—too loud. "IT'S A TRAP."

The Skim runs.

Rion's eyes are lit up with fury.

I yank the rifle off Rion's shoulder and take aim, firing off a single round that brings the Skim down, a heaping pile of flesh splayed prostrate in the mud.

The other Skims spill out from behind trees and statues and headstones, all armed with automatic weapons.

"GO," I yell at Rion, eyeing him severely. He listens to me and veers away, spinning out.

The tires catch. We traverse toward the exit of the cemetery in a blur of heart-stopping noise, faces we pass reduced to a haze of smudged gray and white.

Jac's head lolls back and forth, complexion pale as snow.

Apollo's pressing a strip of fabric he ripped from his shirt against the gunshot wound, but it's barely stifling the blood flow rolling rampantly from both sides of his shoulder.

I turn my attention to Jac. "Breathe," I say after seeing him shudder and twitch. "Breathe and try to stay calm."

I remove my jacket and toss it over him, trying to stop him from shivering. Apollo swallows, his face coated in flecks of mud and splashes of dried blood, hair wet and plastered to his face by a cold sweat.

"He's going into shock," he mutters, nodding at Jac.

I feel my chest tighten as I reflect on how long it took for us to actually reach the city. The quarantine was at least an hour outside of city limits, and we haven't even—

"He'll be fine," I avow quietly, quelling my panic.

The truck whines as we climb an incline, jetting through the heart of the city, darkened by a fast-falling dusk sweeping over the landscape like a stain.

Time passes slowly, every second marked by a heartbeat.

As we leave the city more people filter in, heading not for first or second run, but third. I'll be surprised if there's anything left for them to take. *I can't believe this is the system for distributing supplies to people. This is really the best the United Government can come up with in terms of efficiency?*

We jet through the pitch-black tunnel and are spit out at the city limits at last. As we dip and weave our way through the crumbling outskirts of the city, I see movement—the flicker of twitching limbs as they swarm forth, inundating the streets.

"The Muted," I declare dryly. Rion nods, jaw tight.

Our path is black except for the dull yellow light cast by our truck's headlights, and as time passes the frequency with which we spot the Muted darting out in front of us increases.

Apollo volunteers to take a flashlight and keep a lookout with Merope and Cyb. Though the last thing I want to do is pull the trigger of my pistol again, I follow.

When I exit through the back window, Cyb continues to ignore me altogether, speaking exclusively to Apollo. "We've seen fifty already, at least."

"Merope," I say, glancing at her—cloaked in the bulk of an

extra jacket as she huddles quietly in the truck bed. "M, can you tell us how many you're sensing?"

"Leave her," Cyb retorts curtly. "Let her rest."

"I'm only trying to help."

"Why don't you go back in the cabin, where you're wanted?"

"Are you *seriously* going to be this petty?" I seethe, finding myself nose to nose with her, hands clenched into fists. "Are you really so pathetic? We're fighting for bigger—"

"Hey," Apollo crows loudly. "Now isn't the time to argue!"

"Exactly my point," I say.

"So end it, Eos. Put it to bed." Apollo's comment is enough to keep Cyb from retaliating. "And when they are done being so petty, you can tell them everything you've—"

A cry, shrill as a siren's peal, cuts him off.

The truck turns, skidding over the sheet of ice cloaking the crumbling pavement. Muted flash in front of our headlights in a thick swarm, swooping in and out of the forest lining both sides of the empty highway.

Apollo grips my shoulder, eyeing me. "We need Rion."

"But he's driving."

"It's going to get ugly, and we're going to need him."

"I'll drive," I hear somebody say, a voice weak and fatigued.

"Merope, you're not well enough," Cyb declares, rushing to her side protectively. But Merope shrugs her off, pushing herself up shakily—unsteady, but coherent.

"I am not helping anybody being back here. The least I can do is drive while Rion helps." She drags open the back window and casts us all, including myself, a final glance. "We've got to work together to win. Don't forget that."

Apollo digs through our supplies, clicking on a flashlight as the back window grinds open yet again and emits Rion, who's carrying a rifle and Jac's shotgun.

More shrieking ensues, an utterly chilling sound that rolls over the landscape like a creeping tide.

"We're still forty minutes out," Rion divulges, tossing the shotgun to me. I take it, cringing as my finger finds the trigger.

"So," Apollo says, reloading his pistol. "What plan do you have cooked up for us—soldier?"

Rion pauses, eyes drifting to gaze at the forest—dark and shifting with life—before he cocks his rifle and shoots off a few rounds alongside the highway. Shrieks prelude the distinctive thud of flesh colliding lifelessly against rocky pavement.

Rion takes a stripper clip out of his pack pocket and feeds it into his rifle's magazine. "My plan is to get there," he says simply.

Apollo sniffs, smirking. "Good."

"Hey," Cyb interjects, peering over the tailgate. "Does anybody else see what I'm seeing?"

Apollo raises the flashlight, revealing a large Mute trailing behind us, ravenous and wild—eyes glistening in the beam of white light as puss rolls in teardrops from beneath its eyelids.

My breath catches. "Is that a Haunt?"

"No," Rion replies, strutting to the tailgate. "Maybe in a few more days it would be—but not yet."

The Mute roars as Rion tries deftly to gun it down, but it dips and dodges, as though predicting every shot. The truck swerves violently, causing us all to gasp with alarm.

Apollo looks through the back window. "What's going on up there, Merope?"

"They're trying to make us crash," Rion says, glaring down the scope of his rifle. "Strategizing, throwing us off so that big

231

bastard of a Mute following us can catch up."

We swerve again, but this time we skid sideways, drifting diagonally down the highway.

Cyb screams, dropping to her knees in the truck bed.

We're all thrown off balance—and just like Rion said, as if it was all planned, the big Mute launches itself up, claws raking against the truck's aluminum hide as it boards.

The Mute's fingers are black.

Frostbite.

The entire truck sways as it climbs aboard, diving directly into the truck bed. And before anybody can get a shot off, it falls gracefully, draping itself over me—*and now, if they fire, they risk shooting me along with it.*

Fingers swiping. Teeth bared. Thrashing.

The weight of it against me is unreal, a brick wall built on my fragile chest. My senses are dominated by the smell of rotting teeth and infected flesh, and the saccharine odor of puss dripping from the Mute's eyes, falling in flecks over my cheeks.

I wipe it away, shocked by the acidity of it.

I can't swing my shotgun in such close proximity, fumbling instead for a knife, for *anything*. I reflexively reach up and grab it by the throat—a buzz of electrical energy surging forth, just as it had when I touched the infected woman earlier.

The same smear of steady white noise . . . I can see how the Mute would feel the same way as the infected woman did earlier, but why do they both feel the same way Onyx does?

What does Onyx have in common with a Mute?

"DUCK!" I hear Cyb scream, and without hesitating, I drop to my belly on the bed of the truck. Gunshots ring loudly in my ears as she fires, gunning the Mute down.

It falls, joining me on the bed, sliding in its own blood.

When I look up, I see pure chaos. Rion's firing his rifle off at a series of the Muted clawing alongside his side of the truck, the group so close they could climb aboard any second.

Apollo's guarding the tailgate.

Cyb saved my life.

Rion yells at Jac inside the cabin. "Ditch!"

I follow his line of vision, looking straight ahead of us, over the roof of the truck—to nearly fifty yards away, barely lit up by the headlights. A series of vehicles are wrecked in the ditch.

All of them piled together. Intentionally.

Strategically.

Rion shakes his head, slamming a fist repeatedly into the side of the truck—the first hint of fear I've seen from him, which ignites my chest in a wildfire.

I balance my way beside him. "Strategy."

Rion nods, breathing heavily, before opening fire—pegging the Muted in their foreheads, killing them effortlessly, but it isn't about skill or about weaponry or about precision.

It's all about numbers.

Which we don't have.

Merope speeds up and slows down, swaying to each side of the highway, trying to throw off the Muted, but it isn't even close to being enough—if one Mute misses its mark, the other doesn't.

"Left side, Eos!" Cyb yells, helping Apollo with the tailgate as Rion focuses on what's ahead of us.

I find my shotgun and position myself back on the left side of the truck. Another big Mute gallops alongside as we drive, its jaws snapping wildly, expelling feverish shrieks.

I take aim, squeezing the trigger.

BANG.

The Mute drops, but falls too closely—its body gets caught in the back tire, sucked violently into the wheel well, where it stops the tire from moving altogether.

The whole truck lurches.

We skid over the ice, snagging corpses in our way as we lose control of the truck completely. We spin in circles, ricocheting against guardrails, tilting sideways so fiercely I'm afraid the whole truck's going to roll.

Rion yells as he's thrown out onto the highway's shoulder.

Cyb's forehead collides with the truck.

Apollo swears repeatedly.

I hold the open back window for support, crouching on my knees and squeezing my eyes shut thinking—begging, pleading, hoping that we *get out of this alive.*

For the first time, I don't hear the Muted shrieking.

They are waiting for us to wreck.

We lurch to a stop, colliding against a guardrail alongside the ditch, where the other cars are piled up. My face slams into the back window, and I feel heat rush to my temples, stars bright and exploding behind my closed eyes.

For a few moments, everything is quiet—then I hear Jac in the front seat gasping for breath, shouting wildly, throwing open his door and stepping out.

Once I reorient myself, I realize we've done a 180, twisting totally backward. Ahead of us, which really should have been behind us, Rion's body lies chillingly still in the snow—encircled by a group of the Muted, hissing and spitting.

Jac's a step ahead of me, jogging as fast as he can while also holding his shoulder, trying to get to Rion. Apollo rolls out of the truck bed, groaning in pain, before sprinting off to provide any backup he and his gun can deliver.

Merope swipes at the deployed airbag in her face. "We've got to go help them," she cries, cupping her eye.

"What's wrong with you?" Cyb asks as we pile inside.

"It—it hurts!" Merope's hand peels away, revealing a gaping cut over her right eye, swollen and bleeding profusely.

"You can't drive like this," I say. "Let me."

Merope nods, making way for me to replace her. All around us now, the shrieking of the Muted fills the air, ripening to a high-pitched cacophony.

When I get behind the wheel, Merope's hand clasps mine as she whispers, "You can do it, E."

"I know," I say and jiggle the keys in the ignition. Easy as that and the engine blares back to life.

Up ahead, Jac's trying to lift Rion's unconscious form over his shoulder, leaving Apollo alone in staving off the surrounding group of the Muted—ranks increasing.

Jac tries firing off a round. I hear it *click!*

He's out of bullets.

Apollo swears, raising his gun, readying to use it as a club to beat the Muted to death if he must. He's out, too.

I lean out of the window. "MOVE!"

Jac and Apollo look up, squinting against the headlights for the briefest moment—*and then they run.*

"Hold on," I say, and after a split second of gripping fear and suffocating panic, I slam my foot on the gas pedal.

We're flying. That's what it feels like. We're going so fast that bodies whiz by, blowing dents into the truck's aluminum hood as they're struck one after another, plowed over. The truck skids, free-falling. Raging. It cuts through the Muted encircling the boys like a scythe through a crop of wheat.

Then metal stops meeting flesh and meets metal instead.

With a whiplashing jolt, we're stopped.

Silence.

20

MY CHEEK IS AGAINST the steering wheel, bruised and swelling.

"Are we alive?" Cyb wheezes.

Merope kicks her door open, falling out. "For *now*, we are."

Through my broken window I hear the hissing of air as it's expressed from the truck's tires. *They're flat—or well on their way to being flat. What else happened to our only form of transportation?*

Everything, it turns out.

I heave my door open, which swings so wide it falls off its hinges and lands noisily in the snow. The truck is totaled. Plumes of steam unspool from under its crumpled hood, every window pane cracked, every mirror shattered.

And the tires. *Blown.*

Apollo and Jac are speaking loudly, asking questions.

I hear Rion try to reply—voice like gravel, very much unlike how it usually is—before he doubles over and succumbs to a fit of retching and heaving in the middle of the street.

Rion collapses to his hands and knees. Jac drops beside him and rubs his back soothingly. "Better out than in, buddy."

Jac is, himself, a mess. He's paler than ever, his clothing slick with blood. Pressure hasn't been applied to his wound, leaving it to bleed freely and torrentially.

And now, without a truck . . .

I'm afraid our journey is over.

I stumble forward, feeling as though I'm walking through a sprawling fog. My fingers are numb and freezing. My head aches from getting bashed repeatedly. My composure is fraying.

"He's concussed," Cyb says knowingly.

"Yeah, no shit," Jac snaps, watching Rion roll on his back and begin tracing invisible circles in the sky with his index finger, mumbling incoherently.

Jac sighs, shaking his head. "*Oh god*—we're in for it."

Apollo emerges from behind the truck after a few minutes of digging and rummaging. He's carrying every backpack we've brought with us, stuffed so full their zippers might break.

"They aren't all dead," he warns, nodding at a Mute caught halfway under the truck's tire, twitching. "We need to get out of here before hive mind picks up."

"Hive mind?" Cyb asks gruffly, wiping blood off a split lip.

"They're all connected—like bees, kind of. The longer we stay here, the more likely the ones still alive will send information off to the others, alerting them."

"What about Rion?" Jac asks, nostrils flared. Apollo takes a second too long to provide an answer. "I know you'd just *love* to leave him behind, you fuc—"

"*I'll carry him*," Apollo snaps, handing Cyb and Merope the majority of the backpacks. Jac insists on bringing one, leaving me with the job of forcing Rion to let Apollo carry him.

A near impossible task.

"Rion, stop being so *combative*," I exclaim as he, yet again, finds a way to slip out of my grasp and stagger off. "You're going to get us all killed if—"

We aren't even off the road yet. Already there's noise, startlingly like the Muted, issuing from somewhere beyond the small reach of our truck's flickering headlights.

"Rion," Apollo crows. "Let me *help*."

"Have you carry me? Hard pass," Rion says blearily, swaying on his feet as he dips off the highway and into the forest, swallowed by a thick wall of trees.

The second he dips inside, I can't see him.

It's too dark.

I throw my hands up. "Whatever, let's just get going."

Cyb and Merope follow behind Rion, struggling to get over the guardrail, with Jac and Apollo close behind. It's so dark under the cover of trees, I wonder how we'll manage.

"Hold up a second," I say.

"Wait—where are you going? Don't leave the group!"

"Apollo, *relax*." My legs don't feel altogether steady under my body as I jog back to the truck bed, where a beam of white light screams through the darkness. *The flashlight.*

I take it and move to return, but stop. The rest of my group stands behind the guardrail, their faces white—just barely visible in the truck's dim headlights.

"What's—" I begin but am stopped by my group, gesturing in unison, fingers to their lips, for me to *shut up*.

Apollo nods at Jac and whispers, "Reload."

Jac drops his backpack and slowly tugs the zipper, which is stuck due to the bag being so overpacked. He tugs again. And again and again, but to no avail.

Swearing quietly, he yanks it in full.

The zipper breaks—*loudly*.

Abandoning their plan, I leap into a run—but it seems I'm a split second too late. Something has clamped a hand over my ankle tightly, tethering me in place like an anchor. I feel the same feeling of energy, the buzz and hum of white noise as it blends in a steady stream from start to finish.

I don't get to look down and confirm it's a Mute. My legs are swept out from beneath me in a fast jerk of my ankle, and in the blink of an eye, I'm sprawled on the icy asphalt.

Without a loaded gun.

Without anything but a flashlight.

"RELOAD," I urge the others as I thrash like a fish out of water, limbs flailing against the Mute. When I get a chance to look up at my friends, I see they're also being attacked.

And retreating. Without me.

I slam the flashlight viciously into the face of the Mute that has ahold of my ankle—the very Mute that was trapped under the wheel of our truck, yet is somehow still alive.

Its teeth, soft and rotten, shower out of its mouth, falling like stars as I strike and strike again until it's jaw dislocates and hangs crookedly in a perpetual yawn.

The Mute shrieks, releasing my ankle. A second before it does so, I'm able to identify it as female—a woman who might've had pretty hazel eyes before she gouged them out herself.

The others—which I formerly thought dead—writhe at my side on the asphalt. They're regaining their strength, lured by the scent of lingering prey, prey that should *run*.

I look up and see Merope pull out of Cyb's grip and hurdle over the guardrail, coming after me. She's got a gun. They have managed to reload somehow, but the Muted rise up in a tempest of shrieking and spitting and snarling. I feel their sticky fingers all over my body, my hair, my clothes.

They encircle the others in a swarm so dense I wonder if it's even possible for them to escape. I see them try, only to be set back by the lunge of a Mute, jaws gaping to generate its signature rip of a shriek.

Merope grabs my wrist. "We've got to spilt up!"

The others don't get the opportunity to reply—a flooding surge of the Muted exudes from the forest on the other side of the highway, washing toward them in an angry, violent wave.

I grab Merope's elbow and pilot her away, in the opposite direction of our group. "If they are drawn to groups," I breathe as we sprint together, "shouldn't we all split up—individually?"

Merope ducks behind the cover of a broad tree, pale chest heaving and sweaty. The shrieks in the distance—heading away from us—suggest the Muted aren't following.

They're after the bigger group.

"You really want to face this alone?" Merope asks, her lips as white as chalk. "I don't *think*—"

Our breath catches in unison as, out of the darkest part of the woods, the largest Mute I've ever seen emerges. It is big and deformed and ugly, with bulbous growths bubbling up over its semi-glowing flesh.

Glowing flesh?

It turns, blindly facing us, displaying a bloody maw crowded and overflowing with bristle-thin teeth. Its eyes are veiled by a flap of skin, lumpy with tumors.

Merope raises her gun, shooting the Haunt in the chest.

The bullet does absolutely nothing except infuriate the beast beyond all reason. It lifts a deformed, clawed hand, facing us.

No, not us. *Me.*

I don't dodge fast enough. I feel an invisible hook cling to a place just behind my navel and drag me forward, a force that is downright impossible to resist.

Merope screams, grabbing for me, but I get dragged on.

I kick and flail and cling to the trees and uproot the yellow hibernating shrubs, but nothing—*nothing*—will stop it, not even the full magazine of rounds Merope sends thudding into its chest and eyes and skull.

"What do I do, what do I do!?" Merope cries openly, now, as she watches me be pulled into the arms of the Haunt. "Tell me what to do and I'll do it. I'll do anything!"

Merope drops to her knees, sobbing hysterically, as I feel my feet leave the ground and I'm strung up midair. The Haunt lifts a clawed hand to my body, groping until it finds my throat, and in the second it touches my flesh, I know something's *happening*.

Something very bad.

I choke back a gag. "*Run*—you've got to run!"

The Haunt's contact with my skin causes everything around me to fall behind the veil, a smear of screaming voices—*human voices*—bleating between the hemispheres of my brain. And I see a series of faces, and *know them*—their families, their friends, their lives prior to getting attacked and killed . . .

I know them so well, it's as though they were my own friends, my own family . . . I know everything about them, and their lives before getting attacked.

Their final moments alive are revealed to me like a scroll unrolled before my eyes, and I can feel the searing rip of death as it spreads through their bodies like a black stain—and, strangely, *inexplicably*, I sense they haven't ever fully left. *Like somehow, they are trapped inside the body of this Haunt.*

Merope screams somewhere far away.

Bullets explode, boring holes in the Haunt's chest. I hear it roar somewhere in the distance. I feel its claws retract from its grip around my throat, and its bloody, dripping maw slink away from my lips. But this time, I don't let go.

I hold on tighter. I channel every ounce of my remaining strength into digging deeper, ransacking its ugly, perturbed mind, looking, looking, looking . . .

Looking to find those lost souls.

Looking to free them.

And suddenly the Haunt's energy shifts. It no longer feels like a smear of white noise; it feels vibrant and alive, a beat loud and wild, thudding through its flesh, singing a muddled song.

The edges of my vision sharpen. My group is here, together yet again, eyes wide. They have stopped shooting.

The Haunt's skin glows like a harvest moon, a liquid gold which floods out of its body, siphoned into my own. My grip on the Haunt is a conduit through which the gold is running out of it and into me.

"They suck the souls right out of the living . . .

"I've seen it myself . . . they reap a life and get stronger from it."

I fall.

I WAKE UP TO a world gravely still.

"What happened?" I sit up quickly—feeling so good, I must have slept for three straight days.

The others approach, operating prudently. I hear something at my side and realize it's the Haunt dying slowly, the bulk of its body deflating around a skeleton disproportionately built and terrifyingly inhuman, the loss of the souls living inside its thick hide rendering it a husk of what it once was.

I feel myself coming to, reality sharpening before my eyes.

All around us, the Muted lie dead.

I shoot up to my feet. Everybody freezes, regarding me with a strange hybrid of curiosity and fear. Merope, Cyb, and Jac look like they can't tell if they've witnessed a miracle or a disaster.

Apollo and Rion, though—*they smile.*

"What?" I snap.

"You killed every Mute for miles, I believe," Apollo relays in quiet circumspect. He nods at the Muted, all dead, and I realize they all have something in common.

Snapped necks.

"I—no, I didn't do that," I breathe, but my palms burn like a spate of blisters, and my core feels eerily empty. And in a place even deeper and darker, I feel . . .

Hungry.

Unsatisfied.

"Well, I believe the jig is up." Apollo eyes Rion, whose stiff posture and clenched jaw says, *It was up a long time ago, you just didn't know it, Apollo.*

Cyb drops the supply bags, nostrils flared. "Does anybody care to explain what's going on?" Her eyes glide to me, cold as a block of ice. "Explain how Eos did what she just did?"

But before Apollo can reply, I hear the loud zipper of a bag being opened and the clinking of glass jugs.

Jac holds up vodka. "You're going to want this," he suggests, tossing the fifth to Cyb. "It's a long story and I don't think you'll like it too much." Jac snorts a laugh. "None of your kind do."

Rion tries leaving the tree he's been using for support only to stagger and nearly fall over, caught by Merope, who dips into the crook of his arm, supporting him.

"Let's just . . ." Merope surveys the landscape. "I guess let's make camp right where we are?"

"Well, why not?" Apollo says casually, unpacking the bags of supplies and distributing goods. "Dare I say we may even be able to sleep peacefully tonight?"

Jac grabs a rag out of the supplies and presses it up against his bleeding shoulder. "Not all of us."

"Why not?" Merope asks, lowering Rion to a place where he sits with his head between his knees.

"Rion's got a concussion. Can't let him sleep." Jac gets help from Cyb, who sips from the vodka—only to douse his wound in it all of a sudden, without any warning.

Jac yells, going red in the face.

"Stop being a child," Cyb scoffs, wrapping the bandage over his shoulder now that it's disinfected, securing it so it pinches off the blood flow.

"I'll stay up with Rion," I offer, to no protest.

Cyb cinches the wrap tighter around Jac's shoulder, ignoring how he winces, and goes straight for the vodka. After putting it to her lips again, pulling deep, she glares at Jac.

"Happy?" she asks curtly, tossing the jug to Merope who's at her side, assembling a fire. "Now do you feel like telling us what the hell just happened?"

Rion's head is still between his knees. "Tell them, Apollo."

"Ap—Apollo?" Merope echoes, alarmed by the usage of our real names. She, too, sips deeply from the fifth of vodka, cringing at the spitting flavor of it.

Apollo brushes himself off, sweating slightly as he drags the corpse of a Mute away from camp.

"Where to begin?" he says, issuing a laugh void of mirth and entirely clipped, eyes looking elsewhere.

Cyb snorts. "Might I suggest the beginning?"

Merope blows a fire to life. Jac takes the lighter when she's finished with it, igniting the tip of a fresh cigarette, which he'd previously had the forethought to tuck safely in his pocket.

I glance sidelong, catching Rion's eye. He looks away.

Apollo stops piling the corpses together, swiping at his hair, sticky with sweat. "A while ago, when Rion told Jac to take me to the barn—that was code for letting me speak with Mabel."

My jaw actually drops. "What?"

"They've known about us—all along, they were waiting for our league to deploy. They have profiles of every specimen that has ever landed in this zone, and that's how they knew that I've been working with Mabel Faye for a long time. When they took me to speak with her over a walkie-talkie, she confirmed that."

Cyb stands. "What in the hell?"

Apollo raises a hand, begging for calm. "They are here to help us—all of us—and I only ask that you bear that in mind as they tell you what you're about to hear."

Then, with an abrupt nod before going back to piling up the corpses of the Muted around us, he says, "Do the honors, Jac?"

By now the fire is blazing. Merope takes a blanket out and drapes it over her legs, her face still insipid and moist. The forest is quiet and vacant of the Muted.

"I—well, I've never done this before," Jac confesses, exhaling a stream of smoke. "Usually Mabel does this part."

"Stop stalling and tell us," Cyb barks, getting more hostile with every additional sip of vodka she takes. "Spare us nothing."

"All right, then." Jac clears his throat and takes a final drag of his cigarette before fixing his eyes sincerely on us. "Just over thirty years ago, on the first of September, two things happened to the world. First, it discovered a UFO by the moon, harboring verified, intelligent extraterrestrial life."

Cyb's nose crinkles. "Aliens?"

"An advanced civilization from Coronae Borealis—a place over seventy-five million light years away." Jac's expression steels in a way it never has. "This race made contact with the world at large and announced it was here and didn't intend to leave.

"Three days after the sighting, the plague claimed its first victims by way of infection. A week after that, they flipped into the world's first Mutes."

Jac takes a twig and sticks it in the flames, watching it light up and burn. "The outbreak started in Snowflake, Arizona and was classified as a worldwide pandemic a month later—but the plague wasn't the world's biggest threat."

"The Muted were," Rion slurs, eyes bleary. "They had killed over half of the world's population by the time scientists even decided on a name for the plague: A-42."

"Why A-42?" Merope inquires just as Apollo finishes with the corpse-clearing and reluctantly joins us by the fire. "What do they know about the plague, if anything?"

"The 'A' represents 'alien' and '42' is the hourly average of time before somebody infected flips into a Mute." Jac turns his gaze to Apollo, suddenly. "And we don't know anything about the plague—only that it isn't a virus. Hell, we can't even be sure that it's contagious."

I think back on the Skims, how they employed the usage of gas masks and goggles almost religiously. Clearly there are people who *do* believe it's contagious.

That's what we've always been taught, that specimens have a genetic resilience to the plague. But then again, Onyx has never mentioned a UFO sighting, let alone a correlation between it and the plague at large.

Cyb hiccoughs, shoving the vodka bottle in the ground at her feet where it stays perched in snow. "Are you suggesting an *alien influence* on the A-42?"

"Not suggesting—confirming," Jac says stoically.

"Ridiculous," she scoffs. "What these people saw wasn't a damned UFO. It was our spaceship, a top-secret governmental endeavor, and they *thought* it was a UFO."

"Wrong," Jac says simply.

"And how is that?"

"The United Nations made a public announcement just days after the UFO's sighting to refute all accusations affiliating it with the spotted alien spaceship—"

"It doesn't matter what they claimed!" she hisses. "This is a multi-billion dollar project, and they aren't going to reveal it to the public so easily!"

Jac chucks the twig he's been burning in the fire and fixes her with a steeled gaze. "You're telling me the spaceship was built and piloted and launched *days before* the A-42 existed?"

At this, Cyb falters.

Jac grins in a sympathetic way. "The ship existed prior to the A-42 by three days. The intelligent life it harbored made no effort to hide, in fact contacting government officials—"

"Stop." My throat is so tight, the word's a croak.

"What's the matter?" Jac asks.

"I just—we weren't ever—" I pause, glancing back and forth

between Cyb and Merope, and eventually Apollo, who stands in the shadows rigidly. Nostrils flared, I add, "What the hell are you trying to say, Jac?"

Apollo's lips purse tightly. "What Jac is trying to say is that specimens weren't created by the government—that specimens, in fact, never worked for the United Governments in any way."

"Where do you think your skillsets came from?" Jac chimes in suddenly, jaw flexed. "Humankind doesn't have that kind of technology—and if it did, why wouldn't we apply it to ourselves?"

Apollo's eyes drop to the ground. "The supernatural abilities possessed by specimens aren't the result of *modified* genes—but the result of *implanted* ones."

"Implanted?" I echo breathlessly.

"Specimens aren't just human," Rion says, eyes still as glassy as the still surface of a pond, eyeing me alone. "You're a blend of genetics, creating a human-alien hybrid."

"You're *insane*," Cyb exclaims, nearly dropping the bottle of vodka in all her sudden—and swaying—fury.

Merope grabs it before it falls, drinking it herself. I hold her gaze as she sips, violet eyes cut wide.

Does she believe any of this?

Cyb obviously doesn't . . . but why would the boys lie? And not just that—why would Apollo lie? Does he not realize he's spouting off claims so treasonous, it could get him terminated?

Hasn't he always been unwaveringly on Onyx's side?

I feel too shocked to do anything except listen to the voice haunting my thoughts: *Everyone has an aura . . . Everyone except the mentors . . . Nobody can know they don't have souls like us, that they are different in ways—*

"They refer to themselves as the Borealians," Jac proceeds in spite of Cyb's disbelief. "Aside from that, nobody knows much about them—including why they're here."

"Or why they created us in the first place," I add quietly.

"You believe this!?" Cyb seethes. "You believe we've all been tricked into helping an alien species invade the planet? That we aren't human? That Onyx is a Borealian?"

"None of this make sense," Merope says, agreeing. "If they wanted to take over Earth, why would they create a plague to kill off the world's population and then, subsequently, create us to help save their lives?"

At this, nobody can forge a feasible answer.

Cyb straightens up, eyeing Rion and Jac fiercely—every bit of her posture a threat. "Where are the other leagues?" she asks venomously. "I am going to kill all of you *right now* if you don't tell me exactly where—"

"Sit down, Cyb," Merope warns. "Think of Lios!"

"We need to find the others! What if they were so stupid as to believe all this?"

"Cyb, you've had too much to drink—"

"Quite the contrary," Cyb snaps, putting a finger knowingly to her temple, Persuading Merope to give her the bottle of vodka she's currently holding.

Merope looks like she's been slapped. "Stop *now*, Cyb!"

But Cyb doesn't stop—taking the jug of vodka yet again and raising it to her lips, sipping a deep swig of the alcohol. Her face is red and her eyes wild, every part of her visibly shattered by the presented accusations we can't confirm or deny.

Apollo, Jac, and Rion exchange worried glances.

I bridge the gap between us with a single stride, taking the vodka away from Cyb with a hard yank. "You've had *enough.*"

"Ha!" Cyb waves a hand dismissively before placing a finger knowingly to her temple. An open threat.

"Don't you dar—"

But it's too late, and I feel the pull of her Persuasive skillset ability tug at my muscles, forcing me to walk up to Apollo and extract the pistol from the waistband of his pants.

The cold bite of steel bleeds into my palm, as I raise it up to my own temple, and feel my finger stroke the gun's trigger like an itch it's eager to scratch.

Everybody gets very quiet. I see Rion subtly pull out his own gun, readying it. But Apollo sniffs loudly, giving him a stern glance that tells him to stand down.

Apollo's eyes find mine next, giving me a strange look.

A look of knowing.

A look of *you can do it.*

But what is it you're expecting me to do, Apollo?

Cyb stomps forward, boots breaking twigs and icy snow as she approaches. "Traitor," she breathes.

I feel my finger tighten around the trigger.

Merope ignores Apollo, getting up. "You're not thinking straight, Cyb—this is our *little sister*—"

"She's a traitor!"

"She isn't!"

"She's a traitor, and they will thank me for—"

"*Onyx,*" Apollo interjects, expression so grave as to make him unrecognizable. He holds Cyb's stare. "Onyx would never forgive you."

"You're a traitor too," Cyb snarls, fingertip still pressed to her temple as she Persuades me to take the gun off myself and aim it at Apollo. "You both believe—you *actually* think—it's just *impossible,* because they wouldn't lie to us!"

Apollo gets up, positioning himself directly before the barrel of the gun I'm holding—holding, but not wielding.

"Traitor or not, Onyx would never forgive you for—well, to hell with forgiveness, actually—she might *kill you* herself if she discoverers you're the one responsible for ending the life of her one and only *daughter.*"

Silence.

Cyb's composure slips. "Her daughter?"

What is he . . .

Is he really saying I'm . . . ?

But Onyx hasn't ever believed in me. She tried holding me back from deploying because she thought I wasn't good enough, that I'd be dead weight, or a liability, or . . .

No, there is no way—

My skillset ability whispers for me to regain focus, revealing a break in Cyb's composure, like a fissure snaking through a thick slab of stone. I can practically feel it with my fingers—the edged sensation of it as I pull, dragging it wider.

Exploiting it.

The power I acquired from the Haunt flares to life inside my veins like an electrical current. I use it to my advantage. Not only do I shield myself to Cyb's skillset ability, but I decide to use it against her—*Persuading her in turn.*

I use my ability to rip Cyb's finger from her temple, leaving her gaping and stunned—just like everybody else.

Sit down, I think, and just as the thought crosses my mind she drops down on a log by the fire and stays still. *So this is what it feels like to be powerful like you, Cyb?*

"What the—" she gasps, eyes flashing. "What is going on?

How did—*how did she*—?"

Apollo's lips itch to smile, gazing proudly at me.

Proudly. Like Lios would've.

Like a brother.

Jac flicks ash off the butt of his cigarette, smiling wickedly at both Apollo and Rion—then Cyb. "You haven't let us finish our story, Cyb."

Cyb's face blanches white.

I exhale, handing Apollo his pistol. "We haven't even gotten to the best part yet, have we?"

Merope looks ill. "Best part?"

"Yeah." Rion's lips smile crookedly, dark hair dipping into his eyes as he looks up at me. "We never got to the ending."

21

"ONYX IS THE SPY."

If it weren't Apollo speaking, I might not believe it.

It looks as though confessing as much is physically painful for him—a sheen of sweat masks his face, making it look sallow and waxy, unwell.

I keep Cyb pinned to her seat, though I don't know how.

"My genes are an anomaly. I'm not only immune to the plague itself, but the Muted don't even see me." Apollo's eyes rest on each of ours in turn. "Naturally, if native-borns discovered the way my genes work, if they could replicate it . . ."

"It'd be a hell of a game changer," Jac grunts.

"Ever since she found out, Onyx has been deploying me in secret to Earth for Mabel to conduct tests. She'd meet me at the closest hospital, conduct exams. They have a second spy working at the CORE," Apollo adds, subconsciously looking at the crooks of his elbows, scarred from the needles. "That spy was the one who authorized my podcraft usage."

For a long while, we don't say anything—too shocked by how utterly blind we've been. All along, a member of our own league was deploying to Earth regularly . . . and we never noticed.

"By now, you realize Eos has a skillset ability," Apollo goes on with the eerie poise of a graveyard. "And not only that, but a rare and powerful one—one Onyx asked I try to keep secret from her for as long as possible. I didn't think it would work," he adds with a subtle shake of his head. "Guess I was right."

"Skillset ability?" I inquire shakily.

"The Borealians all have a skillset called Source. I still don't get how it works, only that it grants access to a plethora of other skillset abilities, making it appear like they have more than one."

"So that's my ability?"

"No." Apollo steeples his fingers, lips white. "Source is only for pureblood Borealians. You have a variation of it that's found very rarely in specimens—a strain, so to speak."

I hold perfectly still, feeling my blood harden to ice.

Apollo meets my gaze. "You can Scry."

"Scry?" I say sharply, lifting my hold on Cyb who's just as frozen with disbelief as I am. She doesn't move.

"Like Source. I'm not sure how it works, but I know it has the ability to tap into people's minds." Apollo shakes his head a fraction, lips forming a soft smile as he eyes me. "And based on how protective Onyx has been over you, it can probably do a lot more than that."

"More?"

"That's why Onyx didn't want you to deploy. She knows there's a war going on and she doesn't want you, her daughter, to be a part of it—for your skillset to be misused."

"But I failed all on my own—"

"You didn't, actually," he interrupts. "Onyx tampered with your test scores, making it look like you did so you wouldn't be able to deploy." Apollo's eyes latch onto mine. "And if Pavo ever found out you're a Scrier, you'd be as good as enslaved to him."

I've just lost the feeling in my face.

Apollo stands, then, pacing by the fire. "Your DNA is the first to include Europa lineage—it's known to be powerful, a long living line of Borealians."

Europa lineage? All this time, I didn't even know Onyx's last name was the same as mine—she was always very private, very careful to keep herself as enigmatic as possible.

And she did a great job of it.

I swallow, unable to even *think* about Onyx as my mother.

"Apollo," Merope says pleadingly. "How can you honestly expect us to believe all this?"

"We don't have to," I say after a moment of silence. I stand in front of Apollo, thrusting forward a hand. "Why settle on just taking his word for it?"

My suggestion appears to sober the whole camp.

"Don't tell me—*show* me." My hand stays forward, reaching for Apollo in an open invitation for him to *prove it.*

Prove your claims, Apollo.

"Eos, you've only just discovered this ability, one which is likely unsafe to employ without practice—"

In a flash, I am inches from him, so close I can feel the heat of his body radiating in waves. I fan open my hand, hovering it just above his chest as it heaves for breath.

I look up at Apollo's black eyes. "You have just informed us of a war going on—a war which you're claiming we're fighting on the wrong side of."

I step closer, running my fingertips from his loosely hanging hand up his sleeve, to his wrist—where I feel the buzz of energy flare to life, *thud, thud, thudding.*

Apollo grits his teeth, as though pretending he doesn't feel it as strongly as I do, like he's unaware.

"Show me proof," I say, breathless as the feel of his energy bleeds out of his wrist and into my fingertips, as intoxicating as it is poisonous. As beautiful as it is dangerous.

Apollo's eyes lower, blinking. "I—I can't control what you end up seeing, Eos."

"Do you have anything more to hide from us?"

"No, but—"

"Just do it and get it over with," I say huskily, hardly able to recognize myself. I run my fingertips upward, resting the whole of my palm splayed on his breathing chest.

It's as though I can feel every fierce beat of his heart.

The last thing before my eyes are his. I blink and the world before me fades, a mirror shattered, exposing something new and previously disguised behind it.

I feel like I've just dove into a river pushed by a violent and deadly current, every ripple in the tide a different memory—one of his to which I've gained access, of which I may choose.

I filter through them all—*glimpses.*

Then I see myself, and I stop. Eos as a toddler, lying in a crib in a locked bedroom. Apollo has snuck inside. He's only a young boy, stretching a finger through the bars of the crib for the little girl to hold. *It's a memory I've had before, but never with such stark clarity.*

Flash. I'm holding his finger, laughing.

Flash. He's screaming. Onyx bursts inside, furious.

Flash. Onyx is forbidding him from telling anybody about what happened when he touched me—explaining to his little boy self that I, even at such a young age, managed to Scry him.

I'd tapped into his memory . . . I'd scared him . . .

Onyx knew about my skillset . . .

That long ago, she knew.

Because it only works on native-borns, and she just so happened to have one around—a boy who looked at me like a little sister, because he's for so long perceived Onyx as a mother.

I drift backward, lifting out of the dream the way one might float to the surface of a pool of water, keeping my eyes peeled for anything else—*anything better.*

Farther off, in a different world entirely, I feel Apollo shift under the weight of my touch.

I dip deeper, flipping through his memories like a book.

And that's when I see it. *A newspaper.*

Flash. Mabel hands Apollo the daily newspaper as he waits with a needle in his arm, drawing his blood. His arm throbs as his blood's siphoned from his body, veins tough and his skin a map of track-marks.

Flash. Mabel's revealed to me in a blur, her voice clear but her features smudged. "We must act quickly."

"Why is that?"

"Read," she says, nodding at the paper she's just passed him as she turns in a swivel chair, scribbling swirling, geometric notes in a notebook—using red ink.

Mentor's Language.

The door bursts open, startling them both, and Rion walks in gruffly, shoulders swaying with rage; he's younger, with less scars and slightly shorter hair. The collar of his shirt is torn open to reveal a smooth chest. Bouncing off it with every step is a pair of silver, glinting tags, reading . . . *Pilot.*

"You read the paper, I presume, soldier?" Mabel asks.

"My orders?" he asks.

"We'll discuss them later. My client has yet to be updated on the new developments." Again, Mabel nods at the newspaper in his hands. "You're dismissed for now, soldier. Leave us."

It's as though I'm lodged in Apollo's mind, reading every thought that passes. *He didn't know Rion then. Rion didn't know Apollo, either.* They were two ships passing in the night, reunited years later by serendipitous circumstances.

Flash. Apollo reads the newspaper, which I realize is dated only two years ago.

TAKING BACK EARTH
Fighting the Apocalypse

After nearly thirty years, the United Governments are finally taking action. The UFO harboring intelligent alien life, which has occupied the dark-side of the moon, is officially to be targeted in an open act of war should no surrender be made or compromise found.

"We've anticipated this recourse for decades," says Pol Oclust, the multi-billion dollar man responsible for founding and organizing PIO Morse, and thus reviving the world's chances at redemption. "With the PIO Morse army, and my connections, we are finally ready to strike back in the name of salvaging what's left of humanity."

Targeting the UFO attributed to the A-42 pandemic is the "only option now," a proposition agreed upon globally by all primary government officials.

"The war begins now," Oclust is documented to have said yesterday, during a press release held privately in his gated community, confirming the fight he intends to lead in the coming years against this alien invasion.

My breath is knocked clean out of my lungs.

I stagger backward, lifting my palm from Apollo's chest the way one might after touching something scaldingly hot—and like all the times before, despite feeling shocked, I feel . . . *healthy*.

I feel powerful.

Apollo's nostrils flare. "Believe us now, Eos?"

Merope and Cyb consult me with eager glances, faces and lips white as chalk. I swallow dryly, giving them each a shaky nod of confirmation, two words jittering in my mind.

Alien. Invasion.

Despite knowing it's true, I can't bring myself to accept it for truth—to erase all the lies that for so long I believed, without a shadow of a doubt, to be real.

Who's the real traitor? Nova had asked, her final words to me before dying. *Is it the liar, or the person being lied to?*

You're being lied to, Rion told me, the first information he divulged after I begged him to confirm or deny the legitimacy of my dead friend's claims.

And little did I know, that's *exactly* what he did.

Jac gets up, walks around the fire, and hands Cyb a piece of yellow paper webbed in wrinkles and smudged haphazardly in what appears to be smears of mud.

"Maybe this will help," he says, swigging vodka. I walk up to Cyb's side, peering at the paper from over her shoulder, and recognize it immediately.

Landing coordinates—written in *Mentor's Language*.

The only reason I know it's coordinates in the first place is because somebody—Mabel, I guess—translated it into English.

At the bottom, a signature is scribbled:

The gem. The moon. The stone.

"We don't know the others," Jac says, fists in his pockets as the chill of the night increases in ferocity. "But we're wondering if maybe 'the stone' is Onyx."

Cyb raises her eyes, cold and empty. "Has to be."

"You believe us now?" Jac asks.

"I have to." She lowers the note sadly on her lap, tracing her fingers over the signature line. *The Stone.*

My hand finds her shoulder, resting there until her hand snakes blindly up to mine.

That's as close as she'll get to an apology.

We talk for hours, late into the night, until it's so cold we can't breathe without it burning. By the time we decide it might be wise to sleep, we are all truly convinced.

The Project is a lie . . . Everything is.

Nova was telling the truth.

Merope and Cyb snuggle together. Apollo and Jac take up posts at opposite ends of camp, leaving me to watch over Rion, who isn't allowed to sleep.

We sit together, leaning against the same tree. Hours pass as the night slowly crawls. All the while, we do what we can to avoid freezing: switch positions, trade jackets, burrow our faces into hats and scarves.

Whenever Rion nods off, I shake him awake. The night is a darkness that keeps unfolding, and just as I wonder when it will finally end, I see dawn gnaw at the edges of the horizon.

I think about everything I've learned, trying to absorb it in spite of having it all thrown at me at once. *Nova was telling me the truth all along . . . Is it possible that our mentors, due to being members of an alien race, don't have souls like humans do?*

Is that why they don't have auras?

The clouds shift, exposing the moon; looming beside it is my spaceship. From afar, it looks like a wheel, or a ring, with a green track down the inner part of its center.

What's going on up there today?

My fingers run along the insides of my wrist, feeling for my thin microchip scar. I'm still a blinking red light on the CORE's ever observant radar, trailing alongside my league.

Onyx—*Mom.* The words feel mutually exclusive. It's the one piece of the puzzle patching itself together before my eyes that's too impossible to accept, even more than being *half-alien.*

I feel Rion's body wilt sideways, sagging with sleep.

"Hey," I say, nudging him. "Wake up."

"Wha—who?" In the dawning light, the bruises and cuts all over Rion's face are exposed in full: a split lip, a slice bleeding at his temple, his eyes still glossy.

"Just me," I whisper, patting his arm. "Waking you up."

"*Again,*" he grunts irritably.

"*Again,*" I concede. "Everybody else is still asleep. Maybe we should start packing up our supplies?"

"Might as well." He rolls to a standing position, turning to offer me a hand, which I accept. "There's a highway frequented by our quarantine just over the crest of that slope," he adds with a glance across a sprawling clearing. At the other side, a slope reaches skyward, leveling off in a plateau.

The snow blanketing this crazy, beautiful world is pressed smooth as a fitted sheet over the clearing before us. Trees at the other side thicken dramatically.

"You think there's a chance they will drive by?"

"I do," he says, packing up. "Especially since we didn't come back last night the way we were supposed to."

"Will they look for us?"

"To the best of their ability. For all they know, we could've been taken down by the Skims during the supply drop."

"Rion," I say, speaking so seriously he stops what he's doing to regard me with curiosity. "What about the other leagues? Will we go with them?"

His eyes wince. "Probably."

I drop on the log beside him, keeping my eyes—sharp and unyielding—on his. "They went willingly?"

"Yes."

"And they are staying willingly?"

"Yes," he says again, but after hesitating. I don't know what makes me do it, but I find myself rolling up the sleeve of his shirt to look at the scars lying beneath.

He lets me.

I trace a fingertip along the ridged surface, feeling the buzz of my skillset blazing back to life. But I'm stopped. Rion moves, rearranging himself so our hands rest together—still splayed, not wholly clasped, but touching.

We lock eyes. I look away, feeling uncomfortable, only for my gaze to settle on that crooked smile of his—with one dimple of the left side of lips, full and soft.

He laces his fingers through mine. I don't resist, temporarily awed by my own daring.

I rest a hand on his chest and feel his heart beating.

My skillset begs to be used, but I push it aside. For once, it isn't information I'm after.

It's *him*.

We breathe together—faster, wilder—as my hesitation fades to a wisp and so does his. He rests a hand on my leg, inching up higher and higher, and—

"GET DOWN!"

The whisper-shout is issued from behind us—from Jac, who is squatting beside Apollo, their rifles raised and pointed at some place over my right shoulder.

Rion grabs my wrist and drops, dragging me with him.

"Jesus," he gasps, flinching as snow washes up the lifted hem of his shirt. He extracts a pistol, resting it on the log we were just sitting on.

Jac laughs breathily. "We didn't mean to interr—"

"Shut up," Rion growls, still aiming.

Far too humiliated to look back at the pair, I keep my face where it is: inches from snow, which turns my breath into a veil of rising vapor. Above the log, through the haze of my breath, I see a small group of the Muted staggering into the clearing.

A frantic glance westward confirms Cyb and Merope are awake and aware of what's going on, huddled together behind a large toppled-over tree.

Cyb's finger hovers by her temple—*ready*.

I think to do the same, to Persuade the Muted to stay still long enough for us to gun them down, but even before the tip of my finger touches my temple, I know it isn't going to work.

The power is gone.

But how did I get it in the first place?

And how do I get it back—kill another Haunt?

A cry issues loudly over the landscape, echoing.

As they get closer, I realize they're wearing clothing—that they still have hair clinging to their scalps, and rivers of blood at the base of their eyes that have been freshly gouged out.

"They just flipped." I look to Rion. "Are they familiar?"

"No," he says, before raising his pistol and pegging each of the Muted down in less than three seconds—each disappearing into a puff of snow after they fall.

He exhales hard, then stands back up. This time, he doesn't offer me his hand or even a glance; he simply grabs the bag of supplies he had earlier and walks into the clearing.

I find myself following—*chasing*—after him, jogging into the clearing in his wake. I hear the others gathering the bags we just packed, following fast behind us.

Despite the reach of dawn, the moon looms, big and white and fading in the sky. And beside it the Ora waits.

"Did I *miss* something?"

"No—I did," he says brusquely, not turning even after I'm at his side, matching his stride. "Whatever that was, it can't happen again between us. I'm sorry, Eos."

"You're not *sorry*," I admonish. I'd love to leave without a word, without a care—but as much as it pains me to admit it, I felt *something* moments ago.

Rion faces me. "I am," he whispers. "Really."

I hear the others approaching behind us, filtering out of the woods with our supply bags. *They won't see this. I refuse to let them see me get rejected . . .*

"Yeah, you're right," I say, stomping by. "Huge mistake."

"I never said it was a mistake."

"Didn't you?" My voice is the lethal stillness of a snake as it takes aim to strike—just the way I like it. *Stupid, Eos. Stupid for ever letting your guard down.*

Never again.

Rion's footsteps approach—fast-paced, a jog. "You don't get what I'm trying to say."

"Then speak *plainly,* you ass."

"Yeah," I hear Jac shout from behind us. "Rion, *you ass.*"

Rion scoffs, laughing with a ghost of a smile. But before the others arrive, he glances fervently at me while reaching into the folds of his shirt. Ripping off a necklace.

No, not a necklace—the military tags.

He tosses them to me. I can't imagine why. Even though every part of me begs to catch them, I let them fall and sink into the depths of the snow.

Jac laughs unknowingly in our wake. Cyb and the others strain under the bulk of heavy bags, walking alongside Jac as they coast through the throes of a conversation I can't hear—to me, their words only sound like distant buzzing.

When I look up again, Rion isn't there.

I feel suddenly very raw.

Merope drops a bag in the snow beside me and brushes off her knees, covered in twigs and dirt. "So?"

"So what?" I sigh.

"Do I really need to specify?" I don't answer. "Eos, you look like you're going to cr—" Being my sister, my best friend, she knows all too well to revise that statement. "You look like you've got something in your eye."

"I do—a fleck of dirt or something."

"Can I help?" she asks, casting a precautionary glance at the others who've far surpassed us now. Then, she bends over and extracts the military tags out of the deep snow. "Can I help by holding onto these for you?"

I swallow back the unspent tears, but they still burn.

Breathing deep, I say, "Thank you."

"We've had a trying twenty-four hours," she says, pocketing the tags for safe keeping. "I don't think any of us are ourselves right now, Eos."

"I'm okay, it's just a lot to process."

"That's your problem—you don't process, you *bury*."

"You know me well," I concede as she drapes an arm over my shoulder and pilots me toward our group. "What the hell are we going to do now, M?"

Her arm hangs over my shoulder, still encircled by a puce ring of bruises. I realize, abruptly, that she's forgiving me—that the time I've spent burying Lios's condition instead of processing it hasn't been lost on her. That she understands. That she's *okay*.

"What we've been doing all along, E," she whispers, resting a head on mine. "Find Mabel Faye."

22

"SO HOW'S THAT HEAD of yours?"

Merope playfully ruffles Rion's hair from behind, trying to cheer the both of us up. We've been walking in silence for nearly thirty minutes, the strum of tension as present as the white sky.

"It's fine," Rion says, voice stilted.

"Well that isn't satisfactory!" Jac stops to stoop down on one knee just as we breach the cusp of the forest on the other side of the clearing.

The world is a painting of evergreen, white snow, and scaly, almost-black bark. My nose and cheeks are red with cold and the whiplashed chapping of the wind—my hair a frizzy mess, stuffed back under the hat I didn't realize I'd left at camp after running mindlessly off after Rion.

The hat Lios helped me pick out.

My crazy, ear-flap hat—an equal to his, which I can't seem to mentally locate. Does he have it? Did Mia or Silas mistake it as unimportant and toss it?

Jac shakes his shoulder length, blond hair out of his face and unzips his backpack—digging, as per usual, for his can of tobacco and leafy rolling paper. With it, he takes out a miniature bottle of plumb-colored liquid, contained in a lovely, frosted glass bottle, which he lifts for his friend to accept.

"This will help your headache, if you've got one."

"Port?"

"Found it in the truck." Jac winks, returning his attention to the rolling of yet another cigarette. "Tucked away, hidden in the slot by the footwell where I usually keep my shotgun."

Rion quietly pops the cork out of the bottle's slender neck and takes a sip. Cyb flops down, sitting beside Jac on a log as he works to roll a host of cigarettes instead of just one, as I'd thought. Her face is a map of scratches, bruises, cuts.

I bet mine is too.

Apollo shades his eyes from the bright sky, peering up at the slope ascending like a cresting wave out of the forest a couple hundred yards off. "Stay cautious. Remember, the Muted came from here . . ."

"If not looking for us, who else would be out here, and for what reason?" Jac inquires with a cocked brow, licking the hem of the paper before sealing it.

"They weren't from our camp," Rion confirms, collapsing against the base of a tree with the port in his hands. "We could track them—find their leftover supplies, see if there's anything worth taking."

"That's my man," Jac praises, packing his stuff away.

"I agree that's a good idea, so long as everybody else is okay with the brief detour?" Apollo refers to Cyb, who rolls her eyes in fatigued disinterest at Merope.

"Sounds like a great idea," Merope says, smiling at Rion.

"I'm glad you agree." He gives her a flash of a smile, sipping the port. Merope's face flushes, her black eyelashes long and her face pretty—cut up the least of all of ours.

"Does it look like we're short on supplies?" I snarl, nodding at the bags already weighing us down—straining at their seams so tightly, they're at risk of breaking.

I reach out and snap a twig off a tree angrily. "We should be focusing on getting back. This idea is idiotic and unnecessarily reckless, in my opinion."

I look specifically at Merope. "What do you think?"

That's right, M. You have to pick a side.

"I believe I already stated how I feel. I think it's a brilliant idea that is worthy of our time." Again, her eyes drift to Rion and she smiles. "What if they left behind a working vehicle?"

"Ah, that's a good point," Jac adds.

"Sorry, Eos." Cyb brushes by, finding a narrow path that cuts through the forest and following it. "But a working vehicle could save our lives."

I flirt with the idea of declaring I'll go off on my own, but being the youngest I know that wouldn't fly. It'd only make me look dramatic and foolish.

Foolish, because Merope and Rion . . . smiled at each other?

You're paranoid, Eos. I tell myself she doesn't even know him as a person, doesn't know that he had a little sister named Lindall who was lost to the A-42, or that he talks when he sleeps, spouting off numbers . . .

Merope's in front of me. I speed up, bumping into her side as she scales the path. Trees form walls hugging my periphery, the sky cut into a mosaic by spindly black branches.

"Give me the tags," I bark.

"Okay, fine."

"What's your problem, anyway?"

"What's yours?" she hisses, forking over the tags. They fall in my palm with a clink, silver glistening in the reflection of the obstructed sky overhead. "Eos, I don't understand—"

But I'm not listening.

I look at the numbers etched there.

XII VII IV XIII XXI
PILOT

"That's it," I say abruptly, recognizing the numbers as the exact ones Rion is always muttering in his sleep. "Twelve, seven, four, thirteen, twenty-one . . ."

The footsteps ahead of us stop as Rion, at the head of the stream of us, slows to a halt and looks back—as though trained to hear, and recognize, those numbers.

Even if spoken softly.

"What's going on back there?" Apollo asks, exasperated by yet another delay. Merope moves, accidentally releasing a thin, whip of a tree branch tucked behind her—*right into my face.*

I hiss, seething against the bite of it.

"Eos—I'm sorry!" she says as I run a finger along the welt of the cut, shaped kind of like a smile across the course of my whole left cheek.

My eyes find Rion, who's seen it all. Jaw flexed, he turns to leave just as I see something in my periphery blaze like a scream expelled in total silence.

Color.

A vivid, cobalt-blue cutting through the black-and-white expanse of winter. Off the path, far to the right. I hear the flap of plastic or fabric or perhaps a tent.

No, a tarp.

It's a cobalt-blue tarp.

"Well, it looks like our hunt is over." I dive off the path in a fit of impatience, ignoring the shouted voices I hear in my wake as they try calling me back.

A futile effort.

The snapping of twigs announces an approach—*Rion,* of course, as he catches up to my side. "Hey—*stop.*"

He tugs my sleeve, snagging the chain of his military tags in my hand, pulling them free. They fall to the ground.

Only then, I stop.

We look at each other. His eyes dawn, realizing I didn't just leave them behind miles away in the snow—that part of me, even if it's a part I resent, would never hurt him like that.

Would never think to hurt him *at all.*

The others arrive, Jac in the lead. His cheeks red and shiny as apples, lips peeling and chapped. "Looks like a tarp. Must be their camp, all right."

Rion brushes my shoulder as he passes by, pistol raised as he approaches the nearby camp. "You have a gun?" he asks quietly the second I catch up.

I reply by way of cocking an old revolver. He nods and we walk in tandem, knowing, somehow instinctively, that he's to guard the left and I'm to guard the right.

The others keep their ranks tight. Apollo holds up the rear with a freshly loaded rifle, aided by Cyb.

Rion and I break through a tight crop of saplings, exploding through the campsite's perimeter.

It's been *destroyed.*

A fire reduced to a single dying flame cooks an overturned pot of beans—smoking and charcoaled, plastered hard as concrete to the bottom of its pot.

Then, I see the bodies. The first is tagged against a tree, as though he'd tried to climb it to safety. The left side of his ribcage is ripped entirely off, the other half still attached, but flayed, skin peeled back like a glove.

Blood is everywhere, dripping and mixed in mud.

I step forward, treading carefully around a body still tucked in a sleeping bag. The body is that of a man, his face still visible despite being fixed in a perpetual scream—the crown of his skull broken and jagged, *empty*. Brain gone.

I suddenly feel like I'm about to be sick.

Rion inches closer, arm brushing my shoulder as he keeps his pistol raised—eyes cold, calculated.

Apollo dives in, scouting the camp's supplies. There isn't anything worth keeping. Whoever these people were before they were killed, they didn't have a lot.

"Traveling out of desperation, I bet," Jac mutters, lips white as he regards a third body: slack-jawed and lying sprawled out on its chest, as though trying to crawl away—the sclera of his eyes a solid red, matte after drying out.

"Hey, you guys?" Cyb says, holding up a gasmask and a pair of bulbous, black goggles. "They were Skims."

Rion and Jac cast each other glances, uncharacteristically frantic in nature, setting me on edge. They approach Cyb, taking a look at the supplies.

Rion clears his throat. "There's an extra pair of goggles and a gasmask—at least *one* of their group flipped and started killing the others without warning, maybe more."

A cold chill passes over us all.

The smell of blood gets stronger with every breath, as the

reality of the situation continues to get clearer, more undeniable and real and terrifying.

I lean against a tree, watching the others rummage through what's left of the camp—and suddenly hear a voice huskily speak from somewhere behind my back.

Not a voice. A whisper.

"*Help me.*"

I whirl around, gun raised, moving so quickly as to draw the attention of my whole group. A few feet away from my boots is a withered man, face gaunt, eyes gold with jaundice.

The others are at my side in a heartbeat.

"Who are you?" Jac crows, aiming a rifle at the man's face.

"I was with—this group—but I'm not a Skim," he wheezes as he lies in the mud. I realize his body is badly bruised, but not critically injured; his clothes, even, are barely dirty.

Rion kneels down, pressing the barrel of his gun against the man's sweaty forehead. "That doesn't answer the question."

"I—I'm Eli," he stammers, holding up a hand. "I work for the military, as a recruiter. I was taking those men back to base so they could fight in the war."

This, at least, is so unexpected we can't forge words.

Eli licks his lips. "Anybody involved in PIO Morse gets a roof over their head and free food. Perhaps the six of you would like to be involved?"

The fact that Eli so effortlessly counted our ranks suggests he possibly isn't injured at all; he's thinking clearly enough, or so it appears, at least. *Yet his eyes are colored by jaundice.*

There's something he isn't telling us.

I kneel beside Rion. "What happened to you?"

Eli's eyes are wild, ransacking mine. "We—we were—it was

the *strangest* thing—I think we were attacked by a league of those otherworldly space people!"

"Specimens?" Jac asks, side-eyeing Rion curiously.

"Yes," Eli replies enthusiastically.

"What did they look like?"

"They were older—different than the other leagues—maybe a new breed, I don't know." Eli's eyes widen. "They had a tattoo of a constellation on their faces, cupped around their eyes, kind of like a fish's gills."

Apollo stiffens dramatically. "Cassiopeia," he says.

"Maybe? I'm not—"

"I'm sure it is," Apollo interjects, keeping his gaze averted to the ground as he speaks. "Rion?" he says coolly. "Kill him."

"Don't you dare do any such thing!" Merope steps forward out of our line, shielding Eli. "Our Purpose is to help, not kill."

I raise my own revolver, challenging her. "You seem to have forgotten one thing: we don't have a Purpose anymore, and the one we had originally was a lie."

I look to Apollo. "Why should we kill him?"

Rion surprises me by answering. "Because he's going to die regardless. He's infected."

"I—I can make it back to the base, if you help me—I'd like to be buried with dignity, not die—"

Eli's head snaps backward, pulled by a bullet. Apollo stands with a gun outstretched, his face white. "Sorry, Eli, but there's no way you would've made it."

WE WALK UNTIL SUNDOWN.

Leading the way alongside me, Merope nods to a small rip in

the fabric of night—a space that's clear of trees and shrubbery, doused in the dusty white light of the moon.

We filter out, single-file, into another clearing. The canopy drops off to a clear sky, and like the vaulted ceiling of a cathedral, it arches up high and endless.

The stars are scattered crystals against a backdrop lit up by the glow of a full moon. Farther away, creeping like ivy along the horizon, are the thick clouds of a snowstorm approaching.

Jac staggers, collapsing on a nearby tree for support.

"You all right?" Merope asks, taking in his complexion, which is the color of an eggshell: pale and slightly ashen, a spoiled kind of hue that sets me instantly on edge.

Breathing heavily, he rips off his jacket and exposes a thick bandage heavily sodden with blood—the very bandage Cyb just applied yesterday, last night.

My breath catches and I'm at Jac's side in a beat, taking off the sodden dressing to better examine the injury. The others gather around, faces waxy.

"It won't stop bleeding—why?" I wonder, looking at the gaping hole in his shoulder, still draining blood. "There has to be something we can do."

"There is," Jac grunts, patting my hatted-head fondly. "As long as the injury isn't infected yet?"

"It's not," I conclude. Even in the moonlight, the wound is a clean shot straight through his shoulder, the flesh healthy—no puss or fever or swelling.

Jac nods, running a tongue over his lower lip. "I've gotta take care of this tonight, Rion."

Rion nods, albeit reluctantly. "I'll help."

"No," Jac snaps.

"I'll help." Rion stands inches from Jac's face, speaking with such unyielding finality, I realize he isn't offering his help—he's making an order. "We'll set up camp first. Get a fire going. I've got a knife you can use, and—"

"A knife? For what?" Cyb inquires.

"Cauterizing." Rion's eyes reflect the ivory blanch of the big and bloated moon swelling overhead. "It's the only way we'll be able to stop the bleeding."

Rion marches off and Jac follows, wincing against the pain of his shoulder. Cyb looks at me, as though to say, *They're going to seal his wound by burning it shut?*

How absolutely archaic . . .

I gaze out over the clearing that sags slightly, as though set in a cupped palm. "I wonder," I say, while everybody else picks a place to set up camp and begins working.

I fire off a single round, aiming at the very place where the clearing dips lower. My bullet explodes through something, a veil of ice, and water splashes up in reply.

"It's a lake!" I tell the others, firing off two more rounds to make a triangle shape along its lacy rim.

Kneeling, I pound the triangular chunk of ice free, gaining access to the clean water. We're on our last water bottles. Only three remain, given it's the resource we use the most.

However, being surrounded by snow and ice, running out of water to drink hasn't been a huge concern for us. But I'll always rather have too much instead of too little.

I lower cupped palms into the icy water—so deep as to look endless and black—and draw up a sip, which I drink first, and splash over my dirty face second.

I shiver in the strangest way—a liberating way, as though

all the hardships of the last two days are being slicked off the surface of my skin as I rinse away half-dry blood, patches of mud like sleeves of fish scales, and every lie I once believed to be truth.

Gone. Washed away. Gone.

I torture myself with an upward glance. Beside the moon is my spaceship. Home. Even now, despite it all, I ache for my own bed there, for the people—for Onyx.

Who's my . . .

Who's actually a . . .

The gravity of my situation hasn't fully struck—like Merope said earlier, *I don't process, I bury.*

But this water, there's something about it. I can feel it filter and pool chillingly at my core. I can feel it eroding the hardest parts of myself, and unearthing the place where I've buried all my fears and failures and shortcomings.

Unearthing the grave I've dug inside myself, a grave which is too full and too deep and too angry. And I should've known it would surface one day, and that my cowardice wouldn't be able to outrun it anymore.

And I'd have to face it all again eventually. Harder, fiercer, angrier, and festering.

As I rinse myself off in the water, I remember everything about my experience here on Earth, only in flashes:

Nova's death.

The look Onyx had when she realized I was deploying with or without her consent—and her final words to me as I sat in the podcraft, her cryptic farewell: *I tried.*

Lios's body shook violently by a Mute.

Apollo's panicked face after I'd used my ability to discover his deepest and darkest secrets, my esophagus crushed under the weight of his hands.

Rion, Jac, Silas, and Mia. Natives. When did they start to feel like family? When did I start loving them the way I do the members of my own league?

Fighting alongside them during the supply raid. Trying to help a woman—Amy—and killing a father instead, leaving his two daughters to fend for themselves.

My actions, leading to Jac getting shot in the shoulder.

My actions, leading to us crashing the truck.

My actions, leading myself to Rion.

Discovering we aren't who we thought—that we have been lied to in ways unfathomable. That we aren't people, but truly specimens: genetic creations to facilitate a war we didn't realize we were fighting, forced to adhere to a Project and a Purpose, to fulfill a duty and perform accordingly. *All for what?*

I don't stop. I keep drawing handfuls of water over myself, rinsing and cleansing and concealing. *Why are we even here, what is our*—their—*motive?*

I look up at the sky, glaring at the Ora. *What is it they could they possibly want with Earth's people? Why kill them off and save them all at once? Why create specimens to do the dirty work?*

Shaking my head, I try dislodging the thoughts, but the ache gripping my stomach won't leave—a writhing, seasick kind of feeling that's reminiscent of the time I got really ill and kept throwing up, even when there wasn't anything left.

I hear voices and realize everybody at camp—now set up with a fire and tent and all—are watching.

My face reddens, but I'm not ashamed. For the first time, I think I'm processing. Not burying.

Of all people, Cyb gets up off the snowy boulder she was

sitting on and approaches me at the lake's edge, a serenity to her features that renders her unrecognizable.

Without a word, she sits beside me, drawing water over her arms and face. The first splash is the coldest. After she gets used to the temperature, she goes faster, rinsing herself off altogether in spite of her chattering teeth.

And when she's done—stopping abruptly—she holds out a shaking hand, tinged blue with cold, for mine.

And I take it.

Cyb's silver eyes burn ferociously, finding mine. Her lips are periwinkle, her face clean. But it isn't what I see on the outside that strikes me—it's what lies beneath. What she's dug up from her own internal grave.

Cyb's voice is strong. "We still have each other."

And then she gets up, brushes herself off, and walks fiercely back to camp. All the time I've spent disliking her, the time we have bumped heads, or disagreed, or fought—I thought it was because we were fundamentally different in ways that couldn't possibly be reconciled. But now I realize out of everybody in the league we share, we're the most alike. *And I'm proud of that.*

I'm proud to be like Cyb, who is my sister, and family, and a challenge, and person who's right and wrong—but above all else, somebody who's truly a force unbreakable.

And today, she's right: *We still have each other.*

23

I RETURN TO THE sight of Jac stuffing a pot full of snow.

"You're just in time," he says, sponging a sleeve across his forehead to dab away a band of sweat. "Chef Jac's in the kitchen."

"Which means what?" Apollo replies coyly. "That we'll all have food poisoning by the night's end?"

"Everything we have is prepackaged, Apollo—nothing raw or fresh, alas." Jac packs another handful of snow in the pot and sets it on top of the fire. "Otherwise, yes. Probably."

Apollo scoffs, grinning as he rips off his boots and socks in order to dry them by the roaring flames. Behind him, two tents have been erected—tucked pleasantly in an especially dark pocket of the woods, covered by trees.

We haven't heard or caught sight of a Mute in hours, and though that's a good sign, there's a certain gloom falling over our group I can't deny. *What if we don't get rescued? Do we really stand a chance walking forty miles back to the quarantine, just us and our dwindling supplies? In winter?*

I settle on a log between Merope and Cyb, directly across the fire from Rion, who's whittling a slender sapling into what looks like a crude spear. Meanwhile, Jac digs through our bags of supplies and extracts a series of canned soups, labeled with only a stamp to signify its flavor.

"What are our options tonight, Jac?" Merope asks, her violet eyes flitting over the fire, landing directly on Rion—*where they settle and don't lift.*

I bite down, chewing my lower lip. Rion steadily holds her gaze with an open smile hitched on his handsome lips, eyes freed of their previously concussed fog, and a—

I shoot up to a standing position at once. *Eos, you're being completely and totally absurd. Go somewhere else and distract yourself if this is bothering you, because Rion isn't yours.*

He never was.

Whatever happened before "can't happen again," remember?

Maybe all along it was because he wanted Merope—not you.

Nobody bothers to notice as I dismount the log I was sitting on and walk to the far right, where Apollo sits, warming his bare feet by the fire. *Ew.*

"Is this seat taken?" I inquire casually, nodding to a gap at his side; there's barely enough room for Apollo himself, honestly, but I'm going for it anyway.

Apollo eyes the space. He's sitting on what looks to be a highly uncomfortable boulder—relieved of a layer of snow, but still likely as cold as the ice surrounding it.

"Well, I guess not," Apollo says, brows furrowing.

I wiggle into the gap, snuggling up against Apollo's broad shoulder, his pale skin icy as the snow itself.

"You're freezing," I say.

"Well, it's cold outside, Eos," Apollo replies. Platonically.

"Does anybody," Jac interjects suddenly, squinting to read the labels on the cans of soup, "object to *butternut squash* as our entrée tonight?"

"As long as it's not split-pea." Everybody freezes, realizing that both Rion and I said the same thing in unison. Foolishly, my first thought is, *We both dislike split-pea?*

"Hey!" Jac wields a wooden spoon at us accusatorily. "I'll have no haters of split-pea in my kitchen! Split-pea is a classic, my friends, and you can't *dislike the classics.*"

We all laugh, watching as Jac—still shaky and pale, but not one to lose his humor—digs through the bag yet again in search of something else this time. I know, immediately, what it is the second I hear the clinking of glass-on-glass.

Alcohol.

I should've known.

Jac arranges a half-empty bottle of vodka and a large, unopened jug of whiskey, side by side on a log. Rion reaches for his pocket and extracts his port, lining it up along the others.

"When the world ends," Jac says, uncapping the whiskey at the same time Merope seizes the half-empty bottle of vodka and swigs deeply, "Happy Hour is *every* hour."

I wiggle out of the spot I've wedged myself in, trying to get to the port before it's taken, but am stopped by Apollo.

"Jac's going to get drunk because he's going to cauterize his wound tonight—which will be quite painful," he says, whispering in undertones. "You don't have to."

"Neither does Merope, and she's drinking!"

"She's older than you."

"*Tell me,*" I spit, glowering at Apollo as I snatch one of his drying boots and hit him with it, "*what to do again, and I'll—*"

"Fine, fine!" Apollo laughs, ducking as I strike him playfully with his boot once more. "Do what you want—but if you make any bad decisions—"

"That's exactly what I plan to do." I drop his shoe back in the snow, smiling menacingly. "Why don't you stop being a wet blanket and join in?"

Apollo regards me suspiciously. Then he gets up, accepting a hand I've offered to help, and follows me to the line of bottles awaiting us on the log.

"Bartender, I'll have the port," Apollo declares, taking on a stringent, hyper-sophisticated kind of tone. "The lady will also have a glass—or I suppose, a sip."

"Ladies first," Jac chastises, dodging Apollo's reach in order to give me the port instead. "What kind of gentleman are you?"

Apollo laughs. "A poor one, evidently."

We take up residence beside Cyb, who requests to have a sip of the port as well—it's the first time we've ever tried it, and I'm surprised by how delicious it is.

Far better than the vodka.

Dangerously so.

Merope and Rion are sitting together. It looks as though he's teaching her the rules to some kind of a game. They speak in hushed voices, laughing before taking turns drinking vodka.

"What're you doing?" I say, already feeling the fiery effects of drinking port on an empty stomach.

Merope's eyes flash. "We were trying to decide on a game to play together—a drinking game."

"We want in," Cyb declares on my behalf, patting the place on the log beside her, for me to sit. I sit there, swigging another heavy sip of port, relishing the sweet sharpness of it. Already, I can feel it in my legs and fingertips.

Jac stirs the pot of soup as he asks, "Spin the bottle?"

"Give me that," Apollo says, laughing nervously at the game

suggested, taking the port from me and draining it. "I'm going to need to be sufficiently drunk for this."

Jac walks up, takes a final drink of the whiskey, and hands the rest of the jug to me. "Here—this will speed things up!"

I take a sip. The flavor of it is powerful. Already, I enjoy it the most of the others I've tried, the way it warms me instantly from the inside, out.

We pass it around the circle of us, laughing a bit. Jac brings the pot of soup—bowls unavailable—and we pass it around with the alcohol, taking turns.

Eventually we're full and dizzy, but pleasantly so. I feel like if the desire struck, I could take flight. I'm seeing double and my lips are tingling and numb, a fire lit up in my chest.

Jac leans back to view the sky. "Ah," he breathes, the pain of his shoulder finally eased. "Wait until you guys try tequila!"

"Oh god," Apollo chuckles, eyes drooping.

"So—about this game," Merope goes on, taking the empty port bottle and spinning it on an icy stretch of snow. It spins like a dial, its neck serving as a pointed arrow. "How does it work?"

"Easy," Jac says. "I'll start."

"Lead us by example," Cyb chortles, winking.

"Exactly." He takes the bottle, placing it as closely to the middle of our circle as he can, and spins it—the bottle stops, its neck pointing at Apollo, and the boys roar with laughter.

"Get over here," Jac cajoles, laughing—gesturing with the flirtatious curl of a finger for Apollo to approach. "Now, the rules state he's got to kiss me or perform a dare."

Apollo laughs, dark hair falling messily in his eyes. "Accept a dare from you? I'd be crazy."

Clumsily, Apollo launches forward and kisses Jac full on the lips in front of everybody—and after a startled blip of quiet, we all burst into a round of applause.

Rion sips, eyeing Jac and Apollo strangely.

"My turn," Cyb exclaims, next up. Her bottle spins, landing perfectly on me when it's finished. "Eos, what will it be?"

"Kiss," I say, knowing all too well I'd be making a very grave mistake in giving Cyb the opportunity to issue a dare. I give her a quick peck on her soft cheek.

"Not the way Lios kisses me, but it'll do," she jokes.

"Okay, Rion's up," Merope says from beside me—the three of us girls somehow arranging ourselves together on one side of the small circle.

Rion doesn't look at all interested in the game. But he takes the port bottle and spins it anyway. The bottle skids over the icy surface of snow, screeching to stop a second later, pointing at me.

My every muscle tenses as I hear the memory of Rion's cold rejection echo in my mind: *Whatever just happened between us? It can't happen again . . .*

Standing brusquely, I sway, realizing all at once just how drunk I really am, and feel instantly queasy as the world spins.

"You aren't quitting the game?" Cyb asks obliviously.

"I've got a headache," I say, not really lying. Apollo leaps up to help me, but I shove away his efforts. "I'm fine—I'd rather be alone right now."

"Probably not a good idea," Jac says wisely.

"I promise you, it is." I walk off, trying my best to stumble as little as possible as I trek toward the tents—dipping into the peaceful darkness, the shade of trees.

The air is a wisp of cold, a refreshing reprieve. I'm not ready to go to bed. I just want to get away, to figure myself out. Is this how Cyb feels toward Lios?

This horrible, convoluted, unimaginable feeling?

I lean against a tree—its bark scratchy, dulled by the liquor.

Suddenly, a figure emerges. Rion drifts out from behind a tree farther off, like he's looking for something.

Or someone.

As though he's just heard my thoughts, his eyes click up to my own, discovering me. Neither of us speak. He trudges across a mess of tangled shrubs and trees, bridging the space between us fast and easily.

Before I can register his presence, he's pressing his lips up against mine, kissing me. The heat of the gesture evacuates all of my previously dizzied thoughts, and I relish the freedom of not thinking. Of only doing. Acting and reacting.

Rion kisses me deeply, the broad weight of his body flush against my own. We breathe heavily together. I grab the collar of his jacket and drag him closer.

My eyes are barred on his, drinking in the wild edge stirring beneath his maple irises. He rips off my hat. My hair falls over my shoulders, his calloused fingertips brushing the soft apple of my cheek before gripping my hair, tugging it slightly as my lips raise to meet his once more.

"There's something I've got to tell you," he says, exhaling as his lips softly graze mine—not in a kiss, but in a touch as equally breathtaking.

"I don't want to know," I say, and lace my fingers through his hand, guiding it slowly under the hem of my shirt. Rion's eyes don't leave mine—beautiful and dark and endless—and I wonder if the power of my heart beating will betray how thrilling and terrifying this is to me . . .

287

Betray the fact that I'm new at this.

Breathlessly, he takes it the rest of the way. His touch is at once gentle and fierce—soft and intentional—as he runs fingers up my ribcage, settling at the base of my breasts.

Suddenly his hands drop, holding mine, tugging me toward the tents lingering a few feet away. The others are still sitting at the fire, talking.

We're alone.

We clumsily unzip the tent and go inside, beds already put together—warm and cozy. The light of the fire filters in through the fabric and casts his body in a golden light as he rolls out of his clothes: jacket, hoodie, and shirt.

The military tags blink in the dim light, swinging across the supple plane of his chest. He approaches me slowly—playfully, almost—as he tugs my ankle, pulling me closer.

I've never felt the way I'm feeling.

Not in love. No, I don't feel that full or complete. This feels deliciously filling and emptying at once—like I've been broken and am watching myself get pieced back together.

He leans over me, running a palm along my calf, venturing up the length of my thigh.

My fingertips sail across the stretch of his ribcage and glide up his back—the buzz of my skillset unruly, exposing Rion for what he is inside: all color, music, and fight.

A mixed bag I find myself, despite my resistance, slipping and falling into. My lips on his. The taste of his mouth and the weight of his body cupping mine—until it isn't.

Until I'm no longer in a tent or at a campsite or pinned up against a boy that I can't stop kissing. Until I'm jettisoned into a different reality altogether.

Until I'm looking at his past.

24

I'M STANDING IN SOMEONE'S living room.

Boards nailed over windows—ribbons of morning sunlight knifing through columned spaces, sheets of bronze granting a tiny glimpse of the daylight outside.

There's a television in the corner, but it's long since been rendered unusable: a spider's web of cracks roll outward from a point of impact in the center that destroyed the whole screen.

It's as though somebody *intentionally* shattered it. But that hardly matters when the bulk of the world's populace doesn't have access to TV anymore—this neighborhood, included.

I hear something. A high-pitched cry that collapses into a startlingly monotone weeping—a sound I wouldn't ever believe belonged to a human, if it weren't for the body huddled on the floor in front of the TV.

I inch closer and behold a woman: face coated in a slick film of tears, hair sticking feverishly to her cheeks. Suddenly, she looks up at me: eyes of maple, a syrupy color, cleaved by slivers of honey—a stark contrast to her dark hair.

They are eyes I recognize.

Rion's eyes.

Only these are empty and cold and utterly devoid.

The woman writhes, bare legs stretched awkwardly over the warped surface of the house's wooden floor. She isn't wearing anything but a large, ripped shirt—exposing parts of herself she wouldn't in an ordinary mindset.

Parts which reveal how truly emaciated she is.

Again, she looks up—but she isn't looking at me. No, she's not looking *outside,* she's looking *inside.* The sight of it causes my blood to freeze. I feel my eyes burn—are they my eyes?—against the threat of unspent tears.

"Get the gun," somebody says—a voice unfamiliar, gritty and pitched like the crunch of gravel underfoot. Floorboards whine under heavy, staggering footsteps.

"I can't." My voice is Rion's—my eyes are his too.

"You pathetic fucking coward." Rion's father shuffles into view with bloodshot eyes, a shirt sullied with blooming ripples of sweat stains and dirt splotches. "Worthless. Never contributed a goddamn thi—"

Rion's fist slams into a wall, denting it. "I won't kill her!"

"You just gonna leave her?" Rion's father huffs, then spits a glob of tobacco at his feet before thrusting a gun into his son's hands with a cruel grunt. "She ain't your momma anymore, boy."

As though on cue, the woman shrieks, her vocal cords raw and scratchy, exhibiting the signature voice of a Mute: filled up with phlegm, crackling.

Rion's fist uncurls to reluctantly accept the gun.

I—*he*—begins feeling very ill. Because his father isn't right about many things, but he's undeniably right about this: she isn't a mother, or a wife, or anything anymore—she's a Mute.

And she's suffering.

The cold sting of steel melts in Rion's palm. He flips the gun over, examining it more closely, and I see his wrists have yet to be scarred; they are perfect and soft and ordinary, save for a strip of letters tattooed across the stretch of his wrists.

Not letters. *Numbers.*

A string of roman numerals breathing new meaning to the code Rion's always saying in his sleep.

Twelve. Seven. Four. Thirteen. Twenty one.

Pilot.

I glance at Rion's father, and a shockwave of understanding rolls into place. *He was never a pilot—or a good father, or a brave, strong, admirable man. Rion had only wished he'd been—wished all along he'd had a father worth remembering.*

Rion glowers at the gun in his hand, knowing it is the only thing standing between a world with his mother and a world without her—and it's his choice to make.

"You do it," Rion barks.

"You're a soldier now, aren't you?" His father sniffs, glaring though envious eyes. "You're a big-timer, now! An important soldier—who's afraid of shooting a gun?"

"At my mother?" Rion growls. "You're goddamn right."

"I told you, she ain't your—"

"Leave."

"This is *my* house, and you can't tell me—"

"LEAVE." Rion raises the gun, aiming slightly to the right of the man's broad sternum. Right at his heart. "I'll kill you first if you don't get the hell out."

"You wouldn't," his father scoffs, though he doesn't sound very convinced. "I—I know I've got my own set of problems, like everybody else, but you—my *son*—wouldn't *kill me.*"

Rion breathes heavily, staring unyieldingly at his father with the gun still aimed, tears shaking free. "Leave. It's what you're best at, isn't it?"

"Rion—"

"Just like you left when Lindall—" Rion stops, choking on the fury buoying inside, and cocks the gun threateningly. "You've got ten seconds, Dad."

Noticing a half-empty jug of whiskey left precariously in the cleft of couch cushions, Rion adds, "But don't forget that. You wouldn't get far without it."

Rion's father, for the first time, looks truly miserable—as though he wants more than anything than to prove his son wrong and leave the alcohol behind.

But just can't.

The large man plows shamelessly forward, snatching the jug of cheap whiskey, all the while staring daggers at his son.

Before taking another step, he uncaps the bottle and lifts it to his lips, drinking deeply like a suckling pig. Sweat sparkles on the plane of his tanned forehead, pooling into the tributary-like wrinkles wreathing his pained eyes. If it weren't for his drunken condition, for the insult of time and terror, he would've been a handsome man . . .

When he's finished, he throws the jug at the wall.

It shatters. The smell of whiskey is rife.

Then, after inhaling deeply, he expels a shout so powerful it shakes the house's foundation. "My baby is *dead*. My little girl is dead and rotting—buried cold in the yard—and it's *your* fault, you self-righteous little prick!"

The man lunges for Rion, large and drunk and capable of inflicting an astounding degree of harm, like a bull charging at a red cloak—but is arrested mid-stride when Rion puts the gun against his own temple.

And rests it there, tempted—*so tempted*—to fire.

Rion's father gasps fearfully, sobered by the prospect of not only losing his daughter and now his wife, but also his son. His oldest child and only boy. It seems to dawn on the man's face that this plague obviously hasn't affected him, alone—that it's taken its toll on everybody.

Rion, especially, despite his being so stoic about it.

"I had to," Rion snarls, tether cut. "I had to kill her, because she was infected by the A-42 and she was suffering. You think that for even a second I've forgotten?"

Rion's grip on the trigger strengthens. "I'd *love* to," he says so wholly genuinely, I find myself fearing he'll kill himself right here and now—even though I know he doesn't.

He'll try later. But he won't succeed.

"Mom was distraught," he adds, spitting. "You were *drunk*."

"You're right—"

"You didn't even see it happen!" Rion is sobbing now, his eyes burning and fierce. "You didn't see her screaming—or how she dug out her—"

"I *know!*" his father yells breathlessly. "I *know*. I know what it looks like, and I'm a coward for not facing it—for not being strong enough to face it for—"

"It's too late."

"I know it is, but—"

"Leave." Rion breathes, pained. "I am begging you to go."

"Begging me, eh?" Rion's father sighs heavily, unable to stop himself from looking at the kitchen, where he's likely stashed as much alcohol as possible.

If he goes, he'll be leaving the rest of the liquor too.

But perhaps, after the discussion he's just had, he's eager to earn himself a shred of respect—because he does go, teetering on his feet as he leaves, exiting through a kitchen swarming with flies and bypassing the alcohol altogether.

Adhering to his son's request.

On the floor, a disgusting sucking sound squelches as eyes are dislodged from their sockets, blood and fluid spilling all over the wooden floor. The woman slips in her own mess, lifting her face blindly to the ceiling and crying.

Rion goes to her, dropping fast to his knees. "No, no," he says softly, whispering. "No, Mom ... *stop.*"

He takes her bloody fingers, holding them in his own. Her touch leaves a sticky film behind—a *handprint,* of sorts, which he can't imagine washing off.

And now, as she lies eyeless in his lap, he realizes in full the necessity of killing her—now, or later, or *never.* But she's gone no matter what he chooses.

Rion presses the gun against his mother's sweaty temple but can't pull the trigger. She writhes, resisting his hold. He kisses her forehead, breathing in her scent, trying to remember the sound of her voice, her laugh, the things she'd say.

Trying to memorize the feel of her alive, tucked in his arms, with his chin on her crown, resting. The feel of her breathing and moving and thinking—or is she?

Does she know what's going on right now?

Or is she oblivious? Soulless? Lost?

Is he ... alone?

When she grips his arm with a strength a body as fragile as hers couldn't possibly possess naturally, he realizes it's time to do his mother a favor.

A favor, he tells himself, yet again. *The same favor he gave his little sister, Lindall. The same favor he'd want to be given if the roles were ever reversed.*

The favor, I hear him say, distantly. *The favor of dignity.*

He pulls the trigger.

The woman's head snaps sideways. She falls, collapsing into a brittle, lifeless heap in his lap. Her brains and blood and bodily fluids leak out of the hole he's put in her skull, seeping into the fabric of his clothes as he sits—motionless and empty.

And he doesn't leave. He'd always thought, somehow, that when somebody died, maybe you could feel the weight of their soul leave its body.

But he doesn't feel anything.

And he didn't feel anything with Lindall, either.

It doesn't matter, though—not now, not to him, and most certainly not when there's a way for him to stop waiting to feel something that isn't there.

When he can stop feeling altogether and end it now.

For the second time, he lifts the gun to his forehead—but now he pulls the trigger without fear or hesitation, relishing the sensation of finally—*finally*—finding the nerve.

Except it clicks. Empty.

His father only loaded a single bullet.

Shifting his mother's lifeless body, he extracts a dagger he's kept in his pocket—one he got from the military—and eyes the soft flesh of his wrists and forearms. The veins, blue and bulging under his skin, full of a life he wishes wasn't there.

He rests his mother's head in his lap, blinking away tears as he brushes her dark hair out of her mutilated face—trying in vain to keep her looking nice, lovely, like she used to when she was alive and laughing, happy.

He knows, with a startling degree of calm, that he won't be leaving the place he is now, beside her. Perhaps his father will return eventually, and he'll realize fast what became of his family in his absence—what he's done, what he's responsible for.

But this isn't about vengeance.

It's about *sleeping*—after a long and nightmarish day.

And so, before taking the blade to himself, Rion holds the body of his mother against his chest. "Don't worry, Mom," he whispers. "I'm right behind you."

25

WHEN MY EYES REOPEN, it's to Rion.

A tent cast in the orange haze of firelight—a forest and a campsite and a disaster. *I've just Scried him. I've just invaded his private thoughts; I've violated his trust, looked into the darkest void of his memories and shone a light on it.*

"I'm so—I didn't mean—I'm so *sorry*," I gasp.

"Stop. It's okay," he breathes, but there's a ribbon of sweat at his temples and a dazed look in his eyes, and I know despite what he says, it isn't *okay.*

I've just revived his worst nightmare.

No, even worse: *I've forced him to relieve it.*

Rion shakes his head, scoffing as he subconsciously grabs at the military tags dangling on his chest.

"Thank you," he says, to my disbelief. "I was just starting to forget how much of an asshole—"

"Rion," I whisper, feeling my face blanch ghostly pale.

"No—really, it's okay." This time, he says it while looking at the scars running over the path of his wrists, his whole demeanor shifting and straining—like thunderclouds pulling apart only to collide together again in a purple sky.

"You're the pilot," I say, jaw suddenly tight. Rion nods, his chest rising and falling with breath. There's something stirring in those maple eyes—something I don't like.

A look similar to . . . *sinking.*

"Don't you dare." I suddenly have the urge to slap the look right off his beautiful face. I've got his chin pinched in my palm, forcing his gaze onto my own, holding it steady.

"Don't I dare what?" he asks, a challenge.

"They would thank you . . . if they were alive, if they were in front of you right now, they would *thank you.*" I feel my grip on his chin tighten, our eyes locked, a fierce and wordless exchange taking place between us.

"They aren't in front of me, though, are they?" he says with a sudden pull, freeing himself. "And they never will be—never again, because of me."

"Stop being so obtuse." I scoff, abhorred by the absurdity of the guilt weighing on his shoulders. "They were sick. They had the plague. You knew they weren't getting better—that's why you did what you did—so why are you still punishing yourself?"

"I only did what I did because I thought I'd follow them to wherever it is they went." He rakes a hand through the thicket of his dark hair. "My dad died that day, too. He came back, found me half-dead from blood loss. Tried driving me to the hospital and wrecked the truck."

I feel an icy, rippling sensation fold over my shoulders.

My first vision—*memory*—of Rion's was of a car folded like an accordion, wrecked against the stretch of a rock-wall along the highway taking them from Kipling, Colorado.

Rion's father was drunk.

And now, he's left carrying the guilt of having something to do with every death in his family—though ludicrous, though far from his culpability, logic hardly matters.

"How long ago was that?" I ask through a tight throat.

"Two years." He pulls his hoodie back on, redressing so quickly I wonder if I've imagined everything before. "Mabel was a part of a quarantine near Kipling. There was a breakout that flipped almost everybody there, so we came here together, and—"

Shouting. Loud and angry.

Rion sits straight, listening carefully, his hand held out in a way that says *Don't move, let me investigate.*

Except he must be a fool if he thinks I'll actually adhere to such a primordial suggestion. So naturally, right behind him as he exits the tent, I follow.

We find a very drunk Jac thrusting the knife Rion gave him into the glow of red coals, his shoulder exposed. *Ready.*

Cyb jogs up. "He's going to try cauterizing it on his own!"

Rion doesn't cast her another glance, answering by way of trudging off in Jac's direction. Cyb looks at me suspiciously, with her pink lips coiled in a perfect smirk. "Where've *you* been all this time, anyway?"

I feel so upset—so *angry* with myself—it's hard not to rage.

"I accidentally Scried him," I confess, eyes glued to his back as he argues with Jac. "It was bad—I wish I didn't—it's all my fault, ruining the whole—"

"Apollo told me," Cyb says, quickly interjecting before I get too carried away with myself, "there's a way to *block* somebody trying to Scry you—it's dangerous, but it's possible."

Cyb grabs my shoulder, squeezing. "Rion shared that part of his past with you for a reason. If he really didn't want to, then he wouldn't have, Eos."

I swallow dryly, struggling to believe her—but even if she's only telling me this to make me feel better, at least she's doing that instead of staying angry at me.

"I'm sorry," I confess. "For not being there when Lios—"

"Forget about it." I feel her grip tighten on my shoulder in an affectionate way, our attention turning in tandem to the scene taking place before us.

By the coals, the boys argue. Apollo is trying to put distance between Rion and Jac, who are getting so fired up I'm afraid they might actually get into a fight.

"I don't need *you*," Jac slurs blearily, his shirt ripped down the center to expose his pale, injured shoulder—smudged with streaks of blood, nearly black in the night. He takes the bottle of whiskey in hand and douses it liberally over his wound, cringing as it's cleansed of bacteria.

Jac swirls out of Rion's reach—but only because Apollo's holding Rion back—and clumsily grabs the dagger he's stowed in the coals, now glowing red.

Leaning back against a boulder, Jac readies himself to press the blade against his shoulder—and hesitates. Nostrils flared and face white, he glares angrily at the dagger, as though he's waiting for it to act on its own accord.

Rion shoves Apollo—*hard*—and passes him, ripping the knife effortlessly out of Jac's hand. He clamps a fist around his friend's throat, pinning him against the boulder, and thrusts the glowing strip of metal against the bullet wound.

Jac screams viscerally, his body writhing and bucking.

Rion doesn't relent for a second, turning Jac around so he's facing the boulder. The exit wound is somehow messier—the hole a row of jagged, pulpy flesh. Rion presses the knife against it in a swift motion, as though he's rehearsed this.

Lift, press. Lift, press. Lift, press.

Rion stops only when the hole is sealed completely, leaving abruptly to gather dressing supplies. Jac sways, sobbing openly, ropes of snot and saliva flying in webs caught in the breeze of his labored breathing.

Merope gets up, brushing past me. "I can't watch this."

Cyb looks after her, alarmed. "I'm going with her—you stay with the boys," she says before taking off after Merope, dipping into the forest's veil of darkness.

Rion tosses Apollo the clean dressing—leaving that task for somebody else, apparently—and collapses by the fire. He still has the dagger, folding it over in his hands.

Hands that are shaking.

"You did well," Apollo whispers to Jac upon finishing his job of bandaging the wound, but Jac shrugs him off, still crying and feverish, walking to the edge of camp.

He turns to face us. "I'll be back."

"Don't go far," I croak, though I don't know why he'd ever care enough to listen to me—let alone obey my orders.

"I'll go after him," Apollo says before Rion can move to get up and follow. "Merope and Cyb left in the same direction. Best to round them all up at once, I guess?"

Rion shrugs, unwilling to speak, eyes trained exclusively on the dying flames of the fire. Apollo trudges off, his every step emphasized by the crunch of ice and snow, eventually leaving us in forced company.

The silence between us rings. I find myself at a loss.

What is there to say? To a person like Rion, who's been through so much? Who is both too empty and too full? Who's steeled armor has grown so tight over his skin, I'm not even sure what I'd find if I made my way beneath it?

I get up and begin traipsing off—putting a stale, wintery chill between the pair of us—only to rethink it immediately and turn to see him looking back at me, a question poised in his eyes that's as shrill as a bell crying against silence.

I don't look away. Eyes on him—unafraid to linger, to lean against the embrace of his scrutiny and find the miracle of solace, in a post-apocalyptic world, awaiting me there.

My hands fold into fists, and I turn back. Because he isn't the only one with armor as thick as a slab of asphalt, nor is he the only one with baggage. *I won't walk away from him just because I can't find the right words to say—this isn't about me, anyway.*

I sit beside him, the dying light of the fire glowing in the mirrored reflection of our eyes. The question bubbles up on my lips involuntarily. "What are you so afraid of, Rion?"

At first, he doesn't reply, stoking the fire back to life with the thick dagger in his hands. "For a long time," he says, after a stretched pause, "I felt I'd lost everything—and when you've lost everything, is there anything left to fear?"

I hold his gaze, staying quiet.

He sets a lip between his teeth and grimaces. "It might've been easier, if it had stayed like that—if the world only took away and didn't spontaneously give back."

"I know," I breathe, thinking about how I've lost the life I had aboard the Ora and everybody on it and my life's Purpose all at once—and yet I haven't come away empty handed.

I've come away with Jac and Silas—with Mia, even.

I've come away with Rion.

"When you've lost everything, life gives you more to lose."

Rion nods cynically—then, so fast I barely keep up, he grabs my sleeve and pulls me to a standing position, forcing me to take the knife he's been holding.

"There's something I've got to tell you," he says fiercely, his eyes unyielding. "There isn't time to explain—you're just going to have to listen to me. You've got to run."

"Rion," I say, voice pitched in warning.

"I became a pilot because I wanted to help. I didn't realize it wasn't actually a military camp, but—"

He freezes and I do the same, as a bolt of neon-green light cleaves the sky into halves: a neon-green light I recognize with such brutal familiarity, I can't help but smile.

And then I remember to be afraid.

"Was that a—"

"—podcraft," I say, glaring at the streak of green following in its wake, a sparkling trail. Rion takes my shoulders and pilots me deeper into the cover of the forest.

"If they're here, Eos, then we're already out of time."

"I'm not going *anywhere*," I seethe, whirling on him.

"Eos," he says, tone taking on an edge of severity that roots me icily to the spot. "Whatever you do, don't let Mabel take you to the other leagues staying at PIO Morse. Actually, get as far away from it as you possibly can."

"Why?"

He exhales, eyeing the sky. There's an edge to his demeanor as he rakes a hand through the copse of his dark hair, jaw tight against words unspoken. I wonder what he's thinking . . . why he looks like he's about to do something dangerous . . .

"I won't let them take you," he whispers.

Suddenly a horn blares, lancing through the night's syrupy quiet like the slice of a knife. A *horn*, belonging to what sounds disturbingly like—

"A car," Rion breathes, resting a hand against the small of my back as we run together toward the sound. "It's coming from the same direction Apollo went."

Abandoning camp, we sprint along the hem of the clearing over the lake and toward a bulbous hill—where a dirt road loops back to the highway, a gray ribbon of concrete carving through the landscape.

We dig our hands into the cliff, snagging rocks and fingers burning against ice as the horn continues to sound repetitively—a lifeline to which we cling. I heave over the lip of the road first and extend a hand to Rion, helping him up.

The first thing we see is a spate of familiar faces. Our whole group is here, including Cyb, Apollo, Jac and Merope, as well as the people in the car.

Mia and Silas, their faces lit up intensely.

And in the back seat—

"LIOS!" I cry, voice breaking as he throws open the back door of the geriatric sedan and gets out.

"My little Eos," he says, wrapping me up in arms that aren't quite as strong as they used to be. Though he's pale, with a layer of bandages still thick under his clothes, the sparkle of his light eyes has returned in full.

And perhaps, with a vengeance.

He administers hugs, getting to Cyb last. He falls into her arms and stays there for a while without moving. Cyb cries and whispers in his ears until he eventually breaks away and kisses her full on the lips, despite all of us watching.

"They're coming," Mia says as we pile into the car, the soft fabric of the seats a balm after nights in the forest. "Lios knows everything—we filled him in."

Ignoring this, Jac glares across Silas and at Mia, who's the one driving. "What do you mean, they're coming?"

A beat of silence ensues. The crackle of gravel under tires and a light murmuring of a radio fills up the empty stretch of time as Silas and Mia regard each other wordlessly.

"Mia?" Rion barks, voice pitched low.

"Every quarantine we have alliances with—the ones we get medical supplies from, mainly—flipped at the same time, on the same night, just days ago."

"We're isolated," Silas divulges. "No allies. And with every member flipped into a Mute, we're fighting off pushbacks on a daily basis—and tonight, didn't you see the green light?"

Silas looks at us ominously. "We're the last quarantine on our side of Colorado. By infecting the other quarantines with the plague, they've cut off our resources and all our allies, and there's nothing left stopping them."

"Where's Mabel?" Rion asks.

"Going down with the ship." Silas scoffs angrily, righting himself in his seat. "She says PIO Morse is secure—she's got an insider there capable of taking over if necessary."

Rion shifts, orienting himself. "Where are we going?"

Nobody speaks.

Without another word, he tries ripping the car door open to free himself—an effort that provokes a chorus of disapproving shouts and protests—but we're locked in, not only by the doors but by the windows, which also won't open.

Rion slams a fist viciously against the window. "You don't know what you're doing, Silas!"

"What is wrong with you?" Apollo tentatively asks, gripping

the arm rest like his life depends on it. "The military base is the safest place for us to go!"

The military base . . .

We aren't going back to the quarantine?

"It's not," Rion raves, punching the window again. "We're safest somewhere remote—not the quarantine, or the safehouse, and *especially* not the military base."

"Where, then?"

"Just outside of Kipling, there's a house with a cellar—"

"You're nuts," Jac declares. "The military base has an army ready to fight for our lives—an army with special abilities that might stand a chance against the Borealians." He eyes Cyb, Lios, and Merope. "We're safest around the specimens, aren't we?"

I feel my skin prickle, realizing he didn't meet my eyes.

Intentionally.

I look frantically at Rion—who's more afraid than I've ever seen him before—and make my decision: I rip the revolver out of my waistband and fire it directly at the window, blasting a hole right through its center.

The glass is a web of fissures. Rion lifts a fist, ready to break us out of the car, when we both hear the click of a cocked gun aimed at the space between my eyes.

Jac's chin wobbles, face still pale. "Sorry," he says, less to me and more to Rion, who looks like he's ready to murder. "But we think they're coming for her."

"You didn't—" Lios stops, frazzled. "You didn't say we were giving her over to them!"

Apollo grips Lios's shoulder, agreeing. "If we give Eos back to the Borealians, they win this war," he says with an icy severity that pools in my core. "They will use her as a weapon, and it'll all be over for us, I can promise you that."

Rion inches closer, glaring daggers at Jac. "No matter where she goes, she's a weapon."

Daringly, he pushes the gun down.

Jac swallows hard, throat bobbing, and lets it fall.

"Smart choice," Cyb snarls in Jac's ear, sheathing a knife she'd quietly extracted from her jacket. "I was just about to rake my dagger across your throat."

"We can't forget we're on the same side." Apollo begs for calm with his palms raised. "We aren't turning anybody in, but we also aren't—"

Our car lurches, stopping so abruptly, we're thrown forward in our seats. Shrieking explodes as the Muted flood out of the forest and haphazardly on the dirt road—so thick we can't drive anywhere, stuck.

It isn't long before a Mute smartly discovers the hole in the window I've just shot, peeling back the jagged edges, trying to rip it open and showering Rion and me in shards of glass.

"See what I mean about the pushbacks?" Silas yells over the swelling chaos, just as a Mute blunders through the open window beside Rion, snapping its jaw wildly.

Without thinking, Rion punches it in the face. The beast reels backward, returning a second later.

But I'm ready.

I launch myself into Rion's lap, wielding the dagger he gave me earlier, and stake it into the Mute's skull. It wilts, dragging itself off the blade of my knife, dying just in time for another to quickly take its place.

"Hive mind," Apollo shouts, panicking. "Drive, Mia!"

"But what if they get—"

"DRIVE," everybody yells at once, shrinking away from an influx of the Muted digging their way through the window. Mia puts a foot to the accelerator and we fly.

Our car plows through a cloud of the Muted, killing several in the process before hive mind catches on and they skitter away from the headlights.

We find the highway at last—only to trip into sprawling tide of the Muted so immense it renders us all speechless.

Every inch of ground is packed with the Muted, as though the whole city has flipped at once. The moonlight falls in shafts, exposing their eyeless faces in brutal clarity, all turning to look up in an orchestrated stare.

I feel like I'm going to be sick. Thousands, if not more, are now licking their bloody maws, ready to dig their gummy fingers through our aluminum car doors to get to us, if they must.

They are coming.

Merope wilts, swearing through raspy coughs. "We've got to get out of here, *now*."

But we quickly discover we're too late. We've stumbled into the heart of their nest. Every inch of our car is hugged by the body of a Mute, thudding violently against it.

The window shatters—a burst of glass, which Rion's quick to shield me from. Everybody screams. The Muted reach in, raking fingers over his clothes, tugging at him first.

I cling tightly to him, firing every round of my pistol at the tempest of the Muted trying to infiltrate our car. Lios surges forth to provide backup, as does Apollo. Mia kicks the gas pedal, propelling us forth in a final effort to escape—only for us to crash so violently into a group of the Muted, they break through the windshield.

And I know we're done. We're finished.

This is the end.

The Muted pour into our car—fingernails scraping, jaws set wide and snapping—and there's nothing we can do to stop them from engulfing us, tearing us to shreds.

I think of the campsite littered with Skim corpses: ribcages ripped halfway open, hearts missing; skulls cracked and brains slurped up—*gone.*

That will be all that's left of us.

Rion grabs me, dragging me as far from the open window as we can get. I stay tucked in his arm, our hearts hammering in a furious rhythm, singing together.

And I look for my power, but it isn't there.

Whatever it was the Haunt gave me, I don't have any left.

Mia screams shrilly. Merope and Cyb cling to Lios, who's trying ferociously to protect them—his eyes locked protectively on mine, relieved to see Rion at my side.

A loud crash.

I coil against Rion's chest with my eyes closed.

And then, I hear the enfilade of rapid gunfire gunning down the Muted surrounding us. The Muted fall back, either dying or scared off, providing a temporary reprieve.

Cyb whispers, "Who's out there?"

We get up and look outside, spotting a group of people who strike me as *not belonging.*

They're clean, for one thing. Their heads are shaved almost down to their scalps, girls included, and their eyes are uniformly the color of gemstones, vivid and conspicuously inhuman, with tattoos cupped around them.

Tattooed spots, black and visible, forming a constellation.

Cassiopeia.

They fall back—obeying orders—and a familiar figure slides into view, replacing them. The figure is slender, a silhouette in the moonlight, that I recognize at once.

"Specimens," Pavo booms, his eyes like slivered windows looking out into the depths of space, "I believe it's time for your league to return to our ship."

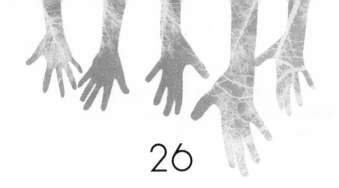

26

PAVO RAISES A HAND, palm facing us.

I feel Rion shift uncomfortably. The others begin thrashing in their seats: Mia, Silas, and Jac lose their breath, casting each other panicked glances.

"What's wrong?" I snap, addressing Rion, who looks as if he's entranced, in the throes of a nightmare: jaw gritted, a band of sweat around his temples, groaning.

Apollo kicks open a door, climbing out of the car. When he speaks, his voice is laced with boredom. "You've decided to blow our cover *why*, Pavo?"

"Well apparently, Apollo, if you want something done right, you better go about doing it yourself." Pavo keeps his palm raised casually in the direction of the car. "Your league is being relieved of its Purpose."

Apollo sucks a bleeding finger. "Why?"

"It's a Purpose we should've given to the Elite." Pavo's lips spread apart, revealing yellow teeth. He nods at the group ringing the perimeter—keeping the Muted at bay. "It just so turns out there's more at stake than I realized."

Pavo's almond eyes click over to mine.

Noticing as much, Apollo intervenes. "We are *days* from

311

getting Mabel Faye into our custody! You can't order us to pull out now that we've gotten—"

Mia screams, a noise as jarring as a chainsaw.

At the same time, Rion breathes heavily, pushing his palms in his eyes like he's trying to quell a fierce headache. In the front seat beside Mia, Silas leans sideways, vomiting a spew of blood.

Okay, that's it.

I'm getting out of the car.

"Eos, no!" Merope gasps, clinging to my sleeve. Her face is still chalk-white in the Muted's presence. "Let Apollo chip away at him first, we'll follow his lead!"

I ignore her and climb through the broken window. The air is crisp and wispy, the horizon edged by a smear of pale sea-green as yet another dawn rises.

"I'd appreciate it if you'd stop killing the very people who will give us access to our target," I seethe, playing along. Apollo nods encouragingly. "You're not ending this until they've taken us to their secret headquarters, *sir.*"

At this, Pavo falters. "Secret headquarters?"

I lower my voice, pretending it's an act of discretion while the others are listening. "Why do you think we're out here—at the break of dawn—in the middle of nowhere?"

Pavo's lips raise to a smile. "Lovely," he concedes. "We'll go there together." But he doesn't lift whatever mysterious power he has over the others, keeping his palm held high.

Noticing my concern, he says, "We'll only need *one* of them to show us the way, correct?"

I hear Mia sigh in relief—being the driver, of course he's going to keep her and kill Silas, Jac and Rion.

"Where's Onyx?" Lios growls, getting out of the car along

with both Cyb and Merope in his wake. "I'd prefer my Purpose to be revoked by my own mentor."

Pavo laughs dryly, flicking his wrist. At once, Silas shrieks in agony, clawing his way out of the car, as though propelled by an invisible force.

"Onyx won't be joining us," Pavo divulges nefariously.

"And why not?" Cyb inquires, lips stiff. "Why would she not be here, as we're *her* league?"

Silas falls to his knees, coughing up blood; the sight lights a blaze of panic in my veins. *What is Pavo doing? As a Borealian, he has multiple skillset abilities, but why kill somebody this way, this slowly and cruelly?*

Pavo steps closer, resting his palm flush against the crown of sandy hair atop Silas's head. The second they touch, Silas looses a breathy cry, losing himself to hysteria: *eyes jaundiced, saliva rolling in beads down his chin, vomiting up blood . . .*

The car doors snap open—Jac and Rion fall out.

Are they next?

Apollo sweats profusely, clearing his throat—his voice still kept light, feigning a general disinterest. "Are you not capable of killing him faster, Pavo?"

"Oh!" Pavo says, delighted to be asked. "My contacts told me your league had learned he truth—the truth about us, about why the apocalypse actually began?"

My league freezes collectively, watching Pavo drop his hand from Silas's head. "Surely you know I'm not killing the boy, but infecting him?"

Just as he says so, I realize Pavo's skin is glowing.

"Infecting?" Merope asks, abhorred.

"I use that term because it's all you know." Pavo tightens a cloak he's got on, chilly. "You aren't yet familiar with the actual terms of my Borealian skillset abilities."

"Abilities?" Cyb asks, playing dumb. "Multiple?"

"Interesting you should inquire about my skillsets over the lineage to which I've just referenced." Pavo's brows raise. "Aren't any of you curious as to what a Borealian is?"

"Your contacts are right." Apollo's face is white—with fear, or anger, or a surge of absolute hatred, I can't tell. "They know as much as I do, Pavo."

"Not everything, then—not why I'm here with the Elite, or why we want Mabel Faye so badly, or why my kind has ventured to this blasted planet in the first place."

Pavo grips Silas's hair, forcing his face up. "And certainly you don't know what I'm doing right now—why the touch of my hand is capable of *this*."

In a flash, I see a glow slip out of Silas's body, filtering up through Pavo's touch, pooling into his chest. A shriek rakes its way out of Silas's lungs, exploding into the quiet night.

The shriek of a Mute.

Silas falls forward, drained of color, and begins digging out his eyes with his fingernails—a feverish clawing that makes my stomach ache, my head spin, and sends my thoughts careening out of control in my mind.

Mia falls out of the car, carrying a gun. "No," she breathes at the sight of Silas. "No, no, no!"

Palm raised yet again, Pavo takes the gun from her custody and claims it as his own. It floats in the air, gliding like a kite from her small hands and into his—a simper elevating his lips as he watches, *amused*, by Mia's anguish.

Pavo's flesh glows brighter than ever, fueled by Silas's . . .

Fueled by Silas's . . . what?

Mia expels a scream, running furiously for Pavo. He raises a hooked finger up high, cutting it through the air like a weapon. Mia falls to her knees, eviscerated from the hilt of her pelvis to the dip of her sternum—guts tumbling out in ropes of steaming red, which she gathers feverishly in her arms before falling over.

Pavo uses the gun he's taken from Mia, shooting a bullet cleanly through Silas's skull, who folds over himself and collapses beside a barely-alive Mia in the snow.

In the car, Jac and Rion writhe in agony, and I feel myself starting to lose touch. Dizzy, feeling ill, I lean against a tree for support as I throw up.

Apollo asks, abrasively, "How is any of this necessary?"

Pavo doesn't reply, glaring meaningfully at Mia and Silas in the snow, lying prostrate together. Losing his patience, Apollo gets in the face of our leader.

"What kind of show are you putting on, Pavo?"

"The *show* has ended, Apollo. What you're seeing now is a cold truth you've been denied—but never fear, I've come to tell you everything."

Tightening his cloak again, Pavo goes on. "I've got my own set of spies here. My sister has been working against our kind for the better half of our stay, and until recently, it always felt like a child's effort to thwart a parent—futile, *vain*."

Pavo faces me. "That is, until I discovered that Eos wasn't defective the way her mentor repeatedly declared, but rather a very special specimen in possession of a very special skillset.

"Which is, of course, why I'm here: no longer is my sister waging a futile war. With Eos's skillset ability, she's turned what was once a game into a real threat." I feel the tug of an invisible force pull me closer, resisting a fruitless attempt. "But if I have her daughter on my side?"

Before I can get a word in edgewise, Pavo's pulled me so close to his face, we're sharing breath. "Europa lineage is one of the oldest Borealian lines alive—and the only one that's capable of producing a Scrying specimen."

"*Onyx*," he seethes, shaking his head. "So dedicated to the cause she made for herself, she contributed her own DNA to the creation of a soldier that would pose a legitimate threat—to a soldier who would always take her side, due to sentimentality."

"That's not why I'm on her side," I snarl viciously, glaring at those big, slivered eyes.

Pavo grabs my throat—a gesture met by fierce retaliation by my league, all of whom leap into action. But with a swift raise of his other hand, they all drop.

Everybody lies limp, eyes blinking and aware, but paralyzed in every other way. Everybody except Apollo—who holds that strange, genetic anomaly granting him immunity.

Pavo's voice is cut like glass. "I am going to kill every person in your league, as well as the natives you've befriended, right now, in front of your eyes."

I struggle against his hold, flailing. "Why, Pavo?"

"Because you'll hate it," he says simply.

"Let them go, or I'll—"

"You've got the ability to stop this, Eos. Onyx will come to her senses if you're on my side, and if she does, she will cut all ties with the PIO Morse agenda."

Pavo's eyes, for once, take on a genuinely fearful gleam.

I realize this isn't about the war, or about moral and ethical repugnance of the Borealian race—but about a brother who loves his sister so much, he'd be willing to forgive and forget all she's done to thwart the Project he's required to defend.

If I don't end this, Onyx will die.

He'll have to terminate her.

"Tell me why you're here," I say, buying time. "I don't want a war either, Pavo. Tell me the truth about the Borealians, and I'll agree to take your side, to go with you."

I see the eyes of my league widen with disbelief and fear.

Apollo stares, horrified.

I'm lying, you fools, I want to say, but can't.

Again, I face Pavo, adopting what is hopefully a look that is convincingly genuine. "Why are we here, Pavo?"

We.

Pavo nods subtly—skin aglow, but waxy and taut. "We, the race of the Borealians, are here because we cannot benefit from the ingestion of physical sustenance."

"You can't eat?"

"Our civilization has always fed on solar energy."

"Energy?"

"When our sun—*Rho,* in *Coronae Borealis*—began to show signs of starting to supernova, our race faced extinction. But we knew of solar twins, which produced the same degree of energy we needed to ingest to survive.

"Earth's sun was the closest. But upon our arrival, we found energy far superior to the sun's in terms of sustenance. This new, foreign energy provided us with abilities and powers which we never could've fathomed.

"All Borealians have *Source*—a single skillset which, so long as it's fueled, can produce a vast multitude of abilities. Feeding off the energy found on Earth fueled our skillsets, extending our life spans, enhancing our quality of existence . . .

"But there was a problem," he adds at last. "The energy we discovered thirty years ago is rare and finite—which we weren't aware of, at first."

He pauses, then, addresses me. "Do you know, Eos, what energy we're talking about?"

My mind leaps yet again to Nova, her final words about her ability to see auras—*soul energy*—in everybody except the few who were our mentors, and everything falls together.

My voice is a croak. "Human souls."

"The more we fed, the more Mutes were born. They were a side effect we didn't expect—a side effect which began killing off the very populace we required to survive. Who knew that a soul's energy was finite? Who knew we weren't killing people, but leaving them soulless, bloodthirsty husks of who they once were?

"That is why we created specimens—hybrids whose human genetics prevented them from feeding on energy, and thus didn't endanger the people in close proximity to them." Pavo arches a brow cleverly, wetting his lips. "But they also required abilities to give them an upper hand against the soulless monsters they were created to destroy."

"My ability to Scry—does that mean I feed off people?"

"No," Pavo discounts straightway. "Not unless you harvest their energy intentionally, no."

"And if I do?"

"You'll adopt powers unfathomable," he says wickedly, and nods at Rion and Jac. "If you are truly on my side, Eos, I'm afraid you're going to have to prove it."

"You—you're asking—?"

"Take a soul," he says, gesticulating casually. "Or choose to deny my offer, take the side of my sister, and I'll kill everybody here regardless of what you do."

"Everybody," he adds suddenly, "except *you*, of course."

"That won't be necessary," I say loudly, eyeing my league before dropping to my knees beside Rion and looking at Mia, who's right beside him.

She's still alive, but barely. Her previously bronzed face is as colorless as a daisy, lips stained a pastel blue, as though she's just kissed a summertime sky.

What do I do, what do I do, what do I do . . .

Mia nods subtly, eyes gesturing at the space of her chest.

At her heart.

Take me, she says. *I'm dying anyway. Take what's left.*

I can't do that to you, Mia . . .

You have no choice.

"Hesitating isn't a sign of confidence, Eos," Pavo prompts ominously from my left—too far away to realize that Mia's still alive and breathing. "Take my side, and I'll have mercy on your comrades, erasing their memory instead of killing them."

Beside her, Rion exhales sleepily, yet pained—the way he looks when he's having a nightmare. Mia's hand finds mine and squeezes softly, encouragingly.

I nod at her. Tears sour, corrosive in my eyes, as I agree to the only option I've got to save everybody else.

Okay, Mia. You're right.

Rion's forearm is as hot as a fever. I grip it, looking over my shoulder at Pavo. "I'll take this soul."

"It's a strong one," he replies approvingly.

"I agree," I say, placing my other hand on Mia's, making sure to keep it hidden, out of sight. I feel the pull of their souls at the same time, bleeding into my palms without coercion.

But when Rion's soul surges, I push it back, letting Mia's trickle in slowly. I gain control faster than expected, staunching the flow of Rion's soul and drinking in Mia's.

I see flashes of her life before my eyes. A periwinkle horizon capped in an inky black. A harrowing cacophony of shrieking in the distance, trailing behind her, and yet she's begging to go back to where she's come from.

"No," a woman snaps—hair silver, eyes a dull gray, like an overcast morning. "They're gone, Mia!"

I realize it's spring, years ago—but not many.

They are surrounded by rich greenery, a landscape rioting with bright wildflowers and looming ponderosas coated in pale moss, their bases haloed with shoots of mushrooms.

The woman grips Mia's arm, dragging her haphazardly out of the forest and onto a highway. "They must be near," she says as she surveys the road, speaking to herself. "Why else would the whole quarantine flip overnight?"

"My parents haven't flipped!" Mia cries, trying again to rip her arm free of the woman's hold and run back. "They could be waiting for me, Mabel!"

Mabel.

The woman—who must be Mabel Faye—traipses up the stretch of the highway, refusing to relinquish Mia's arm, while keeping a close eye on the highway signs.

"Kipling," she mutters, spotting a sign hanging just a few yards away from them. "That's the meeting place—if anybody is to survive, they will find us in Kipling, Mia."

"What's that?" Mia asks, her weeping ceasing temporarily as

they turn a corner and face a recently wrecked car—its hood a series of wrinkles, folded against a rock wall.

The driver is unrecognizable, face destroyed by the impact of the crash: a bloody pulp resting against the steering wheel.

"Look—over there," Mabel says, releasing Mia to sprint to the side of the road where a boy lies inertly. "He's got a pulse but he's barely breathing."

Mia blinks away her tears. "I—I can help him."

"Your parents," Mabel says while ripping off the cleanest parts of her shirt to dress the wound. "They were doctors, were they not, Mia?"

Mia nods, gritting her teeth. I know, somehow, that she's desperate to correct Mabel: *My parents* are *doctors, Mabel—not* were *doctors. We can't know for sure that they're dead, that they've flipped with the rest of the quarantine . . .*

The memory hastens. A car skids to a stop beside them on the highway, driven by a woman with the most incredible, thick magenta hair and bright gemstone eyes.

The woman holds a fingertip to her temple.

Mabel nods appreciatively—*a gesture suggesting they not only know each other, but know each other well*—and helps gather the boy into Mia's lap, who watches him as they drive to the hospital.

They recognize the injury. They see he's military.

Mabel's lips stiffen, recognizing the boy. "Rion," she says in a voice hushed. "He's a pilot—our best."

"He's lost too much blood. I think he's going to die."

"Hold still, Mia," Mabel says, draping a hand over the girl's shoulder while eyeing the woman in the front seat; the pair has a wordless dialogue, make an agreement.

Mia's shoulder tingles. A rush of warmth, pulled from her

very core, unspools and gathers at Mabel's touch—she begins feeling herself get weaker, falling ill.

"That's enough," the driver says abruptly.

Mabel retracts her hand—a glow to her skin unnoticed if it weren't for the fact that I'm already seeking it out, already partly aware of what's taking place.

Mabel closes her eyes and exhales, resting her hand on the worst of Rion's arms. I see the color of her skin fading. The cuts begin stitching themselves back together, a miraculous sight that knocks the breath out of Mia's lungs.

Mabel's face ages—withering and wrinkled—turning to face the girl sitting beside her. "See? I knew you'd save his life."

And then, as though unplugged, the memory goes black right before my eyes and I'm yanked back to reality. My hand is clasped around Mia's, but hers is limp.

She's not holding it back.

She's dead.

A cry escapes my lips, mournful and anguished.

Mia's eyes are ringed in a fan of black lashes, her pupils big and dilated, fixed on the black sky. I notice her eyes are jaundiced slightly and a bubble of blood leaking between the edges of her two perfect lips, and wonder if she would've flipped if—

If she didn't die before she had a chance to.

Her cold hand is cupped in my own.

I can't let go.

I can't let go.

For the first time, I realize the legitimacy of Rion's guilt.

Mia was gutted by Pavo—she was dying a slow and painful death in the snow, and would've died no matter what. And yet I'm technically her cause of death.

I took her soul.

A surge of warmth pools at the base of my spine, and my skin glows golden, and I know *I've done it.*

"Well done, Eos." Pavo approaches, clapping slowly, ready to investigate Rion—who, possessed by the spell he's under, writhes in agony.

Confirming he's alive.

Pavo's nostrils flare with fury.

I feel my feet yanked off balance. I'm dragged mercilessly over the icy snow, propelled by that incredible, invisible force so often used by Pavo to control others.

When I face him, he's glaring at me in open threat.

"You've forfeited their lives," he snarls, throwing up a palm to harvest Rion and Jac's souls before my eyes, to kill my league members—everybody I love.

I feel my fingertips tingle, a power surging forth, pushing up against the underside of my skin, begging for release. *The fight isn't over yet—it's only just begun, Pavo.*

Pavo's hands raise; everybody, including my league, begins to writhe violently in unison. Merope screams. Cyb's voice is a choked cry. Tears roll down the sides of Lios's cheeks as he stares blankly at the night sky, at a slow-crawling dawn.

Jac starts vomiting blood.

Rion rolls on his side, gasping for air.

And Apollo—*Apollo.*

He stands beside Pavo, his posture a soft cower, but his eyes as sharp as a knife's edge.

"STOP," I say, yelling over the surge of cries. "You're going to stop this now, Pavo, or I swear I'll—"

Pavo raises Merope in the air, employing one of his many

skillset abilities—an arsenal he can tap in full, after having taken the souls of so many people. *Every quarantine flipped at the same time, on the same night, three days ago . . .*

That was Pavo.

He's been fueling himself for right now. For this fight.

To fight me.

I feel as though I've just tripped off the edge of a cliff—that dizzying, gravity-less corkscrew. Pavo snaps his fingers and her paralysis is lifted fully, allowing her beautiful violet eyes to regard mine with panicked clarity.

My fingers fold into fists. "RELEASE HER."

Merope writhes, trying to free herself, but her efforts only further infuriate Pavo. "You can't simply *wiggle away,* Poplar!"

"Eos," she gasps, falling limp, giving up.

Giving up.

No, no, you're not giving up. Not yet.

My fingertips burn, a surge of violent power building like the boom of thunder before it crashes. For the first time, I let it loose fully, I free it.

I beg it to make up for lost time.

Pavo's hand reaches forth, forming a strangely remote grip on my best friend's throat—choking her from afar, causing her perfect face to bloat and fade to a sickly indigo.

Merope droops—*suffocating.*

And finally, I free my power. I feel it rip through the course of my whole body like an electrical current—feel it begin as spark and swell into an explosion, which drags itself joltingly through my every fiber. I feel as though I've exploded with it.

There's a loud *crack!* and Pavo falls, neck left bent at a truly ugly angle, lying lifeless in the snow.

27

I'M LEFT STANDING, GAPING and breathless, with the sickening crunch of Pavo's every broken vertebrae still ringing through my grip the way it might if I'd snapped his neck *physically.*

With my bare hands.

The others rise slowly, coherency refining with every gasp of freezing winter air. Jac wipes blood off his chin, glaring at the residue left behind on his sleeve.

"Holy shit," he croaks, crying in full. "Holy shit, *holy shit.*"

"We've got to leave." Apollo eyes the ring of the Elite still at a distance, holding back the Muted. "While we still can, before they realize what—"

"Silas!?" Jac cries, eyes eerily transfixed. "Mia!?"

"What're you talking about?" Rion staggers forth, his hair sticking to the band of glistening sweat at his temples. "Why are you shouting their—"

Jac folds over himself, clutching his stomach as though he's about to be violently sick.

Rion reels, colliding into a tree. "What—happened?"

I feel the burn of their gaze reach my periphery, but I can't look away from Silas and Mia.

325

They were friends.

They were friends who came to save our lives.

Apollo grips my arm, dragging me up only for my knees to give away, buckling. I crash back down, slinking forward so my hands brace the ground, skidding harshly over ice.

Merope's at my side at once. "Eos," she cries, tears trailing down her dirty cheeks. "Eos, tell me you're okay!"

Okay.

The word's the antithesis of what I am, a polar opposite.

But I'm alive.

"Apollo's right—let's go while we can." My legs feel almost as though they aren't there as I stand only to stumble, ramming into the arms of a tree.

Lios ventures forth, offering an arm, which I accept.

"We aren't leaving them!" Jac decries, the sclera of his eyes so wrought with bloodshot they're barely visible. "The second we leave, the Muted will devour their—"

"We don't have a choice." Rion's voice is raw—his eyes just as webbed with bloodshot—exuding a degree of emotion he's not prone to showcasing.

I look back at Mia's body, a shell spilling innards.

We can't take her.

Jac draws the same conclusion, throat bobbing as he gulps away the influx of tears. He looks exclusively at Rion, the pair making a devastating agreement. *Leave them.*

Leave them behind for the Muted.

Leave them because we must.

Wordlessly, they head for the car. We follow, my balance restored by Lios's strong arm. Merope and Cyb drape arms over my shoulders, crying softly.

Apollo's the only one who's staying objective—and I guess, after a lifetime of brutality that began with the death of his whole family before his very eyes, it makes sense.

We pile inside the destroyed vehicle, windows like toothy mouths exhaling stale, wintery breaths.

Rion takes the wheel. "We aren't going to PIO Morse."

Apollo sits, accepting the role of copilot. "You want to go back to the quarantine?"

"Not all of us." Rion's eyes deliberately don't meet mine in the rearview mirror, despite my looking. "We're going to split up as soon as it's safe—Cyb, Merope, Lios and Eos will seek cover elsewhere, while the rest of us fight."

"Like hell," I bark.

"If they get their hands on you—"

"What am I supposed to do?" I lodge myself in the gap set between the front seats. Rion keeps his eyes on the road. "Hide in the forest until the apocalypse is over?"

"Rion's right." Apollo's black eyes find mine. "Let us fight this war for as long as we can. The last thing we need is for you to fall into their custody."

"Have all of you forgotten I just killed a Borealian?"

"You actually . . . didn't kill him." Apollo's correction is met with a stunned silence. "You only deterred him, Eos. You forget that he's soulless, a being that feeds off energy. It's going to take a lot more to truly kill a pureblood Boreal—"

My hand autonomously finds his face, striking it hard.

Apollo recoils, furious. "What the hell?"

"Why didn't you say something earlier? If I knew he wasn't actually dead, I would've—*I don't know*—tried to decapitate him or something, at least!"

Apollo rubs his cheek testily. The car moves faster, alerting the group of Elite specimens to our departure. We all wait with bated breath, expecting chaos.

But we don't get it.

The Elite fall back slowly, allowing the Muted to flood into place like the lap of high tide. From a distance, I see the bodies of our friends—mangled, a heap of meat.

But I don't see Pavo's.

"He's gone," I say breathily.

"I told you they aren't so easy to kill. I'm not even sure that decapitation would do it, Eos." Apollo yanks his eyes back to the road before us, which we slip off and into the forest. "There were times when I thought . . . Well, it's strange . . ."

"Thought what?"

"That maybe the Borealians could shapeshift."

"Are you serious?" Cyb asks.

"Mabel ingests as little energy as possible, keeping her diet strictly to solar energy—but when she's running low, you can see it in her physical appearance."

"Like, she ages?" I ask abruptly, thinking of Mia's memory.

"That's only part of it—aging." Apollo shakes his head in resignation, at a loss. I'm eager for him to explain, but we're all distracted when Rion parks the car, killing the engine.

We look at each other, confused.

Lios asks, "Where . . . are we?"

Jac pops open the car door, leaping out. "The safe-house."

I follow in Jac's wake, stepping out into the dewy daylight of a full-fledged dawn. I feel the last two days weigh at my muscles and eyelids for the first time, exhaustion and hunger rolling into the space adrenaline previously occupied.

After digging at the base of a tree, Rion eventually extracts a dirty key, which he uses to unlock a well camouflaged trapdoor under a carpet of pine needles.

The door rips open, burping a cloud of dust.

Rion's the first to go inside, treading down a flight of steps narrow and twisted, going underground.

Moments later, I see the flickering of candlelight.

The rest of us follow, single file, inside. The room below is extremely small and perfectly square. The ceiling hangs so low, the boys have to duck while walking. I see a vent wheezing cold air into the corner of the room, and a well trickling with the echo of water at the base of the stairwell.

A series of beds make up the far corner, the near corner set up with a chair and a rifle, stationed for lookout duty. Rion gets a second key, also hidden (under a mattress) which unlocks another trapdoor packed with supplies.

Apollo begins distributing water bottles. The cool water is a salve to my raw throat—to the residual burn left in my lungs after all my screaming. We uncover stale energy bars, homemade and wrapped in plastic bags. Though old, they taste great.

I collapse on a bed, staring at the ceiling. I feel the mattress compress and realize Rion's sitting at the very end, focused on reloading the rifle he's taken from the side of a chair stationed at the very bottom of the stairwell.

When he's done, he sighs, lying on his back and staring at the ceiling distantly. The others are upstairs, loading the car with more supplies for the trip back to the quarantine, leaving us temporarily alone.

Rion sits up before I can say anything. With a jacket caked in dirt and grime, he's decided to take it off, leaving it to hang in the far corner of the safe-house.

My eyes skirt the planes of his back, memorizing the dips and curves of his shoulder blades, resurrecting images of the time he was shirtless and I dared to sail my fingertips over and across the stretch of his body.

I think of how there's only one part of him that isn't corded sinew and roped muscle—that isn't masked in brutal scars, fading tattoos, dirty clothes, and messy dark hair.

His *eyes*.

Though carefully guarded and usually edged, I've seen light escape them before—a light that sought out the darkest recesses of myself and fought off the shadows.

He passes a hand through the mess of his hair, as though fighting an internal debate, warring with himself, and then—so fast I barely register—he's kissing me.

Hand cupping his chin, covered in stubble, I break away from his lips and say, "Is this your way of saying goodbye?"

"I don't believe in goodbyes."

"I don't either."

"What should we say instead?"

"Good night?" I suggest, thinking of Lios. It was easier to say good night instead of goodbye. We walk to the door, arms twined together, the warmth of his body a pulse.

Rion must remember my goodbye to Lios, too, because he rests his forehead against mine and breathes, "I'll see you in the morning, Eos."

"Get up early," I whisper.

"I will. I'll get up as early as I can."

"When dawn breaks?"

"Earlier," he says, winking. And then his body peels itself

away from my own—the space between tangible, like a rubber band that strains the farther it's stretched.

At the top of the stairs, he blends in with the others as they rally together, readying to go. Apollo and Jac say their goodbyes to me from the top of the staircase—both knowing better than to tackle me with a hug.

Then I hear an engine rumble, followed by the crackling of pine needles and rocks under tires as they drive away, heading to the heart of the war by themselves.

Leaving us here—the aliens, the *enemy*—to be safe?

Lios, Cyb, and Merope descend the stairs, locking the door over our heads. We're plunged into a dreary darkness, lit up only by the flickering of buttery candlelight.

Lios, the least exhausted of us, offers to be lookout.

Merope, Cyb, and I pile into a bed together, too tired to get under the covers. The edges of my vision blur before I've even put my head against the pillow.

When I fall asleep, I'm not troubled by a single dream.

A WHOLE WEEK PASSES.

The eighth dawn we're awoken abruptly by what feels like an earthquake; cracks split the ceiling into a puzzle, and the floor reverberates violently underfoot.

"Get out, get out!" Cyb yells, shielding her face to a spray of crumbling rocks falling from the ceiling. "Get out—it's going to cave in on us!"

I stagger, following her. Merope and Lios scale the stairs in my wake—all of us operating blindly—as I spill out of the shelter messily, slipping to my knees.

Slipping in a pool of blood.
Fresh blood.

Against a marbled silver sky, a Black Hawk helicopter spits a peppering of bullets at a podcraft—*in broad daylight*—which, in retaliation, deploys a bright green beam of light. that slices the helicopter perfectly in half, throwing it out of the sky, spiraling and careening out of control.

Not a light—*a laser.*

It wrecks nearby, exploding in a plume of vicious yellow fire and a black column of smoke, shaking the ground thunderously the second it makes impact.

We duck and cover, lying together on our bellies, our faces varying hues of ghostly white. *What's going on? What have we missed in the last week?*

Most of all: *Are the others alive?*

My chest tightens, realizing that Rion's a pilot. I stupidly never thought to ask of what. *A pilot of a helicopter, or a jet, or a regular plane? Is he fighting now, in the sky, and I just don't know it?*

The sky blazes, lit on fire. Another helicopter roars out from the graying horizon, heavy artillery spitting bullets at the very craft which glides effortlessly through the sky.

Another joins it, this one a bright violet—not green, as all the other podcraft are—which lights up like a sun, blinding its adversaries with sickening ease.

"HEADS UP," Cyb yells, finger pressed avidly to her pale temple and, just when I think it can't get worse, a scouring wave of the Muted crests the hill, heading straight for us.

Lios shoos Merope and I away, aiming at the influx.

"Hold up the rear!" he orders loudly, yelling over the noise of another Black Hawk wrecking in the distance; he tosses me a pistol, and Merope a knife. "That's all I've got!"

It'll have to do.

We traipse up the hill behind the safe-house—so steeled we're forced to crawl. Peering over the edge, we're subjected to a sight too horrific to articulate.

Bodies.

Everywhere.

"What are they?" Merope cries, glancing at me. Everything seems to happen in slow-motion. Her black hair floating in the gusting wind, eyes cut wide.

The columns of smoke in the distance mark the dead as effectively as headstones—a rigid finger pointing to catastrophe, to stark-smelling death, pools of blood, and splintered bone.

And now, the *bodies.* Piled as high as the hillside itself. They aren't bodies of the Muted, nor are they human beings, leaving us with one alternative.

"Borealians," I whisper, voice swallowed up in the booming chaos exploding around us. "Look at their faces!"

Their faces, narrow and disproportionately large, hanging on disconcertingly elongated necks. Eyes like almonds, large and bulbous, insect-like. Their skin is pallid and cracked, and I think of how Apollo said, when weakened, they aged . . .

Maybe they didn't age at all. Maybe, with energy reserves compromised, so was their human illusion—revealing a haunting peek of what was behind the mask.

They have teeth, but not for chewing—we know, already, they don't eat physical foods—but for killing. Long sabers hang out from under their thin lips, two on top and two at the bottom.

But why would they need them, when they've got skillsets?

Many of the bodies are burned beyond recognition.

They must've wrecked . . .

Or were made to.

Suddenly, a black podcraft emerges. Its tail is like black ink swirling in clouded water as it jets silently through the heart of the white sky.

Merope and I follow, stumbling back down the hill to where both Cyb and Lios are killing the Muted. Cyb holds them, Lios firing at them, slowly and systematically picking them off.

Until they see the black podcraft—*and freeze.*

The Muted, in the presence of the podcraft, flee back into the depths of the forest. To our shock, it settles itself in the ranks of a line of Black Hawk helicopters, deflecting blows fired wildly at them with staggering ease.

"Who is that?" Cyb asks frenziedly, but doesn't have to wait long for an answer. The black craft descends, as though exempt from gravity, with an unnatural grace.

The other podcraft lower, landing as well. I notice there's a fourth that I missed: blue.

Each podcraft exhales a string of Borealians—all apparently in their shapeshifted forms, still visibly human. Most stay behind while their leaders go to meet at the center of a clearing cupped at the base of our hill.

"It's Pavo," Lios announces gravely as a tall, absurdly thin figure drifts out of the green podcraft. He's followed by a female from the blue podcraft, whose hair is as orange as a sunset.

They walk together—chins held high, *dignified*—toward the heart of the clearing, where they wait.

"I recognize that woman," Merope says, nodding at the fiery haired figure. "Andromeda—the leader of the Elite. But what's she doing with Pavo, of all people?"

"She's on his side," Cyb says, sneering. The sight of the two together does something to me: it ignites a rampant fury in the places of myself I thought empty, filling me up.

The black and violet podcraft open, three figures emerging.

They are dressed entirely in black—cloaks whipping in the blustery, winter wind—faces hidden by heavy hoods. They walk in perfect tandem, stride for stride, exuding a power that I didn't expect from them.

A power that Pavo and Andromeda don't have.

A power that suggest they are killers.

They aren't afraid of it.

The figure in the center of the other two rips back the hood of her cloak abruptly, exposing a face I recognize easily, even at such a stretched distance.

"Onyx!" I get up off my belly, rising to see better. "I can't believe she's here, that she's facing—"

"Get down!" Cyb grabs my sleeve, dragging me back onto the snowy ground beside her. "They can see us from here!"

The two others walking beside Onyx shake their hoods free from their faces, exposing a woman I know is Mabel Faye and a lovely, younger woman with magenta hair and gemstone eyes.

"I—I recognize—" I can't articulate myself, too startled by the sight unfolding before us: the women approach Pavo and his rigid ally, the trio as stoic as stone statues.

We inch together nervously, watching our mentor lead her crew of three *traitors* straight to leaders charged with the duty of issuing death sentences for less.

Pavo approaches, lips peeled to speak, but it's clear within seconds that Onyx isn't interested. I see her face flicker and shift before my eyes, the illusion disguising her as human fading away to reveal her Borealian form.

Onyx is a body of thin, marble white. Eyes black and as big as an insect's. Fangs drip out from her jaws, thick sabers that she has capped with vicious, pointed iron tips.

Pavo says something—*a plea.*

Onyx raises a palm, slamming an invisible force directly at his frail chest, sending him flying. Andromeda raises her palm in retaliation only to be levitated vulnerably in the air, lifted high by the magenta-haired woman.

Meanwhile, Onyx and Mabel march toward Pavo, faces lit up with boiling rage, unrelenting determination etched into every rise and fall of their features.

Pavo gets up and cries, "I don't know where she is!"

"Liar!" Onyx yells, blasting him again. This time, however, he's ready for her, parrying the attack and somehow sending it ricocheting back at her.

Onyx soars off her feet, crashing into the snow.

Pavo's illusion lifts, revealing a terrifyingly inhuman body and face beneath: gray flesh webbed with veins, eyes black and depthless, teeth uncapped but sharp.

His fingers light up, literally a beam of fire, which he uses to trace the outline of her body in the snow—a threat similar to tossing a knife inches from somebody's face.

I could've killed you, but I chose not to.

Next time you won't be so lucky.

My eyes drift sidelong to my league. Their facial expressions reflect my own concerns. *Unless Onyx has decided to go against her beliefs, there's no possible way she'll be as strong as Pavo, who's likely already feasted on thousands of souls.*

Onyx gets up, wordlessly striking Pavo with another burst of invisible force—striking him in the chest so savagely, he's left coughing up a sticky, tarlike substance.

The blood of a Borealian.

Pavo's jaws snap, baring his teeth animalistically.

Onyx drops to a crouch, fangs also showing, as she raises each of her palms in his direction.

BOOM.

Pavo skids over the icy surface of old snow, his cloak ripped and flapping in the wind. But he recovers fluidly—with a kind of practiced alacrity—and plunges after Onyx in a sprint so fast, my eyes can barely catch up.

They meet each other halfway, fighting physically—fangs and claws deployed, skillsets firing mercilessly under the gaze of hundreds of startled onlookers.

In the distance, Mabel raises a palm, knocking Andromeda into a coma with the swift flick of her wrist, approaching with a mean glint to her eyes, ready to land the final blow . . .

I cringe, recoiling at the sight. "Onyx can't win," I say at the sight of Pavo and Onyx fighting even harder, no longer holding back in the slightest.

"I don't think she's trying to win," Merope replies wisely.

"What is she doing, then?"

"Making a point."

Pavo and Onyx exchange words in a foreign language, their stiffening postures heralding danger—and then, out of nowhere, they shift back to English.

"Sister, enough of this fighting!" Pavo decries, dropping his fists to his side. "Please," he begs, inching closer. "Please, Sister, we can end this war today—*together*."

"I have two terms."

"Name them," Pavo says eagerly.

"Give me my daughter and let us go free." Onyx's words are met with a strangled silence. The onlookers whisper frantically to each other—and Mabel, standing farther off, winces.

Betrayed.

Onyx has just betrayed her only ally—for me.

Pavo smiles with relief. "I accept."

"I don't," Mabel yells abruptly, raising her palms not to use her skillset ability, but send a signal. "I'm sorry, Onyx."

A signal to her helicopters—to strike Onyx down.

And strike her down they do.

I feel the rip of a scream rake claws down my throat.

But I can't hear anything. I only run, tripping over the lip of the hill, stumbling down the sloped expanse, crawling. I reach the edge of the clearing just in time to see Pavo retreat—*face gray, a stomach full of bullets and bleeding profusely, a leg shattered . . .*

A sister lost.

Just as I ready to plunge into the clearing, I see a figure bolt out of the forest's shadows. *Apollo.*

Folding me in his arms, he whispers, "Be quiet. It's okay."

I notice he's crying.

I notice I'm crying.

Together, we watch Mabel look back at Onyx—her eyes a mess of sour tears, body shaking. She looks as though she's about to breakdown completely. Flanking her sides are an entourage of soldiers—native borns—who usher her off protectively.

Her counsel.

"I've got to go with Pavo," Apollo croaks.

"No—why?"

"Now that Onyx—" He stops, gazing at her body lifeless in

the snow, a stain of black blood marking her grave. "We're going to need a new spy on the Ora."

"Apollo," I cry, holding his face. "I'm so sorry."

"This is not over," he says.

"I know."

"I'll be back for you—I won't forget," he says, kissing the top of my forehead. "Forgive her."

And then he's sprinting off, boarding the podcraft just as it's about to take off. He reserves his final backward glance not for me or for our league at the safe-house . . .

He saves it for Onyx.

The podcraft's door lowers, shutting. It cuts his face out of view and I wonder, truly, if I'll ever see him again—if I'll ever get to make sense of his final words: *Forgive her.*

Forgive who, Apollo?

Onyx or Mabel?

28

WHEN THE CLEARING IS empty, I find Onyx's body.

I kneel beside her, tracing a finger along her arm stretched peacefully at her side, webbed eerily in black veins. And despite being in her unfamiliar, Borealian form, she's still lovely.

I had the chance to go to her—to save her.

And yet I stayed.

"I'm sorry, Mom," I say, throat tight. Without thinking, my fingers slip through hers—spindly, clearly inhuman, but bearing an echoed resemblance to my own.

Just as I go to release her, I feel the tug of energy.

I freeze, tears stopping.

A pull . . . not an influx, the way it usually feels.

My energy wants to . . . filter into her.

And so I let it—exploring the sensation, feeling the rush of my skin's golden glow draining into the marbled skin of the hand lifeless in my own, siphoned mysteriously by the conduit of our physical contact. My head spins, mouth drying.

I don't stop.

I give it all to her, everything I've got.

Just when I feel like I've got nothing left to give, I see a rise and fall to her bony sternum. *She's breathing.*

Breathing. Alive.

My voice is a croak. "Onyx?"

Onyx's eyes drift to our hands clasping. Instantly, she tries to pull away—recoiling.

"You foolish, foolish girl. Don't you realize you're risking your life by doing this?"

"Doing what?" I say, grip tightening.

"You're offering your soul to me." Onyx blinks, those black eyes of hers swollen, sad. I realize she isn't speaking out loud, that her lips aren't moving. *She's speaking telepathically.* "So clever, you are. So headstrong and foolish and brave."

"Not brave enough," I confess. "I didn't—I should've—"

"I knew you were at the safe-house, Eos."

"What?"

"Apollo told me, last night. We've been preparing to face my brother for days. It was all I could do not to go to you, but it was too dangerous."

"Were you planning to betray Mabel?"

"Yes," Onyx says tightly. "I see, now, the lengths she'll go to preserve the cause we're fighting for—the cause we established together, thirty years ago."

"I forgive her," Onyx adds. "Peridot, that is; Mabel Faye is a false identity she's forged to stay covert. Her colleague, and one of her last Borealian allies, is a friend of mine. Io."

Wind rolls forth over the smooth clearing. The chill of it is unlike anything I've felt before, not setting inside me but filtering through me, as though I'm made of nothing.

"I'm getting dizzy," I say, sighing. My eyes drift to gaze at the blindingly white sky thick with churning clouds, a carapace as dense and tight as a lid on a jar.

Helicopters thunder wildly, spewing fire at what I know is the pile of corpses Merope and I found. The smell of cooking flesh fills the air, dizzying me further.

"What do I do?" I gasp, knowing I'm approaching the edge of a precipice fatal should I tip over it. "Who can I trust?"

"Yourself," she says simply. "This is your life—forged by the choices you make—your Purpose is yours to chose, Eos."

I feel something slip out of her hands, into my own: *a knife.*

A long, slender knife—unlike anything I've ever seen.

Onyx tightens her grip, lips firm. "What you've seen today cleaves a path previously straight," she whispers, eyes locked on my own, unyielding. "Which will be yours to follow?"

I don't know what to say. The words ripple through my core as catalytic as a large rock erupting against the glossy surface of untouched water—taking something stagnant, and breathing violent life and passion and purpose into it.

"Eos, it's time to let me go." Onyx grasps my hand in both of hers and eyes me severely, her voice taut. "I've made a lot of mistakes in my life—"

"Onyx—"

"You were never one of them," she ends, tears falling from the creases of her eyes. "You're my best and only triumph."

"Onyx, please!"

"I love you, Eos," she says, peeling my fingers away, ready to leap into the void of death knowingly—*bravely.* "I love you, my daughter—may we meet again."

"*No,*" I sob.

"This is not a goodbye, Eos. I'm going to sleep," she says in a relieved kind of way, smiling. "And the next time I wake up, I hope you're the first I see."

I cling to my mother, for the first time ever, trying to absorb every single detail of her physical existence—the feel and smell and sound and sight of her, because I won't get it again.

"Good night, Eos," she whispers, fingers fanning to steeple my own, resting there temporarily—waiting.

Waiting for me to pull away.

The brink of my periphery coils and darkens, like the burnt edges of paper, and I know I could keep going. I could follow her the way Rion always hoped he could his mother, into that black abyss she's readying to leap into. But she's right . . .

I have a different path to follow.

"You've been brave enough," I whisper. Though my fingers are trembling wildly, I adhere to those words. *I won't make you be brave now. This time, let me be brave for you . . .*

I let my hand fall.

We disconnect to a suffocating silence.

"Good night, Mom," I whisper, stroking the silver hair out of her face and standing to leave. "I love you."

THE OTHERS SAY THEIR goodbyes—or *good nights,* I guess.

We decide, with minimal dialogue, that we're going to raid all the supplies we can carry from the safe-house.

And then, we're leaving.

We ignore the fire feasting on the corpses nearby, the thud of helicopter rotors. We ignore the roar of gunfire. Snow falls as soft as feathers, clinging to my eyelashes, dusting the surface of this crumbling planet with an ill-fitting perfection.

I get to the safe-house first, only to be stopped by a jumble of angry voices—inaudible. I drop down to my belly, peering over the crest of the hillside. The entrance is crowded by a retinue of soldiers filtering in and out of the safe-house; they wear black armor, slick as fish scales, operating in total uniformity.

"Your *duty*," a voice spits angrily, "is *simple:* bring them all to me without slipping up!"

"My duty is to *fly*—not *kidnap*."

"You owe me a debt!" Mabel Faye's gray, overcast-colored eyes are as wide and churning as an ocean. "I'll consider it repaid in totality, if only you comply."

My mouth goes dry as Rion steps out of the trees, his face and body bruised, swelling in places. He's been in battle. *Is he all by himself, now that Apollo's gone?*

Where's Jac?

Mabel postures herself dangerously. "Where is she?"

"I told you," Rion says, turning so we're facing, though still at a relatively safe distance, "I don't *know*—"

The first thing I realize is that Rion's stopped speaking.

The second thing I realize is he's *looking at me*.

Right at me.

"—where," he goes on, strategically turning his body so he's shading me from visibility, "Eos Europa is. Nobody has seen her, or her league, for well over a week."

Cyb crawls to my side, pinching my arm brutishly.

"Let's go!" she breathes.

"Wait—not yet."

"What are we waiting for?" she begs, only to be distracted by the sight before us. Mabel Faye—*Peridot*—rounds on Rion, letting her illusionary human form drop like a veil.

She regards him viciously, fangs dripping with saliva.

"Have it your way," she snarls. "Seize him!"

Rion barely fights as he's forced to kneel—a wad of his hair used as leverage to drag his face upward, giving him no choice but to look Peridot in the eyes.

Her fingers snap, nostrils flared. "Remove your masks!"

The soldiers do.

The first one I recognize is a girl with frizzy hair, as orange as a candle's delicate flame—pale, freckled skin; an upturned nose set under bright, cobalt blue eyes.

Eyes distant and empty.

"Calypso Mar," Merope cries chillingly at my side.

"What's happened to them?" Lios asks. He's holding tightly to Cyb's wrist. "Why are they following her orders?"

I see a black boy wander forth, pressing his palms against the trapdoor of the safe-house and setting fire to it.

Nova's brother, Ares.

They are all here.

Peridot lowers her face, eyeing Rion—who instantly writhes and tries looking away. But she grips his jaw, forcing his maple eyes on hers, as though administering a kind of hypnosis.

"Why so resistant?" Peridot snarls. "You let the girl read your thoughts like a book. Why fight it now, boy? After all, you know what will happen if you do."

What, exactly, will happen, Peridot?

Didn't Apollo say there's a way to resist being Scried—that if you didn't want to reveal information to the person infiltrating your thoughts, you didn't have to?

But at what cost?

Seconds later, Rion begins yelling in earnest—thrashing his head back and forth against the glare of her bulbous, black eyes as they dig deeper, clawing and ransacking, shredding his mind to ribbons as she looks for information on my whereabouts.

As she looks for me.

No—I won't let him die for me.

I won't make the same mistake twice.

I get up, but am stopped. I feel the invisible pull of a skillset ability at work and panic—thinking, at first, that Pavo's back and he's returned with a vengeance.

But it isn't Pavo.

It's Cyb—she's Persuading me.

Eyes glistening with tears, she gives a subtle but stern shake of her head, as if to say, *No, I'm sorry, I won't let you.*

Peridot's eyes shift in color and Rion groans, thrashing.

The sight makes me sick.

Rion's fight gives out—his eyes clouding over, their depth lost entirely, leaving him to stare blankly. The soldiers let him go, his vivacity lost with theirs.

"Pity," Peridot says, breathing heavily, dusting herself off as she walks away—speaking to nobody I can see. Her human veil falls back into place, a curtain drawn. "I thought he'd give in."

WE RUN.

We pass the pit of burning corpses and thread through the trees of the forest. We dodge the eyes of soaring helicopters in the sky and slip in the snow.

We keep going until we can't go any farther.

Exhausted, we stop by a stream trickling lightly, its edges shaped like lace. All the while, I barely notice the acidic burn of tears as they spill acrimoniously over my cheeks.

Wordlessly, I drop to my knees. The stream is icy, carrying a surprisingly strong current.

Merope clings to a tree. "What did we just see?"

Nobody speaks. I keep my focus on the stream—its black water carving into the snowy landscape. The knife Onyx gave me earlier jabs my leg; I've been keeping it in a pocket, with no other place for it, and only now wonder about its purpose.

Onyx doesn't do anything without a reason.

Why did she give me this?

Cyb takes out a pistol, seeing if it's loaded. "It looked like they were all in some kind of a trance. They didn't seem to know what they were doing, did they?"

"A trance," Lios says, brows furrowed, "or something else."

"What else could it be?"

"She could've—well, I've heard of memory swipes being one of the only skillset abilities abolished." At this, Lios's eyes avoid mine completely. "If fought, the victim would lose their mind."

I feel my spine ice over. "Lose their mind?"

I think of Peridot's chilling words:

"Why fight it now, boy?

"You know what will happen if you do."

I roll onto my hip, thrown off balance by the slap of reality as it claps me across the face. *Rion's lost his mind. He's sacrificed his memory for me. To protect me. To keep me safe . . .*

"Rion was right," I crow. "PIO Morse can't be trusted."

"As long as it's affiliated with Mabel Fa—"

"That's not her real name," I say, interrupting Cyb. "That's an alias she's invented. Her real name is Peridot—and the other ally we saw, with magenta hair, is Io."

"PIO," Merope says. "*Peridot—Io—Onyx.*"

"The gem, the moon, the stone," I say, feeling shaky.

Cyb's eyes are cupped in dark circles. "Well, what now?"

"I have an idea," I whisper, extracting the blade Onyx gave me and cupping it in my palms. It isn't thick enough to inflict any real damage—and maybe that's because it isn't supposed to.

It's not a fighting knife. It's a surgical one.

Holding out my wrist—microchip scar visible, rising and falling to the rapid pulse of my heart—I glide the blade over the slender scar, thin as thread.

The others hold perfectly still, staying quiet.

The knife maneuvers effortlessly, dipping between a mess of veins and tendons—though, it's not without pain. If it weren't for the shaking blare of adrenaline, I'd scream.

But I grit my teeth. I lock my jaw.

I keep going.

I keep going until I find my chips.

And when I do, they go straight into the stream, swept up in the surging current—and as far as Pavo knows, my pulse has stopped and my tracker isn't trustworthy.

As far as he knows, I'm dead.

I hold out my wrist for Lios, whose ability to Heal fuses the delicate flesh back together instantly. I stand, shifting so I can look at the sky, at the early moon and the glowing orb beside it.

For all those years—for all my life—I looked out of the window in my pod and gazed at the planet I thought I was created to save.

And now, finally, it's the other way around.

Just as it should be.

"We're the only ones left," Merope acknowledges, her hand slipping into mine as Cyb and Lios close in. She looks up at the four of us, a wry smile parting her lips. "Do we stand a chance?"

Cyb reaches for the knife.

With a swift pull, she's following my lead; the knife's sound zeal for extracting microchips makes it easy, and without the cherry red orb—filled with poison that explodes if a microchip extraction is attempted, which Onyx deliberately left out of our implants for this reason—there isn't anything to fear.

We're free. *We're free.*

Cyb tosses her chips like grenades; they plunk into the swift rush of water, carried away. Turning to us, she smiles. "The real question is: do they?"

I keep my eyes locked on the sky, feeling a dawn buoying to the surface within me. Merope takes the knife, throwing her old life away and chasing a new one—*and just like our first lives, this one was given to us by Onyx.*

Lios watches his microchips float downstream, pressing a clean strip of fabric against his wrist.

"For Onyx," he whispers.

"For Onyx," Cyb and Merope say together—and aboard the ship we've just disowned, I know Apollo's saying the same thing as he sees us, one by one, fall off the radar.

"For Onyx," I say, thinking of her, of where beings without souls go after they die. "They won't even see us coming."

A
DARK
SKY
O·PENS

COMING SOON

PRONUNCIATION GUIDE

Eos (EE-ose)

Merope (MARE-oh-pee)

Cybele (SIB-elle-ee)

Lios (LEE-ose)

Apollo (Ah-PAHL-oh)

Rion (RHY-ahn)

Jac (Jack)

Silas (S-EYE-las)

Pavo (PAH-voe)

Onyx (AWN-ix)

Peridot (PEAR-a-doe)

Io (EYE-oh)

ABOUT THE AUTHOR

When Anna Vera was a girl, she would've told you she was secretly a mermaid, could see ghosts, and teleport to other planets. Now that she's a mature adult, she keeps these things to herself.

Anna currently resides in Arizona, where she continues to write about fantasy realms, post-apocalyptic worlds, and alien invasions. When she isn't writing books, she's practicing hot yoga, playing videogames, and buying too many scented candles.

ACKNOWLEDGMENTS

To my team . . .

To Trisha Leigh (author of *Return Once More*), for being the first perfect stranger to love this story enough to champion it. Pitch Wars 2014 has shaped the direction of my career in incredible ways—and if it weren't for you selecting me as your Mentee, this book likely wouldn't be here today.

To my brilliant editor, Max Dobson of The Polished Pen, for all the incredible guidance—both in track-changes and over the phone on those early, coffee-fueled summer mornings. I can't wait to share the sequel with you this spring!

To Stuart Whitmore of Crenel Publishing, for working against the clock to get this book proofread in time for its release date. You've been such a pleasure to work with, and I hope to see more of you early this year for work on *A Dark Sky Opens*.

To the mind-blowing talent of Qamber Designs, for my perfect cover and internal formatting/design. Najla and Nada—you'll be seeing a lot more of me next year, when I'm publishing more books. Thank you both for your outstanding work!

To my phenomenal critique partners . . .

To Rebecca "Bejon" Frank, for being the first person in the world to read this story, and the first to love it. Your strength—

especially in the face of tragedy—is unparalleled and inspirational. I'm lucky to have you as a critique partner and friend.

To Meredith Jaeger, for taking me under your wing. It's due to your careful guidance through the hazards of this industry that I have made it as far as I have. I thank the Twitter Gods daily for bringing us together and can't imagine taking another step without you in tow.

To my fellow Pitch Warrior, Allie Ziegler. My thanks to you are overwhelming and endless. Thank you for being a buoy when the waves of doubt threaten so frequently to drag me under, for always offering to read and reread, and for taking up residence in my life (where I plan to keep you for the rest of forever).

To Ashley R Carlson (author of *The Charismatics*), for showing me this path is possible. You're a good soul—the best kind, a delicacy amongst the Muted—and I am privileged to have your help in scaling this mountain of self-publishing.

To my family . . .

To Theta Fraser Curry, for impressing upon me the necessity of reading Harry Potter (and let's face it—reading in general) way back in the fifth grade. In so many ways, it's because of you I'm a writer in the first place. Thanks for all your support, Missus. I love you.

To Mom, for instilling my love of Science Fiction. Thank you for all the Star Trek reruns and Star Wars movies—they taught me to look at the night sky, absorb the enormity of the universe, and play with what could possibly exist out there. I heart.

To Dad, for singing me to sleep as a little girl. You were the first to teach me the beauty of the written word—and though I didn't grow up to write lyrics, I hope you're able to sift through my fiction and find the window to my soul I've hidden there. Love you. Always.

To my sister, for everything. Especially the hash tag. You've urged me to run faster and try harder and—most of all—never let go of what means the most to me. This book is for you.

To Karan, for enduring all the early mornings I've left you to wake up alone, all the weekends I've disappeared, and all the late nights I've spent typing by candlelight to write. You make me better.

And last but not least . . .

To everybody on LiveJournal who read and critiqued my earliest stories and gave me the confidence to keep writing. You were my very first critique partners, and I'll never forget you. To everybody I've met on Twitter, who have loyally shouted into the void of social media in favor of advertising my book. To the strangers who told me they didn't usually like Sci-Fi, but fell in love with this story.

. . . and, of course, to every new reader who has taken the time to follow Eos to the last page of this book—and hopefully through the pages of books to come.